Praise for Paul Johnston:

BODY POLITIC

'A hugely entertaining fantasy . . . engagingly
imagined'
The Times

'Think of Plato's Republic with a body count'
The Sunday Times

'An intricate web . . . Johnston is a Fawkes among
plotters . . . Quint's career looks set to blossom'
Observer

'Fascinating and thought-provoking'
Val McDermid, *Manchester Evening News*

'A thrilling hunt-the-psycho novel with countless
twists . . . accomplished . . . offers real proof of the
vigour and class of current Scottish crimewriting'
Ian Rankin, *Scotland on Sunday*

'Imaginative . . . remarkable . . . shows that crime
fiction can be not only thrilling but intellectually
exciting as well'
The Economist

'An excellent satire, and good thriller to boot . . .
Further adventures are promised and eagerly awaited'
Mike Ripley, *Daily Telegraph*

Also by Paul Johnston

Body Politic

About the Author

Paul Johnston was born in 1957 in Edinburgh, where he grew up. He divides his time between the UK and a small Greek Island. He is the author of one previous novel, *Body Politic*, winner of the CWA John Creasey Award for the best first crime novel, and is currently working on *Water of Death*, the third novel to feature Quintilian Dalrymple.

THE BONE YARD

Paul Johnston

NEW ENGLISH LIBRARY
Hodder & Stoughton

First published in Great Britain in 1998
by Hodder and Stoughton
A division of Hodder Headline PLC

NEL edition 1999

10 9 8 7 6 5 4 3

A CIP catalogue record for this title
is available from the British Library

ISBN 0 340 69493 9

Typeset by Palimpsest Book Production Limited
Polmont, Stirlingshire

Printed and bound in Great Britain by
Clays Ltd, St Ives plc

Hodder and Stoughton
A division of Hodder Headline PLC
338 Euston Road
London NW1 3BH

THE BONE YARD

The dung really started to fly on Hogmanay, 2021. The last day of the last month is supposed to be a time for celebrating the good things that happened in the old year and for anticipating the joys of the new one. In Edinburgh that means getting slaughtered. Not even the Council of City Guardians has managed to put a stop to that part of our heritage. But this time someone took getting slaughtered literally. It didn't come as a complete surprise. Ever since the new wave of ultra-keen young guardians took over in 2020, there's been an undercurrent of tension in the "perfect city". Everything's been tightened up so much under the new rulers. They call them the "iron boyscouts" in the ordinary citizens' bars when they reckon there's no informer around, or when they're too pissed to care about being sent down the mines for a month. There's too much supervision of everyone's activities, too many regulations, too much control. And as the city's schoolchildren find out in their sex education classes, if you bottle everything up, you're sure to become a pervert. Or a dissident. Or both.

I would never turn down a murder investigation. The problem was that this case didn't start off being one of those. Or rather, it did. But I just didn't realise.

Christ, I wish I had. Whatever way you look at it, I could never have guessed I'd end up in the Bone Yard. I'd trade my entire collection of blues tapes – W.C. Handy and Big Bill Broonzy included – to have missed that gig.

Chapter One

The weather set its trap with all the cunning and skill of a poacher who invites his extended family round for a New Year's banquet then realises his cupboard is bare. In the early afternoon the sky was bright, Mediterranean blue without a hint of a cloud. Citizens ventured out with only one sweater instead of the usual three and tourists imagined that unbuttoned raincoats would be adequate protection. There were even a few guardsmen and women around without their standard-issue maroon scarves. They all got a couple of hours of reasonable warmth, then the sun went west and the temperature swapped a minus for a plus reading faster than politicians pocketed envelopes stuffed with banknotes in the years before the UK fell apart. I was standing at my living room window when people in the street below started jerking about as if a mantrap's serrated jaws had suddenly closed around their legs. It wasn't exactly warm in my flat, but at least I had a glass of barracks malt to ward off the cold.

"What have you got on tonight, Davie?" I asked, glancing over my shoulder. "For God's sake, leave my guitar alone. The neighbours will start complaining."

The bulky figure on the sofa raised his middle finger, scratched his beard and continued strumming. "And a happy New Year to you too, Quint. If they put up with you playing the blues, I don't see why they should be bothered by this."

"Possibly because they like the blues, while what you're playing is just a wee bit passé."

"Nothing wrong with 'Flower of Scotland'."

"Nothing apart from the fact that Scotland ceased to exist seventeen years ago." I took another pull of whisky. "And the fact that your lords and masters outlawed the song."

Davie discarded the guitar and picked up his glass. "They also banned the blues, Quint."

"Which shows you what a bunch of tossers they are."

"That's enough abuse of the Council, citizen." Davie didn't look too bothered as he poured himself more malt. "Unfortunately I'm on duty tonight. I've got to supervise patrols in the tourist area."

"Which is why you're getting your drinking in now, is it?" I asked. Not that Davie's consumption of alcohol would affect his ability to do his job. The Council may have been struggling to provide Edinburgh's population with decent food, but he was still fit enough to take on anyone in an Olympic wrestling competition. Except there haven't been any Olympics Games for a long time – too many countries have been reduced to warring city-states.

I peered down into the street below. It was rapidly sinking into the gloom of twilight. Under the Energy Directorate's recent electricity rationing plan, the streetlights don't come on until as late as possible.

"So, no chance of a romantic Hogmanay with Fiona, then?" I said. Davie had been spending more time than his rank are meant to with a fellow auxiliary. I did a double-take. "Jesus, look at this. There's a lunatic coming along Gilmore Place."

"Not very likely, given the Council's policy on unproductive citizens. They're all banged up in homes for life."

"Not this one." I followed the guy along the street. First he pressed himself into a doorway on the other side. He waited, then slowly stuck his head out to take a look. And then he sprinted across to the near side in what could charitably be

4

described as an ungainly fashion, narrowly avoiding being hit by a superannuated Supply Directorate van. "Look at him now."

Davie joined me at the window and we watched as the man in the street continued his antics. He was around six feet and thin, like all citizens, in his early twenties, as far as I could make out in the murk. He was wearing an orange woolly hat and the standard dark blue overcoat ordinary citizens obtain with clothing vouchers. From the doorway three down from mine, his head appeared slowly, looking towards the Tollcross end of the street.

"He seems to be checking if he's being followed," Davie said. Then he burst out laughing. "Bloody hell, what a jackass."

Our man belted across the road again, his legs kicking high like a pony that's just seen the vet get out his biggest syringe. Again, the head poked in and out nervously from a doorway opposite.

"Check out your lot and see if they're chasing him." I kept an eye on the strange guy while Davie flipped open his mobile and called the guard command centre in the castle. If it hadn't been for the cold and the location – my flat's on a street where tourists only come if they were born with a jellyfish's sense of direction – I'd have assumed he was a street performer in the year-round arts festival that's the mainstay of the city's income.

Davie signed off. "No. They didn't have a clue what I was on about."

"Don't worry. I think we're about to find out."

The young man had crossed the road, legs all over the place again. We watched as he disappeared from view directly beneath my window.

"You don't think he's on his way up here, do you?" Davie asked dubiously.

"He's a client all right," I replied. "Care for a small wager?"

"Bollocks to that. You know I don't bet with you any more,

Quint." Davie's barracks commander had lost patience with the number of bottles of whisky he used to take from the mess to cover his wagers with me. The one we were drinking now was my Hogmanay present.

I listened for footsteps on the stair. They weren't long in coming. The knock was quiet, just a couple of tentative taps.

"No, I'll get it," I said, waving Davie back to the sofa. "Your uniform isn't likely to turn him on."

I opened up and let in the guy from the street. At close range he looked much more normal. He pulled off the woollen cap – presumably a gift from a doting mother who could only find orange wool in the city's stores – and revealed thick brown hair shorter than the regulation one-inch length. His face was thin and his brown eyes seemed to be far too big for the rest of his features. He smiled hopefully.

"Citizen Dalrymple?" He glanced over my shoulder, but didn't look particularly concerned by the sight of Davie in his City Guard's grey tunic with the maroon heart. If anything his smile got broader.

"The same," I said. "Call me Quint. And that's Hume 253." I didn't give him Davie's name. That would have been too much of a shock for an ordinary citizen – auxiliaries are supposed to be faceless servants of the city and if you don't address them by barracks name and number, you're nailed for non-compliance.

"Em, right." The young man fiddled with his hat then stuffed it into his pocket. "The name's Aitken, Roddie Aitken." He gave another smile, as if what he was called was a private joke.

"Fancy a dram, Roddie?' I asked, holding up the bottle.

He stared at it like he'd never seen whisky before. He may well not have seen barracks whisky before. The look on his face suggested either that he had a massive hangover or that he was one of the few Edinburgh citizens who have an aversion to alcohol.

"Sit down," I said, pointing to the place on the sofa next to Davie. "Don't worry, he won't bite."

Davie wasn't too impressed by that kind of talk in front of a citizen.

"So, Roddie," I said, giving him what I thought was an encouraging smile. "Who's following you?"

The guy looked like I'd just accused him of being sympathetic to the aims of the democrats in Glasgow. He sat bolt upright and looked over towards the door, as if he were gauging whether he could beat us to it.

"Don't panic," I said. "I saw you in the street."

Roddie Aitken relaxed a bit and smiled weakly. "I must have looked like a right . . ."

"Aye, you did," Davie said with a grin.

The young man laughed. He didn't seem to be intimidated by Davie's presence; some of my clients would rather forgo their sex sessions than talk in front of an auxiliary. "I heard you help people out," he said, turning to me. "Is that right, citizen Dalrymple?"

"Quint," I said. "Remember?"

He nodded apologetically.

"And I do help people out, as you put it."

"But you're not in the guard?"

"Not any more. I have contacts though." I nodded at Davie. "Why? Have you got a problem with the guard?"

Roddie Aitken shrugged. "No, not at all. It's just that I told them about my problem and they . . . well, they haven't followed it up."

It wasn't the first time I'd heard that story. There aren't enough auxiliaries in the Public Order Directorate to deal with every citizen's request for help. One of the reasons I didn't rejoin the directorate when I was invited a couple of years back was that there's plenty to do cleaning up their omissions and lapses.

The fact that I'm regarded as Mephistopheles without a disguise by the new wave of headbangers in the Council is neither here nor there.

"What exactly is your problem, citizen?" Davie demanded with typical guardsman's subtlety.

"Yes, you'd better give us a clue, Roddie," I said, gesturing to Davie to lay off him. "Don't be shy. Hume 253 often works with me."

Aitken thought about it for a few moments, then got stuck into his story. It often happens like that. Clients spend the first few minutes with their noses twitching like dogs carrying out extensive research on an unfamiliar leg, then they suddenly start rubbing themselves up against it like the trousers are on heat.

"I told the guard about the hooded man yesterday morning. They said they'd get back to me today, but they haven't. The thing is, I'm not sure what it's all about. Jimmie reckons that the guy was trying to have a real go at me, but I didn't see the knife . . ."

Davie's eyes were rolling and mine probably weren't too stable either. "Hold on a second, you've lost us," I said. "We've got a hooded man, a knife, a Jimmie, the guard and you. Make some connections, will you?"

Roddie Aitken laughed and his face took on an even more boyish look. It was hard to tell how old he was. Maybe that's why he was dubious about the whisky. "I knew it would sound crazy," he said.

Davie got up and went over to the window.

Suddenly the young man's face looked older. His eyes were wide open, fixed on the figure in uniform. "Is he there?" he asked in a taut voice. "Can you see a big guy in a long coat with a hood?"

Davie stared down at the street, lit now by the dull glow of streetlamps on low power. Then he turned back to us, shaking his head slowly. "No hooded men, no one dressed up as Santa Claus who's got the date wrong, no one chasing people down the road with a knife. How many beers have you had today, laddie?"

Roddie looked offended. "None." His face reddened. "I don't like drinking that much."

"Let's start from the beginning," I said, giving Davie a look that he ignored. "Someone in a coat with a hood has been following you, right?"

He nodded, glancing at Davie with an injured expression. I felt a bit sorry for him.

"So how often have you seen him? When did all this start?"

Roddie sat up and pulled his orange hat out. "Look, I think I'm wasting your time. I didn't really want to come. It was Jimmie who—"

"Hang on," I said. "You can't just walk out. I've got my tongue hanging out like a kid whose girlfriend's decided she won't undo her blouse after all."

He grinned shyly, then sat back again. "Fair enough, citizen . . . I mean Quint."

"Right. Fill me in then."

"The first time I saw the guy was on Christmas Eve. I work in the Supply Directorate – the Deliveries Department. Food mainly, sometimes some booze, cigarettes for the nightclubs, that sort of thing."

I was interested. It's unusual for someone as young as Roddie Aitken to get a job as a delivery man. The older members of that department hog the driving duty because it gives them the chance to pilfer – if they have the nerve to risk a spell on the city farms or down the mines.

"It was in the Grassmarket, across the road from the Three Graces. I couldn't see a face or anything. It must have been about half seven in the evening and they hadn't turned all the lights on. Anyway, I was in a hurry – they'd suddenly realised they were short of whisky."

"How did you know he was interested in you?" Davie asked.

Roddie Aitken raised a finger to his lips and shook his head slowly. "I didn't really. It was just . . . he was staring at me, really hard. You know, giving me the eye."

"Nothing else happened?" I asked.

"No. I went into the club and made my delivery. When I came out, he wasn't there any more."

Davie leaned towards him. "You say 'he'. How do you know it was a man?"

Roddie's forehead wrinkled as he thought about that. It looked to me like he did more thinking than the average citizen. I wondered why he wasn't an auxiliary.

"Can't say for sure. He was big – not huge, but big enough to be a pretty unusual woman." He smiled at the idea. "The hood part of his coat had a kind of high neck as well; that's why I couldn't see much of his face."

"Not much to go on so far," Davie said.

"I know. Then I saw him again three days ago, last Saturday night about half nine. This time it was on Nicolson Street, near my flat. I looked round a couple of times and he was still there, about twenty yards behind me." He shrugged. "Then I turned into Drummond Street where I live and he didn't show."

I wasn't too excited so far. Christ, the guy himself didn't seem to be very bothered. But something about his expression, a tightening of the skin around his eyes, suggested the punchline was worth waiting for.

"Then he showed up again the night before last." Roddie turned to me, his eyes wider. "I'd been working late. One of my mates in the department was sick – pissed, I should think – so I was delivering vegetables to the shops. I got back to Drummond Street just before curfew at ten. The sky was dead clear and there was a frost. That must have been why the footsteps sounded so loud. This time I didn't see him till I was about fifty yards from my door." He stopped to catch his breath, looking at both of us. "Then he started running. I turned round and saw the figure in the long coat and hood. He had something in his hand.

I ... I couldn't see what he could possibly want with me so I didn't run, just walked a bit more quickly."

I began to get the distinct feeling that Roddie Aitken was too laid back for his own good. I reckon I'd have been down the road faster than the mob in London after the millennium when they spotted anyone who looked like a city trader or a lawyer.

"I didn't really see what happened next," he said. "Jimmie, my neighbour, opened the street door and pulled me in as the guy hurtled past. Jimmie swears blind he saw a big knife, but I don't know ..."

"What exactly was this Jimmie doing at the door?" I asked.

Roddie smiled. "He's a nosy old bugger. Always sits at his window. He said he saw the man in the hood and didn't like the look of him, so he came out."

Davie stood up again and headed for the window. "And you reported this to the guard?"

"Jimmie told me I should." Roddie Aitken shrugged. "I suppose he had a point – after all, he saw the knife. There are some crazies around, even in Edinburgh."

He was right there. But I couldn't figure out why even a crazy guy would follow a delivery man around. "Is there anyone who's got a grudge against you, Roddie? At work, for instance?"

He looked at me innocently, as if the idea were ridiculous. "No. I get on fine with everyone, Quint. I reckon it's just a piece of nonsense." He paused and glanced down at his hands. They had suddenly started to shake. "At least I did, until I saw him behind me as I came along Lauriston Place on my way here."

That explained why he'd been acting like a five-year-old on speed in the street. Davie was already on his way towards the door.

"What colour was the coat?" he asked.

Roddie shrugged. "I'm not sure exactly. Dark – maybe navy blue or black."

The door banged behind Davie.

"Have you got a complaint reference?" I asked.

"Aye." Roddie handed me a crumpled piece of official paper numbered 3474/301221. It told me that citizen Roderick Aitken, address 28f Drummond Street, age twenty-two years, next of kin Peter Aitken of 74m Ratcliffe Terrace (relation: father), had reported an attempted assault by a person unknown (probably male). The location and a description of the assailant were also given. I was pretty sure that the guard would have paid about as much attention to Roddie's report as they pay to the city's few remaining Christians when they complain that the Moslem tourists get more religious tolerance than they do. The thing is, the Christians are right. Maybe Roddie Aitken was too.

"Look, how do you feel about this, Roddie? Do you reckon the guy is really after you?" I fixed my eyes on his. "You'd better come clean with me. Are you in trouble?" I was thinking of his work — maybe he'd got in some heavy-duty black marketeer's way.

Roddie opened his arms to protest his innocence. "I haven't got a clue, Quint, honestly. I'm straight." He looked at me with his wide brown eyes. "All I ever wanted was to be an auxiliary, but I failed the exams two years ago because my maths is so crap. I'm having another go next month. I don't do what some of the others in the department do — pilfering, selling black and the like."

I opened my mouth to speak but he beat me to it.

"And I haven't been telling tales either. None of my workmates knows I'm doing the exams."

I believed him. He was a pretty wholesome citizen, the kind who should have been in the guard instead of arselickers who don't give a shit about the city. Like all of us, he could have done with a better diet and a shower more than once a week. But he gave the impression that he was proud to be an Edinburgh citizen. There aren't too many like that these days.

"All right," I said. "I'll see what I can do."

"Great. I can't pay you very much . . ."

"Don't worry about that. The Public Order Directorate subsidises me. After a fashion." I looked at my watch. "There isn't much I can do tonight though."

Roddie stood up. "No problem. I'm going out with my friends."

"Right. Stick with them and ring my mobile if you see the guy again." I scribbled the number on a piece of paper. "I'll come round to your place tomorrow and talk to your neighbour."

He pulled his hideous orange hat down over his ears. "What time do you think you'll come?" He suddenly looked a bit awkward.

"Some time in the middle of the day." I wasn't going to let him off the hook. "What's the matter? You don't like drinking, so you won't have a post-Hogmanay hangover. Not planning an illicit sex session by any chance, are you?" Citizens are only supposed to have sex with officially approved partners.

His face was red, but he looked pleased with himself. "Well, I've got this girlfriend, Quint, and I'm hoping . . ."

"It's okay. I won't tell Hume 253."

A second later Davie came back shaking his head. "No sign of the mystery man."

I went to the door with Roddie and put my hand on his shoulder. "I'll see you tomorrow then. Don't worry about the idiot in the hood. Have a great Hogmanay."

"Thanks, Quint." Roddie headed down towards the street. "Same to you."

"Not much chance of that," I called after him. "I'm going to the guardians' annual cocktail party."

"Lucky you," he replied, without a trace of irony.

He'd have had a great future as an auxiliary.

Chapter Two

I pulled on the least crumpled of my black sweatshirts and a reasonably clean pair of strides, also black. I wouldn't wear anything smarter to a Council do on principle and anyway, my only suit is retro enough to be banned on the grounds that it might bring about a 1990s nostalgia cult. Then I checked myself out in the mirror. The usual suspect. One thing to be said for food rationing is that it keeps you trim. My jawbone looked like it was about to break through the parchment of my face and I didn't seem to be big enough for my clothes. My half-inch-long hair was continuing its deep and meaningful relationship with greyness, but at least my teeth hadn't fallen out. Yet.

Coming up to seven. They'd soon be kicking off at Parliament House, not that I intended to arrive on time. I took a last pull of whisky, decided against having a blast of B.B. King then hit the road. Davie had offered me a lift in his guard Land-Rover when he went off to the castle for his shift, but I prefer walking. You never know what you might come across on the perfect city's streets. Hooded men lurking in doorways perhaps.

As I headed past Tollcross towards West Port and the Grassmarket, I found myself trying to put the last year's chaos into some kind of order; 2021 wasn't likely to take up too much space in Edinburgh history, not even in the make-believe version the Information Directorate was no doubt working on at this

very moment. Most of the old guardians had been eased out in
2020 – thanks mainly to my mother, as senior guardian, at last
coming to her senses and resigning – and for the rest of that year
the new guardians kept their eye on the ball reasonably well.

"How are you doing, Quint?" The old man who hands
out the *Edinburgh Guardian* at the corner of Lothian Road and
Fountainbridge interrupted my reverie. "On the piss tonight?"

"After a fashion. How about you, Andy?"

He opened his worn duffel coat. "Look. I managed to get
hold of a bottle of stout to bring the New Year in."

I nodded, suddenly feeling guilty about the malt I'd been
gulping. Christ, even last year the average citizen managed to
find enough bevies to do the job. "Have a good one when it
comes, Andy," I said.

"Aye, laddie, you too."

I walked on, seething. This is how Edinburgh is now. Things
were buggered from the start of 2021. The city prides itself on
being independent, but that doesn't mean it can survive in a
vacuum. There was a disastrous flu epidemic in the Far East
and that sent tourist numbers from China, Korea and Japan right
round the U-bend. Then the Russian mafia thought it would be
a neat idea to lob some former Soviet warheads into the Middle
East to screw up oil production and, all of a sudden, a lot of
Arabic-speaking tourists had better things to do than mess about
in Edinburgh's shops and clubs. So revenues did a nose-dive and
we only get meat once a week, a beer at the weekend if we're
lucky and enough coal to keep ourselves as warm as penguins
on an ice floe. It's a pretty good recipe for civil unrest. But the
iron boyscouts – fifty per cent of the guardians are female but
somehow "iron girlguides" doesn't have the same ring to it –
instead of patting us on the back and sweet-talking us about how
the good times are just round the corner, decided to apply the
thumbscrews. Everything's by the book now, no leniency. Step
out of line and you're in the shit. But as they say on the streets,
at least the shit's warmer than your average citizen's flat.

The castle rose up before me. It was lit up like a flagship in pre-independence times on an evening when the admiral had his pals round for a pint or two of pink gin. That was the kind of thing the Enlightenment Party, the Council's forerunner, had vowed it would put a stop to. Everyone in the city would be equal, the same opportunities for all and so on. And here I was on my way to a reception where guardians and senior auxiliaries would be offering foreign dignitaries the best food and drink the city could provide, without an ordinary citizen in sight. If we could eat hypocrisy, there'd be no problems with malnutrition.

I came down into the Grassmarket and my nose filled with the delicate odour of cow dung. A couple of days a week, cattle are run in here by herdsmen dressed in seventeenth-century costumes as a spectacle for the tourists. The Agriculture Directorate swears the beasts are all BSE-free. I hope they're right — there are sometimes rumours about outbreaks in the city farms, followed by the secret culling of infected herds. I edged round the cowpats. A squad of labourers was clearing them up without much enthusiasm. Beyond the skeletal trees in the middle of the broad street is the Three Graces Club where Roddie Aitken had his first sighting of the hooded man. It's another example of the Council's double standards. Strictly tourists only are allowed to watch a floorshow that gives the imagination the evening off, especially when the Three Graces themselves are on. I suppose Canova's marble sculpture of the goddesses in the City Gallery might be a turn-on to a few perverts, but the performers in the club make sure everyone in the audience gets the point — using a lot of pointed accessories that the sculptor didn't find space for.

I looked across at the replica of the ensemble on the pavement outside the nightclub. Even at this early stage it was surrounded by potential customers who were running their hands over the Graces' rumps. When the original was first brought to Edinburgh for some ludicrous amount of money in the 1990s, I can remember people referring to it as the Six Buttocks. I can also remember my mother giving me a major earbashing when I did the same. She never was one for levity. Then again, when she was senior guardian she did plenty to establish the city's reputation as the Bangkok of the North. I never quite understood how she managed to reconcile that with the Council's ideals of sexual restraint and the inviolability of the body. Obviously filling the city's coffers took priority. Ah well, I couldn't hold it against her now. She died last January. I didn't see her much after her resignation and the lupus she'd been suffering from for years gave her a bad time near the end. But I sometimes feel an unexpected sense of loss. I reckon my old man does too, not that he'd ever admit it.

As I walked up the West Bow past souvenir shops bedecked with tartan scarves and plastic haggises, it occurred to me that perhaps I was being too hard on the present Council. After all, they were only continuing the policies of their predecessors, with a zeal my mother and her colleagues would have approved of. Then again, there's nothing worse than a young zealot. I should know. In a previous existence I was one. Before Caro died seven years back and my career in the Public Order Directorate became about as meaningful as a 1990s European Union directive on the configuration of bananas.

I stopped outside a shop and watched a Chinese family buying what looked like Edinburgh's entire stock of souvenir playing cards. Their faces were wreathed in smiles, from the aged grandmother with suspiciously black hair to the infant cradled in her father's arms. I shivered and stamped my feet as the cold bit hard. But it wasn't just the chill that was getting to me. In the rush to establish a just and equitable society, we forgot about friendship and affection, not to mention love. We get physical at weekly sex sessions, but there are no sessions for emotion. Then I thought of Davie and his Fiona. Even though auxiliaries aren't supposed to get emotionally involved, they seemed to manage all right. Maybe it was my own fault. I was still hung up on a woman I hadn't seen for nearly two years. Katharine Kirkwood. She came to me because her brother had gone missing and we ended up in a multiple murder case. Then Katharine left the city. God knows where she was. She'd probably erased all traces of me from her memory by now.

I walked up to the Royal Mile and glanced at the gallows where they give the tourists a thrill with mock hangings. I was going through one of my regular depressive phases. There's only one known cure – taunting guardians and senior auxiliaries. I headed to the reception with a spring in my step.

I resisted the temptation to spit on the Heart of Midlothian as I passed in front of St Giles. It used to be the tradition, but if you do that kind of thing nowadays you're asking for trouble. They don't mention it in the City Regulations (a document which I've come to know intimately in my line of work) and I don't imagine anyone would complain if a tourist who'd read Walter Scott gobbed on the brass plaque that marks the site of the old Tolbooth. But the maroon heart is the emblem of the city and the guard are pretty touchy about it being messed with by ordinary citizens. Christ, I'd almost talked myself into emptying out my throat.

But I was interrupted. A horse-drawn carriage with a group of Africans in colourful robes missed me by about an inch on its way to the neo-classical façade of what was once known as Parliament House. It's called the Halls of the Republic now – you can't get away from Plato in this city. The Council only uses it for over-the-top receptions like this one. They prefer the Gothic pile of the Assembly Hall for their daily meetings. They have a point in one respect. This building was where the Scottish law courts were based before the Enlightenment won the last election in 2003. Since the Council rapidly dispensed with the concept of an independent judiciary and gave the Public Order Directorate responsibility for the administration of justice, they'd have been pushing their luck in the irony stakes if they'd located their base here. Besides, the draughts in the Halls of the Republic are even worse than down the road.

The guardsmen and women on duty at the entrance took one look at my clothes and moved towards me *en masse*, hands on their truncheons. Then they recognised me and stepped back. Some of them nodded as I came up – they were the ones who'd heard that I'm good at what I do. The rest belonged to the persuasion who regard me as a boil on the body politic. The way they were glaring at me suggested they'd like to take me round the back and use their service knives to lance me.

Inside the building a red carpet leads to the main hall. Auxiliaries dressed in medieval costumes lined the corridors. Maybe they gave the foreign dignitaries a thrill, but they did nothing for me. The old hall was another story though. It was packed with people who'd already got well stuck into the magic, but I wasn't paying attention to them. It was the seventeenth-century roof that caught my eye: great oak hammerbeams arcing over the throng like the stained bones of some gigantic creature that had perished in the dawn of time. There were open log fires roaring in the ornately decorated fireplaces, their flickering light glinting on the varnish of the beams and catching the colours of the painted windows. One of them shows the charter of the newly independent city being handed over by a suspiciously well-fed citizen to the first senior guardian.

"Is that outfit the best you could do, Dalrymple?"

I gave up perusing the decor reluctantly and grabbed a crystal glass from a passing waitress who was dressed up as one of Robert the Bruce's camp followers, complete with disembowelling knife.

"Tell the truth, Lewis. You couldn't bear the disappointment if I turned up in a suit." I took a slug of the whisky. It was a dark, smooth malt that the Supply Directorate must have been keeping in reserve for this sort of occasion: there are no trading links with the Highlands any more and the whisky produced by the city's two distilleries is a sight worse than this.

The public order guardian shook his head in disgust and sipped mineral water. He used to be famous for his rum and cigarette consumption before independence, but guardians don't allow themselves any vices. In the case of coffin nails, they don't allow anyone else that vice either: they banned them, along with TV and private cars, not long after they came to power.

"So, have you been enjoying youself telling the foreigners how little crime there was in Edinburgh last year, Lewis?" I was pleased to see my use of his name in public was giving him the needle. Guardians are supposed to be addressed by title only.

"And what if I have, citizen?" he said combatively. "The directorate's kept things under a tight rein."

I laughed. "That's true enough. No murders, not many muggings—"

"None at all in the central tourist area," he interrupted.

"Only a few burglaries in the suburbs," I continued. "And officially, there's no drug consumption, no rape, male or female, no gunrunning" – I glanced up from my glass and saw that Lewis Hamilton was beginning to look pleased with himself – "no pornography – at least among ordinary citizens – no bribery, at least none reported." I gave him a smile before skewering him. "And a black market that runs as efficiently as any other department in the city."

He looked around, eyes bulging, and stepped closer. "Keep your voice down, man. You know perfectly well that a carefully regulated black market is necessary to maintain equilibrium."

Yet another example of Council hypocrisy. Citizens get nailed if they're caught skimming off goods from city stores or delivering short, but all the time auxiliaries are keeping tabs on the black economy. Actually, to be fair to Lewis Hamilton, it's something that's come about under the iron boyscouts and I reckon he's not too keen on it himself. But he's one of the few survivors from my mother's team, so he hasn't got much room for manoeuvre.

The guardian moved back and eyed me balefully. "I don't understand your attitude, Dalrymple. The directorate gives you your ration vouchers and allows you to work in your idiosyncratic fashion. Why do you have to be so bloody bolshy?"

I couldn't help laughing. Lewis sometimes sounds like a caricature of a mid-twentieth-century colonel. But he had a point. I could have gone back into the directorate on my own terms after the murder case in 2020, but I didn't fancy the boneheaded hierarchy. Better to stay outside, keep up my private investigations and help him chase dissidents when he gets desperate. I thought I might come across some trace of Katharine that way too, but I've never even had a sniff.

"Good evening, citizen."

I turned and was confronted by another reason I've kept my distance from the directorate: Hamilton's deputy, known in the trade as Machiavelli. A scheming, arse-licking piece of slime who'd stab his boss in the back if the lights went out. Fortunately for Lewis, the directorates have their own power supply and their electricity doesn't go down like it does in ordinary citizens' houses.

"How's life, Raeburn 03?" I said, pronouncing his barracks number like it was a virulent strain of groin infection.

He returned the favour by giving me a supercilious smile from beneath his feeble beard as he drew his superior away for a private chat. I watched them as they retreated to the area in front of the statue of Viscount Melville. The body language was revealing. Raeburn 03, wavy blond hair gleaming in the light, was doing a Uriah Heep, rubbing his hands like they were covered in best barracks lard and bending his skinny frame towards Hamilton, who was bending over backwards to keep his distance.

I grabbed a refill and caught sight of my father with another former guardian. The Council usually ignores ex-members but it invites them to the Hogmanay reception to keep them sweet. Hector didn't use to turn up, but since my mother died he's been more assertive. I went over.

"Hello, old man."

"Hello, failure." The skin around my father's eyes creased and he nodded to me slowly. "I wasn't sure you'd come, Quintilian." He loves to use my full name. He should do. It was his idea.

"I wouldn't miss a chance to network with the city's movers and shakers," I said ironically. "How are you, William?"

The shrivelled figure at my father's side quivered as if the force of my breath was almost enough to knock him over. He used to be science and energy guardian when my mother was in charge, but it didn't look like he had a lot of energy reserves left now.

"William," he repeated in a querulous voice. "I'd almost forgotten my name. They still call me 'guardian' in the retirement home. William Augustus McEwan," he said slowly. Then he seemed to revive. "I'm still going, Quintilian. Hector has been telling me about your exploits."

"Uh-huh. Don't believe everything the old man says."

"But I do, Quintilian, I do." William McEwan smiled sadly. "The city needs more like you." He looked around blearily at the mass of people. "The new guardians, they're going to throw everything we worked for away." He shook again and held on to my father's arm. In their faded tweed jackets and worn brogues, surrounded by loud-mouthed drinkers gabbling away to hard-faced young auxiliaries, the pair of them had the appearance of time travellers who'd got stuck in the wrong millennium.

I tried to inject a light-hearted note. "The Council has about as much desire for more citizens like me as it has for an outbreak of AIDS among the city's nightclub staff."

William McEwan shook his head weakly. "You're wrong,

my boy. They're going to need you, all right. They don't know what they're letting themselves in for."

I've rarely seen anyone look more solemn. Even Hector, never one to keep his feelings about the boyscouts to himself, looked dubious. "Have another whisky, you old misery guts," he said. "You don't get this quality of dram in the home."

But his companion was peering round the room again, apparently looking for someone. As he was doing that, I caught the medical guardian's eye and raised my glass. Despite her sober black dress and flat-heeled shoes she stood out, her short, silver-blonde hair and high cheekbones a striking combination even among a gaggle of ambassadors' wives in expensive outfits. She raised an eyebrow at me. If she hadn't been a guardian, and therefore sworn to celibacy, I might have tried to forget Katharine by having a go. As things are, there's no chance.

Hector started mumbling about some less than fascinating discovery he'd made about Juvenal's sexual peccadilloes. My father's spent years combing the pages of the old Roman misogynist, presumably because it keeps him close in spirit to his wife. A waiter in a pair of tartan trews came up with a silver tray full of canapés that ordinary citizens wouldn't have recognised as food. As a representative of that body, I did my duty and grabbed as many caviar, lobster and *foie gras* dainties as I could.

"Here, William," I said, turning to the ex-guardian. "Have some of . . ."

But he was off, piling across the hall like a man with a mission. I almost choked on my vol-au-vent when I saw who he'd approached. Then he started waving his arms about with surprising force.

"Oh, Christ," said my father.

"Oh, Christ is right." I handed him my evening meal and went to rescue William McEwan. The person he'd chosen to give a piece of his mind to was the senior guardian; and although

23

the senior guardian is supposed to be a leader among equals, the present one's more like a deity than a servant of the city. He'd been groomed for the top since the day he started the auxiliary training programme. He had the kind of record that other auxiliaries would sacrifice their closest colleagues for – triple As in every exam he ever sat, four bravery commendations during border duty and numerous prizes for his knowledge of Plato. His calm authority seemed to inspire worryingly mindless levels of devotion in his supporters. The tall figure in an immaculate powder blue suit turned to William like he was an irritating insect, smiling apologetically at his guests. But as I approached, it seemed that the guardian's brow furrowed and it even looked like he was being shaken by what he was hearing. His eyes, pale blue between the black of his hair and wispy beard, held the old man in an unwavering stare. Which meant that young blue eyes didn't register my arrival.

"And what about the Bone Yard?" William McEwan demanded, all traces of querulousness vanished from his voice. "What about those poor—"

He broke off and gasped as the senior guardian gripped his wrist.

I put my hand on William's shoulder and pulled him gently away. That broke the senior guardian's flinty gaze and he swung his eyes on to me, briefly stopping to take in my missing right forefinger.

"Citizen Dalrymple." The deity favoured me with a thin-lipped and very brief smile. "I'm afraid the former guardian is not very well. I suggest you remove him before he makes a spectacle of himself." He turned back to the men in suits he'd been addressing and ushered them away from us.

"What was all that about, William?" I asked as I led him and Hector to the nearest corner. "What's the Bone Yard?" But he was shaking, all the energy he'd summoned up now spent like a battery's last surge, and I didn't get any answers to my questions. Not long afterwards I put Hector and him into a guard vehicle and sent them back to their retirement home. What a way to spend Hogmanay.

It didn't get much better. I hung around and consumed as many canapés and as much whisky as I could manage. And I chatted up a few foreign businessmen's wives, but never got beyond them telling me how much they liked shopping in Edinburgh because of the low prices. When midnight came, I joined hands and sang "Auld Lang Syne" like the rest of them. It was worth staying that long to see how awkward some of the guardians looked when they tried to be spontaneous. Machiavelli in particular had the horrified expression of a snake that's just slithered into a convention of secretary birds. That's when I decided I'd seen enough.

Outside by St Giles I took in a few deep breaths to clear my head. Bad idea. My lungs tensed up like they'd just been injected with ice water. For a moment I even thought I was going to pass out. It was the idea of landing on the frozen pavement that made me get a grip. I headed home, the distant singing of revellers in the suburbs echoing in my ears like it did when I was a kid and Scotland won the rugby Grand Slam. Tonight was the only night of the year when the curfew isn't enforced. I suddenly felt wide awake, the whisky only a faint throb in my temples, dead certain that I wasn't going to sleep for hours. I stopped at the corner of George IVth Bridge and Roddie Aitken flashed into my mind. I wondered if he was all right. I even considered walking down to Drummond Street and knocking him up. Then I remembered he had a girlfriend. I'd be really popular if I turned up at this time of night.

So I wandered back to my place and shivered through the wee small hours listening to the blues at low volume. When I eventually crashed out, Katharine Kirkwood and the medical guardian refused to keep me company, even in my dreams. That was a great start to 2022.

Chapter Three

It was still dark when I came to. Workmen seemed to have been round during the night and poured a ton of gravel down my throat. My feet had made an abortive break for freedom but hadn't got any further than six inches from the edge of the bedcover. They were so cold that I was forced to get up and knead the circulation back into them. After that I was wide awake and there was no point in going back to bed, despite the fact that New Year's Day is one of the few official holidays recognised by the Council.

I worked at what the Supply Directorate describes as my "desk, plywood, ordinary citizen issue" — more like a picnic table with rickety legs that I've had to shore up with volumes of ancient philosophy — and brought some of my missing persons reports up to date. Most of them were just people who'd been called up for extra duty in the mines or on the farms. The Labour Directorate is supposed to notify their next of kin but the paperwork is for ever going astray. And then there are the citizens who get sick of the Garden of Edin and cross the border without having the nerve to let their family know. I've lost count of the number of times I've had to tell tearful mothers and disbelieving partners that their loved ones have done a runner. I try to do it with a bit more delicacy than the City Guard.

I gave Roddie Aitken until eleven to do what he had to do with the girlfriend he was so bashful about, then headed off to his flat. There was no point in trying to call him since the only phones available to citizens are the public ones at the end of every third street. In the early days of the Enlightenment it was claimed that the telephone system was too expensive to maintain and that the mindless nattering it encouraged wasted time which could be put to more productive use. Everyone knows the Council just wanted to control the flow of information.

It was still cold enough to make deep breathing a hazardous occupation, the sky clear and deceitfully bright. I walked along Lauriston Place, the soot-stained granite of the City Infirmary on my right and what used to be George Heriot's School on my left. Its flag-topped turrets and octagonal dome now house a hotel dedicated to the wealthiest of post-communist China's businessmen and women. No prizes for guessing which building is better looked after. I walked on through what used to be university territory. The Medical School is an auxiliary training centre, while the McEwan Hall is now called the Edinburgh Enlightenment Lecture and Debating Hall – the dialogues of Plato which underpin the city's constitution are analysed on a daily basis here. The D-shaped building's former name reminded me of the ex-science and energy guardian and his performance at the reception last night. What the hell was he on about to the senior guardian? And what the hell was the Bone Yard? I didn't like the word much. It made me think of graveyards, cities of the dead, tombstones canting over as the corpses beneath decomposed and the earth subsided. Very cheerful on the first morning of the New Year.

Drummond Street is across the road from the university Old College, a great Adam building around a quadrangle topped by a dome high above ground level. They still light it up at night. Since the university was the spiritual home of the Enlightenment – a lot of its early leaders were professors like my parents – I suppose the current Council feels it's worth the electricity to commemorate the place, although most of the iron boyscouts fancy themselves more as hard-nosed enforcers than intellectuals. But they still aren't practical enough to sort out the city's bureaucracy, as my missing persons files show.

I wandered down Drummond Street towards number 28. There was no one about; even the kids seemed to have hangovers. I stopped and cocked an ear. Dead quiet for a few seconds, then in the distance the raucous cries of the gulls desperately hunting for scraps in this underfed city. It struck me that I had nothing in the flat to eat and the food shops were closed for the day. Maybe Roddie Aitken would have some bread. He seemed like the kind of guy who'd be organised enough to stock up on provisions.

I pushed open the shabby street door and let out the usual reek of disinfectant failing to mask sewer gas and citizens who only shower once a week. It was tempered with the acid stink of vomit, as you'd expect after Hogmanay. Flat f was on the second floor. Someone across the landing from Roddie had defied Housing Directorate regulations and put a pot on the floor containing a gigantic plant with wide leaves so shiny they looked plastic. The branches had almost reached the filthy skylight. I didn't blame them for trying to find a way out of the dingy staircase.

I went up to Roddie Aitken's door and knocked. Not too hard – I didn't want to sound like the City Guard – but hard enough and long enough to wake him even from a sex-induced slumber. No answer. I knocked again. While I waited, I looked at the faded blue door. Down by the keyhole there were some recent scratches, quite deep. He probably couldn't get the key in last night while pissed. I pressed my fingers on the panel. It swung open on hinges that badly needed oiling.

"Roddie?"

Still no answer.

"Roddie, where are you? It's Quint, Quint Dalrymple."

Like most flats, mine included, the door opened straight on to the living room. Chaos. I'm not the most tidy person, but even when I'm arseholed I don't wreck the joint like Roddie had done. The standard-issue armchair and sofa were upside down, their fabric torn and cushions shredded; the books citizens are encouraged to read (philosophy texts, classic novels, that sort of thing) had been scattered around the floor; the kitchen cupboard had been emptied, cereals and potatoes all over the place. Even if Roddie had invited the city rugby champions round, he wouldn't have had this much cleaning up to do.

Then I noticed his orange woollen hat. It was lying on the underside of the inverted table and it had been ripped to shreds. I began to get a seriously bad feeling about the scene.

I knocked on the bedroom door. Nothing. I opened it hesitantly, then drew breath in so sharply I almost choked.

Roddie was there all right. I saw immediately why he hadn't been answering.

His throat had been torn out.

I was bent over the kitchen sink, gasping and shaking. Trying to throw up, but aware very quickly that even though I hadn't seen a murder victim for nearly two years, I'd still seen too many in my life to be able to react like a normal human being. I wasn't sick in my stomach, but in what passes for my soul — sick that I'd abandoned Roddie to this, sick with responsibility and guilt. Jesus, I liked the guy and his naïve enthusiasm.

I splashed water on my face and stood up in front of the mirror. Shook my head and called myself a lot of names. And swore a solemn oath that I'd catch the evil bastard who slaughtered the boy who came to me for help. Then I went back to the door and looked at the horror on the bed.

I forced myself to be dispassionate. It's not difficult if you've been an auxiliary, even one who was demoted seven years ago like me. Auxiliaries pride themselves on being able to handle any crisis. One thing I definitely was not at that moment was proud. But I had to do my job. Roddie deserved the best I could give him even though it was far too late.

The first thing I did was call Davie. He was asleep after his night shift, but I heard the exhaustion vanish from his voice even over the mobile.

"Fuck." The word rang out like a pistol shot. I knew it was one aimed at himself. "Bloody hell, Quint, I thought the lad was just imagining things." He shot himself again with the same word. It sounded like we were both guilty about what had happened to Roddie Aitken. "I'm on my way."

I called Lewis Hamilton. He'd have to be directly involved as there hadn't been a violent death since the last murderer ran riot. I hoped to the god I don't believe in that we didn't have another one like that on the loose. I also called the medical guardian and asked her to handle the post-mortem herself.

Before the guard arrived and turned the staircase into even more of a war zone, I carried out a quick private inspection of the flat. I didn't go far into the bedroom because there was a lot of blood on the floor and the killer would have left prints and traces. But the living room was another story. There were no visible signs of blood here, suggesting that the murderer had worn protection over his feet in the bedroom then removed it. I was thinking about the hooded man Roddie had described. What could be his motive? Smuggling? Black-market goods? There was no need to kill for those – plenty of people would willingly provide whatever you wanted for a price. But the way the place had been trashed, it certainly looked like a search had been undertaken. I hunted around for any evidence of pilfered supplies. Roddie Aitken definitely hadn't struck me as that kind of delivery man, though he might have sold me a dummy. But I found nothing in the living room. Perhaps there would be something in the bedroom. Or perhaps the killer had found what he was after.

In the distance I heard the high-pitched wail of sirens. It wouldn't be long before I had to face Roddie close up.

Hamilton came in looking pale, a team of people in white

plastic overalls at his heels. "Good God Almighty, Dalrymple, what have you found?" He peered over my shoulder into the bedroom and flinched. The public order guardian never did like dead bodies.

I filled him in about Roddie's visit and request for help, though I kept quiet about the hooded man for the time being. Scene-of-crime personnel were already starting to take photos and sketch the room layouts; they seemed to have memorised the manual I wrote when I was in the directorate.

The medical guardian turned up, also in white plastic. "I'm impressed, citizen," she said with a tight-lipped smile. "You even work on city holidays."

"You don't mind handling this personally, do you?" I asked. "It's the first murder for—"

"I know my job," she said tersely, then handed me some overalls. "Who's in charge on the public order side?"

"I'm taking the case." I glanced at Hamilton, who looked a bit dubious. "I know I found the body, but that doesn't disqualify me." If Hamilton knew how fired up I was to catch Roddie's killer, he'd have been even more dubious about letting me run the investigation, but I wasn't planning on telling him about the oath I'd sworn.

Davie came in, a grim look on his face. I beckoned to him to come over. "I'll need Hume 253 to work on this with me, guardian."

"Very well, Dalrymple." In the old days Hamilton wouldn't have let me lay down the law — that was his party piece. Now he's too busy protecting himself from the iron boyscouts, who were well pissed off when he refused to resign with most of my mother's gang.

I got Davie to oversee the scene-of-crime squad and told him to look out for any sign of illicit goods. Then, when the photographers finished with the longer-range shots, the medical guardian led me into the bedroom. We had to step around some large patches of partially dried blood on the worn carpet. Standing by the bed, we looked down at the mangled upper torso; a heavily stained sheet lay over the lower part of Roddie's body. His chest and arms were bare, splashed with blood from the gaping wound in his throat. The medical guardian, known to citizens who were prepared to take a chance as the Ice Queen because of her silver-blonde hair, was making preliminary observations into a small tape-recorder. The trachea had been ruptured and over two square inches of skin and cartilage torn out.

The guardian was bent over the wound, a magnifying glass in her hand. "The tears in the tissue are uneven," she said, standing up slowly. "It looks like a bite."

That was the way it struck me too. "A human bite?" I asked, pretty sure what the answer would be.

The Ice Queen nodded. "I think so. I can't see any signs of the deep laceration you get with bites from dogs and other animals with long canines."

"Any teeth marks we can match up with dental records?"

She was bending over the body again. "It's a terrible mess, citizen. We might be lucky."

"Look." I pointed to the swollen skin on Roddie's wrists. "He was tied down." Whatever was used, the killer had taken it with him. The thick marking suggested rope.

"That would have helped the assailant to bite his victim, but you'd still expect him to have been writhing around. I wonder if he was knocked out." The guardian examined Roddie's head. "No sign of any blows here."

I had a sudden flash of the hooded man running down the street. The neighbour said he'd seen a knife. I looked at the bloody sheet over the lower half of the corpse. Christ. What were we about to find underneath it?

The Ice Queen glanced across at me. It seemed she was on the same wavelength. "Ready?" she said in a low voice, her fingers on the edge of the sheet.

"Go."

Carefully she lifted Roddie's shroud. I forced myself to take a deep breath, blinked my eyes once and focused on his lower abdomen.

"Oh, no." Even the medical guardian, highly qualified stomach cancer specialist and fully paid-up member of the ultra hard-hearted wing of the iron boyscouts, was having trouble with this vision of horror. "I can't believe someone could do this to one of his fellow human beings."

I parted company with her there. I'd come across several vicious bastards who happily sliced open their fellow human beings. But I saw her point. This was gross even by their standards. Where Roddie's genitals should have been there was nothing except a great hole stretching right up into the groin.

"The penis and scrotum are missing," the guardian said.

I had a look under the bed. Nothing.

"It seems the killer took them when he or she left."

The Ice Queen's glare lived up to her nickname. "Citizen, are you seriously suggesting that a woman carried out this atrocity?"

"We're hardly in a position to rule anything out so far." But I didn't want to fight with her. "Forget that for now."

She'd already done so. Her head was over the wound. "Citizen," she said, her voice registering surprise. "There's something inside here."

"What is it?"

"It looks like the edge of a clear plastic bag."

I bent down and caught a glimpse of it. "Get it out," I said. She hesitated. "Get it out," I repeated impatiently.

She shook her head. "No. I want to wait till we get him on the slab. Pulling it out now might compromise other traces."

She was right there. I looked up at Roddie's face, something I'd been avoiding doing much of so far. The eyes were bulging and his lips were drawn back from his teeth. There was blood on the teeth. I had a piercing flashback to Caro dying on the dirty floor in the barn on Soutra, her foot jerking spasmodically.

"Oh, Christ," I muttered under my breath. "How come nobody heard him screaming?" I looked over at her. "Guardian, we're going to have to prise his mouth open. I think his tongue's been taken too."

She nodded slowly. "That'll have to wait for the mortuary too. I estimate he's been dead for at least nine hours. Rigor mortis is well advanced."

I thought of how I'd almost gone to see Roddie when I left the reception, then spent the early hours listening to Robert Johnson and shivering under a blanket. Not for the first time I felt pitifully inadequate.

Davie shook his head slowly as the body was removed by Medical Directorate personnel.

"Jesus, Quint, who did that to him? Do you think the hooded—"

I raised a finger to my lips and motioned in the direction of Hamilton. "Keep him to yourself till we finish up in here."

He nodded. "Right you are." He looked round at the auxiliaries who were dusting for fingerprints and itemising what was on the floor. Some of them had moved into the bedroom now. "What do you reckon went on in here last night?"

The public order guardian came over to us, his face greyer than the guard tunic he often wore instead of his guardian-issue tweed jacket.

"Well," I said. "For what it's worth, we're not just dealing with a drunken argument that got out of control. I think the victim was tortured because the murderer wanted to know where something was — something that was valuable enough to kill for. There's no way of telling at this stage whether he found what he was looking for."

"Is there a sexual slant to it as well?" Hamilton asked.

"Could be, in a seriously perverted way." I shook my head slowly. "I'm not sure though. It's all a bit contrived. We'll have to wait and see what's been put inside the body."

Hamilton gave an involuntary shiver. "I've never heard of a plastic bag being secreted inside a murder victim before."

"Me neither."

"I gather you think the killer cut the tongue out as well," the guardian said, avoiding my eyes.

I nodded. "At first I thought it was to keep him quiet, but there would still have been some noise. We'll probably find out from the neighbours that there was music playing." One of the Supply Directorate's standard-issue cassette players was lying smashed on the floor.

"Do you think the victim knew the killer?" Hamilton asked.

I shrugged. "Your guess is as good as mine. What else have we got? The scratches round the lock suggest that whoever put the key in had a pretty unsteady hand."

"Drunk? Shaking?" Davie suggested.

"Maybe the latter. Maybe the victim was being threatened at the time."

There was some shouting outside the door. A guardsman stuck his head round.

"Neighbour, guardian," he said. These days auxiliaries often speak like words are rationed. Why not? Everything else in the city is.

I remembered the old man Roddie mentioned. "Let him in, guardsman."

A small figure almost ran in, slewing to a halt in front of us.

"It was Roddie, wasn't it?" he demanded desperately. "It was Roddie they carried out."

"You're Jimmie, aren't you?" I looked at the short, stocky man in front of me. He was bald on top, but he made up for that with the largest pair of eyebrows I'd ever seen. It was like Nietzsche's moustache had acquired a twin and migrated.

"Aye," he said, peering at Hamilton and Davie with the

mixture of fear and loathing affected by most ordinary citizens. "Jimmie Semple."

I put my hand on his arm and led him back towards the door. "Why don't we talk in your place?" I glanced over my shoulder in an futile attempt to pacify the guardian. "I'll be back soon." It was obvious to me that the old man would clam up like a 1990s government minister in front of a parliamentary committee unless I got him away from anyone in the guard. Hamilton still fondly imagined that citizens would do anything an auxiliary told them.

"Who are you, son?" Jimmie Semple said as he took me into his flat on the ground floor. "You don't exactly have the look of one of them bastards."

"Quint's the name. Quint Dalrymple."

The old man sat down in his armchair at the window. "Oh, aye, I remember you. You were the one who caught that killer a couple of years back." He shook his head. "Something like this has been waiting to happen ever since the fucking boyscouts turned the screw." Then he caught and held my gaze. "What's happened to Roddie, citizen?"

"Call me Quint." I didn't look away, though I'd have liked to. "You were right upstairs, Jimmie. It was him they took away."

"That bastard in the hood got him. I knew he would. I told Roddie to be careful, but he didnae listen."

"You're wrong," I said, sitting opposite him and leaning forward. "He did listen to you. He came to me for help."

"Did he tell you about the crazy guy with the knife?" the old man asked.

I nodded.

He swore under his breath, spittle landing on the carpet by the toe of my boot. "So congratulations on a job well done, ya shite."

I couldn't think of anything to say for a bit. "Look," I said eventually, "I liked the lad. He only came to me yesterday afternoon. It was when I came round today to follow up on his problem that I found him."

Jimmie Semple looked back at me, his expression softening. "So you didn't think he was just wasting your time?"

I shook my head.

"Aye, well, I'm sorry if I was a bit . . ."

"Forget it. Will you help me find the man in the hood?"

His eyes were wide, bloodshot, under the dense growth of his brows. "Aye, son, of course. But what can I do?"

"Tell me everything you saw and heard. Last night and the night Roddie was chased down the street."

He told me about the hooded man first, but there wasn't much to it. He hadn't seen a lot more than Roddie, confirming only that the attacker was tall and solidly built and that the face had been obscured by the hood. He wasn't sure about the colour of the coat either – another triumph for the Council's enlightened policy on streetlamp brightness. He didn't even have much to say about the knife. It might have been a hunting blade, or even a carving knife. Christ. A blood-freezing image of the Ear, Nose and Throat Man came up before me like a spirit from the underworld: he used long knives to butcher his victims as well as to take off the end of my right forefinger. But he was long dead and buried, of that I was certain.

"What about last night?" I asked. "Did you see Roddie?"

"Aye, he came by on his way out." The old man glanced over at the dusty clock on his mantelpiece. "Must have been about eight o'clock. He was on his way out to meet his pals for Hogmanay."

"How did he seem?"

"Och, he was fine. He wasnae bothered about that lunatic." Jimmie brought his hand down hard on his knee. "He should have been though."

"He mentioned a girlfriend."

"Aye. Good-looking lassie. I don't know her name. I only saw her from the window a couple of times."

"Jimmie, did you hear Roddie come back last night? Did you hear anything at all from his flat?"

He shook his head and looked at me with an expression of infinite sadness. "No, son, I didnae. I wish I had. I had a half-bottle of whisky I'd been saving all year, you see. I was dead to the world long before midnight." He gazed across at me, a sheen on his eyes. "How did Roddie die?"

I mumbled some bullshit about the case being subject to Public Order Directorate security regulations and left him to the view from his window.

He was better off not knowing what happened to his friend upstairs. Roddie would be on the mortuary table by now, the medical guardian waiting for me before she started the post-mortem. I wished I was on another planet. Preferably one on which I was the only human being.

Chapter Four

I left Davie in Drummond Street taking statements from the rest of Roddie's neighbours. Hamilton dismissed the guardswoman who was behind the wheel of his maroon Land-Rover and drove towards the infirmary. It was mid-afternoon by now, the sun already low in the western sky and the shadows lengthening in the city. The air was even colder than it had been, making the breath of the people unfortunate enough to be out on foot plume around their heads like the ink squirted by a nervous octopus.

"What kind of monster would do that, Dalrymple?" The guardian glanced at me. "Don't tell me you think it's an auxiliary." Two years ago he'd never come to terms with my idea that the killer was one of the city's servants. I had the feeling he was less sure about the rank below his these days. Then again, he didn't think much of his fellow guardians now either.

"I haven't a clue, Lewis. It's too early to say," I said. "You haven't heard any reports of a hooded man in the city centre, have you?" I tried to make the question sound nonchalant.

He looked blank and shook his head.

I told him what Roddie and Jimmie Semple had seen.

"It isn't much to go on, is it?" he said morosely.

"It might be all we get." I looked out the side window as we passed the Potterrow Entertainment Club. It was once a famously shitty student union, but ten years ago the Tourism

Directorate converted it into an electronic games centre. No Edinburgh citizens are allowed in, of course. The building's concrete walls are heavily stained with the soot that has built up since coal was reintroduced as the main heating fuel; the nuclear power station at Torness was shut down soon after the Englightenment came to power. A gaggle of Filipinos stood around outside the entrance stamping their feet and waving their arms in the cold. The amount of tartan knitwear they had on should have kept them warm. Maybe the quality of wool isn't as high as the Marketing Department claims.

"I don't think I'll bother with the post-mortem, Dalrymple. I've got some paperwork to catch up with." Hamilton had always been squeamish during autopsies. He used to attend them just to keep an eye on me, but apparently he'd got beyond that stage. Progress indeed. Then he spoilt it all. "You can manage on your own, can't you?"

"What do you think?" I said sarcastically. That was always the problem with the first generation of guardians: they treated everyone like primary school kids.

"All right, all right," Hamilton said wearily. "Obviously you'll need to attend the Council meeting tonight."

"Obviously." I relented a bit. "I'll give you a call beforehand and let you know what we find."

He pulled up and let me off outside the infirmary's grey-black granite façade. It seemed like years since I'd walked past it at midday on my way to Roddie's. Sometimes I wish I'd found another line of work. But, like the Labour Directorate says, "Every citizen has a talent that the city needs." Every citizen except the bastard who did for Roddie Aitken.

I found the Ice Queen in the mortuary antechamber, fully kitted up and ready to go. She gave me a brief nod, then handed me a set of protective clothing. Even in layers of green medical gear she looked pretty amazing, her figure firm and her complexion smooth. I made sure she didn't see the way I was looking at her. You don't want to play that kind of game with guardians, especially not guardians who can handle a scalpel.

"All right, citizen," she said. "Let's see what we've got."

I usually try not to get too affected by what's laid out on the mortuary table. Otherwise I'd keep away like Hamilton. But this time was different. I'd seen Roddie Aitken alive less then twenty-four hours earlier. He'd been sitting on my sofa talking in his boyish voice without much concern about the strange person who was following him. Watching the medical guardian and her assistants going about the normal procedures – removing the plastic bags over feet and hands, scraping fingernails, plucking sample hairs – made me feel seriously uncomfortable. From the bottom of the table I could clearly see the corner of the plastic bag that had been pushed into the wound in the groin. But the guardian wasn't to be hurried. She was examining the torn skin on the neck.

"I'll cut this whole area away now," she said. "It looks like there's at least one reasonable impression of bite marks."

"Good," I said without much enthusiasm. "Now all we can hope is that the killer visited a dentist in the city." The problem was that state-funded dental practices more or less died out in the years before independence and there were plenty of people growing up then who couldn't afford treatment. Even though the Council set up free dental care for all Edinburgh citizens not long after it came to power, a lot of them steer clear of the surgeries. The fact that the Medical Directorate spends as little as it can on pain-relieving drugs may have something to do with that.

"What do you reckon was the cause of death?" I asked. No harm in hurrying the Ice Queen along.

Her head was over Roddie's chest. "Still too early to say. Possibly heart failure brought about by the shock of what was done to him." She pointed at the deep cuts in the flesh of the upper thighs as well as at the gaping hole.

The senior pathologist who was assisting her nodded vigorously in agreement. I got the feeling that he would rather have gone for a walk in the badlands beyond the city border than contradict his superior.

The door opened and a thin figure wearing a green gown over a guard tunic entered. One glance at the hands which almost immediately started rubbing together was enough for me to identify Hamilton's number two, Machiavelli. He bowed his head punctiliously at the medical guardian, who completely ignored him, then at the lower-ranked auxiliaries in the room. They had to acknowledge him as they couldn't risk showing what they really thought of him. Apparently I'd recently turned into the invisible man. No way was he getting away with that.

"What are you doing here, Raeburn 03?" I asked in a loud voice. "On work experience?"

His body stiffened. "I could ask you the same question, citizen," he said after he'd run his eyes over the body in front of him.

I didn't like the way he was looking at Roddie. "Presumably you haven't spoken to your boss recently," I said. Mentioning an auxiliary's senior officer is the best way to make him flinch. Machiavelli flinched. "I'm in charge of this case," I continued. He didn't look at all pleased at that piece of news. Maybe he'd thought this would be an opportunity to make a different kind of name for himself in the directorate – Sherlock Holmes or Inspector Bucket instead of the Renaissance schemer.

The medical guardian had moved down to the middle of the table. She extended the incision she'd already made in the upper part of Roddie's abdomen to the point where the wound began. I glanced at Machiavelli and was surprised to see that he looked a lot less queasy than his boss used to when the dissecting knife went in. His eyes were fixed firmly on the Ice Queen's rubber-sheathed fingers. She parted the skin, examined the area, took some samples and finally laid hold on what had been rammed in to the cavity.

"There you are, citizen." The guardian held up the plastic bag. It was about six inches square, covered in blood and dotted with bits of internal debris. Something I couldn't make out was weighing down one corner.

"What is that?" Raeburn 03 asked in a strangled voice. Maybe what he'd been watching was getting to him after all.

I let the photographer do her work, then took the bag from the guardian. On the scrubbed surround of a sink I ran a finger between the sealed opening — it was one of those bags that are used for frozen food and the like. Machiavelli was at my shoulder.

I turned the bag up and let its contents slide out.

"What on earth . . ." Hamilton's deputy stretched his hand out.

I grabbed his wrist and squeezed hard. "Excuse me, Raeburn 03. You're on my territory."

He gave me a glare that Medusa would have been proud of then stepped back a few inches.

I concentrated on the find. It was a cassette tape, made of clear plastic with the brown tape visible inside. There were no paper stickers on the outside and no writing to identify what had been recorded on it. I was, however, willing to bet my collection of Johnny Guitar Watson tapes that something had been recorded on the cassette. It looked to me like the killer was playing a very nasty game indeed.

"It's not a standard-issue cassette," Machiavelli put in. "There's no Supply Directorate serial number on it."

He was right. Citizens are only allowed to listen to music approved by the Heritage Directorate, which they can obtain free from the city libraries.

I looked at the cassette again. Near the top edge was a line of what looked like Chinese characters. Standard-issue cassettes are imported from Greece as part of the deal involving package holidays in Edinburgh for Greek nationals. So what we had here was technically a piece of contraband. More important, it suggested that the murderer had links with the world outside the city borders. Which raised the spectre of dissidents or gangs of psychos. Bloody hell. This was getting worse by the minute.

"Shouldn't we listen to find out if there's anything on the cassette, citizen?" Hamilton's number two had changed his tone. Now he was almost conciliatory. Bollocks to that.

"We're going to," I said, putting the cassette into a bag of my own. "At tonight's Council meeting." That dealt with him. Unless Hamilton was hit by a bus in the next couple of hours, Machiavelli wouldn't be deputising for him in the Council chamber and so he wouldn't hear a thing. At least until he wormed it out of one of the numerous iron boyscouts who liked his style. He must have been doing them a lot of favours.

"Citizen?" The medical guardian was back at the top end of the table. Her assistants had been wrestling with Roddie's jaws. "You were right. His tongue has been removed."

I got a lift in a guard vehicle back to Drummond Street. Davie had spoken to most of the neighbours. They'd all been well into the bevy from the early evening, but some of them said they heard music coming from Roddie's flat after midnight. The guy across the stairwell had knocked on his door to wish him happy New Year but got no reply and assumed he was pissed like the rest of them.

I told Davie about the cassette. "Let's borrow a machine and listen to it. I don't want to go into the Council meeting blind. Or deaf."

We borrowed Jimmie Semple's cassette player and set it up in Roddie's flat. The scene-of-crime people had finished, having found, so Davie told me, no fingerprints apart from Roddie's and no sign of illicit goods. They'd left the place as it was, so we had to step over books and cushions to get to the single power point. I pushed what was left of Roddie's orange hat under the sofa — it was giving me a lot of angst.

I stuck the cassette in and waited for what I was pretty sure was some kind of message from the killer.

What I got was a hell of a surprise.

"Is that what I think it is?" Davie asked after a minute.

"If what you think it is is Eric Clapton playing 'Tribute to Elmore', then yes, guardsman, it is."

We listened until the music stopped and left the tape running. There didn't seem to be anything else recorded.

Davie rubbed his beard. "Well, boss, you're the expert. What does it mean? What's this got to do with Roddie Aitken?"

"And why was it stuck inside him?" I looked into the darkness outside, then glanced both ways in the street below. No hooded man. "God knows."

"A non-standard-issue tape with banned music on it." Davie nudged my arm. "It must mean something, Quint."

I wasn't arguing with that. A series of unpleasant thoughts had struck me. The blues had been banned not long after the Enlightenment came to power because the drug gangs that used to terrorise the city took them as their trademark. The leader of each gang gave himself the name of a famous bluesman – Muddy Waters, Howlin' Wolf, John Lee Hooker – and the gang members followed suit. My love affair with the blues had started before that. When I was a kid in the nineties, contemporary music was so poor that my friends and I ended up turning to what we thought was the genuine tradition. But I couldn't say the blues were only a source of pleasure to me. The psycho who killed Caro and eleven others called himself Little Walter. And now we had a clown messing about with Clapton and Elmore James. This was bad news almost on a par with the Stop Press from Sarajevo in August 1914.

"It's an instrumental," Davie said, breaking into my thoughts.

"A chance for 'God' to show off his skills on the bottle-neck that Elmore was famous for. What's your point, Davie?"

He shrugged. "I was just thinking that if there had been a lyric, it might have told us something."

I headed for the door. It was half six and I needed to talk to Hamilton before the Council meeting at seven. "It might have," I said over my shoulder. "But then again, we might not speak this particular language. The message is presumably directed at someone who does."

Davie's boots clattered down the stair behind me. "I thought you knew all there is to know about the blues, Quint," he said.

I shook my head. "Not when they're being played by a lunatic, my friend."

Some of the most unpleasant experiences of my life have occurred in the Council chamber. As a result, I hate the place. The building used to be the Assembly Hall where the Church of Scotland had its annual knees-up. It was an attempt at steepling Gothic splendour, but its blackened façade strikes me more like the castle of a vampire with a taste for coal dust. Hamilton was doing an imitation of a sentry on autopilot outside. Behind him the central tourist area was lit up brighter than a Christmas tree in the days before trees became an endangered life form. In the suburbs beyond, where the ordinary citizens live, the lights were a lot dimmer.

"Are you aware of the fact that Raeburn 03 was at the autopsy?" I demanded, warming up for the fight I was about to have with the boyscouts.

The guardian looked surprised. "I was not. Did he get in your way?"

"He did, Lewis. Pull his chain, will you?"

Hamilton smiled grimly. "With pleasure." His face darkened. "We're in trouble, aren't we, citizen?"

"I reckon so. This killer's more than just a butcher. He's playing mind games too." I told him about the tape.

The guardian swore under his breath, an action which would have definitely convinced his colleagues that he was past it. Guardians pride themselves on being above coarse language. Me, I'm a big fan.

"Come on, guardian, we're going to be late." I let him go first through the doorway and up the wide staircase. Busts of Plato were all over the place, the philosopher's wrinkled brow and featureless eyes giving a greater impression of fallibility than the first Council intended. He was their master, *The Republic* and *The Laws* the cornerstones of the new constitution. Unfortunately he didn't specify how to deal with murderers who stick music cassettes inside their victims.

We were admitted into the chamber. When my mother was senior guardian, there had been a vast horseshoe table. The Council members sat round it and people like me who had to give reports sat between the horns and felt small. The iron boyscouts have changed things. In an attempt to show that they're even more devoted to Plato than their predecessors, they emptied the hall of all its furniture and remain on their feet throughout the daily meetings. As the meetings sometimes go on long into the night, they've taken to moving around the hall – the senior guardian playing at Socrates wandering the streets of ancient Athens with the rest of them as his interlocutors. I suppose it keeps them off the freezing streets of Edinburgh.

"Good evening, guardian. Citizen." The senior guardian nodded briefly at us and led us into the middle of the hall. The other thirteen guardians gathered around. They were all carrying clipboards. I saw the medical guardian. She had her notes under her arm and her hands stuffed into the pockets of her light brown tweed jacket.

"The meeting is in session," said the senior guardian, his head held high and his hands behind his back. He looked like a preacher about to address a congregation, the thin beard backing up his earnest expression. "I understand from the public order guardian that Citizen Dalrymple is to lead the investigation into the unwelcome discovery at Drummond Street." He glanced at Hamilton. For a moment I thought there was going to be trouble about control of such a serious matter being given to a non-auxiliary, but the senior guardian let it pass. He knew I could do a better job than anyone in the Public Order Directorate. "Perhaps you will favour us with your report, citizen," he said, turning his unwavering eyes on me.

"All right," I said. I've always got a kick out of trying to stamp my authority on the guardians. Shocking them out of their routine is a good ploy. "Let's start with a bit of music." I pushed through the ring of tweed jackets and put the cassette in the player that was kept in the chamber.

I couldn't really say that Clapton went to the top of the Council charts. Most of the boyscouts were too young to have much more than a vague idea of what kind of music they were hearing. Those who did know – like the heritage guardian, an expert on eighteenth-century Scottish art who had the look of a poorly preserved mummy but was actually five years younger than me – tried to appear scandalised that the blues should be heard in the Assembly Hall. As for the senior guardian, he kept his head held high. There was a faint smile on his lips but I couldn't make up my mind if he looked more like a tolerant saint suffering for his faith or a public-school headmaster about to use his cane in the old days. The music stopped and there was a long silence.

"Thank you for sharing that with us," the senior guardian said eventually. "I presume this was the cassette that was found inside the victim."

Obviously the grapevine was working well.

"It is, guardian," I replied.

"And what exactly is the significance of this particular . . . how shall I describe it . . . piece?" The guardian moved towards where I was standing by the cassette player, his colleagues close behind.

I shrugged. "Search me, guardian."

He gave me a thin smile. "But you know what it is and who performed it?"

"Oh, aye. It's Eric Clapton's 'Tribute to Elmore'. Elmore being Elmore James, leading proponent of the bottle-neck guitar."

Some of the guardians made a note but most didn't bother.

"Very interesting, citizen," said the heritage guardian, holding his pen vertically like a child trying to attract the teacher's attention. "But what did the murderer mean by putting it—"

"I think we're getting ahead of ourselves, guardians," interrupted Hamilton. I'd been wondering how long he'd keep quiet. "Clearly some information about this case has become available to you already." He looked around balefully. "I'd like to know how."

Nobody volunteered an answer. Gossip between the directorates is the lifeblood of the system, but none of the iron boyscouts could admit that openly — certainly not in front of an ordinary citizen like me. I let them stew for a few moments, then outlined what I'd found in Roddie Aitken's flat. This time all of them took notes.

"So, to summarise," the senior guardian said when I'd finished. "We are dealing with a murderer who took care to leave no fingerprints, who took advantage of the only night of the year when there is no curfew to effect his escape, who tortured his victim to discover the whereabouts of some object as yet unknown and who left this piece of music as some kind of message."

Not bad for a scientist. And the senior guardian isn't just any scientist. He was a senior researcher in the mechanical engineering faculty at the age of twenty-one and a key member of the Science and Energy Directorate a few years later. The word is that when he became senior guardian he never even considered assigning his original directorate to someone else. But no matter how much they fancy themselves, guardians aren't investigators and he hadn't mentioned everything.

"Correct — as far as it goes," I said. Then I gave them something else to chew on. "I'm assuming the murderer was the hooded figure seen by the victim four times before he was killed. What does that tell us, guardians?"

Rustling of papers and eyes definitely lowered. I felt like a professor leading a seminar for a group of students who were never given reading lists.

"What are you getting at, Dalrymple?" Hamilton asked suspiciously. He wasn't impressed that I was springing something we hadn't discussed on him.

"Simply this. The hooded man – not that I'm necessarily convinced it's a male at this stage – showed himself several times to Roddie Aitken. Why? Why didn't he just follow him back to his flat the first time and do what he did last night?"

The senior guardian was nodding, his lower lip caught between his teeth. "I see what you mean, citizen. He was trying to frighten his victim."

"Very good, guardian," I said. "The killer was trying to frighten him into handing over something."

"But what was that something?" Hamilton said, his brow still furrowed.

"I don't know," I said, shrugging my shoulders. "Either he found what he was looking for in the flat or—" I broke off. It had occurred to me that maybe Roddie never had what his killer wanted. He didn't seem to be the kind of guy who was into the black market. So why was the bastard after him? Could it be a case of mistaken identity or was it something more sinister? Possibilities started to bombard me.

"Wake up, citizen," said the medical guardian, her pale face looking unusually impatient. "Or what?"

"Or . . . I don't know," I said, smiling lamely.

The senior guardian gave me a dubious look then turned to the Ice Queen. "Very well. Let's have your report." He paused momentarily before addressing her. "Guardian."

One of the problems the guardians have constructed for themselves is how to address each other in front of ordinary citizens. I'm bloody certain they use their first names when they're on their own, but they can't do that in front of the likes of me.

The medical guardian ran through her preliminary report, putting the time of death around two a.m. and the cause of death shock-induced heart failure. She thought the knife the killer used had a large non-serrated blade – possibly a hunting knife. (Or possibly a standard-issue auxiliary knife, but I didn't feel like raising that point for the time being.)

"We are carrying out tests on matter removed from the

victim's fingernails," the guardian said. "No other traces of the killer have been found, apart from the bite mark on the throat. This is being analysed as I speak and I am cautiously optimistic that we will have sufficient data to carry out a search of dental records." She looked around her colleagues, ending at the senior guardian. "I hope to be able to provide further information at tomorrow's meeting."

"Thank you, guardian." The senior guardian turned to me. "Anything else you feel we should know, citizen?"

I could think of a lot of hints concerning the way they run the city, but I bit my tongue. "We'll be looking at all aspects of the victim's background and following up leads." I gave the information guardian the eye. She was a nervous-looking redhead who had survived from my mother's time. "Are you intending to publicise the killing?"

"That is a matter for the Council," the senior guardian said, his gaze hard. "I suggest you get back to your investigation, citizen."

I headed for the door, then decided to give them a farewell gift. "Guardians," I said over my shoulder, "we're not dealing with an average murderer here. This one walked away with Roddie Aitken's tongue and genitals as well as leaving us a cassette. A cassette that was not standard issue and suggests some connection with the world beyond the city border." I turned and faced them. In the air above the guardians' heads I could almost read the word "dissidents". It has the effect on senior auxiliaries that "Brussels" used to have on Conservative politicians in the 1990s.

I hadn't finished with the Council. I wasn't going to sleep easy tonight and I didn't see why they should. I moved to the door then turned back to face them.

"One of the few things I'm certain about in this case so far is that this isn't the end of the killer's activities. This is just the beginning. Pleasant dreams, guardians."

Chapter Five

———◦◦◦◦◦———

"Where to?" Davie asked from the driver's seat of the guard Land-Rover he'd laid his hands on for the duration of the investigation.

I stood by the railing looking out over the racecourse in Princes Street Gardens towards the ravaged stump of the Scott Monument; the top twenty yards of the space-rocket-shaped steeple fell off a few years back, making a mess of a tourist group from Hong Kong. Frost glistened on the floodlit grass while voices from the tourist restaurants and bars on Princes Street echoed around the surfaces of the ground, the granite buildings and the castle rock. Everything was hard, like the guardians wanted to be and the killer definitely was.

"The hooded man's out there somewhere, Davie," I said, turning to him. "Somebody knows him."

"His friends and relatives maybe don't know that he likes biting people's throats out." Davie shook his head slowly. "Why Roddie, for fuck's sake? Why him, Quint?"

"Let's see if we can find out." I climbed into the rust-spattered Land-Rover. "To the City Archives, guardsman. At the double."

"Now you're talking." Davie gave a sardonic smile as he started the engine. "There's nothing I like better than an evening with the files."

"Sorry. You'd better call Fiona."

"I already have. She's not expecting to see much of me in the immediate future."

We crossed the Royal Mile on the way to the main library which houses citizen archives. I felt sorry for the disruption to Davie's love life, but not too sorry. At least he had a woman in the city. All I had were memories of one who was dead and one who had disappeared.

"Right, what have we got?" We'd been through Roddie Aitken's records and compiled lists of people to be interviewed — questioned, the guard would call it, but I prefer the subtle approach.

Davie leaned back in his chair and stretched his muscular arms, then picked up the checklist we'd made. "Parents: Peter and Morag, 74m Ratcliffe Terrace."

"I'll do them." That promised to be a lot of fun. The local bereavement advisor would have been round by now, but they're often unfeeling enough to make things worse for the families. I'd been coming across this more and more in the last few months. In the past, auxiliaries in the social care and welfare departments had been trained to cope with the needs of citizens. Now most of them were like miniature iron boyscouts, with all the social graces of the worst football fans in the years before the sport was banned by the European Union because of match-fixing and street warfare.

Davie made a note. "Friends: apparently three close male friends and two close females, one of them his cousin."

The Council keeps tabs on citizens by making them declare the friends they see more than once a month. God knows how many auxiliaries that occupies updating files and carrying out spot checks.

"Do you want to make a start on them tomorrow?" I said. "We'll need to try and track down this girlfriend he had. Maybe she's one of those two. If not, he might have met her at a sex session."

Davie nodded. "Then there are his workmates."

"We'll check them out in the archives first. The likelihood is some of them will have black-market offence notifications. We may need to put them under surveillance rather than blunder in."

"Right." Davie raised a finger. "I've just thought of something else. The report Roddie made to the guard about the hooded man."

I grinned. "Well done, guardsman."

Davie's finger was now simultaneously moving up and down and swivelling. "I suppose you had that on your personal list?"

"Of course I did. You're the expert on the City Guard. See if you can find out why no action was taken."

"I can tell you that now, Quint. You know how busy we are, especially over the Christmas and New Year period."

"You never know what you might come across." I stood up and looked around the high shelves packed solid with grey files. They ran for over fifty yards to the far end of the basement which was thirty yards wide – and these were only the archives for citizens like Roddie Aitken who live in the central areas because of their jobs. There are six other citizen archives, not to mention each of the twenty barracks archives where auxiliaries' files are kept, and the central guard archive in the castle. Christ, what had the Council done to the city? Turned it into a paper mausoleum, where people's souls are confined to the archives and their lives programmed more carefully than the computers the guardians keep to themselves. This wasn't why the Enlightenment won the last election. Or why, even until recently, Edinburgh citizens preferred Council rule to the chaos caused by the drugs gangs in the past.

I roused myself. "Come on, Davie. We'll be late for your chief." Hamilton had called an hour earlier and suggested we meet at my place to co-ordinate tomorrow's activities. Now I came to think about it, the guardian had never been in my flat before. He must have fancied a change from his rooms in the castle.

I felt a wave of exhaustion wash over me as we drove towards

Tollcross. It's always the same at the beginning of an investigation – there are so many angles to cover, so much you're unsure about. Sleep is the first casualty, but you can usually rely on the odd adrenalin rush to keep you awake. I got a very large one as we turned into Gilmore Place.

"Jesus, Davie. Pull in. Look down there." I pointed down the street towards the door of my staircase. The curfew had been in effect for a couple hours so there was no one about. Apart from a figure in a long coat with a hood.

"Bloody hell." Davie cut the engine and drew in to the kerb.

"Leave the lights on," I whispered. "We won't see a thing otherwise."

We both leaned forward and watched the hooded man. He was leaning against the wall by the doorway, head bowed. It was difficult to gauge his height and weight because of the voluminous coat and the limited light we were casting.

"He must have seen us," Davie said, his hand straying down to his service knife.

True enough. I knew what he was thinking. The bastard looked like he was waiting for me. I can recognise a challenge when I see one. He had some nerve showing himself on the streets, especially after curfew.

"Stay here. I'm going a bit closer."

"Are you out of your—" Davie shut up when I raised my finger to my mouth.

I opened the door carefully and set my feet on the icy pavement. Then walked slowly out into the middle of the street.

A movement came from the hooded figure, a twitch of the head to tell me I'd been spotted. But he stood his ground. I stepped forward, my heart doing a passable imitation of Willie Dixon producing a particularly thunderous riff on the bass guitar. I got to within ten yards and could see that the coat was dark grey.

Then everything moved into overdrive.

I heard the roar of a clapped-out diesel engine and more lights came round the corner behind me. Hamilton. I'd forgotten about the guardian and his sodding rendezvous. In the few seconds it took me to wave at Davie to get in his boss's way then run forward to my door, the hooded man was off like a greyhound.

I went after him, but he was always going away from me; he obviously kept himself in a lot better shape than I did. I knew where he was headed. Round the corner to the right, there's a yard where the Tourism Department store scaffolding for the tattoo they put on in the summer. If he got over the fence into it, he had a good chance of getting away altogether. My lungs were bursting as I came round the turn. The hooded figure was a good fifty yards ahead, his legs apparently unhindered by the coat. He would hit the fence any second now and it isn't high enough to put off someone as fit as him.

I ground to a halt, spitting something sticky and salty from my mouth, and pulled out my mobile phone.

"Davie," I gasped, "send vehicles round to the other side of the store in Gilmore Place Lane. Quick, he's over the fence."

Over the fence didn't do justice to the fugitive's leap – he sailed over like he was a champion vaulter with his pole concealed about his clothing. I waited for a minute then walked painfully back to Davie and Hamilton.

They were following the chase on their mobiles. I could tell from their expressions that the hooded man hadn't been sighted. We drove round and watched guardsmen and women comb the piles of scaffolding. There was nothing.

And nothing over the next few hours from all the guard units across the city, despite Hamilton's fierce instructions to spare no effort in the chase.

It was beginning to look like we were after one of the supernatural creatures that filled the world's TV screens before the millennium – our very own file stamped "X".

*   *   *

In the morning Hamilton was apologetic. He had to be. I made it clear to him what I thought about the timing of his arrival in Gilmore Place. He muttered something about wanting to see how the other half lived. Jesus.

"Still no trace of your hooded man, Dalrymple," he added dolefully.

I was at the leaded window of his office in the castle, looking out over the ice realm that the city had become overnight. The suburbs were wreathed in smoke from the coal fires while the glass frontages of the shops across the gardens glinted in the sunlight. To the right, tourists slipped and slithered their way up the Mound. It was closed to buses in the early morning. In the old days there had been an electric blanket under the road, but the Council gave up using it a couple of years ago because of the electricity restrictions.

"You'd have thought there would have been some footprints around the depot he passed through," I said.

"Scuffmarks and the like. Nothing useful."

I had another bone to wrestle over with him. "So the Council decided not to publicise any details of the murder?"

He looked up briefly from his papers. "Majority decision, yes." Hamilton often fell into using the clipped sentences favoured by professional army officers and robots.

"And were you one of those who voted in favour?" I asked, sitting on the edge of his wide desk. That always got to him.

"No, I wasn't actually," he replied, glaring at me.

"What's happened?" I asked sarcastically. "Have you suddenly become a supporter of the free flow of information?" As far as I was aware the Council hadn't brought April Fools' Day forward.

"Certainly not." That was more like Hamilton. "I simply feel that in a murder as gruesome as this one we stand more chance of catching the perpetrator if we have the citizen body on our side."

"Very good, guardian." I got off his desk in surprise. "We've finally found something we agree on."

He looked at me and shook his head hopelessly.

My mobile rang.

"Good morning, citizen." The Ice Queen's business-like tones. "First the bad news. There were no traces of the murderer under the victim's fingernails. But the good news is that I have a profile of part of the killer's upper jaw. Do you want some of my people to help with the archive search?"

Two guardians trying to be helpful in one day. That was unusual. I handed her over to Hamilton to co-ordinate their directorates' efforts. And went to interview Roddie Aitken's parents.

Ratcliffe Terrace. When I was a student a year before the Enlightenment we used to go to a bloody good pub there which had an antique panelled bar and a moulded ceiling. The beer wasn't bad either. It got burned down by one of the drugs gangs not long after independence. Now it's a day care centre — all mothers are working mothers in the perfect city, and children are looked after by city staff from six months.

I slipped for about the tenth time that morning as I got out of the guard vehicle and headed for number 74. Davie'd just called to say that he'd spoken to two of Roddie's friends and was on his way to the third, one of the women. He hadn't found anything that looked significant so far.

The stairwell smelled the same as mine and every other in the city — boiled root vegetables, dodgy sewage and rancid citizens. I climbed up to the fourth floor, feeling the muscles tight in my legs from my ineffectual sprint last night. The place was dead quiet, everyone except the Aitkens at work. I'd asked them via the guard to stay at home.

The door was in surprisingly good nick — it had been repainted recently. I wondered where the paint had come from.

The Housing Directorate hasn't been doing much maintenance of citizens' houses in the last few years.

"I'm Dalrymple," I said to the tall, balding man who eventually opened the door. He was stooping slightly, an expression of childlike bewilderment on his slack face. "You can call me Quint."

"Quint?" he repeated blankly.

"Come away in," said a strong voice behind him. A woman who was nearly as tall as Peter Aitken appeared, nudging him gently out of the way. "I'm Morag, Roddie's mother," she said, offering her hand. "You'll be the investigator we were told to wait for."

I repeated my name.

"Quint? Is that short for Quintus, the fifth born?" Her eyes were dark brown like her son's and lively. Although her hair was pure white, the softness of her face suggested she was younger than her husband.

"No, it's short for Quintilian."

"The Roman orator and grammarian," Morag Aitken added. She'd probably taken advantage of the Education Directorate's continuing education programme. She led me and her husband, who was lagging behind, into the living room. It was a bit larger than mine and efforts had been made to decorate it distinctively. Someone had provided a series of pretty impressive watercolours depicting Edinburgh skylines.

"Mine," Roddie's mother said, following the direction of my eyes. Then the façade cracked momentarily. "Roddie always liked them." She took a deep breath then made an attempt at smiling. "Sit down, the pair of you."

"I met your son," I said, forcing myself to look at them. "I . . . I liked him a lot."

"Aye," his father said. "Everybody liked him." His voice broke towards the end of the sentence.

Morag Aitken was studying me. "How did you come to meet Roddie, Quintilian?"

"He visited me on Hogmanay." I was watching them carefully to see how they would react. "He had a problem he wanted my help with."

"What sort of problem?" Their voices came simultaneously. They glanced at each other in surprise.

It was obvious Roddie hadn't told them about the hooded man. Was he keeping it secret or did he just not want to scare his folks?

"Oh, just a minor hassle at work," I said, looking down at my notebook.

"What was it?" Morag Aitken asked insistently. "Roddie never had any problems in the department."

"That's right," her husband said. "All the other delivery men thought he was a great lad. His superior told me he had high hopes for him."

I would be checking that, but the impression I was getting from the parents tallied with my own. Roddie was a genuinely good lad. So why had he been tortured and killed?

"I'm sorry if this seems like an insulting question, but it may be important." I found it difficult to look these seemingly decent people in the eye now. "Did Roddie ever . . . em, bring anything home from work?"

Morag Aitken drew herself up like a lioness about to remove a jackal's head. "That *is* an insult, citizen. Roddie was brought up to be totally honest."

I glanced at Peter. He was nodding his head. I believed them. "If it's any comfort to you, that's what I expected to hear."

Roddie's mother gave me a long stare, then nodded sternly. "That is some comfort, Quintilian."

I was quiet for a few moments.

"He mentioned a girl. Do you know her?"

"A girl in the romantic sense?" Morag asked, giving me a sharp look.

"I think so. He wasn't too specific. We're talking to some of his friends . . ." I showed her the list of names.

"Those are his oldest friends from school," his mother said. "But he never said anything to me about a girlfriend."

I wasn't particularly taken aback by that. If Morag Aitken had been my mother, I don't think I'd have been too open about my sex life.

"In this city, girlfriends are hardly encouraged," she said. Neither are married couples like Roddie's parents, but the Council allows citizen weddings if people are insistent enough.

I stayed for another half-hour filling in Roddie's background and finding nothing at all to suggest that he'd ever been a bad boy. On the contrary, he would have been an ideal trainee auxiliary — apart from the fact that he wasn't the callous type favoured by the iron boyscouts.

They showed me to the door. Something about the way Peter Aitken was looking at me made me think he wanted a private word. I said my farewells to his wife, then engaged him in conversation about the paint he'd used on his front door. That got rid of her quickly enough. It turned out that he'd had it from a friend in the pub and not from his son.

"That girl you were asking about," he said in a low voice. "He did mention her to me once. He was very pleased with himself." He glanced back into the flat. "Morag's a bit ... well, she never liked the idea of Roddie being with a woman."

"Do you know her name?"

He shook his head. "Sorry, son." Then he gave me a conspiratorial smile. "But I do know that he met her at a sex session."

"Cheerio, then, citizen," I said loudly, seeing Morag Aitken's white head looming in the hallway behind.

"Find the bastard who did that to my lad, son," Peter Aitken said in a feeble voice.

I hadn't forgotten what I'd sworn at Roddie's bedside. I might have known it would be this way. *Cherchez la femme*. The story of my life.

*   *   *

I met up with Davie at my flat. We found some stale baps and floppy slices of cheese and ate them for lunch. I glanced through the letters requesting help that people push under my door, while Davie told me about Roddie's friends. It was as his parents said. He'd known them all from primary school. None of them had the faintest idea why he'd been killed. What was interesting was that he'd kept his girlfriend secret from them all.

"Look at the state of this writing," I said, holding up a tattered standard-issue recycled brown envelope.

"What is it?" Davie said, his mouth full. "One of the Dead Sea Scrolls?"

The tiny, perfectly formed letters certainly looked like those of an ancient scribe. My namesake Quintilian must have got letters like this all the time. I opened the flap carefully and pulled out a single piece of the off-white writing paper citizens get from Supply Directorate stores. When I deciphered the address at the top, I discovered to my surprise that it was from my father's retirement home in Trinity. I looked down at the signature.

"It's from William McEwan."

"The former guardian who misbehaved himself at the reception the other night?"

"You heard about that, did you?"

Davie grinned before taking another bite. "The story goes that the senior guardian froze him out in a big way."

"'Quintilian,'" I read, "'I fear there is nothing even you can do about the great injustice of the Bone Yard.'" I looked over at Davie. "The Bone Yard. I heard him mention that at the party. Have you ever heard the name before?"

Davie sniffed suspiciously at a bottle of milk from my tiny citizen-issue fridge. "The Bone Yard? What is it? A new nightclub?"

I read on. "'I am breaking the Council's confidentiality oath by writing this letter, but I cannot keep silent any more. The next time you visit your father, come to my room. We are guilty of a great wrong and I must share it with you before it is too late.'"

Davie was making tea on my electric ring. "Bit melodramatic, don't you think?"

"You never know with the old ones." I remembered William at the reception. "He was wound up about it enough to go for the senior guardian's jugular."

"I'd have it black, unless you're keen on tea-flavoured yoghurt," Davie said, handing me a mug. "So what does it mean?"

"God knows," I said, shaking my head. "I'll check it out when I next see Hector." I looked at my notebook. "Right, then, back to the files. Let's check out Roddie's workmates."

We spent the afternoon in the archives. Some of the guys who worked with Roddie had been done for black-market activities, but none of it looked too serious. I turned my list over to the public order guardian – he'd enjoy terrorising them.

Meanwhile Davie and I went off to Roddie's local sex centre to hunt the mysterious girlfriend. The poor woman was probably looking forward to her next meeting with him, completely unaware of the murder. I hoped to hell I wasn't the one who would have to tell her.

Chapter Six

The tourists braving the cold on the Royal Mile had forced smiles on their bluish faces. The sky was overcast now and the temperature had gone up by a few degrees. I suppose that was as good a reason as any to feel cheerful. But tourists are only in the perfect city for a week or two. The rest of us have to live here permanently – no foreign holidays, no dancing in the streets (apart from Hogmanay) and no time off for good behaviour. All that most citizens have to look forward to is the weekly sex session. Even that's less exciting than it sounds, especially if, like me, you haven't ever really come to terms with having sex with complete strangers. Then again, you can get used to anything.

"Don't you think it's a bit strange that none of Roddie's friends knew anything about this girlfriend of his?" Davie said as he turned down St Mary's Street.

"Not necessarily. Maybe he was just keeping her to himself. He wouldn't be the first guy to do that."

I looked out at the grimy buildings on both sides. As soon as you leave the Royal Mile the atmosphere changes. No more souvenir shops, expensive tea rooms or restored medieval façades. You're into ordinary citizen land, although the Council has made a bit of an effort to tart up the Cowgate further down. It's here they run the cattle along to the Grassmarket and the tourists who watch sometimes venture into the pubs. They're still pretty shitty though. When I was a student we used to call the Cowgate the ninth circle of the inferno. The bars stayed open all night and the road was full of paralytic lost souls bewailing their fate and desperately searching for friends who'd long since buggered off home. The curfew's put paid to all of that.

Davie pulled up outside the Pleasance buildings. A sign on the wall described them as Citizens' Leisure Centre Number 13. In pre-Enlightenment times they were part of the university – there was a theatre, squash courts, bars and the like. Now it's a licensed knocking shop. Unusually for this city, tourists are not allowed in. They're catered for in the much more upmarket facilities run by the subtly named Prostitution Services Department. And they have to pay. At least citizens get laid for free. But we pay for that privilege in other ways.

"How do you want to play this?" Davie asked before we got out.

I knew what he meant. Guardsmen are about as welcome in sex centres as a tingling in the urethra. The places are run by low-ranking auxiliaries who do their best to convince clients that they have only citizens' interests at heart. Of course, copies of the records they keep are collected in the middle of every Sunday night by plain-clothed guard personnel. Where would the Council be if it didn't know exactly who was screwing who? Maybe that's how the celibate guardians get a thrill.

"Let's go in together," I said, grinning at him. "It's a bit chilly for you to stay out here." Davie's a useful guy to have around auxiliaries who think they're something special. Which means more or less all auxiliaries.

The middle-aged reception clerk looked me up and down with a practised eye but ignored Davie completely. Then she picked up the phone on her desk.

I cut the connection. "Hold on, citizen Macmillan," I said, reading the badge on her flat chest. "A few questions before you call your supervisor." I showed her the Council authorisation Hamilton had given me earlier in the day.

"I'm only on the door," the woman said in a dull voice. "I don't know anything." Her face was fleshless, the skin pocked with scabs. Another triumph for the medical guardian's Dietetics Department.

"You don't know anything about what?" I asked, giving her an encouraging smile. "I haven't even told you what I'm after yet."

"I don't know anything," she repeated sullenly. This is how citizens are nowadays. Hyper-suspicious of the Council and all its works.

I showed her the photograph from Roddie's file. "Recognise him?" I saw her eyes flicker.

The skin around her mouth loosened and she almost smiled. "Oh, aye, that's Roddie. Roddie Aitken. He's been coming here for a long time."

Five years, I calculated. Citizens attend weekly sex sessions from their eighteenth birthdays.

"Roddie's fine. We all like him here," she said, her face suddenly hardening again. "What's he done?"

"Don't worry, he hasn't done anything," I said. That was true enough. I sat on the end of her desk and gave her another smile. All that did was make her look down at her thin thighs, which were poking out from the short skirt sex centre staff are required to wear. "Who was he with in the last few weeks?"

Citizen Macmillan seemed to freeze for a few seconds before she answered, her eyes still lowered. "I can't remember. I'm only on the door. It's not my job to—"

"It's not your job to do what, citizen?" The man's voice was as smooth as the duvet cover in a tourist hotel bedroom. I almost believed he was unconcerned.

He didn't wait for the receptionist to answer. "And you are?"

"Dalrymple," I answered, flashing my authorisation again. "I need to see your files."

"Where's your barracks number badge, auxiliary?" Davie demanded. You can't take him anywhere.

The supervisor smiled urbanely. "I do apologise, guardsman. I must have left it on my desk. I'm Moray 37." His low barracks number indicated that he'd been a member of the Enlightenment before independence. He led us down a corridor, his long legs sheathed in an unusually tight pair of cream trousers. He didn't look like he would last a day on the border, but he'd have got in as an auxiliary before the boyscouts restricted the rank to heavy-duty headbangers.

"Well, here we are," he said, tossing carefully tended locks of black hair back from his forehead. "*Chez moi.*"

The room we were in was a file-spotter's paradise. Apart from the table and chair a couple of paces in from the door, the furniture consisted entirely of gunmetal filing cabinets. Judging by the neat array of pens, pencils, notepads and proformas on the tabletop, I reckoned Moray 37 was that file-spotter.

Davie picked up a barracks number badge and tossed it to the auxiliary, who gave him a brief smile.

"Well, gentlemen, tell me how I can be of service." The supervisor sat down in front of us and propped up his head on the extended fingers of one hand. He was probably tired after a hard morning with his pencil and rubber.

"A citizen by the name of Roddie Aitken," I said. "Do you know him?"

"I think not." Moray 37 almost pulled it off. If his eyelashes had quivered for a micro-second less, I'd have gone for it. "Should I?" he asked with a studied lack of interest.

"Citizen Macmillan at the door says he's very popular around here," I said, watching him carefully.

The auxiliary fluttered his lashes deliberately this time. "Citizen Macmillan doesn't know the meaning of the word popular." He leaned back and pulled open a drawer in the nearest cabinet. "Aitken, Roderick. Here he is." He pulled out a grey cardboard folder and opened it. "Aitken, Roderick." His features were blank. Too blank. "I can't say I remember him. It appears he's one of our people though. Next due in on Saturday."

No chance of that. I wondered whether Moray 37 had really heard nothing on the grapevine about the murder or whether he knew more about Roddie than he was letting on. Time for the third degree. I gave Davie the nod.

"Do you think I'm funny, auxiliary?" Davie asked mildly.

Moray 37 raised an eyebrow. "You're about as far from funny as I am from playing in the front row of the barracks rugby team."

Davie leaned over the table until his face was a few inches in front of the supervisor's. "So why are you laughing at me?" he demanded.

"I can assure you, guardsman ..." There was no way that sentence was ever going to reach the finishing post.

"You're taking the piss. My boss and I come in here asking questions and what do you do?" His beard was close enough to tickle Moray 37's cheeks. Davie brought his fist down hard on the table. "You give us the runaround."

The supervisor's eyes sprang open wide, then his gaze dropped. "I ... oh, very well ... you can see the file for yourselves."

"Thank you." I took it and looked down the attendance sheet. Next to the dates of sex sessions is entered the name of the partner. Unmarried ordinary citizens must, as the city regulations put it, "enjoy sexual congress" once a week with a different member of either sex, depending on whether they have declared themselves hetero or homo. (Bisexuals aren't catered for – they made the original guardians feel insecure, don't ask me why.) This was supposed to be a way of widening people's sexual experiences and ensuring that everyone screwed everyone, whether they were handsome, ugly, fat (not many of them nowadays), thin, spotty, greasy-haired or whatever. Believe it or not, the Council actually reckons this improves social cohesion. I've had sessions with women who definitely did not have that effect. No doubt there are several female citizens who would say the same about me.

There wasn't anything special about Roddie's attendance

sheet. I made a note of the last six female names he had been with. Then I flicked through the other pages. One detailed his sexual preferences (oral sex was one – how unusual); another, the comments made by his partners to centre staff afterwards. They were mostly complimentary, although one woman didn't think much of his technique. The last page gave the results of his most recent medical check-up, which were clear.

"Satisfied, citizen?" Moray 37 asked. His voice sounded just a bit tense.

I smiled at him. "No. Show me the reception records."

The auxiliary went as grey as the white bread in the city's bakeries. This looked promising.

"I'll come with you," Davie said as Moray 37 got up and headed back to citizen Macmillan's desk in the entrance hall. He suddenly seemed to be carrying a great weight.

They were back in a minute, Davie holding another grey file. The auxiliary sat down slowly.

It only took me a few seconds to discover what he was worried about. "Well, well," I said. "The Council is going to be very upset. You haven't been balancing your records, have you?"

Moray 37 now looked like he was about to lose control of his lunch. He shook his head distractedly.

What I'd found were the check-in slips for Roddie's last three partners. And the juicy bit was that, while the attendance sheet showed three different names, the slips all had the same one. Moray 37 could be demoted for this. Regulations state that citizens are forbidden to enjoy sexual congress more than once with the same partner unless what's called a "long-term relationship permit" has been issued.

"Did you know about this, Moray 37?" I asked, showing him the slips.

"I . . . no . . . I . . ." His shoulders dropped. "Well, yes, I did have some idea . . ."

"Some idea?" Davie yelled. "What the fuck does that mean?"

The auxiliary shifted around on his chair as if a burrowing creature had just broken through the fabric of his trousers. "You know how it is, citizen," he said, looking at me hopefully.

I did but I wasn't going to tell him that.

He started shuffling paper. "Sometimes citizens form emotional attachments. They like to see the same partner every week."

"And what do you get for arranging these romantic trysts?" I asked.

"What do I get?" Moray 37 tried to look outraged. "I'm an auxiliary. My job is to serve citizens."

Davie sounded like he was about to choke. "Your job, in case you've forgotten, is to serve the city."

"Which isn't exactly the same thing," I said. "Don't tell me you did it in the cause of young love."

The supervisor squirmed again. "Obviously you have no understanding of the feelings experienced by young people."

He was wrong there, but I still wasn't buying it. Auxiliaries, even older ones, aren't known for acts of charity to citizens. Maybe someone was pulling his chain, but short of taking him up to the castle and setting Davie loose on him in a big way, it didn't look like I was going to get much more out of him.

I looked at the name on the last three check-in slips. It was an unusual one. "Get me Sheena Marinello's file, auxiliary."

Now Moray 37 had the look of a pre-independence banker whose company car had just been surrounded by a crowd of ex-customers objecting to the way their savings had gone walkabout to the Cayman Islands. He moved away.

"I'll be right behind you," said Davie with a death's-head grin.

They went to the filing cabinets, where Moray 37 put on a performance of failing to find the file that would have won an Oscar in the days when Hollywood producers made the occasional watchable movie, rather than the Christian fundamentalist garbage they come up with now.

"Apparently the file's been — how did you put it, auxiliary? — misplaced," Davie said from the far end of the room.

I can't say I was surprised. "Can you describe how she looks, Moray 37?"

He shrugged. "Medium height, dark brown hair, shoulder length, freckles on her cheeks — nothing particularly special."

"Don't discuss this conversation with anyone, auxiliary," I said as I left his office. "That way, if you're lucky, you might stay in your job."

He looked ridiculously grateful.

In the corridor I heard the usual noises from the cubicles where citizens get their weekly hour of congress: music, lowered voices, grunts, moans, even a soft, satisfied sigh. I can't remember the last time I emitted one of those. Well, I can. It was with Katharine, and it was in my flat rather than in public.

The late afternoon shift of clients had started and there was a queue in the entrance hall. The receptionist was checking in a middle-aged couple who were glancing at each other dubiously. I waited for them to head off down the corridor, clear space between their bodies. There's nothing worse than being allocated a partner you don't even vaguely fancy.

"Citizen Macmillan," I said. "One question."

Her mouth slackened and her eyes opened wide.

"Don't worry. I'm not investigating you."

She didn't look like she believed me.

"Sheena Marinello. I know you've seen her. Describe the way she looks, will you?"

"Describe the way she looks?" The thin citizen laughed once, with surprising bitterness. "She's a bloody stunner. The kind that men do anything for. Beautiful body, perfect face, legs up to her neck." She shook her head slowly. "Roddie couldn't believe his luck."

We walked out into the cold past more ordinary citizens: young lads with lust in their eyes and standard-issue condoms in their pockets, women who'd seen it all before standing wearily in line. Roddie Aitken had got more out of his sex sessions than most. But who exactly was Sheena Marinello, and why had the supervisor been so vague about her charms? Time for another trip to the archives.

Where I discovered something very interesting. There weren't many women called Marinello in the citizen body, and only one whose first name was Sheena.

"Look at this, Davie." I showed him the front cover of the file. A single word had been rubberstamped in black on it.

"Bloody hell," he said. "Was Roddie Aitken having sex with a ghost?"

"Marinello, Sheena Pauline, deceased 12.3.2021." I read the handwritten date from the middle of the stamp, then opened the file. "She was past the age for compulsory sex sessions anyway."

Davie looked at the photograph. "Over sixty by a mile. So what's been going on at Moray 37's sex centre?"

That made me laugh. "You're not on parade now, guardsman. I know what goes on in barracks."

"All right, all right," he said with a scowl. "One of my female colleagues fancied a bit of rough."

I nodded. Occasionally auxiliaries got bored with barracks sex sessions and got themselves into ordinary citizen centres. That explained why the supervisor had looked guilty and why Sheena Marinello's file had been misplaced. It wasn't the first time dead citizens' identities had been assumed.

"Are we going to pick Moray 37 up?" Davie said as we got back into the Land-Rover.

"Hang on a minute. Let's see if the dental records search has turned up anything." I rang the medical guardian on the vehicle's mobile phone. She sounded totally unexcited to hear my voice, but she did inform me that no match had been found for the bite mark in the records so far.

Great. I looked up George IVth Bridge to the corner of the Lawnmarket where the gallows stand and thought about taking

Moray 37 in. It would mean curtains for the supervisor's career if we did. I didn't reckon he deserved demotion and the rest of his life being shunned by citizens for being an ex-auxiliary just because he'd done a colleague a favour. On the other hand, this mystery woman might be the only lead we had to Roddie's killer. Before I could decide, my mobile rang.

"Dalrymple? Hamilton here."

I knew immediately that he had something shit-hot to tell me – he'd never use his name rather than his title on the phone unless he was seriously wound up.

"Another body's been found."

I signalled to Davie to start the engine.

"Where is it, Lewis?"

"Among the ruins of Holyroodhouse."

"The palace?" Not a million miles from Roddie's flat or from the sex centre. I pointed to Davie and we moved off at speed. "We're on our way."

"As am I. And Dalrymple?"

I had to hold the phone to my ear with my shoulder as both my hands were otherwise involved. Davie had taken the corner like a Formula One man in the days when spending millions of dollars driving round and round in circles was an acceptable part of popular culture. "What, Lewis?"

"It's a woman this time."

I felt my stomach somersault.

"Not an auxiliary by any chance?"

"How on earth did you know that?" Hamilton asked in surprise.

"Call it a hunch, Lewis. Out."

I could live without that kind of hunch.

Chapter Seven

We raced down the lower reaches of the Royal Mile past bright lights, flags and startled tourists – into the black hole straight ahead of us. In the last hour night had fallen on the city. The ruins of the palace were as dark as anywhere in Edinburgh. Holyroodhouse had been the epicentre of the catastrophic riots that followed the heir to the throne's second marriage to the daughter of a Colombian drugs baron before his coronation in 2002. It wasn't only his fault. We'd been strung along for years by political parties who'd set up devolution but kept their sticky unionist fingers very much on the controls. The crown prince's attempt to improve his family's cash reserves wasn't a brilliant public relations exercise though. His involvement with a drugs heiress went down like a lead zeppelin at a time when the UK was being torn apart by drugs-related crime. Just as well he wasn't staying at the palace. The masses would have had no problem blowing him up as well.

"Hope you've got a torch," Davie said.

"Hope the directorate manages to find a generator." The Council had left the ruins exactly as they were. It liked the idea of them as a reminder of the bad old days, but it didn't like the idea enough to put up any lights.

"We're okay," Davie said. "They're way ahead of us. A generator must have been authorised as soon as the body was found." He pointed at the glow that was faintly visible beyond the first line of stones.

"Course it was. There's no expense spared when it's an auxiliary who's been murdered."

"Thank you for that observation, citizen." Davie's imitation of Hamilton's solemn tones made me laugh.

Not for long. Guardsmen and women were moving around among the crush of official vehicles, their faces drawn and pallid in the headlights. The main thing they're taught during auxiliary training is how to put a lid on their emotions. It looked like the collective pressure cooker was about to blow. I got out and immediately felt my feet begin to freeze.

Another Land-Rover pulled up, sending a shower of gravel over my tingling legs. Hamilton and the medical guardian got out.

"Over there, guardian." A guard commander had arrived at Hamilton's side like a dog that was desperate to please. "Raeburn 03 arrived with the scene-of-crime squad."

That was all I needed. Machiavelli had been out of my hair for the last twenty-four hours. I might have known the louse would try to lay his eggs again.

Hamilton strode away angrily towards a fifteen-foot-high section of the ruins that had been part of the picture gallery wall. Light from the generator that had been set up shone round the shattered edges. It was a good sheltered place for a murder. Not many citizens or tourists bother to walk here, especially in winter.

I went round the back and found Hamilton laying into his subordinate.

". . . and I specifically told you to keep your nose out of the murder case, Raeburn 03. Dalrymple's in charge."

Machiavelli stood there rubbing his hands and bending forward in a way that combined acquiescence with a complete lack of respect – a good trick if you can pull it off.

"I heard the initial call for assistance, guardian. I judged it was a serious matter and—"

"You judged it was something your friends in the Council would like inside information on, auxiliary," Hamilton roared. "Well, that's my job. Get back to the castle and play with your files."

Machiavelli straightened himself up, shot me a vicious glance and moved off slowly, trying to salvage some credibility in front of directorate personnel. I don't think he pulled that trick off.

"Did Raeburn 03 touch anything at the scene?" I asked a heavily built guardsman with a grizzled beard.

He shook his head. "I arrived with the first squad. We were told to keep everyone back until the guardian arrived."

"Who found the body?"

The guardsman nodded at a tourist with a pair of binoculars round his neck who was leaning against the wall further down. His knees didn't look too steady.

I turned to the Ice Queen. "Shall we have a look then?"

She was already kitted out in plastic overalls. I pulled mine on and walked with her to the tarpaulin that lay in the centre of the lit-up area. The ground was rock hard, with no sign of any footprints.

The guardian nodded to the guardsmen at the tarpaulin corners. They lifted it and rolled it back, averting their eyes.

It was a bad one. I've seen a lot of victims' bodies, but this one was in a hell of a state. She was on her back, naked apart from the remains of a brassiere, the cups of which had been ripped apart with a sharp blade. I couldn't see initially if she fitted the description we had of Roddie Aitken's girlfriend because her head was tipped back, displaying a bloody hole in her neck. The blood was frozen. The icy sheen of the body made it look even more grotesque – like a frozen mummy rather than a woman who'd recently been alive.

"She's been here for at least twelve hours, probably more." The medical guardian was on her knees beside the upper body. "The throat appears to have been bitten in the same way as the previous victim."

"That's not the only similarity," I said, pointing to the groin. The corner of a plastic bag was protruding from the mutilated vaginal opening. There were several deep cuts in the flesh of the upper thighs too.

"The wrists were bound as well." The guardian indicated ice-flecked weals in the skin.

"How did she die?" I asked.

She went back up to the head.

"Difficult to tell. Could be shock again, especially in an ambient temperature like this." The guardian examined the ground beneath the neck. "Loss of blood perhaps."

"How about the mouth?" I bent over the victim's head. There were frozen traces of blood around the chin. As with Roddie, the jaws were locked together and the teeth bared in a ghastly rictus.

"You'll have to wait, citizen. It's certainly a possibility that the tongue was cut."

"He'd need to keep her quiet, even out here in the middle of the night." I shook my head. "Why can't the butcher use a gag like anyone else?"

The Ice Queen stood up and stretched her arms. "Excuse me for encroaching on your territory, citizen, but didn't you have some theory about the tape being a message?"

"So?"

"So the removal of the tongue isn't just a way of stifling screams – it's symbolic too. The music speaks, not the human voice."

It wasn't a bad idea, especially as the Clapton track was an instrumental. It made me shiver though. What kind of lunatic leaves symbolic messages in his victims? Serial killers aren't usually too hot on semiotics.

"How do we know she was an auxiliary?" I said, turning to Hamilton, who was keeping his distance and looking in the opposite direction.

"I know her," said the grizzled guardsman I'd already spoken to. "She's in my barracks. Moray 310 is her number."

Was her number, more like. So she was in the same barracks as the sex centre supervisor. Things were beginning to connect.

The face of the tourist who found the body appeared behind the guardsman. The guy was in his late fifties, grey-haired and shaking from the cold.

"I insist you take me indoors," he said in a caricature of what was once called the Queen's English. "I explained to the officer that I was perfectly willing to make a statement, but I am not enamoured by the prospect of freezing to death before you can be bothered to take it."

Davie asked for the man's passport. "US national," he said. "Oliver St John Stafford."

He was probably one of the numerous ex-British citizens who jumped ship when crime in the UK made life less than rosy. You don't get any tourists from England itself in the city these days – the Council regards England as a wasteland harbouring hundreds of drugs gangs in search of new markets. It's one of the few things the iron boyscouts have got right.

"We'll send you up to the castle in a minute, Mr Stafford," I said with a brief smile. I wasn't keen on the prospect of permanently losing touch with my feet either. "Just tell me how you found the body, please."

He touched his binoculars. "I was birdwatching in the park. I thought I caught a glimpse of one of the American thrushes which sometimes make it across the Atlantic and—"

"What time was this, Mr Stafford?" I asked with an even briefer smile.

"It was about four, I suppose. The gloaming was well advanced." He looked pleased with himself for having got a Scots word in, not that his vowels were very convincing.

"Did you see anyone else in the vicinity?"

"Good God, no. Far too cold for anyone except a dedicated twitcher like me."

"What did you see when you arrived here?"

The fatuous smile was wiped from his face. "What did I see? I . . . Well, I was after my thrush and I came round the corner over there and found . . . found the woman."

"What was the first thing you noticed?" I gripped his arm to focus his mind. It's surprising what sticks in people's memories.

"The first thing I noticed were her clothes and the things from her bag." He moved his head rapidly from side to side. "They were all over the place." Then he lowered his chin to his chest. "My first impression was of the mess a bird of prey makes when it catches a smaller bird – feathers torn out and left all around."

I hadn't noticed the woman's clothing because of the restricted range of the lighting. Looking around in the surrounding gloom, I made out the white overalls of scene-of-crime people collating objects. Clothes and possessions scattered about. I remembered the mess in Roddie's flat. The killer had been looking for something again.

I sent Davie off with the birdwatcher.

A guardsman came round with plastic cups of black tea – the Public Order Directorate often fails to get hold of enough milk.

"What did the killer do for light?" Hamilton asked, cursing under his breath as he scalded his tongue.

I took hold of his elbow and led him out of the ring of artificial light. "Look above Arthur's Seat."

The moon, a day past full, had just cleared the summit of the hill. It shone out with frozen radiance over the aptly named Enlightenment Park.

"Would that have been enough for his purposes?" Hamilton asked.

"He might have had some kind of portable light as well." I beckoned to the nearest scene-of-crime officer. "Any sign of the victim's torch?" Auxiliaries are issued with torches and the batteries to run them; ordinary citizens are denied access to both, in order to restrict movement after curfew.

The young guardsman shook his head.

"So the murderer took hers," the guardian said.

"That doesn't mean he didn't have one of his own too," I said, stamping my feet. Circulation was long gone below my knees.

Hamilton's nostrils flared. I knew they would. As far as he's concerned, my chief suspects are always auxiliaries.

"Can we wrap this up, citizen?" Even the medical guardian looked like the cold was getting to her.

I nodded. "What about the post-mortem?"

"Tomorrow morning. She needs to thaw out."

I could have insisted on having it done during the night, but I had plenty of other things to be getting on with. Like why the victim was wearing a bra that was a lot flashier than the standard-issue number.

I went over to the pile of clear bags that contained the rest of her clothing and held them up to the light one by one. Black track suit bottoms — fair enough. White T-shirt and maroon and white running shoes — ditto. But black fishnet stockings? And high-cut white silk knickers matching the bra?

"She was in the Prostitution Services Department, citizen." The guardsman with the grey beard was at my side.

"You amaze me."

"Worked in one of the clubs. She must have been on her way back to barracks when the piece of excrement caught up with her."

"Any idea which club?"

He looked at me and nodded slowly. "The Three Graces in the Grassmarket. She was one of them."

The Three Graces was where Roddie Aitken made deliveries and had his first sighting of the hooded man. Coincidence?

"I need a photograph of her," I said.

The guardsman set off towards one of the directorate personnel who'd been at work around the body.

"A photograph of her alive," I called after him.

"Oh, right. If you come back to Moray with me, I'll get you one from her file."

I called Davie and told him to meet me at the sex centre. Then I followed the guardsman to his vehicle. The moon was higher in the inky sky now and my feet were blocks of ice dug from the deepest glacier in Greenland. But they were nothing compared with the freeze-dried heart of the beast who was loose in this benighted city.

Citizen Macmillan recognised the photograph I'd been given at Moray Barracks immediately.

"Aye, that's Sheena Marinello all right." She shook her head and muttered something abusive. "So she was an auxiliary." The photo showed the dead woman wearing a guard tunic, her hair plaited in the requisite female auxiliary style. "I thought she was a stuck-up bitch."

"Is the supervisor on duty?"

"Is he fuck. He left about half an hour ago looking like his arse was on fire."

We left her to the queue of customers that had built up behind us.

"We've got two choices," I said as we got back into the Land-Rover.

"And neither of them involves eating, I'm sure," Davie complained.

"Oh, guardsman, I'm sorry, are you hungry? We'll just stop the investigation for an hour so you can refuel. After all, it's only a double murder."

"Up all your orifices, Quint," he replied. "So what are the two choices? Check if the supervisor's gone back to his barracks and . . . ?"

"Actually, you might get a chance to eat at the other one."

"Great. Let's go there." He turned the key and waited for the prehistoric starting motor to engage.

"Fair enough." I picked up my mobile and called Moray

Barracks. They hadn't seen the supervisor since midday. So I called Hamilton and asked for all barracks to be alerted about the missing auxiliary.

"Where are we going then?" Davie enquired when I finished.

"To the Three Graces in the Grassmarket. Or rather, the Two Graces as it now is."

"A sex club." Davie shook his head vigorously. "I couldn't possibly, citizen."

"Uh-huh."

We got there in under three minutes.

Although it was only eight o'clock, there was already a large crowd of tourists around the replica of the Three Graces outside the club. We were told to get to the back of the queue in at least ten languages as we pushed our way through. At least I think that's what was being said.

A couple of gorillas in dinner jackets three sizes too small blocked my passage. Then they saw, in rapid succession, my authorisation and Davie. They let us through. Next we were greeted by two girls in toga-like robes which showed more than they covered up. The things some people have to do for the Council – and auxiliaries can't say no to any duty they're assigned.

"Who's in charge?" I asked.

"Watt 94, citizen. You'll find her at the bar."

"Good. I could do with a drink."

The girls parted the curtain and we went down into the club proper. It was large but there still weren't enough tables. The air was full of smoke – tourists being the only people in the city allowed tobacco products – and I had to blink my eyes to see what was happening on stage. Then I had to blink them again to convince myself I hadn't fallen into wet dreamland. So did Davie and he's about as prone to shock as the journalists who covered what MPs got up to in the days before MPs became extinct like the dodo and the elephant.

On the raised stage there were three nymphs cavorting to the sounds of a seriously languid saxophone. Cavorting doesn't fully cover what the women were doing. They were all completely naked, their hair done up in ribbons like the originals in Canova's sculpture. They were also standing close together. There the similarities with the work of art ended. Each of them was holding a pair of very large, knobbly dildoes and applying them to any opening they could reach. One of the three, presumably the dead auxiliary's replacement, was definitely not having a good time – or at least wasn't covering that up very well. The crowd, which contained a lot more men than women, was yapping and cackling like a pack of exceptionally ravenous hyenas. The noise got even louder when one of the Graces lay down and spread her legs. Another got down between them and started lapping at her colleague's groin. Meanwhile the third, the unhappy one, simultaneously plunged a green dildo into her own fanny and a purple one into the crouching auxiliary's arse. Wonderful stuff.

"Duty calls, guardsman." I manhandled Davie away to the bar that ran down the left side of the room.

"You didn't exactly have your eyes lowered, Quint," he said with a grin.

"I'm following up an important line of enquiry."

"Oh, aye."

I leaned against the polished mahogany of the bar. The burly barman was looking a bit uncomfortable in his Doric chiton and sandals. I asked him for whisky and Watt 94.

"What can I do for you, citizen?"

I turned to see a tall, middle-aged woman in lace blouse and tartan evening skirt. She had short black hair, bright red lips and eyes of burnished steel. You can always spot a senior auxiliary, even when they're out of uniform.

I flashed her my authorisation and emptied the glass that had appeared in front of me. It was tourist-quality whisky – a sight better than even barracks malt.

She eyed my glass coldly and nodded. "I was expecting you."

"Were you now? How come?"

She glanced over her shoulder then sent the barman away. "You know how it is. Bad news travels fast. You're here about Moray 310, I take it." Her voice was so deep I had trouble picking it up over the drone of the saxophones in the band.

"I'm also looking for a male auxiliary from her barracks – Moray 37. Seen him in here?"

She shook her head. "My men on the door would have told me if one of our own people had tried to get in." Auxiliaries are supposed to get their kicks only in barracks sex sessions.

"So tell me about the dead woman."

She shrugged. "I was only posted here a couple of days ago. I can show you her file . . ."

"I'm a big boy, Watt 94. I can find files by myself."

Spots of colour appeared on her cheeks, then that reliable old auxiliary self-control kicked in. "Really. Well, instead of wasting my time, you should go behind stage and talk to the club co-ordinator. She knows everything there is to know about the Three Graces."

I pulled Davie away from a plate of deep-fried miniature haggises. The Dietetics Department would never let Edinburgh citizens overdose on suicide food like we used to before independence, but the tourists can eat as much of it as they like.

On stage the Graces had got bored with their sex aids and were fiddling around with a trio of rough-looking young men in leather shorts. The Three Disgraces, presumably. We passed through another curtain and entered a shabby backstage area manned by a stage crew who were paying no attention to the show. Two of them were hunched over a chessboard. That's the way your more old-fashioned auxiliary spends his leisure time.

"Where's the co-ordinator?" I asked.

One of the guys stuck a thumb out and jerked it in the direction of a dim corridor.

Davie was about to take issue with the guardsman's manners, but I shook my head.

At the end of the corridor was a row of mirrors and sinks. At the last sink was someone I hadn't seen for some time. "Patsy? What the hell are you doing out of your cell?"

"Well, well, the great Quintilian Dalrymple." The woman took a step back and appeared in all four of the mirrors between her and me. Suddenly I had four ex-brothel keepers in their mid-fifties to deal with. They all looked in pretty good nick, blonde hair perfectly coiffured and well-stacked figures squeezed into black velvet dresses. On the other hand, none of them looked particularly pleased to see me.

"What are you doing here, Patsy?" She'd once been in charge of the Prostitution Services Department.

"New career," she said, giving me an acid smile. "You can't be sure of anything in life."

"I didn't have you down as a philosopher."

She ignored that. "So what's happened to my star performer? All they told me was that she's had a accident."

"You're going to have to spend some time training up her replacement."

Patsy turned to me, her face suddenly slack. "What happened to her?"

"Someone bit out her throat and cut her apart," I said, watching her closely. Patsy used to know a lot of the city's hard men. "She wasn't the first, either. Any idea who might have done it?"

"I'm just an ordinary citizen now, Quint. I only know what I hear around the club." She looked up at me, her eyes wide apart. "Is there another lunatic out there like the last time?" Suddenly she looked like a frightened old woman despite the layers of make-up and the tough talking.

"Maybe. So what have you heard around here? What can you tell me about Moray 310?"

"Oh, for fuck's sake, Quint, she had a name."

"I know," I said in a conciliatory voice. It's usually me who gets pissed off when auxiliaries are referred to by barracks number. Maybe I was turning back into what I'd once been. Shit. "What can you tell me about Moira?" The guardsman who gave me the photo had told me the victim's first name.

Patsy rested her rump against the edge of the basin. "She was a complete natural. I couldn't teach her much. Men just had to look at her and she had them under her spell. It was the way she moved. Slow and seductive, like a snake. She made the guys feel it was them who were shafting her, not that piece of rubber." She laughed softly and looked over at me. "I've only seen two other women who had that kind of power."

I knew what she was about to say.

"Your friend Katharine was one of them." She held her eyes on me to see how I reacted.

"Thank you for that, Patsy," I said with a scowl. "Let's get back to Moira, shall we? Was she involved in anything else?"

"Anything the Council wouldn't approve of, you mean?" Patsy gave me a bitter smile. "Why would you believe what I tell you, Quint?"

She had a point. She'd been known to have trouble with the concept of truth. But we were friends once, in the far distant past when I was in the directorate and she was turning herself from the city's number one madam into a high-ranking auxiliary.

"I trust you, Patsy," I said, smiling back at her and glancing around at the decrepit washroom. "Why would you lie? Things don't get much worse than this."

"That's true enough," she said, nodding. "Moira was … clever. Cunning. She was one of those auxiliaries who pretend they have the city's interests at heart but are really only looking after themselves."

"There are a few of those around," I said ironically.

"Aye, a few." She laughed. "Well, I can spot that type a mile off, so I always kept an eye on her."

This was getting interesting.

"But I never picked up on a thing."

No, it wasn't.

"She was smart, kept a tight grip on herself, even when the punters got her pissed."

"So this conversation's been a waste of time," I said, putting my notebook back in my pocket.

Patsy shrugged and turned back to the mirror. "If you say so, Quint."

I headed for the door.

"But there's one thing I can't work out . . ."

I hit the brakes.

"She was on the phone in the corridor a few days ago." All facilities like this have phones for the staff to keep in touch with their barracks control room. "And she was really scared. Shouting and screaming. Till she saw me at the other end of the passage."

"What was she saying?"

"She kept repeating the same thing. I couldn't make any sense of it."

I went up to her and took hold of her fleshy arms. "What was it, Patsy? What was she saying?"

"'The electric blues.'" She looked at me uncomprehendingly. "She kept asking, 'What about the electric blues?'"

I let go of her and stepped back, thinking of the tape we took out of Roddie Aitken. Eric Clapton playing electric blues. Then I thought of the auxiliary's semi-frozen body, the legs splayed wide apart.

I was bloody sure another tape had been left inside her. The question was, what had been recorded on it?

Chapter Eight

━━━◆◆◆◆◆━━━

It was a long night. Davie and I waited for the surviving Two Graces plus the victim's replacement to take a break from delving into each other. They were no more ecstatic about our delving into their relationships with the dead Moira than the new girl had been on stage. It soon became obvious that they thought their ex-colleague was a supercilious cow who kept herself to herself outside business hours. None of them had any idea exactly what she got up to when she wasn't at the club, but the general idea seemed to be that she was doing a lot of freelance whoring among the wealthier tourist clientèle. Patsy had the same impression. So where had the dead woman stashed her loot?

"Moray Barracks?" Davie asked as we came out into the freezing night air of the Grassmarket.

I nodded. "She was asking for trouble if she kept currency or jewellery in her barracks, but we have to start somewhere."

Davie pulled away from the even larger crowd that had gathered outside the club. Performances go on until four in the morning — no wonder the performers have trouble looking enthusiastic. "Do you think it could be a tourist who killed her?" he asked, swerving to avoid a Japanese guy in a Black Watch kilt.

"Christ, Davie, don't let Hamilton hear you saying that. That would be even worse than an auxiliary. Think of the dilemma that would give the Council. As far as it's concerned, tourists' arses exist primarily for us to kiss, not for tourists to shit out of."

"It's not quite like that, Quint," he said testily. "Without the income from tourism, the city would be more or less insolvent."

I love it when Davie turns back into a model auxiliary and spouts the Council's standard line. I didn't find it very convincing. "So you approve of your fellow auxiliaries spreading their legs for the tourists, do you?"

He gave me the glare guardsmen use when citizens are massively out of line. "Of course I fucking don't, but how else are we going to attract the business? These days people from the successful countries don't just want package tours that take in a few museums and medieval banquets. They want cheap sex."

I nodded, looking out at the crowds of half-cut foreigners wandering around the Cowgate. They want cheap sex, horse-racing in Princes Street Gardens, casinoes on every street corner, whisky and tartan knitwear. What they don't want is to bite people's throats out and hide music cassettes inside them. I didn't have much idea of what was going on, but I was sure of one thing: Edinburgh's latest multiple murderer was a home-grown product, born and bred in the city like his victims. Which led me back to another thought. Where was the bastard hiding out? Someone must know him; someone probably saw the bloodstains on his clothing after the second killing. So where the hell was he? I called Hamilton and asked him to get his people to check all the barracks' patrol reports. We might be lucky. Perhaps some vigilant guardsman had spotted a suspicious character in the early hours but failed to pull him in. Perhaps some citizen on his or her way to the early works buses had reported a strange man in a long coat. And perhaps Edinburgh citizens go to bed every night reciting "Our Senior Guardian who art in heaven . . ."

We would have got a warmer reception at Moray Barracks if we'd walked in sporting bubonic plague sores. Eventually my Council authorisation prevailed. I looked up from signing the sentry's log and saw Hamilton's deputy Machiavelli exiting at speed. The guardsman at his side had a guard rucksack on his back.

"I hope you're not going to lower morale even further by asking awkward questions," said the barracks commander, a doleful guy with bald head and thick brown beard who'd been called down to meet us. He looked like Friar Tuck after a particularly heavy night, except that he could probably count the number of times he'd smiled in his life on the fingers of one hand.

I gave him a smile of my own to show him he was already out of his league. "Awkward questions, Moray 01? Of course not. The morale of your barracks is much more important than the threat posed to the city by a psychotic killer."

That had some effect. The commander stepped back like I'd propositioned him, then struggled to regain his composure. A vein pulsed prominently in the middle of his forehead.

"Show us her cubicle. In person, please."

Moray 01 glanced at me to check I was talking to him, swallowed when he realised I really did want him to act as barracks porter and headed slowly down the corridor.

Moray Barracks is a seventeenth-century mansion that used to be a teacher training college before the Enlightenment. The Council decided it would serve their purpose better as the barracks covering the lower end of the Royal Mile and the Cowgate, not least because teacher training is now part of the auxiliary training programme. Auxiliaries learn hand-to-hand combat, survival skills (useful when they do their tour of duty in the notoriously dangerous border posts) and what are called public order skills; then those of them who want to teach are deemed ready for action and chucked straight into schools. At least there aren't many discipline problems in the classroom. The downside is that Moray House has been wrecked, its decorated walls knocked through to make dormitories and its moulded ceilings left in partial ruin. Very enlightened.

*   *   *

The commander led us through a female dorm, then a male one. I was on official business of course, so I paid attention to the semi-naked bodies on display in the first room. The female auxiliaries glanced across briefly, then ignored me as effectively as prime ministers used to ignore cabinet members in the old days.

We left the second dormitory and went up a wide staircase that had once been elegant and ornate and was now high quality drab, the steps chipped from heavy auxiliary boots. Moray 01 stopped at the first door on the next floor and pointed.

"This is Moira ... I mean Moray 310's cubicle." The commander made to depart.

"I haven't finished with you yet," I said, pushing the door open. The room beyond was quite large, containing a sofa, armchair, table and desk as well as a single bed. I looked at Davie then at the Friar Tuck lookalike. "I definitely haven't finished with you yet."

The commander was suddenly finding the carpet, which was in unusually good condition for a barracks, a source of great fascination.

"What's going on here, Moray 01? Why did the dead guardswoman have a room of her own instead of a dorm cubicle?"

He mumbled something about her overnight shifts and heavy workload.

"Come on, commander, all auxiliaries have times when they have to do the night shift. Why did Moray 310 – sorry, Moira, as you called her – get special treatment?"

The vein on his forehead had turned dark blue. Eventually he raised his head and faced me. "I'm not able to say. It's a Council matter, citizen."

"And this is a Council authorisation."

He turned to go. "So address your questions to the Council."

I glanced at Davie, who looked like he fancied playing

basketball with the commander's head. "Wait a minute. Raeburn 03, the Public Order Directorate official I saw leaving when we arrived, has he been in here?"

Moray 01 stopped but didn't turn round. "I don't see why he should have been, citizen. Now, if you don't mind . . ."

"Thanks for your co-operation," I shouted after him.

Davie stepped up. "Cool it, Quint. You aren't among friends here."

I nodded and looked around the well-appointed room. "Get a scene-of-crime squad down here, Davie, including a fingerprint guy. We're going to have to tear this place apart."

We did so. And found nothing special. Prints that were soon matched to the victim and other barracks members; underwear that was definitely not standard issue, but that came from the Prostitution Services Department stores rather than smugglers; and a couple of books of Eastern erotica that were presumably source material for the nightclub act. So either the killer got what he was looking for or she'd hidden it elsewhere. We spoke to some of her colleagues, but none of them was very close to her. They claimed to know nothing about her trips to Roddie Aitken's sex centre and I believed them. Most auxiliaries are very bad at lying.

At one in the morning my mobile buzzed.

"Dalrymple?" came Hamilton's voice. "We've picked up the missing auxiliary Moray 37. He's being brought to the castle."

"We're on our way."

Adrenalin and black coffee are the main things that keep you going during investigations, but it helps if you get a little help from your leads. With the sex centre supervisor we got the big zero.

Sample question: "Moray 37, why did you allow Moray 310 to impersonate a dead citizen and have sex with Roddie Aitken?"

THE BONE YARD

Sample answer: "I was doing her a favour. I knew her in barracks when she was a trainee auxiliary."

Sample question: "Why did you risk your own position to do a favour for an auxiliary who didn't exactly lack the means of obtaining all the sex she wanted at the club?"

Sample answer: "Because she asked me."

Sample question (one of Hamilton's – you can tell by the stilted Council diction): "Why did you absent yourself from the sex centre without authorisation?"

Sample answer: "Because I panicked when I heard about the murder."

And so on. I kept after him, the guardian kept after him, but his answers didn't change. Eventually I concluded that he really had been doing the dead woman a favour. Maybe she fluttered her eyelashes at him and he couldn't say no, despite his sexuality (his file confirmed what his demeanour suggested). He had solid alibis for both murders and a search of his cubicle revealed nothing incriminating. At five in the morning we let him go, putting one of Hamilton's best undercover operatives on his tail. I had the feeling he was a dead end.

Davie and I got a couple of hours' uncomfortable sleep on the sofas in the guardian's outer office. I had a hazy dream about a drugs gang boss called Elmore, but that didn't do me any good. There never had been such a character – or one called James, or Eric, or Clapton, or God. Sometimes you can't even trust your subconscious.

Hamilton woke us up with more big zeroes. Apparently none of Roddie Aitken's workmates was into contraband any juicier than Danish bestiality magazines. And none of the barracks patrols had seen any hooded men with tell-tale bloodstains on their coats.

Then it was time to set off for the infirmary. For the next post-mortem.

I walked into the grey granite building in the pitch darkness that passes for morning at this time of year in Edinburgh. I felt the cold biting at my hands with sharp, insistent teeth, making the stump of my right forefinger tingle like it had just been touched by the blade of the Ear, Nose and Throat Man's knife again. That sick bastard would have enjoyed all this. But not even he went to the extent of planting tapes in his victims.

"Mind if I come with you?" Davie asked, catching me up. "I've never seen a post-mortem."

I looked at him in surprise. "Haven't you?"

"How could I? There haven't been any murders since the last ones you solved."

"No, I suppose there haven't. And you spent most of that investigation on surveillance."

"Aye. So can I come?"

I led him through the entrance hall with its patient line of thin, coughing citizens. The place was busy even at this early hour. "Suit yourself," I said. "Personally I can think of better ways to start the day."

"And I can't?" Davie stared at me fiercely. "You're always telling me to educate myself in the ways of the criminal."

"All right, big man, I said you could come. But promise me one thing."

"What?"

We stopped outside the mortuary and showed ID.

"Don't let the side down by losing your grip on your breakfast."

Another ferocious glare. "I'm an auxiliary, citizen. We never lose our breakfast."

"Right."

We robed up.

"We've got another bite mark," the medical guardian said, bending over the victim's neck.

"Which will no doubt match the last one but, like it, won't match anything in the records." I joined her at the upper body.

The skin was no longer under a sheen of ice and lividity was visible towards the underside. The auxiliary's teeth were still clenched, with dried runnels of blood leading down to the ragged hole in the throat.

The Ice Queen moved down to the lower abdomen. "Severe lacerations to the thighs and vagina. Mutilation of the outer labia and . . ." She lowered her face. "And removal of the clitoris."

I heard a sharp intake of breath from Davie. His face was about the same shade of green as his gown. "Before or after death?" I asked.

"I'll need to run more tests. It's difficult to be sure of the time or cause of death yet." The medical guardian looked up at me. "But given that the victim's hands were bound, at least some of the knifework could have been carried out while she was alive."

"Her feet weren't tied though."

She nodded. "True enough. You'd imagine she'd have been thrashing around."

"Maybe he stunned her."

"There's no indication of any blow to the head." The guardian took a pair of forceps and applied them to the object in the dead woman's vagina. There was a noise like the sound of an oar entering the surface of the sea as she pulled. Davie's breathing was very loud. I nodded towards the door but he paid no attention.

"There you are, citizen." The Ice Queen held the blood-encrusted plastic bag up. It was caught for a second in the flash from the photographer's camera.

"What a surprise," I said, blinking my eyes. "Another cassette."

"Not much doubt it was the same killer," she said.

"Have you got a cassette player in the vicinity, guardian?"

She had moved back up to the top of the table. "In my office."

"Let's have a break from this, Davie." I led him towards the door. His legs weren't too steady.

The guardian's voice came as I put my hand on Davie's elbow. It was sharp, the pitch suddenly higher.

"For the love of God."

Guardians, like all auxiliaries, are sworn atheists. Normally I would have been entertained by one of them referring to the supposedly non-existent deity. But not this time. I looked round to see her leaning against the slab. Her assistant was bent over the corpse's jaws, having just wrenched them apart, his head turned away. The Ice Queen was holding a pink and black shrivelled object in her forceps.

"It's a penis, citizen," she said, the timbre of her voice now deep and throaty. "A penis severed at the root by a very sharp knife."

Davie blundered out of the door, but I went back slowly to the table. There was no escaping the thought that it was Roddie Aitken's member which had been placed in the dead woman's mouth.

The Council chamber, seven o'clock in the evening. I had several things to share with the iron boyscouts and another couple I was going to keep to myself. Davie and I'd had a busy day.

"I trust you are making every effort to trace this homicidal maniac, citizen," the senior guardian said as his colleagues gathered round me like a family of tweed and brogue-clad vultures.

I resisted the easy shot; of course, the fact that the latest victim was an auxiliary was having an obvious effect on how seriously the Council treated my investigation.

"I'm making all the efforts I can, guardian," I said. "Unfortunately, so's the killer." I glanced at the chief boyscout. "But I don't think he's a maniac. He's been smart enough to avoid all the patrols, he's got a plan and he's running rings round us."

The senior guardian looked at Hamilton. "Is citizen Dalrymple out of his depth, guardian?"

"I'd like to see anyone else do any better," he answered brusquely. That was about as close to a vote of confidence as I could expect from Hamilton.

The senior guardian nodded at me slowly. His wispy beard made him look like a forgiving Christ, but the tone of his voice was more Old Testament. "Very well. Your report, citizen."

"If you don't mind, guardian," interrupted the Ice Queen. She was looking particularly stern tonight, her white-blonde hair combed back close to her scalp. "I have some test results that citizen Dalrymple is unaware of." She gave me a perfunctory glance.

"Enlighten us," said the senior guardian. If that was a reference to his other role as science and energy chief, no one seemed prepared to acknowledge it. There's no chance it was anything as flippant as a pun on the Enlightenment Party.

"Moray 310 died from loss of blood. I put the time of death at between five and six a.m. on Thursday 2 January." She looked around at her colleagues with their clipboards and their bowed heads. "Tissue and blood tests have confirmed that the penis found in her mouth was that of the first victim, Roderick Aitken." The heads remained bowed. The medical guardian caught my eye briefly. "Moray 310's tongue was removed as well."

"Is there some significance in that, citizen?" the senior guardian asked.

I shrugged. "The medical guardian thinks it's a pointer to the other messages he's sending."

"You mean the tapes?"

"Before we get on to that, senior guardian," the Ice Queen interrupted again – she really was taking her life in her hands – "I found something unexpected in the victim's stomach."

Now I was paying close attention. "What was it?" I asked.

The medical guardian suddenly seemed a lot less sure of

herself. Her head was bowed now as she flipped over pages on her clipboard. Then she looked up. "It showed up in the toxicological analysis of the stomach contents."

"It?" I shouted and was instantly surrounded by a ring of startled faces. "What is 'it', guardian?"

The Ice Queen pursed her lips at me. "'It', citizen, is a trace of a stimulant."

"A drug?" said Hamilton, his eyes wide. The years he spent fighting the gangs that used to traffic in controlled substances had left him scarred for life. "What kind of drug?"

"I told you," replied the Ice Queen. "A stimulant."

"Not one of those that are sometimes prescribed for guard personnel on the border?" I asked.

The senior guardian looked down his nose at me. "Those are not controlled substances, as you well know, citizen."

I did, but it's always worth winding the guardians up. Very occasionally they even lose their tempers. "So what is it?"

"A compound of one of the known methamphetamines and another substance that the Toxicology Department hasn't been able to identify." The medical guardian glanced at Hamilton. "Where did she get it, guardian?"

"Don't ask me," he replied, his cheeks red above the white of his beard. "We haven't found banned substances in the city for years." He glared at her. "Maybe you should check that none of your people has been experimenting in the labs."

"That'll do, guardian." The chief boyscout wasn't impressed with inter-directorate scrapping, at least not in front of an outsider like me.

I had a thought while they were squabbling. "Maybe that's what the killer's been looking for. Maybe this is all about drugs."

"Bloody hell," said Hamilton, to be given a bowel-liquefying look by his superior. "You don't think the drugs gangs could be forming up again, do you, Dalrymple?"

"Who knows what's going on beyond the border? There have

been plenty of drugs in the democratic states like Glasgow since they decided legalising them was a good idea."

Hamilton wasn't giving up. "They also still have high levels of criminal activity."

It wasn't the time for a debate about public order policy. "We'll need to close the Three Graces down immediately and see if we can find any sign of this new drug," I said. "All the staff will have to be searched and questioned."

That was more to Hamilton's taste. He was so anxious to get started that for a moment I thought he'd forgotten his incontinence pants.

The tourism guardian was in a similar plight – until the senior guardian assured him that none of the customers would be hassled. I might have known.

All of which overshadowed what I had to say about the tape that was inside the dead auxiliary. This time it was Jimi Hendrix playing "Red House"; the original studio version from 1966 – slow, sexy, very electric blues. And at least this time there was a lyric. So what the hell did it mean? The guy in the song hasn't seen the girl in the red house for ninety-nine and one half days; his key doesn't fit the door and he ends up going back across the hill to chase her sister. The expression on the Council's collective face said "And?" I didn't have much to suggest, except that Holyroodhouse where the auxiliary was murdered was now a kind of red house. They didn't buy it. Christ, I didn't buy it myself.

"Anything else, citizen?" asked the senior guardian.

Time for some more fun and games.

"A couple of things," I said, giving the group around me a smile to soften them up. "Why did the dead auxiliary have a room of her own rather than a cubicle in a dormitory? Her barracks commander suggested I take it up with the Council."

Silence for a time, then the senior guardian let out a long sigh. "What is the point of your question, citizen? Do you think that a single room is proof of corruption in high places?"

If only. No, I was just rubbing their noses in the reality of their supposedly equitable system.

"The Tourism Directorate recognises that certain key personnel need privileged treatment," the chief scout continued. "For the good of the city."

I let that pass without comment. "One last point. Roddie Aitken reported that he'd suffered an attempted assault by a hooded man to the guard."

They were still in a ring around me, like a herd of cows congregated in the middle of a field. I went into biting fly mode.

"Someone's removed that report from the guard operations file."

"What?" Hamilton looked like he was about to do serious damage to his cardiovascular system. I hadn't had a chance to tell him about my discovery before the Council meeting started. "How can you be sure the report was logged?"

"They are filed in numerical order, are they not?" said the senior guardian. He seemed to be very well informed about guard practices.

I nodded, unable to protect Hamilton from the bucket of shit he'd just thrown over himself. "The docket was torn out in haste. I found a small piece of the edge in the binder."

The public order guardian was shaking his head slowly. "I'll find out who took it, you can be sure of that. Probably the idiot who forgot to follow the report up."

Maybe. Or maybe there was someone in Hamilton's directorate who didn't want Roddie's complaint to be followed up. I wasn't sure how many other people in the Council chamber had the same thought.

We closed the nightclub and spent the rest of the evening looking for illicit drugs. We didn't find any. Davie and I were mobbed by a crowd of irate tourists when we left. They wanted naked flesh — not ours — but all I wanted was my bed. And I still hadn't turned forty. Pathetic.

Chapter Nine

———◆◆◆———

"Stop!"

"What the . . . ?" Davie stood on the brakes and pulled up in the middle of the deserted junction at Tollcross.

I put my shoulder to the door and leaped out on to the tarmac. I managed two paces, then fell flat on my face. My old friend the ice was back in force.

Davie pulled me to my feet. "What are you playing at, Quint?"

I started running again. "He was over there, in the shopfront."

"Who?"

I reached the butcher's. Even though it was chained up, the sour reek of meat well past its prime was still about the place. Nothing human though.

"The hooded man," I said. "I caught a glimpse as we went past." I ran out into the middle of the road and looked around in every direction. It was dead quiet, all the local citizens housebound by the curfew a couple of hours back. Nothing moved except the city flags under every streetlamp gently flapping in the chill breeze.

"Are you sure?" Davie joined me and peered about doubtfully. "I didn't see anyone."

I rubbed my eyes and tried unsuccessfully to swallow a yawn.

"I'm not sure of anything much at the moment, guardsman," I said eventually and headed back to the Land-Rover. The idea of the hooded man hanging around the vicinity of my flat again suddenly struck me as farcical. It was probably just my imagination messing me about. So I got Davie to drop me off and fell into a sleep so subterranean that not even the killer in my worst recurring nightmare could locate me.

And then, over the next couple of days, everything in the investigation went quiet. You get that sometimes – a burst of headless poultry activity at the beginning, followed by a becalmed state like the one the Ancient Mariner enjoyed so much. So what was going on? Had the killer found what he was looking for? Maybe the dead auxiliary had somehow got her hands on a new stimulant. Or maybe Roddie Aitken had pulled the wool over everyone's eyes and managed to smuggle it in. You sit around with ideas swooping through your mind like swallows catching flies on a warm summer evening when you haven't got anything else to go on. But unfortunately this was the freezing heart of winter and the leads we were chasing up didn't give us much to bite on. At one stage I tried to convince myself that the killer had found the drugs and departed to seek his fortune in a more liberal city like Glasgow. But I wasn't that gullible, not even for a fraction of a nanosecond.

The Council's policy towards tourists didn't help much. I wanted to check out any who were regulars at the Three Graces. It would have been easy enough to do as customers have to fill in a card giving their name and hotel, but the tourism guardian accused me of wanting to harass the city's customers. I assured the Council I would apply all my well-honed diplomatic skills, but they weren't having it. So instead I had to stick to what used to feature in twentieth-century police procedural novels, i.e. chasing up every boring detail. Meaning that Hamilton and I had undercover surveillance teams tailing as many of the two victims' friends and contacts as we could manage, including the sex centre supervisor and Patsy Cameron; that we searched all their cubicles or flats while they were absent; that Davie compiled a list of everyone who had access to the guard complaint register; that the bite mark and DNA data from the second victim were checked against dental and medical records (no joy); and that, in my spare time, I tried to work out what the point of the blues tapes was. It was all as about as useful as an enema during an epidemic of dysentery.

Then, on Sunday afternoon when I was walking across the ice rink that the castle esplanade had become and trying hard not to use my buttocks as skates, I got inspired. Sex reared its purple rosebud head and I immediately stuck my hand in my pocket – to pull out my mobile and tell Davie to meet me at the centre where Roddie and Moira had achieved congress. I'd just remembered that citizens can be allocated lockers if they want to keep personal equipment secure.

"What's up?" Davie said when I got there, his backside against the rust-shot maroon door of his vehicle. "Getting desperate?"

"Very funny, guardsman. You know former auxiliaries like me aren't allowed to defile ordinary citizens." That's why I have to spend every Thursday night with weird demoted women. One thing to be said for the investigation was that I had a reason for calling off my last session. The last thing I needed just now were distractions of a carnal nature. Well, almost the last thing.

It was a Sunday so there was a long queue outside the sex centre. As usual, citizens were grumbling about the fact that they had to meet here for sex rather than in their flats. The official line is that this way health standards are maintained, but everyone knows it's so that a firm grip is kept. It's not a joke though – any citizens caught having it off in unapproved premises get to acquire an intimate and long-term knowledge of potato picking and turnip tending on the city farms.

I pushed through to the front. Citizen Macmillan gave me a reluctant nod from her desk.

"Back again, citizen? Did you forget something?"

"Now you come to mention it . . ."

"Well, don't take all day. People behind you have got things to do."

I glanced round at the sullen faces in the reception area. They looked like children who've got to the front of the school dinner queue only to see that the last tray of chips has just run out.

"I won't keep you long," I said. "Roddie Aitken and Sheena Marinello. Did they have lockers?"

The receptionist's eyes flashed open at the mention of Roddie's name. "Where is Roddie? Why do you keep asking questions about him?"

I knew she didn't expect any answers. In some ways I would have liked to tell her what had happened to him – she was obviously quite friendly with him. But she was better off not knowing.

She shook her head slowly, her gaze lowered. "Roddie didn't. He wasn't one for sex aids or any of that kind of stuff." Then she looked up at me again and her lips pursed. "But she was. The cow always had a bag with her. She took a locker the day she registered."

What had been a dull murmur from the citizens behind me was beginning to get louder. I heard Davie clear his throat and everything went quiet again. It was one of those times when a guard uniform is a handy thing to have around.

"Were you wanting to have a look at her locker, citizen?"

The tone of citizen Macmillan's voice made me suspicious. "Don't tell me it's been cleared out."

She smiled triumphantly, pleased with herself for having got one over an authority figure, even one as marginal as me. "No, no, not yet. The supervisor told me to go through the locker file yesterday, but I haven't had the time yet."

"Or the inclination?" I said, returning the smile that had momentarily transformed her face. These days there are a lot of citizens who don't smile much. It wasn't always like that. For years after the Enlightenment, people were almost pathetically grateful that the Council had managed to restore order after the nationwide chaos the drugs gangs had caused. The fact that everyone had work and a place to live was a major improvement. But things have got a lot harder recently.

"Can I have the key?"

She handed it over and got back to checking in clients.

Davie and I beat a rapid retreat down the corridor.

"You don't want to mess around with citizens' sex lives," he said. "They were getting pretty restless back there."

"For a lot of them it's all they've got to look forward to every week," I said. "They don't have the privileges your rank enjoys."

"Oh, aye?" he said belligerently. "Privileges like patrolling the back streets of Leith in the middle of the night? Privileges like burying your tongue in the arse of every drunken tourist who asks for directions to the nearest brothel? Privileges like . . ."

I smiled at him. "Only joking, guardsman."

"Fuck you, Quint," he said, shaking his head in disgust.

"Here we are. Number 238." I put the key in the lock. "Any chance of a result in here?"

"I'm not betting on it, if that's what you mean," he replied testily.

"Cheer up, Davie. There might be a gold-plated clue lying waiting for us in this locker."

"Aye, and you might stop taking the piss out of the likes of me."

"I take it you're not optimistic then?" I said, pulling the door open.

At first glance it looked like he was right. The auxiliary hadn't left much behind. There was a bright orange dildo with a ridged top that could have done service as a witch's nose in the days when kids were allowed to dress up on Hallowe'en. And there were some pieces of good-quality black underwear, including a bra with holes for the nipples to poke through. I don't know why, but I found it comforting that Roddie at least had the chance to experience imaginative sex with a professional. Exactly what she was doing impersonating an ordinary citizen in order to screw a raw young guy like him I still found puzzling. I pulled out an object covered in light brown foil.

"What's that?" Davie asked.

"It's a malt whisky-flavoured condom, guardsman. Don't they have those in your barracks?"

"Not the rubber, jackass." He pointed past my leg at a small dusty blue object in the bottom left corner of the locker. "That."

"Bloody hell." I dropped to my knees and whipped my magnifying glass out. Then pulled a plastic bag over my left hand, picked the thing up between thumb and forefinger and reversed the bag. "Well spotted, Davie."

"So what is it?" he asked, peering as I held the bag up to the light. "A tablet?"

"Yup. We'll need to get it to the toxicology lab sharpish. Look at the colour. I've got a feeling it's what the killer was after."

"What do you mean look at the colour?"

"Wakey, wakey, Davie. Remember the music on the tapes? Remember what the dead auxiliary was saying on the phone?"

His eyes opened wide.

"Exactly. I reckon what we've got here is a prime example of the Electric Blues."

That was what I reckoned, but scientists don't deal in snap judgements. The chief toxicologist took my mobile number and sent me about my business without showing the slightest concern at my demand for a high-priority analysis. I considered pulling the senior guardian's chain since it was his directorate I was dealing with, but decided against it. He would probably just spin me a line about how the complexities of science aren't subject to being rushed.

So Davie and I went back to the castle and sat in the Land-Rover on the sunlit but still ice-coated esplanade. We went through the list of guard personnel who had access to the complaint file. There were twenty-three people on it, including the public order guardian and his deputy. I wondered about Machiavelli. He seemed to have taken Hamilton's warning to stay out of the case seriously. I hadn't seen him for a few days. Then I remembered where I'd last caught sight of the shifty bastard: departing rapidly from the dead auxiliary's barracks with a guardsman carrying a rucksack. What had he been doing there?

"I suppose you know Machiavelli?" I said to Davie.

He nodded. "Unfortunately."

"His reputation in the guard's that bad, is it?"

Davie shifted in the well-worn driver's seat. It wasn't the Land-Rover's luxury upholstery that was making him uncomfortable. He always gets fidgety when I start questioning him about his superiors. Auxiliary training and discipline are hard to get over. Except in my case, of course.

"Raeburn 03's . . . well, he's the kind of guy who gets up people's noses. He's devious, always gives you the impression that he's working to his own agenda. Or at least some agenda that the rest of us don't know about."

Those were more or less my thoughts too, but I'd have used plainer language. As far as I was concerned, Machiavelli was a shite on legs.

"He's got friends in high places though," Davie added. "He always makes sure everyone knows how close he is to the guardians."

"Apart from Hamilton."

Davie laughed. "Aye. The guardian really hates the contents of his abdominal cavity."

"For someone who failed to make it through his first post-mortem, I'd recommend cutting down on the anatomical imagery."

"Very funny."

I looked at the list again, then out on to the glinting tarmac. "I can't see why the docket should have been torn out of the file deliberately, Davie. Maybe it's just a coincidence."

"Could be. It's not exactly unknown for bits of documentation to go missing."

I nodded and looked out towards the northern suburbs. In the distance behind the equestrian statue of Field Marshal Haig — someone who got away with murder on a grand scale — flashes of icy light sparked from the dreadnought grey surface of the Firth of Forth. Cold sea, cold sky, and, somewhere out there, the latest butcher of the city's young.

I shivered. "Time to check some more files. That should warm us up."

It didn't, but the chief toxicologist's phone call did. We ran out of the guard archive in the castle and burned over to the labs. They're in what used to be the university science area at King's Buildings. The site was secured with razor-wire as soon as the Enlightenment came to power because of the interest the drugs gangs had shown in the equipment and chemicals stored there. The Council has never bothered to take the wire down, even though it could make better use of it on the border these days.

"What is the provenance of this tablet, citizen?" the scientist asked after we'd cleared the security checks and got into his lab.

"You mean where did I get it, Lister 25?"

The chief toxicologist's thick lips gave a brief and surprisingly delicate twitch, like an actor greeting a colleague across a crowded room in the days before that profession became superfluous to modern society's needs. Lister 25 must have been very overweight in pre-Enlightenment days, but twenty years of auxiliary eating had left him with great folds of skin hanging from his face like an elephant on a controlled diet.

"Sorry, that's classified," I said, avoiding any excessive lip movements in case I encouraged him.

"I see." He turned to the lab table and picked up a test-tube with a pale-coloured sediment in the bottom. "It's just that this is very interesting, citizen. In fact, as far as I am aware, it's unique. In several ways."

That certainly was very interesting. "And what ways are those? I presume it matches the trace that was found in the dead auxiliary's stomach?"

"Indeed. But that trace was so minute that, though I say so myself, I did very well just to identify it. I won't bore you with the intricacies of its chemical structure, but this drug's chief claim to uniqueness is its strength. The dosage contained in a tablet this size would be enough to cause massive increases in mental alertness and sexual potency in an average-sized person."

It seemed a fair bet that was why they were called "Electric" Blues.

"How else are they unique?" Davie asked.

Lister 25 carefully lodged the test-tube in a rack and turned back to us, then gave another twitch of his lips. "The compound is also exceedingly dangerous for anyone with a weak heart. The effect of a dose this size taken more than once in such cases would be severe nausea, stiffening of the muscles, convulsions, coma, respiratory collapse and then death."

"Fucking hell," I said under my breath. "But the post-mortem on the dead auxiliary didn't report those effects."

"As I said, citizen, in her case the dose was minuscule. She was doubtless a healthy specimen and it appears that she put a tablet against her tongue for a few seconds." The scientist looked at me seriously. "You understand now why I asked you about the provenance. If there are quantities of this drug in the city, I can promise you that you will be picking up bodies on a regular basis. I am certain that no clinical trials have been carried out on this little beauty."

"Wonderful," I said, with a scowl. "I'll take your report to the Council this evening. What about manufacturing the drug? What kind of facilities would be needed?"

Lister 25's expression lightened. "That's the good news, if there's any to be found in this sorry tale. The compound is so complex that only a top-level chemist could produce it, and a well-equipped lab would be essential." He opened his arms and looked around the room we were standing in. "The labs in this building would fit the bill. Come to think of it, the six chemists on my staff would too. There aren't many other installations in the city that could do it." He raised his hand to pre-empt me. "And before you ask, citizen, neither I nor any of my people have had anything to do with these tablets. Whoever produced them should be put up against a wall."

He was bound to say his people were clean. And I wasn't capable of understanding their technical capabilities. I only did chemistry for a term at school before begging to be allowed to change to something that had more to do with my experience of the world. As far as I was concerned moles were small blind creatures that used to be turned into trousers, not something to do with chemical structure.

We left him to his test-tubes and bunsen burner. Before independence chemists would have worked for years to come up with a face cream to deal with those pachydermic wrinkles. Now they've got better things to do – or have they?

That evening's Council meeting was an uncivilised affair. I was the barbarian at the gates, of course. The boyscouts didn't take kindly to my demand for searches to be carried out on all regular customers of the Three Graces. Eventually they went along with it; that's the power the spectre of drugs-inspired chaos still has. They were even less impressed when I told them I'd already started checking airport records to see if any tourists with the symptoms described by the toxicologist had been flown out of the city over the last few days.

The toxicologist was also the cause of a set-to I had with the senior guardian. I asked him, in his capacity as science and energy supremo, if what the guy had told me about his team of chemists was true. Maybe I should have put it a bit more tactfully, but I've always thought that tact is for people who don't want anyone to know what they're really thinking. I positively enjoy sharing my thought processes with auxiliaries, especially guardians. Apparently the enjoyment isn't mutual.

The senior guardian immediately leaped on to a horse so high you could have got the entire Greek army besieging Troy into it. "Citizen Dalrymple," he said, his boyish face with its unlikely beard set hard, "I can give you my personal assurance that no laboratory in this city has been used to produce this drug."

I shrugged, trying not to look impressed but actually quite surprised. It's unusual to get a credible personal assurance out of a guardian – they aren't that different from twentieth-century politicians. He hadn't finished either.

"I can also assure you that no scientist in Edinburgh would have anything to do with an illicit substance such as this one." He looked at me like a heron that's just speared a fish and then decided it's not worth eating after all.

I left shortly afterwards, my tail more down than up. It's a bad idea to go into battle with the Council when you're short of ammunition. So far this investigation had come up with about as many bullets as a conscientious objector playing Russian roulette.

Outside it was another polar evening, the cold piling into my lungs faster than a crowd of tourists stampeding into the Tourism Directorate's whorehouses at opening time. Sunday night. I had to make the weekly visit to my old man. Even though I saw him at the reception not long back, he'd give me hell if I didn't turn up as usual. Davie was off trying to convince his regular skirt he still fancied her, not that he ever seemed to have much trouble pulling that off. So I called a guard vehicle and directed the driver to the retirement home in Trinity.

On the way down I found myself thinking again about the cassettes the killer had left in his victims. Had he used Clapton and Hendrix just because they were masters of the electric blues? And if it was some kind of message, who was it directed at?

Then I thought of the person who was my best friend when I first listened to those guitarists as a spot-ridden, music-crazed teenager; the guy who played drums in my first, ear-shattering band at university; the guy who used to run all the city's most profitable deals until I caught up with him. William Ewart Geddes. Billy. This smelled like the sort of dead smart, high-profit, totally immoral deal he'd have got himself into right up to his shifty grey eyes.

But then I shook my head and made myself come back to the real world. Billy was so crippled that he could hardly even move around in the wheelchair they strapped him into every day. There had been talk of him being allowed to continue making the deals the Council depended on when my mother was still senior guardian. But the iron boyscouts took one look at his record and packed him off to a home for the disabled. Not exactly the place to run a drug trafficking operation from. No, I was dreaming. I was also guilty as hell that I hadn't been to visit him for over a year.

In the end there's only so much you can do for your friends when they go bad. With relatives it's different. They can tear you to shreds every time you see them, they can turn out to be completely cynical in the pursuit of whatever they lust after – power in my mother's case. But when they go, they still leave you with a hole inside bigger than the one in the ozone layer our predecessors bequeathed us.

The Land-Rover pulled up outside the house in Trinity. I was a bit shaken. For a moment I almost thought I was getting sentimental.

Chapter Ten

The house was set back from the road, its front lit by the bright lamp above the door and the much dimmer ones in the old men's rooms. I looked up to the third floor. My father had the only room up there, just below the lookout tower that the early Victorian sea captain who built the mansion had insisted on. Hector had dug around in the archives – like son, like father – and discovered, to his great amusement, that the first owner had been drummed out of the Royal Navy for sodomy before he turned to trade. He was probably one of the few who got caught.

I knocked on the door and was admitted by the usual sour-faced nurse. I couldn't blame her for looking less than enchanted with life. Who would volunteer to be in charge of a bunch of semi-incontinent old curmudgeons who spent most of their time working out scams for getting their hands on the contents of the alcohol cabinet? Like the buggers in the navy when such an institution existed, retired citizens are entitled to a shot of booze every day – unless they misbehave, in which case it ends up in the nurse.

There wasn't much misbehaving going on tonight though. I walked across the hallway, breathing in the familiar reek of boiled fish and the wind it inspires, and popped my head into the common room. There was still an hour till bedtime and normally they were gathered around Scrabble boards or chess tables chuntering and rabbiting on like a convention of geriatric trainspotters. There were a few of them playing, but no one was saying much. I didn't have to ask why.

I wasn't too worried. The nurse would have told me if it was Hector who'd died. Then I remembered the note I'd received. Jesus, surely not. I took the stairs in threes and miraculously reached the top without hamstring damage.

"Who was it?" I said, stumbling into Hector's room. "Don't tell me it was . . ."

My father looked up from the array of books spread across his desk. "Ah, there you are, failure." He shook his head irritably. "I wish you'd learn to formulate comprehensible sentences."

"Not now, for God's sake. Who's died?"

That seemed to be comprehensible enough for him. He dropped his gaze. A shiver convulsed his long, thin body and suddenly he looked even older than he was. "Poor William. He should never have been in a second-floor room. He had trouble with his eyes . . . couldn't judge distances properly . . ." His voice trailed away.

I leaned over him and swung his chair round so he was facing me. "I need to know exactly what happened to him, Hector."

His eyes flashed as they met mine again. He was never down for long. "Why? He's not the first former guardian to go. You're not normally this interested."

I suppose that was a reference to my mother, but he was being a bit hypocritical. For years my parents regarded each other with maximum suspicion and he didn't exactly collapse with grief when she died. Then again, neither did I – it hit me later. But he had a point. I wasn't too sure myself why the former science and energy guardian's death had given me a frisson.

"How did it happen?" I asked quietly. Raising your voice with my father is always a waste of time. His time as a guardian and, before the Enlightenment, as professor of rhetoric at the university made him more or less invincible in verbal combat.

"He fell down the stairs this morning. Broke his neck, the silly old sod." The words were harsh, but the tone wasn't. I knew my father had been close to William.

"Did you see him?"

"I heard him, lad." He gave me a weak smile. "I was sitting here reading some Quintilian, curiously enough."

"What time was it?"

"Before seven. You know how early I wake. I heard his door open down below, then there was a sliding noise like he'd lost his footing. Then a series of bumps that I didn't fathom immediately, followed by a godawful bang." He looked up at me, his face white as he relived what had happened. "I got up from my chair and looked down the stairwell. I could see him, legs crumpled and his head at an impossible angle. He must have hit the floor head first. You know how hard it is in the hall."

I nodded. "Was anyone else about?"

"I started shouting. The woman dragged herself out of her pit and called an ambulance, but there was no point."

"Did William usually wake early too?"

Hector glared at me. "I didn't sleep with him, you know." He fumbled with his pen and eventually managed to screw the cap back on. Then he looked at me curiously. "No, as a matter of fact he didn't. When he arrived here after your mother cleared out the Council — apart from the stubborn buggers like Hamilton — I remember him telling me how much he was looking forward to staying in bed in the morning. Apparently he never liked getting up at the crack of dawn."

I had the strong feeling that something peculiar had taken place in the retirement home.

"Did you see anyone unusual around here this morning?"

Hector threw up his hands. "The place was full of stormtroopers. There was so much noise I couldn't concentrate on my reading."

"No, I mean before William fell. Any vehicles outside?"

"This room might be in the lookout tower but I'm not a bloody sentry, Quintilian." More glaring, then a reluctant sigh.

"I did glance out when I got up. There was nothing in the street." His eyes began to open wide and I backed off. "What are you suggesting, laddie?"

"Nothing. Nothing at all." I headed for the door. "I'll be back in a minute."

William McEwan's room was easy to spot. It was the one with the wide-open door and the stripped bed. The nurse hadn't wasted any time getting the place ready for its next occupant. I bent down and examined the carpet on the landing. It looked like a herd of waterbuffalo had been stampeding over it for centuries. The same could be said for the rug in the old man's room. I stood there for a few minutes and asked myself exactly what I was playing at. I'd heard the ex-guardian having a go at the chief boyscout, giving him grief about something called the Bone Yard. Then he'd sent me a note mentioning it again. Now he was dead. So what? I'd seen two people on the mortuary table who definitely hadn't died accidentally. And what was I thinking anyway? That the senior guardian had been so pissed off by the old man's harangue that he'd had him done away with. Even someone as cynical as I am about the effects of power on the individuals who exercise it would laugh at that idea. Then I saw the mark on the wooden floor beyond the rug.

I suppose it could have been made by William himself. Except that it was recent, and surrounded by several indentations that looked distinctly like those made by the nails on the soles of guard-issue boots. There's no way a retired guardian would have a pair of those; if he was lucky, he might have managed to keep a hold of his guardian-issue brogues like Hector had done. If Davie had been there, I would have bet him that someone had dug a heel in while dragging a reasonably heavy weight off the bed. The odds would have been pretty short as well.

I went back up to my father's room and tried to look nonchalant. I've never been much good at that. He knew I was on edge and conversation became sketchy.

I got up to leave before the nurse came round to turn the light out at ten. "When's the funeral?"

"Tomorrow morning, nine o'clock. Full Council attendance." Hector gave me a dubious look. "Are you planning on coming?"

I nodded slowly, suddenly wondering why William's death hadn't been mentioned at this evening's Council meeting. Surely they weren't trying to keep me away? That idea got up my nose in a big way. "I'll be there all right."

I said goodnight and went back to the Land-Rover. I'd already decided I wasn't going to wait till morning to visit the crematorium.

If the driver thought it was weird to be directed there, he didn't show it. His rank is taught to treat surprise as if it's the bad boy at the back of the class — ignore it and it'll eventually give up and find someone else to annoy. Oddly enough, I used to have problems with that tactic when I was an auxiliary. Probably something to do with my highly strung temperament.

Which was actually about as taut as a Hendrix e-string as we drove through the darkened streets to the northern of the city's two crematoria. It wasn't only that I was going way beyond my authority. That was limited to investigating the murders but anything's fair game in a murder case as far as I'm concerned. No, it had just struck me that I hadn't been back there since my mother's funeral. It was suddenly very clear to me that I didn't want to go anywhere near that soulless brick and concrete dump. So why didn't I just redirect the driver and forget about William McEwan? I'd have been hard pressed to answer that question. Suspicion? Hunch? Curiosity about this Bone Yard that seemed to be eating away at him like a liver fluke? I wasn't sure, but there was no one in the Land-Rover actually expecting answers to those questions so I let them ride.

The steel gate at the entrance to the crematorium driveway was chained up. I got out and pressed the intercom button. Even through the crackle I made out the voice that responded. I'd been hoping the city's chief ghoul might have taken the night off. Or gone back to the underworld. He didn't exactly sound overjoyed to hear my voice either.

In a minute he appeared on the other side of the gate.

"Citizen Dalrymple," he said drily, the stiff parchment skin on his face even yellower than usual in the artificial light. "You're almost becoming a regular."

"I'm pleased to see you too, Haigh. Hurry up. Unlike you, I'm not a creature of the night."

He finally got the chain open and let me in. I signalled to the driver to wait where he was. The less he knew of what I was about to do, the better for his future career.

"I imagine you have an authorisation, citizen," Haigh said. He put out his hand for it like a vulture flexing its claw as we walked into the dingy low building. The guardians have a very pragmatic attitude towards death. All that matters to them is disposing of the body efficiently, so what funds they've spent on the crematorium have been to maintain the furnace, not to tart the buildings up. It's never occurred to them that the bereaved might like to see off their relatives and friends in slightly more salubrious surroundings. No doubt that was why they kept Haigh on as facility supervisor too. His bony bald head and elongated limbs made even atheists cross themselves.

"Now, let me see, when was the last time we met?" the old bastard asked, handing back my authorisation.

"You know very well it was at my mother's funeral, Haigh," I answered, giving him the eye. "Shall we get on?"

He smiled, lips drawn back over seriously far gone teeth. "I also know that any personnel arriving at this facility during the hours of curfew have to be checked with guard headquarters. I'll just go and make the call."

I grabbed his fleshless arm before he could move off. "I don't think so, citizen. What I'm going to do now will be our little secret."

His jaw dropped. "What do you mean, citizen?" he asked suspiciously.

I gave him a smile to encourage him. All that did was make him look like a vampire who's just noticed the garlic festooned about the chosen virgin's negligée.

"William McEwan. You have him here?"

Now the virgin had whipped her cross out. "The former guardian?" he said haltingly. "Yes, he's here. Why do you ask?"

"I want to have a look at his papers."

The old bureaucrat's expression brightened. "Only his papers?"

"Before I take a look at the body."

He was back to being the panic-stricken vampire, this time with the first rays of dawn appearing over the eastern Transylvanian uplands. "You ... you can't do that. It's against regulations. I'll have to call ..."

"You'll have to calm down, citizen," I said, leading him briskly into his office. Then I gave him the eye again. "You'll also have to comply with everything I request." I glanced around his impeccably neat room with its cabinets full of perfectly organised files. "Otherwise an unexpected wave of chaos might suddenly burst over your records."

As I thought, the threat of messing with his files did the trick – anally retentive bureaucrats are easy to intimidate. He unlocked the drawer of his desk and took out a maroon file. Deceased ordinary citizens and auxiliaries get grey, but guardians are honoured with maroon. So much for death the great equaliser.

I flicked through the pages. I was after the post-mortem report, but all I got was a big zero from the Medical Directorate.

"How come there was no post-mortem, Haigh? It wasn't exactly death by natural causes, was it?"

The crematorium supervisor looked away shiftily. "Yes, I did notice that. I rang the Medical Directorate and was told that a post-mortem was not required. They didn't give me a reason."

"And you were happy with that?"

Haigh gave the smirk of the bureaucrat who has covered his arse with fifteen-inch armour plating. "If that's what the Medical Directorate decides, it's good enough for me. I logged the call, of course."

"Of course you did." I handed the file back. "Got your screwdriver ready?"

His face slackened again. "Isn't this enough for you? What more do you need to know?"

I went over to the nearest cabinet and grabbed a handful of folders.

"No, put those back. I . . . oh, very well." Haigh put the file away, took out his screwdriver and locked the drawer again. He was nothing if not careful. I wondered how many other people he expected to be interested in the recently deceased former guardian.

The hall and corridors of the crematorium were bloody freezing. I followed the supervisor down to the room where coffins were stored for the brief period allowed by health regulations before their contents go up in smoke (the coffins themselves are reused, of course). The place had hardly any lights and I suddenly had the nasty feeling I was being led into a fairy-tale fiend's lair. As if to reinforce that, Haigh looked over his hunched shoulder and gave me a grin Beelzebub would have been proud of. For all his protestations, I was sure this was the part of his work he liked best — messing about with the bodies.

"Here we are, citizen," he said, turning into a windowless room and putting on the light. There were three coffins on stands, all of them showing signs of wear and tear. The one Haigh headed for was in the best condition of the three.

"Screwdriver," I said, holding out my hand.

He handed it over reluctantly.

"Now, off you go back to your files," I said. I was pleased to see he could barely contain his disappointment. He wasn't giving up though.

"Regulations clearly state that a member of crematorium staff must always be present when coffins are opened, citizen Dalrymple."

"Are you attached to this screwdriver?" I asked.

He didn't get my drift.

"Would you like to be even more attached to it?" I brandished it at him like they taught us in the auxiliary training programme. The door closed behind him rapidly and I set to work.

Actually, I could have done with his help to lift the lid off when I'd undone all the screws, but I didn't want him to see what I was looking for. That was the problem. I didn't know what I was looking for myself. I took a deep breath and manhandled the lid off. And looked upon the face of William McEwan.

But it wasn't much like Schliemann looking upon Agamemnon's features. No gold mask, not even much attempt to arrange the face in a condition of repose. The poor old guy's eyes were wide open, his lips and teeth parted, giving him the expression of someone who's just woken up from a disturbing dream. But there would be no more lie-ins followed by leisurely breakfasts for this sleeper – only the ultimate substantial slumber.

I loosened the maroon and black striped Council tie and the white shirt under the tweed jacket that they'd dressed him in. His neck had that clammy chill feeling we all acquire eventually. I felt for the fracture, lifting him up. The head lolled loosely to the side. His neck was broken all right, and there was no obvious bruising to suggest that hands had been laid on him. And there was a large contusion on his forehead consistent with a fall. So far everything was in order. What had I thought I would find? A label saying "Assassination carried out by Council order"?

I shook my head and stepped back from the open coffin. I had a decision to make. It didn't take long. There was no point in getting this far if I wasn't going to go through with it.

I stepped forward again and started to undo the buttons of his shirt. I didn't want to, but I was going to have to examine the whole body for marks showing if William had been manhandled to the top of the stairs. This was what should have been done in the post-mortem that someone had decided wouldn't take place.

I was unzipping the former guardian's trousers when Haigh tried to come in. I shouted at him so loud that I was lucky William McEwan didn't come round and ask me what I thought I was doing. I asked myself the same question after I'd struggled to get his trousers off and found nothing; the fact that the laces on his scuffed old brogues were double knotted didn't help. Then my eyes fell on the shoes. They were lying on their sides on the floor where I'd dropped them. Why the hell would anyone tie double knots on a dead man's shoes?

I went to the bottom of the coffin. Even before I pulled his socks off, I could see William McEwan's feet were badly swollen. The black bruising all over the top of both feet showed that he didn't just have bad circulation. Some piece of shit had trampled all over the old man's feet, which probably had nothing more than bedsocks on them at that time of the morning. No doubt it was the bastard who'd left the marks of his boots on the bedroom floor. There was no way William had fallen down the stairs accidentally. Christ, with these bruises he'd hardly even have been able to walk two paces.

I backed away again and squatted down on the concrete floor. This time the decision I had to make took a lot longer.

After I put the clothes back on William's wasted limbs and tried unsuccessfully to close his eyes, I was nearly consumed by rage. Haigh saw how I looked as I stormed down the corridor and veered out of my way. I tossed over his screwdriver without making any effort to miss him and told him to put the lid back on the coffin himself. At that moment I was dead set on driving straight to Moray Place and asking the senior guardian what the fuck was going on. Then I got outside and the Arctic air brought me to my senses. Suddenly suicide didn't seem like such an attractive option.

Back in my flat I gulped whisky and tried to work out a plan of action. Whoever killed the ex-guardian had friends in high places, as the lack of post-mortem showed. On the other hand, I had very few friends on the Council. Hamilton might class himself as one if he was feeling charitable, but his own position in the Council was isolated. No, the only sensible way was to keep what I knew to myself and nail whoever was responsible when I had the whole story.

So I put on my black suit and turned up uninvited to William's service. Hector beckoned to me to sit beside him but I preferred to stand at the side where I had a good view of all the guardians and senior auxiliaries on parade. I saw Haigh lurking in the background and wondered if he'd told anyone about my visit. If he had, no one seemed to be too bothered. Judging by the lack of eye contact I was receiving, I might as well have stayed at home. The medical guardian was the only one who even batted an eyelid in acknowledgement of my presence, but I wasn't getting my hopes up – she looked as beautiful and as glacial as ever. Machiavelli was standing next to Hamilton with his nose in the air and his head angled away from the guardian in another tell-tale piece of body language.

What I was hoping might be interesting was the senior guardian's address. I reckoned I'd be able to spot if he was harbouring any guilty feelings about the old man's death, but I'd forgotten what a skilful performer the chief boyscout had become during his time at the top. He ran through William's achievements at the Science and Energy Directorate, expressed the city and the Council's gratitude and held his head high as the coffin disappeared into the floor. A statue would have given more away.

Outside, no one was inclined to hang about. The temperature was doing its usual impression of Tromsø on a bad day and there was no wake afterwards; since the guardians don't permit themselves alcohol, there wouldn't have been much point. I had a few words with Hector then led him towards a guard vehicle.

"Aren't there better ways for you to spend your time, citizen?"

I turned to face the senior guardian. I'd been wondering if he'd have the nerve to approach me.

"It's important to mark the passing of the old guard," I said with a thin smile. "Even if the passing is a bit premature."

I was hoping to catch even a hint of regret but there was nothing.

"Citizen, it's someone who hasn't passed away yet who you should be after – the murderer. Kindly get back to work." He strode off without a glance at my father.

"What did he mean?" Hector asked. "Are you working for the Council again?"

I nodded slowly.

Over the crematorium a cloud of smoke rose from the chimney. It was the last breath of William McEwan, floating away into the chill blue sky above the "perfect" city he'd served.

Chapter Eleven

———◆◆◆———

I was running down an ice-rimmed street under a bright moon, my legs flailing, trying to catch up with a figure in a long, hooded coat. Then the figure stopped and turned to face me. I slowed to walking pace, my breath rasping in my throat and a stitch fastening my liver to my lowest rib tighter than an industrial sewing machine could. As the figure's face came into view I felt myself falling into an abyss. It was Roddie Aitken, lips bared and blood trailing down his chin. Then everything went black, darker than the universe before the big bang went off, darker than the soul of the killer I was trying to find. But I could hear voices. Not Roddie's, not any man's. They were women's voices, the voices of the women I'd lost. My mother, Caro, Katharine Kirkwood. They seemed to be getting closer, asking questions plaintively, accusing me of failing them. But I'd also lost the power of speech. Like Roddie, like William McEwan.

I woke up in a sweat-soaked bed reeking of nettles and seaweed. It took me a couple of minutes to work out that the smell came from the cup of barracks tea on my bedside table.

"Nice dream?" Davie asked as I staggered through into the main room of my flat. "You looked like you were well into an imaginary sex session."

"Sod off, guardsman. It was a nightmare actually."

Davie grinned. "That's the problem with random selection of partners."

I shook my head. "No, it was a real nightmare. Christ, this bastard case. We're going nowhere with it. Just waiting for the butcher to kill again."

"You read my mind," Davie said. "When you'd woken up properly I was going to tell you that none of the tails we've got on the two victims' friends and contacts has come up with anything significant." He tossed over a sheaf of papers. "Their reports up to yesterday evening."

At least the City Guard's bureaucracy was still doing its job, though personally I'd have given the undercover people an extra hour's relaxation rather than make them write up the day's events before they sign off.

"No more pills found anywhere either," Davie added, flipping the pages of his notebook then closing it. "So what are we doing today?"

I knew what I was going to do, but it was something that I didn't want to risk involving him in. "Can you keep an eye on all the leads we're following, Davie? I want you to keep Hamilton off my back as well. I'm switching my mobile off today."

"Oh, aye?" he said, raising an eyebrow. "And where exactly are you headed, Quint?"

"You don't want to know, guardsman. You do not want to know."

I reckoned I had about an hour at the most. I still had an "ask no questions", one of the cards issued by the Public Order Directorate to undercover operatives, from the murder investigation in 2020. It would get me into the Science and Energy Directorate archive all right, and my disguise would buy me some time from the senior guardian. If he was advised that someone answering my description was in his directorate files, he'd be down faster than the Archangel Gabriel when Lucifer got uppity.

And so it came to pass. I used the blue overalls I had when I was in the Parks Department a few years back, supplementing them with a bag of tools to make me look like a plumber. Pipes are always blocking up or cracking in the Council's Edinburgh and plumbers bring out the best in even the most granite-jawed sentry. I was also wearing a bright blond wig I'd picked up in one of the ragshops that ordinary citizens rely on when their clothing vouchers run out.

I strode purposefully up the steps to what used to be the Royal College of Surgeons in Nicolson Street. Trust the Enlightenment to choose a Playfair neo-classical temple for the city's science and energy base. The original Council members had little time for science. It had been misused so much in the late twentieth century, what with cloning (until the American religious right put a stop to that), the development of new, even more addictive consumer drugs and the nuclear industry's increasingly unchecked expansion. Such scientific experiments as were allowed took place in the King's Buildings where the toxicologist worked and at a few other locations, but the headquarters were symbolically situated in a building Plato would have approved of.

I got into the archive room and diagnosed a supposedly explosive leak. That scared all the file shufflers off. Then I locked myself in and headed for the records covering the years when William McEwan was guardian. In the limited time I had I was unlikely to find some as yet unidentified needle in this particular stack of bureaucratic hay, but I owed it to the old man to have a try. If he'd been keeping any documents to show me at the retirement home, they were long gone by the time I searched his room. I took a deep breath and started pulling open cabinets and maroon-coloured "guardians' eyes only" files.

As it turned out, I got even less than the hour I'd estimated. By the time the banging started on the steel-plated security door, I'd found nothing. But as nothings go, it was a very interesting one. What I wanted to know was, why was there a full set of top-security files covering one particular hot subject except for four months of William McEwan's period of tenure? That particular subject was what used to be the city's main source of electricity until the Council shut it down – the advanced gas-cooled reactor power station at Torness.

Whoever was laying into the door was doing a fair imitation of a blues drummer who's taken too many pills from the bag marked Speed Kills.

"Who is it?" I shouted, trying to stall them.

"Davie."

I was impressed. "How did you find me?"

"Are you going to let me in, Quint?"

I finished putting the files back and opened the door.

"There's been a sighting of the bastard in the hood," he said hoarsely. "A sentry's been attacked – knocked senseless. He's regaining consciousness now."

"The attacker got away?"

"What do you think?"

We came out into the watery sunlight. Clouds had been gathering while I was inside and it didn't feel as cold as it had. No doubt the weather was laying another ambush.

"Where are we headed?"

Davie started the Land-Rover's engine. "Raeburn Barracks. Apparently the sentry was patrolling the waste land where that school used to be when he saw a guy in a long coat in the bushes. I don't know any more."

"I know the feeling," I muttered as we roared down the South Bridge. "So how did you find me?"

"I was in the ops room when the sentry here reported a plumber with an outrageous wig," he said, turning to grin at me. "Who else could it have been?"

I looked away, pissed off that he'd clocked my disguise from a mile off. On the bridge a small boy in the maroon sweater all the city's schoolchildren wear flicked us a well-practised V-sign as we passed. I liked his spirit but I didn't give much for his chances if he tried that with the auxiliaries in his school. The Council is keen on the three Rs, but it's an even bigger fan of the three Ds: Discipline, Direction and Drill. I should know. My mother was the first education guardian.

Raeburn 497 was six feet two and about fifteen stone. That's how he survived. As it was, he was definitely a candidate for the small number of plastic surgery operations the Medical Directorate carries out each year – the Council has been having a big downer on non-essential use of resources.

"Shouldn't he be in the infirmary?" I asked the barracks commander.

"My medical officer's had a good look at him. She says his skull's undamaged."

Which was more than I could say for the young auxiliary's face. It looked like someone had been tapdancing on it with steel-toed boots.

"Can you describe the man who laid into you?" I asked, bending over the swollen purple features.

A brief shake of the head. "Not really."

I had to lean closer to make out the words. He'd lost most of his front teeth.

"The collar of his coat was pulled up and the hood was hanging down low."

Sounded like our man all right.

"What colour was the coat?"

"Dark brown. It was long, almost down to his boots."

"What colour were they?"

"Black. High, up to his knee. Badly scuffed." He shook his head a couple of times. "Not like any I've ever seen before." He tried to laugh and only succeeded in coughing up blood. "Except in the Westerns they show in the Historical Film Society."

Cowboy boots? I hadn't seen a pair of those since the ones I saved up for when I was sixteen fell to bits years later. Another pointer to someone from outside the city. No doubt you can buy all sorts of exotic footwear in democratic Glasgow – if you can fight your way to the shop. It didn't look like our man would have any problem doing that. But something was bothering me. I didn't have any recollection of the hooded figure I'd chased from my flat wearing that kind of footwear. I was pretty sure I'd seen an ordinary pair of work boots.

The sentry's breathing was heavy and he was obviously in a lot of pain. I turned to his commander, a barrel-chested specimen in the standard iron boyscout mode. Before I could ask exactly where the sighting had occurred, the door to the barracks sick bay opened and Machiavelli walked in. His face immediately turned greyer than the contents of the pies ordinary citizens have to put up with. I couldn't tell whether that was because of the guardsman's injuries or my presence.

"What happened here?" he asked, his eyes opening even wider as he approached the bed. "It's Raeburn 497, isn't it? He's inter-barracks unarmed combat champion."

I left the commander to fill him in. So our killer had taken out the city's best fighter. That made my day.

"Where were you when you saw him?" I asked the sentry.

He suddenly looked a lot worse, his head lolling over in my direction. "Fettes . . . near the foundations of Carrington House. He was in the bushes by the gates . . . here, I've lost my knife . . ."

He passed out. Just as well. His commander would drag him over the coals in the barracks boiler room for mislaying his auxiliary-issue weapon. I was overjoyed to learn that the murderer's collection of sharp blades had grown by one.

"Commander," I said, interrupting the conversation he was having with Hamilton's deputy, "This man's in a very bad way. For Christ's sake get him to the infirmary."

For a sworn atheist, Raeburn 01 showed surprising alacrity in complying. Maybe he was just programmed to obey anything in the imperative mood.

❋ ❋ ❋

Davie and I drove up to the place where the guardsman had been attacked. It was only about a hundred yards from Raeburn Barracks, which shows you the nerve of the guy. But what the hell was he doing here?

Before the Enlightenment what's now a lattice of foundation stones with untended grass growing over them had been one of Scotland's most expensive public schools. Which is one reason why the drugs gangs, who started out in the urban nightmare of Pilton up the road, decided to blow the place up. A lot of the stone had been carted off and used in other less exclusive building projects – though since most of them were tourist facilities, that isn't exactly accurate. Down by the remains of one of the boarding houses, the city's number one headbanger had been given a lesson in unarmed combat by the city's number one murderer.

We hunted around the area that was cordoned off by City Guard tape. Apart from a few scuffmarks on the bone-hard ground, there was nothing to see. I don't know what I expected. The killer had been careful enough so far not to leave anything he didn't want us to have. After a while I squatted down by the unkempt bushes and looked up through the trees at the dull red ball of the sun to the west.

"You know what I think?" Davie said.

"Surprise me, guardsman."

"He was waiting for someone."

"In the bushes, within spitting distance of a barracks? Doesn't seem too likely. What citizen would willingly come here? It'd be a real risk." Then I raised my eyes to his. "You're not suggesting he was meeting an auxiliary, are you?"

Davie was suddenly looking uncomfortable. "Well, it's a possibility, isn't it?"

I thought of how Machiavelli looked in the sick bay. Something had washed all the colour from his face and I didn't think it was just the smell of antiseptic. But that was hardly conclusive. After all, Raeburn was his barracks. He had every right to be there even though his current billet was in the castle.

I stood up and shook the stiffness from my legs. "I wonder. Maybe the hooded man didn't have a meet arranged." I turned to Davie. "Maybe he was doing the same thing as we are."

"What do you mean?"

"Maybe he was looking for someone."

"An auxiliary?"

"It wouldn't be the first one he's targeted."

"Great. That means we've got the five hundred members of this barracks to check out."

"Forget it, my friend. The Council would never allow it. Anyway, what would we be looking for? All Raeburn personnel with guilty looks on their faces?"

I headed back to the Land-Rover. As we were driving away, I remembered the last time I'd been in the public school's grounds. It was when I was investigating the murders two years ago. An ex-drug gang member called Leadbelly who was one of the few remaining prisoners in the city's prison had been clearing stones from the site. He gave me some information that turned out to be useful and I gave him some blues tapes in return. As we turned south and the long line of spires and gables leading along the Royal Mile to the castle swung into view, I wondered what had happened to my informant. Then my mobile rang and the thought exited my mind as quickly as a warm spell on an Edinburgh spring day.

"What exactly were you doing in the Science and Energy Directorate, citizen?" The senior guardian's voice didn't suggest that he was making anything other than a mundane enquiry, but I sensed he was a lot more interested than that.

"Checking on labs with personnel who could have produced the Electric Blues," I lied.

"In disguise?" There was a silence that the chief boyscout presumably thought was meaningful. "You are wasting your time, citizen Dalrymple. No auxiliary would have anything to do with the manufacture of such drugs without a specific order from my directorate. No such order has been given."

I was sure that if it had been given, there wouldn't be any reference to it in the archive. I considered passing that thought on to him but decided I was enjoying my freedom too much.

"Are you still there, citizen?" The senior guardian almost sounded impatient, an unusually human characteristic for him.

"I am."

"What are you doing?"

I've never been able to handle close supervision. "Sorry, guardian, you're breaking up. I'll see you at the Council meeting. Out."

Davie glanced across at me. "Are you messing the senior guardian about, Quint?"

"Why? Are you going to do me for insubordination, guardsman?"

He shook his head, but the expression on his face was grim. "He might look like a saint in a Renaissance painting, but he used to have a reputation in his barracks for breaking people he didn't like." He slowed at the checkpoint on Raeburn Place and raised his hand to acknowledge the guardswoman on duty. She gave him a smile that would get her a job in the Prostitution Services Department any day.

"Friend of yours?" I asked.

"Auxiliaries don't have friends," he replied with a grin.

"Sorry. Close colleague?" I said, using the official term.

"Close enough a few years back."

"You seem to have been close enough to every female auxiliary under thirty-five in the city, Davie."

"Jealousy's a fearful thing, citizen." The smile died on his lips. "Listen, I meant what I was saying about the senior guardian. Are you going into battle with him?"

I looked out at the citizens trudging up the hill towards the centre for the evening shift in the city's hotels and restaurants, casinos and strip joints. Their backs were bent, their faces drawn in the cold. Was this really the best the Council could offer them after nearly twenty years? The Enlightenment's ideals of education, work and housing for all were still intact, but only just. I didn't have much faith in the iron boyscouts and I wasn't the only one. The question was, could anyone else do any better?

"Well, are you?"

Davie's voice roused me from my thoughts. "Am I what?"

"Are you going into battle with the senior guardian?"

I looked ahead into the grey, lowering sky. "I don't know, Davie. I'm beginning to get the feeling that he's declared open season on me."

A snowflake hit the windscreen and stayed there on its own for a few seconds. Another joined it. Then they got our range and a flurry of the white stuff carpeted the glass. The frayed wipers immediately had trouble clearing it. The Land-Rover slowed as Davie took his foot off the accelerator and peered out through the glass.

"Shit," he said. "This is going to cause chaos. You know what the city's like when it snows."

Buses with worn, remoulded tyres slewing across the roads, citizens late for work, tourists complaining – it's the same every winter. But I had a nasty feeling that the murderer wasn't the kind of guy to be deflected from his plans by a change in the weather. Of course, it would have helped if I had the faintest idea of what those plans were.

The snow kept pelting down, some flakes even managing to slip through the holes in the Land-Rover's bodywork. I felt them on my hands for a moment before they melted away, leaving as little behind as the hooded man who was haunting the city. And me.

The Council meeting was a lot of fun. Hamilton told them how none of his operatives had turned up anything and I told them about the attack on the guardsman at Fettes. There was a brief burst of outrage at this second assault on one of the city's servants, but as it wasn't in the same league as the murder of the female auxiliary, they soon shut up.

"Citizen Dalrymple." The senior guardian paused for effect after addressing me. His lips twitched in a brief and unconvincing smile. "I have the strong impression that you are merely waiting for events to occur in this investigation. Surely there is more that you can do to pre-empt the murderer." The tone of his voice was suddenly sharp and I remembered what Davie said about the chief boyscout's reputation. He was trying to muscle in on my territory. Normally I give anyone who tries that the verbal equivalent of a knee in the bollocks, but that would just have ended up with me being booted off the case. No, I had to keep the senior guardian sweet: that was the only way I'd be able to find out if he or any of his colleagues had anything to do with the production of the Electric Blues.

So I grovelled like a trainee auxiliary who's failed all his assessments and has to beg for one last chance before being reassigned to ordinary citizen's duties like cleaning the bogs in the city's nightclubs.

"I'm sorry my investigation hasn't uncovered anything significant yet, guardian. I'd appreciate any help you can give." Out of the corner of my eye I caught a glimpse of Hamilton's face. He looked like he'd just seen a tourist voluntarily donate all his winnings from the racetrack in Princes Street Gardens to the Council's urban renewal fund.

As I suspected, the senior guardian didn't have any specific advice to offer. He'd just been laying down the law. It's interesting how many guardians in this supposedly equitable city get a kick out of doing that.

"I won't tell you again, citizen," he said, fixing me with a steely glare. "Concentrate on finding the killer and leave the Science and Energy Directorate to me."

As far as I was concerned, that was as good as him hiring a mason to engrave in stone the words: "I have a secret that I'm not at all keen on you finding out about."

❊   ❊   ❊

Hamilton caught up with me on the stairs outside the Council chamber. "What on earth was going on in there, Dalrymple? I know the investigation's ground to a halt, but there was no need to make us look quite so cack-handed."

I wasn't really listening to him. What was much more intriguing was the sight of his deputy Machiavelli racing up the stairs towards the senior guardian. His face was still greyer than a corpse's. I turned and watched as the pair moved out of the throng of guardians to a secluded corner. Then Machiavelli started waving his arms about like a windmill in a hurricane.

I'd have given a lot to hear that conversation.

Back in my flat I sank into the faded, lumpy cushions of my citizen-issue sofa, took a pull of what remained in the whisky bottle and considered my options. When I was in the directorate, people used to accuse me of excessive cynicism. This manifested itself in a distrust of authority – meaning Lewis Hamilton – and a predilection for conspiracy theories. Nothing had changed. In this particular investigation I definitely distrusted the city's top dog and I was bloody sure there was a conspiracy around the Electric Blues. Whether the two were connected was anybody's guess. Then I remembered Roddie Aitken sitting on this very sofa and telling his story. I remembered the way he'd laughed off the hooded man as if he were a harmless crazy guy and went off into the dark to bring in the New Year. It looked more and more like he'd been set up. I hadn't forgotten the oath I swore. I was going to find the bastard who cut him open. I was also going to find the bastards who put the killer on to him. No matter who they were.

This time I was sprinting up a hillside in the moonlight after a shadowy figure, my breath rasping in my throat and my legs brushing through bracken. For all my efforts, I couldn't gain on the figure. I caught a glimpse of a long coat as it breasted

THE BONE YARD

the summit. Then I slipped on the wet vegetation and went my length, knocking the breath out of my lungs. That woke me up with a jerk.

There was a faint light in my bedroom. As my senses cleared from the dream, that began to puzzle me. I'd made sure the candles were extinguished before I crashed out at midnight. I sat up in bed and looked towards the door. The light was coming in through a slight gap between the door and the jamb. My heart skipped a few beats. The seal on the bedroom door is good and I always pull it to. It never opens itself during the night. I put my breathing on hold and listened carefully. Nothing, not a sound. But what was the source of the light? It couldn't be Davie. His arrivals were about as subtle as a herd of rhinos. An icy thought stabbed into my mind. The hooded man. He'd been in the vicinity at least twice. I felt my hands tremble then the rest of my body followed suit. The auxiliary knife that I should have handed in when I was demoted was in my bookcase, behind my copy of the collected works of Sir Arthur Conan Doyle. All I had in the bedroom were my clothes. I forced myself to take a series of deep breaths. As I completed the fifth, I heard the unmistakable sound of the strut creak in the middle of my sofa. Jesus, there was definitely somebody there. I felt around under my bed for my boot, the only offensive weapon I could think of, gripped it hard and tensed every muscle in my body. Then powered myself out of bed and through the door.

Although the light from the single candle on the coffee table wasn't bright, it was enough for me to make out a single figure sitting on the sofa. The figure was wearing a long, dark-coloured coat.

Chapter Twelve

A moment of gut-freezing shock as what the killer had done to the groins of his two victims flashed in front of me, then I was put out of my misery. The figure raised its head and the light cast by the candle fell on the face.

"Hello, Quint. Still in love with your bed, I see."

I tried to step forward then decided against it. My knees were suddenly weaker than those of a 1990s prime minister confronted by a backbench revolt. A series of shivers ran up my spine. I tried to make out the features, which were ringed by crewcut brown hair, but there was no need. I knew this person from the languid, hoarse voice.

"Katharine?" I managed to get the name out, but inducing an auxiliary to tell a joke about Plato would have been easier. "Is it you, Katharine?"

She stood up and let the coat drop from her shoulders. "At least you remember my name. Should I be pleased?"

It came to my attention that I was standing in an unheated room wearing nothing more than a pair of grubby citizen-issue underpants and brandishing a well-worn size eight boot. For some reason this irritated me.

"What the bloody hell are you doing sneaking around other people's flats in the middle of the fucking night?" I threw the boot to the floor, narrowly missing my bare and very cold feet.

"You'd better put some clothes on, dear. You'll catch your death." A smile flickered across Katharine's lips, making her face look less gaunt. The shortness of her hair had the effect of increasing the size of her green eyes. I felt them on me.

"Make yourself even more at home than you have already," I said, turning tail and heading back to the bedroom. "Nothing much has changed since you were last here."

I sat down on the bed and tried to get a grip. Katharine Kirkwood. I never expected to see her again. After the murder investigation a couple of years back, she jumped the border fence. Edinburgh hadn't been too kind to Katharine in the past so what was she doing back here? Surely she wasn't risking arrest for her unauthorised departure from the city just to say hello.

I fumbled with my flies and pulled on a heavy sweater. It's against regulations to burn coal after curfew and I didn't fancy risking another run-in with the senior guardian – he was energy supremo, after all.

Katharine had pulled her coat round herself. It was brown and had a high collar, as well as a hood. I sat on the sofa, forcing her to move over. As she did that, I noticed her footwear – worn work boots rather than the cowboy variety.

She turned to look at me, her face eventually loosening to a faint smile.

"You look all right, Quint," she said.

"Oh, thanks. What were you expecting after two years? All my teeth to have fallen out and my hair to be whiter than the stuff that's clogging up the streets?"

"Why are you angry with me?" she said, her eyes flashing. "I've taken a lot of chances to get to you."

I nodded. "Yes, you have, haven't you? I was impressed by that leap you made into the storeyard. Course, you've always been good at jumping."

"Haven't I just? Was that Davie with you in the Land-Rover?"

I ran my eyes over her. She was thinner but fitter-looking than before. Like all of us, she could have done with more to eat. Still, whatever she was involved in wasn't doing her too much harm.

"Didn't you want to hang around so you could lay into him like you used to?" I asked. Davie and Katharine had never got beyond the stage of intense mutual suspicion.

"I wasn't sure it was him. Then that other Land-Rover arrived. I don't want the guard to know I'm back."

"What about at Tollcross the other night? Was that you too?"

She looked at me uncomprehendingly and shook her head. So that had either been the killer or my imagination playing tricks.

I picked up the whisky bottle and held it up to the light. Enough for a slug each. I offered her it.

"No, thanks. Try this." She handed me a half-litre of Russian vodka.

"Jesus, where did you get real vodka?" I let the spirit wash down my throat. Warmth instantly spread through my abdomen.

"We can get anything from the traders — when we have something to trade." She took the bottle from my hand. For a moment I felt her fingers on mine. The flesh tingled as if she'd spilled acid. That was my body's way of reminding me that the first time we had sex was in this room. I didn't actually need that reminder.

Neither did Katharine. "Are you pleased to see me, Quint? Or have you been through too many sex sessions to remember what we did in that armchair?" Her eyelids were wide apart and the corners of her mouth twitched.

I leaned forward and kissed her. For a few seconds she was still, then she put her hand against my chest and gently pushed me back.

"You're not answering my questions," she said, her voice even hoarser than usual.

I shrugged. "All right. Yes, I'm pleased to see you. No, sex sessions haven't erased the memory of our love."

"Fuck you," she said with a laugh. "I don't remember anything about love."

I took the vodka back and drank. "Don't you? Why are you here then?"

"That's just typical of a man," she said, shaking her head. "Not everything revolves around your cock, Quint."

I gave her a weak smile. "Very little has been revolving around that recently. I'm on a case."

She looked interested. "Are you now?" She pulled the bottle from my fingers and drank. "Any chance of you telling me what it's about?"

It was time to be masterful. "No."

She laughed and I felt the hairs rise on the back of my neck. She had the most arousing laugh I'd ever heard. I reached out for her hand. The long, thin fingers were another part of her that used to fascinate me.

"Don't, Quint. This is serious."

"So's this."

She stuck both her hands inside her coat. "You want to know why I came? All right, I'll tell you, mister investigator. You're about to have a major drugs problem in this city."

I sat up as if a hatpin had just worked its way through the cushion.

"And that's not all," she said, turning towards me and fixing me in her gaze. "The gang boss who's setting it up is a complete psycho."

She wasn't telling me anything I hadn't begun to suspect but how did she know all this? "Anything else?" I asked, trying to conceal my surprise.

She nodded, her expression quizzical. "I don't really understand this bit. The guy who told us about the drugs had escaped from one of the local gangs. He was delirious most of the time and he kept saying the same words over and over again."

My mind was in turmoil. What was she going to hit me with now?

"It seems to be a place," she continued. "Or at least the code-name for a place."

"Tell me, Katharine."

She ran her fingertips down her cheek then twitched her nose like she'd just sniffed industrial-strength disinfectant.

"The Bone Yard," she said, shrugging her shoulders. Then she realised I was as jumpy as a male tourist near the stage in the Three Graces. "What is it, Quint? Have you heard of it?"

I nodded slowly and reached for the bottle again. It looked like it was going to be a very long night.

Katharine shivered and closed her eyes. After a couple of minutes I began to wonder if she'd fallen asleep. Then she gave a start and sat up straight again.

"Where have you been hiding out in the city?"

"We've got some contacts here." She frowned and looked at me suspiciously. "Are you working for the Council again, Quint?"

"Yes, but not full time. Don't worry, Katharine. I'm not going to hand you or your friends over to the guard."

"You'd better not try," she replied, her expression harder than a barracks rugby player's. Then she shivered again, this time uncontrollably.

I put my arm round her shoulders. "What is it, Katharine?"

She let out a sob then swallowed hard. "Food," she said with a gasp. "I haven't had anything for a couple of days."

"Glad to see your people have been looking after you," I said on the way to the kitchen that takes up one corner of my main room. "I haven't got much myself. I've not been in a lot recently."

"You don't have to tell me that," Katharine said weakly. "I've been looking for you all over the city."

I found a can of stew that had escaped Davie's notice and opened it. The electricity was off so the cooker was no good. "Have this," I said, handing it to her. "You're taking your life in your hands eating it cold. God knows what state the meat's in. There are rumours that the Supply Directorate's been having problems with diseased cattle."

She started wolfing it down. "You'd have been much better off coming with me out of the city, Quint," she said between mouthfuls. "At least we have clean herds on our land."

Some dissidents run collective farms, defending them against the lunatics and criminal gangs who maraud about the country.

Katharine had finished eating but she was still trembling. I touched her hand. It was freezing. There was only one solution.

"Come on," I said, pulling her to her feet. "You're the one who's going to catch her death. The bed's the only warm place in this flat."

She didn't resist, but as I pulled off her coat and bundled her under the covers she looked at me sternly. "I haven't forgotten what they taught us in auxiliary training about keeping each other warm on night exercises. But that's all that we're going to do, all right?"

I gave her my best salute and crawled up against her. After a while she stopped shivering and moved so that there was a gap between us.

"Right, Quint. Let's get down to business."

Her business in the past had been purveying sexual services to tourists in the city's biggest hotel, but I didn't think mentioning that would be a good idea. She seemed to have lost interest in carnal matters.

"Okay," I said, letting my head sink into the sack of straw that the Supply Directorate classifies as a pillow. "What do you want to tell me about first? The drugs, the psycho or the Bone Yard?"

She glanced down at me and twitched her head. "It doesn't matter. As far as I can see, they're all part of the same story."

I was afraid she'd say that.

"Our fields are in what used to be East Lothian, south of Dunbar," she said after a long silence. "There are about a hundred of us — enough to look after the animals, work the crops and guard the fences. I made sure we got a hold of rifles and ammunition not long after I arrived. Most of the gangs keep their distance." Katharine glanced at me dispassionately. "Any who don't, we shoot."

"Which is why firearms were banned in Edinburgh," I put in. "Mob rule's a dangerous thing."

She glared at me. "We're not a mob. Anyway, it's not as simple as that and you know it, Quint. This city's got plenty wrong with it from what I've been hearing."

I got my hands out from beneath the covers and tried to calm her down. "All right, cool it. I'm even less of a fan of the Council than I used to be."

She kept her gaze on me, then laughed. "And you never exactly gave the guardians your unconditional support in the old days." Her face became serious again. "Quint, I heard your mother died. I'm sorry. You must have had a hard time."

Those words affected me more than the official tributes at the funeral. Katharine had first-hand experience of the catastrophic mistakes my mother had made when she was senior guardian, but she was still sympathetic. I'd missed her openness.

"Anyway, our fence guards found the guy who deserted a couple of weeks back," she said, leaning over me to reach for the vodka. My nostrils were filled by the reek of unwashed clothing and sweat which didn't completely obscure the delicate smell I remembered from the few times we'd been naked together.

Katharine gulped then quivered as the spirit fired up inside her. "He was in a bad way physically and mentally. He took a couple of bullets in the abdomen when he slipped out of the gang's camp. And he was raving. At first we thought he'd messed himself up permanently on some brain-damaging drug."

Electric Blues, for instance? I took the bottle and swallowed from it. There wasn't much left. At least we were keeping ourselves warm.

"So what did he say that sent you back into the city you love so much?" I asked.

Katharine gave me the kind of look that guardswomen reserve for the barracks jackass when they draw him as sex session partner. "In one of his relatively lucid periods he told me about this formula for a hot new drug that his gang leader had got a hold of. Apparently it was pretty complicated and needed a good chemist in a well-equipped lab to produce it."

"And his gang boss had a contact in the city who could arrange that?"

She nodded then looked at me sternly. "Am I telling you something you already know, Quint? This isn't a one-way transaction."

"I'll tell you what I'm working on, Katharine." I squeezed her arm. "Honest."

She pulled her arm away. "You'll tell me after I tell you? Sounds like kids playing doctors and nurses."

"We can do that too if you like."

Her face went blank and her body jerked away from mine.

"What is it, Katharine? What's the matter?"

She was gazing straight ahead into the darkness, the candle on the bedside table casting its dim light on to her profile. Although she looked thinner, the lines of her features hadn't changed in the two years since I'd last seen her. But she'd been strong then, hardened by her experience of prison and the Prostitution Services Department. Now her toughness seemed more of an act.

"I . . . I had a bad time after I went over the wire. There are a lot of animals out there."

"Tell me, Katharine."

She kept her eyes off me. "No, Quint. I can't. It's over now."

I touched her hand with one finger. "No, it isn't. You're still in pain." I sat up and moved closer to her. "Remember when I told you about Caro? You persuaded me it would do me good to share the pain. I didn't believe you at first, but you were right." Her eyelashes quivered and for a moment I thought she was going to weep, but she kept control. "Let it go, Katharine. You can trust me."

She turned slowly towards the light and looked into my eyes. Then she shuddered briefly and dropped her gaze, like a deer that senses the stalker's gun but can't find it in herself to turn tail.

"There was a gang in the hills east of Lauder," she said slowly. "They lived off the sheep that have run wild there since the original farmers were massacred years ago." She lifted her eyes to mine and I saw the hatred in them. "They really were animals, Quint. They called themselves the Cavemen. The morons had burned down all the cottages in the area, so they had to dig themselves holes in the ground. Bastards." She spat out the last word and lapsed back into silence.

"They caught you?" I asked haltingly.

She gave a bitter laugh. "I thought I could look after myself. But not against those madmen. They even slashed each other with their skinning knives in their desperation to get at me." She looked at me, her gaze suddenly unsteady as she finally began to lose control. "I was tied to a tree for a month before I killed two of them and escaped."

"Jesus." I tried to put my arm round her.

"Don't!" Her shout must have woken most of the neighbours. "Don't, Quint," she repeated, her voice back to something approaching normal volume. "I . . . I haven't been with a man since then."

I moved away. "I understand, Katharine."

She looked at me in disbelief.

"Or at least I'm trying to understand." In fact I was way out of my depth and suffering from cramp in both legs.

"So now you know," she said, her face loosening into a faint smile. "After years spent satisfying tourists, I've turned into Katharine the Untouchable. Funny, isn't it?"

I wasn't laughing. Suddenly I had a great urge to change the subject. "The guy who told you about the drug formula. What did he say about the psycho who was running the deal?"

Katharine nodded, happy to stop talking about what she'd been through. "He was completely terrified of him. Remember, this was a man who was delirious most of the time, but even when he was raving he kept going on about the Screecher."

"The Screecher?"

She nodded. "That's what the leader of his gang was called. He was terrified the Screecher was going to track him down and cut him to pieces for deserting."

Cut him to pieces? That sounded familiar.

"What else did he say about him?"

Katharine shrugged. "Nothing very coherent. I had trouble making sense of it. About the drugs, his boss . . ."

"And what about the Bone Yard?" I asked, trying not to sound too interested.

"He kept repeating that and moaning — not just from the pain of his wounds, but as if it were something horrendous that he could barely live with."

Like William McEwan, I thought. But not like the senior guardian. I hadn't seen many signs of spiritual disturbance on his saintly face.

"He never explained what it was though." Katharine settled back on her pillow, her eyes flickering. She was about to pass out, but I needed more.

"So where is he, the wounded gang member? I need to see him for myself. It sounds like he could do with hospital treatment as well."

She shook her head weakly, her eyes firmly closed now. "He's long past that stage, Quint. He died a week ago."

"Shit." The first half-decent lead I'd got in the case and it vanished quicker than the beggars on Princes Street after the Enlightenment came to power.

Katharine turned over, her back towards me. "Look in my coat pocket. I've got his ID."

Santa Claus does exist after all. Even though he'd arrived a bit late this season.

*　　*　　*

I came to as the front door slammed.

Katharine sat up straight. A wicked-looking knife that I hadn't noticed before glinted in the faint glow from the streetlights. "Who's that?" she whispered.

"Davie. Get back under the covers."

I jumped out of bed and reached the door before he came in.

"You're up early, Quint," he said. "It's only seven o'clock. What happened? Guilty conscience keep you awake?"

"Something like that," I mumbled, suddenly aware that I was seriously short of shut-eye.

"Here." He tossed me a brown paper bag, which I failed to catch.

"Croissants? Jesus, Davie, where did you get them?"

He looked over from the kitchen where he was starting to make coffee, a grin spreading across his bearded face.

"Fell off the back of a Supply Directorate van, did they?"

"Are you suggesting that a guardsman is capable of dishonesty? That's a serious offence, citizen." His face didn't look very serious.

"Aye, and so's nicking tourist provisions." I headed back to the bedroom with my share of breakfast.

Katharine's head emerged from the covers.

"Take these," I said in a low voice.

"What about you?"

"I'll pick something up later. Now listen. Stay here all day. I'll get back as soon as I can. It's not safe for you on the streets." I pulled on my trousers and put the dead gang member's ID card in the pocket.

She raised her eyes to the ceiling. "I can look after myself."

"Please," I said, putting my hand on hers. "There are some serious crazies out there."

She pulled her hand away, not too fast, and looked at me accusingly. "You never told me about the case you're working on."

"I will." Then, before she could move, I leaned forward and kissed her once on the lips. "Later."

If her expression was anything to go by, I was lucky not to walk into the main room with the haft of her knife protruding from my chest.

Chapter Thirteen

———◦◦◦◦◦———

Davie and I went out into the cold. Darkness still prevailed in the sky overhead and the underpowered streetlights weren't making too much of an impression on it. They were helped a bit by the thick carpet of snow that was lying on all the surfaces. It reflected their feeble glow and muffled the sound of the buses on the main road. Citizens unlucky enough to be working in the mines were already heading for the collection points, scarves wrapped around their faces. Eyes were sunk as deep in their sockets as those of the prisoners on Death Row after the last, desperate UK government reintroduced capital punishment.

Davie had parked the Land-Rover away from the pavement as the snow had drifted near the buildings. Walking into the road, I caught sight of thin parallel tyre tracks about two feet apart. Probably some poor sod in a wheelchair going to the infirmary for an early morning appointment.

"Where to then?" asked Davie.

"The main archive on George IVth Bridge."

"Not again," he groaned as the starter motor whined and eventually fired. "This case is about as much fun as the paper chases we did during auxiliary training."

"Don't knock it, guardsman. It's the only lead we've got." He was about to ask me about it. I'd have to tell him eventually but I didn't want him to know about Katharine yet. I spoke before he could. "Did the guardsman who was attacked yesterday have anything more to say?"

Davie shook his head. "I checked with his barracks commander late last night. Apparently he was still pretty shaky."

"He took a hell of a pounding."

Davie swung carefully round the snow-covered junction at Tollcross, slowing to walking pace as we passed a City Guard emergency unit. A Mines Department bus had mounted the pavement and turned an *Edinburgh Guardian* kiosk into firewood. The passengers were standing around looking dazed and confused, but happy; whatever happened next, they'd missed at least part of their shift in the frozen earth.

"I wouldn't worry," Davie said as he accelerated up Lauriston Place. "I played rugby against that guardsman once. He used his head like it was the business end of a battering ram. He probably bangs it against a wall himself if he doesn't get his daily ration of hits."

At the archive I sent him off to see if Hamilton's people had reported anything overnight. That made him very happy. Then I told him to come back as soon as he'd finished, which didn't impress him so much.

Even at eight in the morning there were plenty of auxiliaries in the archive. Paper has come to dominate this city in the eighteen years since the Enlightenment came to power. Here were large numbers of highly educated people spending their lives chasing files. Winston Smith in *1984* would have felt very much at home, though his first name wouldn't have made him popular with the Council – too redolent of what's still seen as the bankrupt legacy of the British establishment. The Enlightenment regarded computers as socially divisive and educationally sterile, so they got rid of as many as they could. Those the guardians have kept are used to run the Council's classified records, but there aren't enough to go round for that. Just as well. That means I can still find a lot of sensitive information in the archives.

I found a quiet corner and took out the ID card Katharine had given me. Under the bright reading light it didn't take me long to discover something very interesting. The card proclaimed that Hamish Robin Campbell had been born on 27.11.1970, had the status of ordinary citizen, was five feet nine inches tall, weighed twelve stone six pounds, had light brown hair, a complete set of teeth and an appendix scar; he was in the Leisure Department of the Tourism Directorate, lived at 19b Elgin Street and his next of kin was his wife Muriel Campbell. The photograph that stared out dully from the laminated card was of a balding, sad-faced man who looked like he'd been working too hard for too many years. In that respect he was no different from most of his fellow citizens who'd invested their lives in the Enlightenment. Except they don't carry fake ID cards. If you've seen as many as I have, you can spot a ringer faster than the annual strawberry ration disappears from the city's foodstores.

I had a pretty good idea where this particular specimen came from too. The City Guard's Documentation Department is staffed by skilled forgers and graphic designers. The problem is, they're all auxiliaries and auxiliaries are by training and nature perfectionists. They make a really good job of every false ID they produce for undercover agents, with the result that those IDs often look more convincing than the real cards the Citizen Registration Department issues.

So what was going on here with Hamish Robin Campbell? Was he a former guard operative who'd deserted? Or could he be an active undercover man who'd penetrated the gang that was run by the crazy guy he called the Screecher? The obvious person to ask would be Hamilton, but that wouldn't prove much. I'd never heard of covert guard operations being run outside the city borders and, anyway, Campbell might have been handled by one of the iron boyscouts without the public order guardian's knowledge. I also wanted to keep this to myself till I found out more about the dead man and his links with the drug formula.

I had a plan about how to do that but it would need careful timing. In the meantime I checked the Deserters Register for

Campbell's name. It wasn't there. Either he'd managed to leave the city without being missed or his name had been deliberately kept out. Then I checked the Accommodation Index and discovered that there had once been a Muriel Campbell living at 19b Elgin Street, but she died in 2016. That was as much confirmation as I needed that the ID had been produced by auxiliaries. It's standard procedure to use an address that checks out superficially, but the forgers in the castle aren't required to update secondary details. Now I was sure the card was fake. But I wasn't looking forward to what I had to do next.

"Davie, I need to get Hamilton out of his office for a while."

If he was surprised, he didn't show it. "You're keeping something to yourself, aren't you, Quint?" He made a skilful adjustment to the Land-Rover's steering as we came on to the esplanade. Judging by the way other guard vehicles were slewed about the snow-covered expanse beneath the castle entrance, most drivers had decided that parking in the normal neat ranks was not essential today.

"Is it that obvious?"

"Aye." Davie laughed. "You get this faraway look in your eyes when you're on to something tasty. Like a kid opening the *Enlightenment Encyclopedia* at the page headed 'Human Sexuality' for the first time."

"Very funny, guardsman." I gave him a stern look. "What page number is that again?"

He pulled up by the sentries. "Volume three, page four hundred and thirty-seven." He undid his seatbelt and looked back at me thoughtfully. "I suppose I could get the guardian to come down to the operations room to go over the roster of personnel involved in the investigation. These days he almost licks your feet if you ask for his advice."

"Poor old sod. The iron boyscouts think he's a joke."

"Well, I don't," Davie said defensively, "and neither should you. He's been asking what you're up to."

"Has he now? Tell him I'm checking on the guardsman who got his brains rearranged yesterday."

Davie nodded. "Okay. Give me ten minutes before you go to his quarters."

I put my hand on his arm. "There's the small matter of the clerk in his outer office."

Davie grinned. "Oh, don't worry about Amy. I'll tell her you're on official business."

"I can do that myself."

"Aye, citizen. But will she keep quiet about your visit afterwards?"

He headed off through the gate, acknowledging the guards. I sometimes wonder if there are any female auxiliaries in the city who he hasn't provided with an unforgettable sex session.

Hamilton's clerk was middle-aged and faded, her hair as grey as the auxiliary-issue suit she was wearing. But there was a red glow about her cheeks. Whatever Davie said to her seemed to have done the trick. As soon as I went in to the outer office she looked down at her papers. As I went in to the guardian's office, I heard the outer door close behind her. I was on my own. The question was, for how long?

The last time I used Hamilton's computer was during the search for the murderer two years ago. I was banking on the chance that he hadn't changed his password since then. I sat down, logged on and entered the word "colonel". Then I hit the return key and waited, feeling my heart pounding in my chest. The screen flashed and the Council Archive main menu came up. I highlighted the City Guard line, then the Confidential Operatives line in the subsidiary menu that followed. I was asked again for a password. As in all systems, users are instructed not to use the same one that they use for initial access. But Lewis Hamilton was a leading proponent of the Enlightenment's anti-information technology position and he used his terminal about as often as I agree with current Council policies. The chances were that he used the same password. I entered it and waited for alarm bells to ring. They didn't. The menu of the file containing details of all the guard's undercover operatives appeared. I was in.

I glanced at my watch. Nine thirty-three. I hoped to hell Hamilton was buying Davie's strategy. Tea is brought round at quarter to ten in the castle. That would give Davie an extra chance to stall the guardian.

I went into the Operatives' Aliases option and entered the name on the ID card. There was a brief pause and then the file came up. Hamish Robin Campbell: alias approved 12.8.2018. That was interesting. It showed that the guy had been undercover for three and a half years. I noted down the barracks number of the auxiliary who had assumed the alias, which was Watt 103. Things were looking promising. Then I requested the reports Campbell had filed on his activities and my luck ran out as comprehensively as the guy's at the end of the queue when the whisky runs out on a Saturday night.

The screen told me that Campbell's reports were "Not Available". That's jargon for "So Secret That Even Guardians Don't Have Access". There was only one person who could call up "Not Available" files and that was the chief boyscout. Who knows what his passwords were? "Baden" and "Powell"?

I went back into the main menu and tried to bring up Watt 103's service record. All auxiliaries' data are held in the Council Archive, but I was pretty sure this particular servant of the city had officially died a long time before Katharine came across him. And so it turned out. Watt 103 didn't feature as a serving auxiliary, but there was a reference to him in the "Auxiliaries – Deceased" archive. According to that, he had died of a heart attack in the infirmary on 4 December 2019. Unless he'd come back to life like a cataleptic character in an Edgar Allan Poe story, someone had been messing around with the records. And whoever that was had fallen foul of the cross-referencing system, suggesting he or she didn't have a complete grasp of the archives but also hadn't wanted to involve a professional clerk.

I heard the outer office door bang. After a delay that made my heart shake, rattle and roll there was a knock on the door of the inner office. Then another knock. I waited, frozen to the seat in front of the terminal, ready to claim I was a technician updating Hamilton's software and fully aware that wouldn't do anything more than buy me a little more time. Then I heard footsteps moving away and the outer office door close again. The guardian's notorious temper seemed to have put the visitor off entering without permission. That was the first time I'd ever felt grateful that Hamilton was such an irascible old bugger.

It was obviously time to get out but I still wanted to know more about Watt 103. I scrolled down his personal details and came to a piece of information that made all the tangled nerves I'd suffered in the last twenty minutes worth while. The auxiliary who staggered to Katharine's collective farm south of Dunbar had been trained as a physicist before the Enlightenment. Not just any kind of physicist either, but a nuclear physicist. After the Council was established, he'd been involved in the decommissioning of Torness nuclear power station. I sat back in the chair after I logged off and looked out through the leaded windows towards the gull-grey water of the Firth of Forth. Torness nuclear power station went out of service in 2007. So what was one of the few remaining nuclear physicists in a city where coal has been the main fuel for fifteen years doing over the border? And what was he doing in a gang that operated close to the city's former main source of energy?

I smelled a very large mutant rat glowing brightly in Edinburgh's Enlightenment gloom.

I met Davie and the guardian in the corridor outside the operations room.

"Ah, there you are, Dalrymple." Hamilton was looking twitchy, which isn't usually a good sign. He started running his hand back and forward through his beard as if the Council had just decreed that auxiliaries must be clean-shaven but that razors aren't allowed. "There seems to be a bit of a problem."

It was unlike him to be vague, even when he ran into trouble.

"What is it?" I asked, glancing at Davie. He didn't look particularly bothered.

"It's my bloody deputy," the guardian replied.

"Raeburn 03? He hasn't fallen under a bus, has he?"

Hamilton glared at me. "That isn't funny, Dalrymple. I don't think much of him as an individual but he's an excellent administrator."

Most of that was for Davie's benefit. I wondered if the guardian knew that his number two was known as Machiavelli by everyone else in the guard.

"So what's the problem with your excellent administrator?" I asked.

"We don't know where he is," Davie put in. "No one's seen him since yesterday evening."

That sounded interesting. "When you say no one, you mean no one you've asked so far," I said.

Davie looked at his notebook. "All personnel on duty in the castle, all personnel in Raeburn Barracks . . ."

"How about the senior guardian?" I looked at Hamilton.

"He's been informed. He hasn't seen him since the end of the Council meeting last night."

I nodded, remembering Machiavelli's urgent conversation with the chief boyscout outside the Council chamber. "I think we'd better run a check on your deputy, guardian. Is your computer operational?"

Hamilton strode away down the passage. "It was the last time I looked. Useless piece of junk. I don't know what you expect to find there."

"It's amazing what you come across in the database sometimes," I replied, grinning at Davie.

We set off after him, our boots ringing like drumbeats on

the flagstones. I wondered where Machiavelli's auxiliary-issue footwear was at this moment; and if he'd gone there willingly.

Hamilton was overjoyed when I offered to handle the computer. I was pleased too. That way he wouldn't notice the tell-tale line informing him that he'd logged off ten minutes ago. I remembered to ask him for his password. He went all coy and wrote it down rather than say it in front of Davie.

I got into the senior auxiliary section of the Serving Auxiliaries archive and typed in Raeburn 03's barracks number. It was then that the guardian began to have second thoughts.

"Em, Dalrymple," he said, leaning over my chair. "What exactly do you expect to find out about my number two? You know how many checks personnel have to go through to reach his level in the hierarchy."

I looked up at him. "He's a missing person, isn't he? Guard regulations state that anyone absent from their post for more than three hours is required to attend a review board."

Hamilton looked at me like a medieval abbot who'd suddenly detected signs of demonic possession in one of his monks. "Since when did you care so passionately about guard procedure?"

I shrugged. "I did write most of the regulations when I was in the directorate."

"That was a long time ago, citizen. You surely can't suspect Raeburn 03 of any involvement in the murders."

Even I wouldn't have gone that far, at least not yet. "Look, guardian. He's been very interested in the case since the beginning. He turned up at the first post-mortem, he was in the second victim's barracks not long after her body was discovered, he's been—" I broke off. Telling Hamilton that I was suspicious about Machiavelli's friend the senior guardian was probably not a very good idea.

"Well?" demanded Hamilton. "He's been what?"

I gave him a smile to pacify him. "He's been someone the Council has had its eye on for promotion."

My smile had the wrong effect. "You mean when it manages to get rid of me?" the guardian said, his cheeks scarlet. "Well, I'm not going anywhere. This is my directorate and I'm staying till I drop."

Behind him Davie had his eyes raised to the inlaid ceiling. "I know that, guardian," I said, scrolling down Machiavelli's service record. I realised that I knew as little about him as I knew about his superiors in the Council. They'd all appeared out of the woodwork when my mother's regime began to crack.

"Auxiliary training 2010 to '12, then a year on the border, a couple of years in Raeburn Barracks administration, three years in the guard, a year in the Tourism Directorate ... that's interesting, guardian. Your deputy was in the Prostitution Services Department."

"Get on with it, Dalrymple."

I could see from Hamilton's expression how impressed he was by that aspect of his deputy's career. "Then he was in the Science and Energy Directorate for a year. As assistant to the present senior guardian no less."

"That's probably why he follows him around like a lost sheep," the guardian growled.

"Uh-huh." I kept on scrolling, then stopped abruptly. "And his last posting before this one was in the Finance Directorate, from 2019 to '20." I paused. There was no way Hamilton was going to let that pass without comment.

"Yes. As one of your friend Heriot 07's assistants." The guardian sounded like he'd just inhaled deeply in a pigsty. "I wonder what he learned from him."

"My ex-friend Heriot 07," I said, trying to stall him. Heriot 07 was the barracks number of Billy Geddes, who used to run all the city's money-making scams. I was beginning to wish I'd kept a much closer eye on him since he'd been confined to a wheelchair. Jesus. There were wheelchair tracks in the street outside my flat this morning.

The door burst open.

"What is Citizen Dalrymple doing at your terminal, guardian?" The senior guardian's voice wasn't exactly sharp. He still sounded like he could sweet-talk the Lord God Almighty into passing on to him the secret of eternal life, but there was an edge to his voice that would have put the wind up Satan. "Kindly leave us, guardsman." Davie didn't hang around.

Hamilton hit the shutdown function. "I was supervising the citizen, senior guardian."

"Never mind that." The chief boyscout moved into the centre of the room and looked around like a pre-Enlightenment estate agent working out his percentage. "About Raeburn 03. I am handling the search for him personally." He gave me a stare that he no doubt hoped would send my body temperature through the floor.

"I think there may be some connection with the murders," I said, looking straight back at him. You could almost hear the clang of invisible sabres crossing.

"I will be the judge of that, citizen. If any such connection exists, you'll be the first to know." The senior guardian turned his attention back to Lewis Hamilton. "In the meantime, guardian, you will not pass any information from the Council Archive to citizen Dalrymple. Understood?"

The guy was about thirty years younger than Hamilton, but he was treating him like an auxiliary trainee on his first day in uniform. Lewis had his face set hard, but there was nothing he could do.

"I wish to speak with my colleague, citizen." That was guardian-speak for "Close the door on your way out, scum."

I left them to it.

And spent the rest of the day trying to work out how to dig up more information on Machiavelli, Billy Geddes and the dead physicist Hamish Robin Campbell. By the time I went back to the flat, I was beginning to make progress on two of those fronts.

Chapter Fourteen

There was a tap on the door just after eight o'clock that evening.

"Where the fuck have you been?" I yelled. "I told you to stay indoors."

Katharine stood in the doorway of my flat, shaking off melting snow like a dog that's been in a river.

"You told me?" she said, eyeing me blackly. "And who exactly are you to tell me what to do?"

I got up and went over to the kitchen area, not wanting to show her any more of how I felt. "You must be freezing. I'll make coffee."

She spread her coat over a chair and sank down into the sofa. "Coffee," she said wistfully. "I haven't had that for a long time."

"Not many people in the city have — at least, not decent stuff. You can still find it if you know the right people."

"How corrupt."

I turned and saw that she was smiling ironically. "How realistic, more like. Since you object so strongly on moral grounds, can I have your share?"

She didn't reply but the smile remained on her lips.

"So where have you been?" I asked, handing her the least chipped mug I possessed.

She laughed. "Now he wants to know where I've spent my day."

"For Christ's sake, Katharine, there's a double murderer out there." I gave her what I hoped was an unconcerned shrug. "Anyway, it's better for me if you don't hang around here. I don't fancy being done for harbouring a deserter."

She was about as far from buying that line as the city was from purchasing a fleet of Chinese limousines to ferry citizens to the mines.

"If you must know," she said with a nervous flick of her head, "I was trying to score some drugs in the Cowgate."

"You were what?" My voice went soprano.

"Don't worry. I was pretty subtle about it."

Somehow I managed to get a grip on myself. "Let me just get this straight, Katharine. You went down to the street in the city that's most infested with undercover operatives and tried to find out if a new drug has appeared. You do know that Edinburgh has what *Time* magazine described as the most ferocious anti-narcotics programme in the western world, don't you?"

She gave me a monarch-of-all-she-surveys look that would have impressed the long dead Margaret Thatcher. "Of course I know about the Council's drugs policy. I also know that there are ways and means for tourists to get hold of stuff."

I slumped back on the sofa beside her. "Don't tell me. You pretended you were a tourist."

She shrugged. "Obviously it worked," she said in a remarkably convincing sing-song Scandinavian accent. "The guard haven't turned up on my tail."

"Not yet they haven't," I said, resigning myself to the idea that my staircase might at any moment become a physical training location for most of the auxiliaries stationed in the castle. "Did you get a sniff of anything?"

Katharine shook her head. "Bugger all, apart from some hash that even schoolkids in the old days would have laughed at."

"So for some reason it's not being distributed yet. That confirms what I know from guard sources."

"Well, I'm glad I've been of some service," she said acidly.

"It wasn't worth the risk, Katharine."

"I can look after myself, Quint. You know that."

Except when there's a gang of Cavemen around, I thought. I didn't share that with her.

"What about you?" she asked. "Found out anything interesting?"

I had to make a decision. I looked across at her, wondering if it was a good idea to involve her in the case. I'd get shat on from the stratosphere if the Council discovered I was sharing classified information with a deserter. On the other hand, I needed all the help I could get if it turned out that senior auxiliaries like Machiavelli had been bad boys. She turned towards me when she felt my eyes on her and fixed me with her bottomless green gaze. It was no contest. But I needed to check something out first.

"Did the guy who died ever say anything about the old nuclear power station at Torness?"

Her eyes were still on me. There was a long pause before she spoke. "No, he didn't. At least not that I understood. He was raving most of the time. Like I told you, he just kept going on about the Screecher and the Bone Yard."

I'd begun to wonder if there might be some connection between Torness and the Bone Yard. But even if there were, what could that have to do with the Electric Blues and the killings in the city?

"That was truly disgusting," Katharine said, pushing her empty plate away.

"Sorry. It's not like it was when supermarket chains still existed. These days, if something's out of season, you don't get it, end of story."

"So in winter the only vegetables are potatoes, turnips and

kale. They don't have to be half rotten though. And as for the tinned soup . . ."

"I suppose you're spoilt on your farm."

"You obviously haven't tried growing root crops without the benefit of machinery." She sat upright. "Anyway, you still haven't told me what you found out today."

I nodded. "I'm going to. But, Katharine . . ." I waited for her to look at me. "It won't be like it was the last time we worked together two years back. You won't be an official member of the team. Davie and the others can't know about you."

"Suits me," she replied. "What makes you think I wanted to be in the team?"

"Nothing. But you risked your freedom by coming to tell me about the drug formula, so you must still have some feeling for the city."

She laughed harshly. "I don't give a shit about the city, Quint. The Council has always done exactly what it wants with it." She broke off and looked down. "But you're right in a way. I was an auxiliary once and I swore an oath to serve the bloody place. As far as I'm concerned that means the people. And the people are being fucked by the system."

"You'd get on well with the democrats in Glasgow."

"I'd have gone there long ago if there weren't so many gangs of lunatics between us and them." She looked up and her eyes flared in the dim light. "Are you going to tell me what you know or not?"

"Okay. I'll just put some music on." If my place had been bugged, Katharine and I were already up the Crap River without a punt-pole. But at least the bastards wouldn't find out the latest news. Muddy Waters seemed appropriate.

"You remember Billy Geddes?" I asked as the master belted into "The Hoochie Coochie Man".

"Your schoolfriend? How could I forget him? I thought he was crippled."

"He is. And even though the Council under my mother would

probably have kept him on as a deal-maker, the iron boyscouts cut him loose without a second thought. Or so the archive shows. He was demoted and packed off to a disabled persons' home in Merchiston a year and a half ago."

Katharine opened her hands. "And?"

"And I found when I went there this afternoon that he hasn't been seen since 18 November last year."

"Maybe he died."

I shook my head. "There's no record of that. And no record of a transfer to another home. Christ, the guy's in a wheelchair. He can't go far on his own."

"So what are you saying, Quint?"

I sat back, shaking my head. "I don't know exactly. But it's too much of a coincidence that Billy the arch-fixer disappears at the same time a new drug is developed." I took a deep breath and filled her in about the Electric Blue we found in the dead auxiliary's locker. She was unimpressed that I hadn't told her last night, but I made up for that by mentioning Machiavelli's disappearance.

"I remember that bastard from the guard," Katharine said, screwing her nose up. "I might have known he'd lick his way to the top."

I nodded. "The problem is, both he and Billy are dead-ends until we can track them down. I've got Davie doing a check on all the city's disabled facilities, but I don't reckon he'll turn anything up."

Katherine looked at me, her forehead lined in frustration. "What are we going to do then?"

I raised the stump of my right forefinger. "Never fear, Quintilian's got a plan."

She looked seriously unconvinced. "What is it then, smartarse?"

I tried to make it sound impressive, even though it was a last resort. I could only think of one senior scientist to consult. "I've been feeling a bit under the weather recently. I'm going to see the chemist."

I'd got Davie to find out where the chief toxicologist lived. It turned out he was one of those typical first-generation auxiliaries who was totally dedicated to the job. Either that or his manner put off even other scientists, because he avoided his barracks and spent his off-duty hours in a room above his laboratory. I deliberately didn't give him any advance warning of what I thought would be *my* visit.

Katharine saw it as *our* visit. "I'm coming with you, Quint."

"No, you're not. Word about you will get back to the Council."

She smiled at me sweetly. "We'll just have to make sure he keeps quiet about us, won't we? Don't worry, I'll think of a way to do that."

"What about the driver?" I demanded. "Oh, forget it." I called the castle and asked them to send me a vehicle. The auxiliary who brought it down would have to call for another Land-Rover to pick him or her up, but that was someone else's problem. My problem, and Katharine's, was whether I could remember how to drive after two years on my bicycle.

"I'd rather have ridden a mad cow," Katharine said, jumping down outside the labs as soon as I skidded to a halt in the snow. Mixing concrete with a straw would have been easier than finding gear in the clapped-out vehicle.

"Was I that bad?"

"No wonder cars were banned by the Council. You'd have reduced the population to double figures on your own by now."

"Thanks very much. I take it you'll be walking back." I led her to the gate. The guardswoman on duty waved us past when she saw my authorisation and the "ask no questions" which I'd passed to Katharine. I got directions to the chemist's room.

"Let me do the talking, all right?" I said as we walked into the building.

"Oh, you know what you're going to say, do you?"

It was a fair comment. I reckoned the city's chief toxicologist would answer my questions because something about him had given me the impression that he wasn't the iron boyscouts' number one fan. That didn't mean I had a very clear idea of how I was going to get him started.

We climbed to the fourth floor, our footsteps ringing down empty corridors which smelled of noxious substances and the sweat of scientists who, like everyone else in the city, don't see the communal baths often enough. At the far end of a long passage we came to a door. A scrap of paper with the words "Chief Toxicologist" had been stuck to it with a drawing pin. The city has better things to spend its money on than laminated signs, even for senior auxiliaries.

I put my ear to the faded black surface and heard the faint sound of music. I couldn't make out individual notes but the rhythm was familiar.

"He'll keep quiet about our visit," I whispered to Katharine with a smile.

"Why?" Her face was blank.

"Watch." I raised one hand, knocked twice quickly and turned the handle. The chemist hadn't locked it. He was probably too caught up in the music. "Good evening, Lister 25."

"What?" The chief toxicologist's pachydermic features appeared from behind a lateral shelving cabinet filled with files, beakers, test-tube racks and pot plants. "What do you think you're doing, citizen?" He moved across to the cassette player.

"Leave the music," I said. "Robert Johnson was a genius in my book."

Lister 25 stood still, his ungainly form bent over the low table. "You like Robert Johnson?" he asked in amazement. "You know who Robert Johnson was?"

I shrugged. "Like I said, a genius. This is one of my favourites." I glanced at Katharine. "'Kind Hearted Woman

Blues.'" She ignored me. "I don't think you're a genius though, Lister 25. Playing banned music in a Council building isn't going to do your career much good."

The chemist turned the volume down and twitched his lips at me. "My prospects are severely limited as it is, citizen. Who's your friend?"

"You don't want to know," I said.

Lister 25 nodded slowly. "I see. But you do want to know something."

I smiled. "Correct."

"And if I help you, my illicit addiction to the music of black America will remain unknown to my superiors?"

"Correct again. You can trust me. I'm a blues freak too."

"Sit down," said the chemist, waving expansively at a pair of unsound-looking plastic chairs. "I will endeavour to comply with your every demand. Is it about the matter we discussed on your last visit?" He looked doubtfully at Katharine.

"The Electric Blues?" I said with a laugh. "What do you think of the name?"

The toxicologist gave me a supercilious glance. "Electric blues were a travesty of the original Delta sound, citizen."

"You reckon? Well, whatever. I'm not here about them."

He rubbed his jowls pensively. "Really. I'm intrigued."

"Did you ever know a physicist by the barracks number of Watt 103?"

He went pale faster than a tourist who's put the last of his holiday money on a donkey masquerading as a horse at the Princes Street Gardens racetrack.

"Are you all right?" Katharine said, moving quickly to the sink and running him a glass of water.

Lister 25 was trying to take deep breaths. "Why are you . . . why are you interested in Watt 103, for God's sake?"

He must have been about the same age as the dead man. "How long have you known him?" I asked.

"Since the first year of university," Lister 25 gasped, finally bringing his breathing under control. "Alasdair was a brilliant physicist."

"A nuclear physicist," I said, watching his reaction.

The toxicologist nodded, then looked down. He'd started to knead the loose skin on the back of his left hand.

"When did you last see him?"

He shook his head weakly. "I don't remember exactly. Two or three years ago."

"What was he doing then?"

Lister 25's breathing again began to sound like that of a diver who's had his oxygen line slashed. "I . . . I . . . don't . . . don't . . . know. Class . . . classified work."

"You're going to do him an injury, Quint," Katharine said, settling the chemist gently in his chair. "Stop this. Stop it now."

I nodded reluctantly. "Just one more thing," I said. "The Bone Yard. Have you ever heard of it?"

Between more gasps and choking, the toxicologist managed to nod that he had. But he seemed not to know anything about what the word referred to.

"Ask . . . ask the senior . . . the senior guardian," he said as we were leaving. "He . . . he has . . . he has all the files."

I knew that already. And the chief boyscout was the one person I couldn't ask about the Bone Yard. He'd warned me off already and I had a nasty feeling that if I asked again I'd end up in a box like his predecessor as science and energy guardian. And anyway, what did all this have to do with the murders? I couldn't see what the link was. But I was getting more and more convinced that there was one.

Katharine decided against walking back through the snow-carpeted streets of southern Edinburgh. It wasn't a good decision. I still couldn't make much sense of the Land-Rover's gearbox.

"You take the bed." I put the candle I'd lit on the table.

Katharine shook her head. "I'm all right on the sofa. I haven't had much to do with beds recently. We sleep on sacks of straw on the farm."

"All the more reason to renew your acquaintance with a mattress now. What do you think Supply Directorate beds are?" I sat down and pulled out my notebook. "Anyway, I've got work to do."

She came over. "I can help."

"I wish you could. This investigation's going nowhere faster than the old parties at the last election."

"That bad?" She smiled then looked at me seriously. "What does the Bone Yard mean, Quint?"

"If I had any clue about that I wouldn't be sitting here chewing the end of my pencil."

She shook her head impatiently. "No, I'm not talking about your investigation. What do the words 'bone yard' refer to?"

I shrugged. "Cemetery, according to the dictionary."

"So have you checked out the city's cemeteries and grave-yards?"

"Checked them out for what? There are dozens of them. And since the Council brought in mandatory cremation back in 2006, nothing much has gone into them."

She smiled grimly. "Which means they'd be good places for illicit activities like drug trafficking, doesn't it?"

I sat back and heard the flimsy chair creak beneath my weight. "But there hasn't been any trafficking, Katharine. We'd have found bodies by now. The Electric Blues are fatal for people with weak hearts."

She nodded slowly. "Okay. What other angles have we got?"

I grinned at her. "You should have taken up my mother's offer to join the Public Order Directorate."

She was quiet for a minute. "I suppose if I'd stayed in the city, the Cavemen wouldn't have got me," she said eventually in a low voice.

"Christ, I didn't mean that, Katharine."

"It's all right, Quint. It was a long time ago." She got up from the table and moved towards the bedroom. "I'll see you."

"Yeah. Goodnight." I watched her svelte figure move into the darkness, then heard the door close tight. She might think it was a long time since she'd been abused by those neanderthals but she wasn't anywhere near getting over it. Then I thought of Caro. It was nearly seven years since the Ear, Nose and Throat Man had killed her and I still had vivid dreams of her. Not often, but enough to make sure I felt guilty at every sex session. That's what the Council's managed to do in its relentless search for the utopian state. It imagined it could appeal to people's desire for knowledge and self-advancement, but all it's ended up doing is pandering to their animal appetites. All anyone thinks about apart from screwing is getting enough to eat.

Which brought me back to the Bone Yard. It suddenly came to me that the city is indeed full of bone yards. But unlike the cemeteries, these ones operate to full capacity. Every day of the year Edinburgh has to feed thousands of tourists as well as its own citizens. So the perfect city is extremely well endowed with slaughterhouses.

Chapter Fifteen

———⟨◦⟩———

I woke up to a thud from the direction of the front door and looked at my watch blearily. Six thirty-two. The postman had beaten Davie. I staggered over from the sofa and picked up a brown A4 envelope. Then all traces of sleep were blown away as quickly as the smoke from the city's myriad coal fires when the east wind kicks in.

I'd recognised the small, ultra-neat handwriting. I received something from the same correspondent only a few days ago. It was William McEwan. I looked at the postmark. It was dated 4 January 2022, the day before the old man went head first down the stairs. The post in Enlightenment Edinburgh doesn't run to standards Mussolini would have approved of, but it gets there in the end. And the envelope was unopened. It had escaped the random checks the Public Order Directorate makes on citizens' mail.

I ran my left forefinger under the flap and pulled out a sheaf of stapled pages. On the front was a brief handwritten note, which read:

> Quintilian,
>   In case your regular visit to the home is delayed, I am sending you this classified minute. I have other documents which I copied illicitly before I left the directorate, but

they are too sensitive to trust to the post. I hope this will bring you down to Trinity soon.

W.M.

Not soon enough, unfortunately. I stood in the centre of my freezing living room flicking through the pages. Then sat down on the sofa and took a deep breath. No wonder the Science and Energy Directorate archive was missing a lot of files.

The minute was of a meeting between McEwan and the senior guardian dated 14 October 2019. Of course, the chief boyscout wasn't senior guardian at that time. My mother was. At the meeting they agreed to follow the recommendations made in the Science and Energy Directorate's feasibility study, which was written by none other than Watt 103, a.k.a. Hamish Robin Campbell, the man who had died at Katharine's farm. And what did he write a feasibility study about? Whether the two advanced gas-cooled reactors at Torness nuclear power station could be reactivated.

I sat back and tried to work out what the hell was going on. The minute was marked "Senior Guardian/S.& E. Guardian Eyes Only", which was interesting. It suggested that the rest of the Council – which, in an unusual link with the pre-Enlightenment UK cabinet, is defined in the city's constitution as a body bearing collective responsibility – hadn't been briefed about what was a major policy change. After the horrendous disaster at the Thorp plant at Sellafield in 2003, nuclear power became about as popular as a doctor with syphilis. So the Enlightenment had come to power with a promise to shut down Torness at all costs. What were my mother and William McEwan doing planning to start it up again?

I went over to the sink and splashed water on to my face. Maybe they hadn't actually gone ahead with the plan outlined in the minute. Surely some news of a big operation like that would have filtered out. On the other hand, why had the files gone from the archive? And why had William McEwan been so agitated about the Bone Yard? It looked like my idea about the city's abattoirs was off target after all.

Katharine came out of the bedroom in a pair of my faded citizen-issue pyjamas. I was so engrossed in my thoughts that I didn't give her anything more than a mumbled greeting. And completely forgot that Davie was both late and in possession of a key.

He chose that moment to make an entry.

"Hello, Davie," Katharine said without any sign of surprise.

He took in her short hair and gaunt features, then what she was wearing. "Oh, aye?" he said, turning to me. "Got your fancy woman back, have you?"

I was never one for pig in the middle. "I'll just sit down and let you two get on with it." When they worked together in the last murder case, Davie and Katharine had what could best be described as a relationship based on mutual loathing. He didn't like her dissident record and work in the Prostitution Services Department, and she thought he was a typical boneheaded guardsman.

"I am not anybody's fancy woman," Katharine said haughtily.

Davie ran his eye over her again. "I see what you mean. Times been hard on the other side of the border?"

"Not as hard as the ones the females in your barracks must go through waiting for the sex session roster to be posted."

"Children." I waved the minute at them. "I've just got a big break in the case. Can you postpone the verbal boxing contest?"

"Not really, Quint," Davie said, his cheeks red above the thick curls of his beard. "She's a deserter. I should take her in."

"Just try it, guardsman," Katharine said, leaning forward on the balls of her feet like a lioness about to pounce.

"Oh, for God's sake, what's your average age?" I demanded, glaring at them. "Above eight, by any chance? Look, this investigation's just gone critical in more than one way. For the next few days we need to keep our canines out of each other's throats."

Davie and Katharine exchanged glances that were still hostile enough to petrify a Leith hard man in the days before they all joined the guard, but at least they both kept quiet.

"That's better," I said. "Davie, I hadn't intended to tell you about Katharine, but since you've got into the habit of coming in without knocking . . ."

"You said I could," he protested with a pained expression.

"Go and make some coffee, will you? We need to have a serious look at what we're going to do next."

Outside, the noise of the early morning traffic suddenly seemed a lot quieter. I drew the curtain and saw a cloudful of large snowflakes so thick that I could hardly make out the flats across the street. As visual metaphors for how much Edinburgh citizens know about the activities of their guardians go, it wasn't bad.

I filled them both in about the Torness minute and tried to make it clear how dangerous it might be if they were to tell anyone else. Then I mentioned a pretty dodgy strategy I'd worked out for getting into the senior guardian's personal archive. It involved a lot of dressing up and judicious use of the "ask no questions". Neither Davie nor Katharine looked impressed, but since they weren't liable to end up down the mines for impersonating a rodent control technician, they couldn't complain too much. As things panned out, I didn't need to open my make-up bag after all.

My mobile buzzed and Davie answered it. "It's the guardian," he said, handing it over. "Sounds hot."

It was nothing like the inside of an advanced gas-cooled reactor, but it was still enough to get my circulation going.

"Dalrymple? We've found Raeburn 03."

"Dead or alive?"

"The former." Hamilton's voice took on the usual diluted quality it acquired when he had to talk about violence. "Cut up like the others."

"You haven't touched anything, have you?"

"I haven't," he said defensively. "The guardswoman who

found the body brushed off the snow to find his barracks badge."

"What's the location?"

"The summit of Blackford Hill."

"We're on our way." I grabbed my jacket. "Come on, Davie."

Katharine was standing by the table. "What do you want me to do, Quint?"

"Stay here and don't answer the door."

Davie turned from the front door. "You could always do a bit of early spring cleaning."

She raised her middle finger.

If Katharine stayed inside my pit all day I'd perform oral sex on the senior guardian. I didn't tell her that though. She was always one for a challenge.

"What was Machiavelli doing up here?" Davie asked as he steered the Land-Rover up the steep slope of the snow-covered road past the observatory. Scene-of-crime people were already taking photos of tyre tracks and cordoning off the area.

"Good question. We'll have to see if he was killed here or somewhere else." My mind was already racing ahead. What if he'd been in the surrounding area before the murderer got to him? I could think of one place he might have been visiting – the laboratories at King's Buildings. Maybe he'd recently acquired an interest in chemistry.

There was only a faint line of light in the sky to the east. A generator was being set up ahead of us by the directorate's technical squad. The guardian loomed out of the darkness.

"Jesus Christ, Dalrymple," he said, shaking his head slowly. "I don't know how much more of this I can take."

"What's the problem?" I asked lamely.

There was a shout from ahead of us, then the flood-lights came on in a sudden blaze. I blinked and tried to focus.

"See for yourself," the guardian said, tramping off to his vehicle.

I moved towards the light.

Davie was on my right. "Bloody hell," he said with a rapid intake of breath. "I see what he means."

The body was lying just below the trig point at the summit. There was a carpet of fresh snow on it. Machiavelli was in a rough crucifix position with his legs about six inches apart, feet towards us as we laboured up the hill. But the position wasn't what caught the eye. Despite the snow, a great crimson gout was visible. It was about six feet long and a couple of feet across and stretched out from the neck to the concrete pillar. From the neck. The body in the grey guard tunic had been decapitated on the spot. And I could see no sign at all of the head.

You'd think the snow that had fallen on Edinburgh overnight would be a useful source of traces – footprints, spots of liquid and so on. The problem is it also covers things up.

"What have we got then?" I said to Davie after we'd spent more than enough time crawling around in the snow beside the body.

"Not a lot," he replied, blowing on his fingers and then trying to flip over the pages of his notebook. "Except terminal bloody frostbite."

A guardsman came up with plastic cups of tea that was as grey as a citizen-issue block of writing paper. I gasped as my lips soldered themselves to the rim of the cup.

Hamilton came up to where we were standing about five yards from the body. His face was looking a lot redder than it had done earlier. Maybe he'd supplemented his tea with barracks whisky.

"I don't suppose there's any doubt that it's my deputy."

I shook my head. "We checked that. Obviously another body could have been dressed in his uniform, though God knows why anyone would bother impersonating him."

"Have some respect, Dalrymple," the guardian said, giving me a ferocious glare. "The man's been butchered."

"Sorry," I said. It is a bit out of order to talk ill of the dead, even those who've been behaving suspiciously. "He had a distinguishing mark. A scar on his pelvis from a bone-marrow graft. It's Raeburn 03 all right."

The medical guardian came over, peeling off surgical gloves and dropping them into a bag held out by one of her assistants. Her ice-blonde hair almost merged into the snowy backdrop – apart from the wide red stripe that extended from where Machiavelli's head should have been. "Clearly the victim was alive when he was decapitated because of the spurting," she said. "But he may well have been unconscious. He'd been badly tortured like the others."

I nodded. We'd logged knife wounds on the thighs and abdomen, but no organs had been cut out to make a cavity and no tape had been secreted.

"The deep rope burns on his wrists suggest he was kept tied up for some time," added the Ice Queen. "I'll know more about the state he was in prior to death once I've run tests on the stomach contents and so on. The same goes for the time of death. I'd tentatively put it at around four a.m." She turned to go.

"I'll see you in the mortuary when I've finished here," I said.

"I'll be waiting for you, citizen."

Davie and I watched her move off across the trampled snow, her shape still eye-catching in the protective white overalls that made the rest of us look like semi-inflated rubber dolls.

"To get back to business, gentlemen," Hamilton said irritably. "Did the killer leave any traces?"

"We're still looking," I replied. "The snow's an effective shroud."

"There are Land-Rover tracks leading down the road," Davie said. "They may well come from the guard vehicle used by Mach . . . by Raeburn 03."

Hamilton looked like he was about to ask Davie about the dead man's nickname so I intervened. "And the guardswoman who found the body at ..." I checked my notes. "At six twenty-one a.m. saw no sign of anyone."

"What brought her up here?" Davie said.

"She told me she saw wheel tracks leading up from the main road and followed them," I replied. "She did well considering the amount of snow that had already come down on top of the tracks."

"Amazing, Dalrymple," Hamilton said with a snort. "A good word for the guard from you of all people."

I smiled at him. "I've got no problem with individual guard personnel. After all, I have a very good assistant." Davie looked about as comfortable as politicians in the old days used to when someone mentioned poverty in the Palace of Westminster. "Of course, that may have something to do with the training manuals your directorate uses, guardian."

Hamilton decided this was a good time to depart, his boots crunching into the snow as he headed for his Land-Rover.

"Thanks a lot," Davie said. "My career in the directorate just took a major nosedive."

"Because you're identified with a demoted auxiliary like me?" I laughed. "Tell the truth, guardsman. You love it when I have a go at the guardian."

"No, I don't." He started stamping his feet up and down and clapping his hands together. "Anyway, guard procedures work well enough, no matter which tosser wrote them. And what have you found out here that the rest of us haven't?"

He had a point there. Even if we had found plenty of traces, they wouldn't necessarily have got us any closer to discovering the killer's identity. Or motive. I watched as Machiavelli's headless corpse was wrapped up by Medical Directorate personnel. Beyond them the city's skyline stretched out in the light of morning which had been gradually increasing while we were on the scene. I ran my eyes along from the castle's turretted bulk and down the Royal Mile's line of spires and rooftops. In the east Arthur's Seat crouched like a somnolent lion, its flanks albino white apart from the vertical black scars of the crags. The Ice Queen's staff carried the shrouded body to a battered pre-Enlightenment ambulance that the mechanics in the Transport Directorate had miraculously managed to keep together. The city was going to pieces in all sorts of ways, and someone was taking individuals to pieces. But why had the murderer removed a senior auxiliary's head from this frozen hilltop in the middle of the long Edinburgh night?

I spent the day at the autopsy and checking out Raeburn 03's rooms in his barracks and in the castle. There were no traces of Electric Blues in his stomach and no bags full of the drug in his wardrobe. That would have been too easy. Machiavelli and his accommodation were as clean as a model would-be auxiliary's locker in the tented training camp in the Meadows. I did find copies of his namesake's works on his bedside table, but they're required reading for his ranks so I didn't even smile.

In the evening I attended the Council meeting. I thought there was a chance that the senior boyscout would be shaken up by Machiavelli's gruesome death but if he was, he wasn't showing it. What did get me going was his reluctance to accept that the latest murder was connected to the earlier two. Fair enough, there was no tape. But the other similarities convinced me that it was the same killer. Not for the first time I had the impression that I would make plenty of progress with the case if I tied the senior guardian to a chair and gave him the third degree. There was about as much chance of that happening as there used to be of insurance companies responding quickly to claims in pre-independence times. I considered trying to get Hamilton to give me access to his computer again so I could check out his deputy further, but that would have been a waste of time. What the senior guardian says goes. Unless you're an insubordinate schemer like I am. I went back to my flat to scheme.

"What do we do now?" Davie asked.

We were sitting in the Land-Rover in Gilmore Place under the light of the streetlamps. It was glowing dully on the grey sludge that the morning's snow had become.

"Good question," I said. "We haven't exactly got much to go on." There had been no reported sightings of Machiavelli's Land-Rover during the time he was missing, so we had no idea where he'd been before the killer caught up with him. The vehicle had been found in a back street near the King's Buildings with only Machiavelli's and other guard personnel prints on it. The sentry's log at the chemistry labs had no record of Hamilton's deputy being there. And there were no witnesses around Blackford Hill – everyone had been asleep in their uncomfortable beds.

"What did the medical guardian have to say in the Council meeting?"

I shrugged. "She just confirmed that the time of death was around four in the morning and that the cause of death was severing of the carotid arteries. The wounds on the thighs and abdomen and the rope marks on the wrists were similar to those of the previous victims."

Davie looked up from his notes. "And the weapon?"

"A sharp knife with a large blade, would you believe?"

"Great." He closed his notebook. "Like I said, what next?"

I opened the Land-Rover's door. "Ask me that tomorrow morning, guardsman."

"Don't do anything I wouldn't with that deserter woman, Quint," he said, leaning out of the window.

I looked back at him sternly. "As a loyal auxiliary, I know you wouldn't do anything at all with a deserter, my friend."

"That's exactly what I mean," he replied, slipping the vehicle into gear and pulling away.

What I called him was drowned out by the racket from an

exhaust pipe shot through with more holes than a 1990s election manifesto.

In the stairwell's feeble light I made out a hooded figure sitting on the floor across the landing from my front door. My heart seized up for a couple of seconds, then I remembered who else wore a long coat.

"Katharine?" I moved towards her. "What are you doing out here?"

She raised her head slowly. Her face was pale, the rings around her eyes so dark that for a moment I thought she'd gone three rounds with the city's female boxing champion. She opened her mouth, whispered a few words I didn't catch and pointed with an unsteady hand at my door.

I followed the direction of her arm. And froze as solid as the ground around the concrete post at the top of Blackford Hill that morning.

"Tell me it's not what I think it is," Katharine said faintly.

I pulled out my mobile. "Davie?" I shouted. "Get back here. Now!"

"Tell me, Quint," Katharine repeated insistently, her breath catching in her throat. "Tell me."

I stepped carefully over the flagstones and knelt down in front of the discoloured bag that had been hung from my doorknob. I could make out the stamp of the Supply Directorate. It looked like a flour sack but I knew very well it didn't contain that substance. More like a single, heavy object the shape and size of a football. On the floor beneath the sack were spatters of coagulated and partially frozen blood.

"Fucking hell," I said under my breath, then jerked backwards as the street door below slammed. The sound of nailed boots sprinting up the stairs filled my ears.

"What is it?" Davie yelled as he careered on to the landing, narrowly avoiding Katharine's legs.

I pointed at the sack. "What do you think's in there?"

His eyes widened. "Oh, no."

"Oh, yes." I pulled on rubber gloves then lifted the weighty bag off the handle and set it down gingerly. "Knife."

Davie handed me his service weapon. I took a deep breath and cut through the string round the top of the sack. Parted the flaps of material. And looked down on the severed head of Raeburn 03.

I heard Katharine move and waved to her to keep back.

Davie leaned forward, his lips drawn back in a rictus of disgust. "Bloody hell," he hissed. Then he clutched my arm. "What's that in his mouth, Quint?"

"Give me your torch."

I tilted the head over and shone the light at the senior auxiliary's swollen lips. The teeth were apart and a flat object covered in transparent plastic was protruding about two inches from them. I looked closer. There was no way I'd be able to open those hardened jaw muscles without an expanding clamp. That was a job for the medical guardian. But I already knew what was in there. The killer had provided another piece of music. And it had been personally delivered to me.

Chapter Sixteen

—————◇◆◇—————

As I knelt down beside Katharine, the staircase lights flashed three times.

"Come on, that's the curfew," I said. "Let's get you inside." I looked over my shoulder at Davie. "Call the medical guardian, will you? And don't let anyone inside the flat."

He nodded, glancing down at the sack and what had been inside it. "This should keep everyone occupied out here."

I pushed Katharine in gently as the lights went out and lit a couple of candles. She slumped down on the sofa, her chin resting on her breastbone. Her breathing was uneven. She looked like an explorer who'd given everything and was now resigned to the end.

"Hey," I said, sitting beside her and touching her hand. It was ice cold. "How long were you out there?"

She shivered but no words came.

I squeezed her chilled skin. "Tell me, Katharine. I need to have an idea of when the . . . the sack was put on my door."

She shivered again, this time more violently then laid into me. "You only care about your fucking investigation, don't you, Quint? It was the same the last time. I should have known better than to come back. I don't mean anything to you, do I?"

I left the question unanswered, feeling the sting of her words turn into a warm sensation deep inside. So it wasn't just concern about the drug formula that had brought her back to the city. Apparently she had some interest in me after all.

"I've only been back for about half an hour," she said, looking away from me. Then she let out a great sob.

I took a chance and put my arm round her shoulders. She resisted for a few seconds, then moved towards me.

"I . . . I couldn't touch it," she said, her voice quivering like a frightened child's. "I couldn't get to the door handle."

"It's all right, Katharine. I didn't exactly have a great time touching the sack myself."

She raised her head and looked at me in the candlelight. "No, there's more to it than that." Her eyes burned into mine. "You see, I knew what it was."

I stiffened involuntarily, suddenly gripped by the horrific thought that she had some involvement in the killing. "How, Katharine?" I asked, my voice unsteady.

"I've seen a man's head in a sack before," she said, her eyes still fixed on mine. Whatever else I read in them, it wasn't guilt. She'd been in bed with me all last night.

Outside on the stair there was the pounding of many feet. Davie knocked and stuck his head round the door. "They're here."

"I'll be out in a minute," I said, then turned back to Katharine. "When did you see a head before?" I got her to her feet and steered her towards the bedroom.

She sat down on the bed and wrapped her arms round herself. "The time I told you about with the . . . the Cavemen . . . the leader was a madman and he used to lay into his own men all the time." She glanced up at me, then looked down again. "Two of them started fighting over me . . . Christ, I don't know why . . . they all had plenty of time to do whatever they wanted . . . and the leader, he just waded in and grabbed one of the guys by the hair . . . he had this long bayonet and he . . . he hacked the head off . . . then he put it in a sack and made the other Caveman wear it round his neck . . ."

"Jesus, Katharine."

She looked up again and shrugged. "I was happy at the time, though I made sure I didn't show it. One animal less." Her voice broke. "But you don't forget things like that."

I sat down beside her. "No, you don't. You wouldn't be a normal human being if you could."

Katharine laughed bitterly. "No way am I a normal human being, Quint."

"You think anyone else in this room is?" I stood up. "Look, I'm going to have to get out there. Stay here. I'll be back."

She fell back on the bed like she'd been poleaxed. "I spend my life waiting for you, Quintilian Dalrymple."

As I pulled the covers over her, it struck me that there were plenty of less encouraging things she could have said.

"What do you think, guardian?"

The Ice Queen looked up from the mortuary table on which Machiavelli's head had been placed. Behind her the body had been laid out on another table. In the bright lights it looked like a scene from one of the television pathologist series that were so popular in pre-Enlightenment times. Except that hospital finances in the 1990s wouldn't have stretched to two tables for the parts of a single body.

"What do I think?" the medical guardian asked irritably. "I think there are better ways to spend an evening."

I was surprised. I'd always assumed that the Ice Queen was in the habit of shutting herself up in the morgue's refrigerated storeroom overnight.

"On the other hand," she continued, "I know that this head belongs to that body and I know that this is our killer's third victim."

That was more like it — competent analysis a robot would be proud of. "What about the tape?"

"Quite so." The guardian straightened up and beckoned to her assistant to remove the contents of the dead auxiliary's mouth.

I followed her over to the sink. "Any thoughts on the victim?"

The Ice Queen gave me a sidelong glance. "You surely don't expect me to speculate on matters outside my field, citizen."

I grinned. "They aren't exactly outside your field. Mach . . . Raeburn 03 was very well connected in the Council. If he was a target, who's next among your colleagues?"

She shook the water from her hands and made a passable attempt at indifference. "I really don't see what you're getting at. The other victims had no such connections."

I handed her a paper towel. "Maybe the killer's working his way up the hierarchy. Ordinary citizen, auxiliary, senior auxiliary — next, a guardian?"

She dropped the towel in a bin, managing to imply that my line of thought should go with it. "I'd keep that idea to yourself, citizen," she said, looking across to the table. "Your tape's been ejected."

I almost fell over. Verbal humour from the Ice Queen was about as likely as spontaneous cheering during a debate on *The Republic*. I took the tape from her sidekick and headed for the machine.

Before I got there the guardian's mobile rang. She spoke briefly and signed off.

"An emergency Council meeting has been called, citizen. Your presence is required."

I started walking again. "What, now?"

"Now."

I slotted the cassette into the cassette player, desperate to hear what was on it. I wasn't disappointed.

Great music, but not exactly consistent with the other pieces. Then I got the message. And experienced meltdown.

The Council chamber. If the senior guardian was shocked by the discovery of Machiavelli's head, he wasn't showing it. That wasn't the case with his colleagues. They were standing around him with their mouths open like a group of statues in the middle of a fountain. Fortunately the water supply had been turned off.

"What is on the tape, citizen?" the chief boyscout asked after the medical guardian had confirmed that the head went with the body.

I went over to the machine and hit the play button. The exquisite sounds of Paul Kossoff's guitar washed over the guardians. I was pleased to see that at least one of them looked to be getting into the rhythm surreptitiously.

"And that was . . . ?" the senior guardian asked when the music finished.

"'Fire and Water' by Free," I replied. "There are those who say that Paul Rodgers had the finest voice of all British rock singers."

"Really?" said the senior guardian in a voice that sounded interested but I was bloody sure wasn't. Then his expression livened up a bit. "Did you say rock singers? The other pieces of music were blues, were they not?"

I shrugged. "Free were influenced by American rhythm and blues like a lot of bands in the late 1960s. Paul Rodgers sang plenty of blues standards in his time."

The senior guardian's eyes locked on to mine. "So why exactly was this song chosen, citizen?"

I was pretty sure he was squaring up to me, daring me to come out into the open. In fact, that was probably why he'd called this emergency meeting – to make sure I came up against him in front of the other guardians rather than in private. He knew I'd been digging in the Science and Energy Directorate archive and he knew I'd heard William McEwan mention the Bone Yard. But he didn't want to give me the chance to ask him any awkward questions. Like whether the song had anything to do with his directorate. I reckoned it did. "Fire and Water" sounded to me like a pretty unsubtle hint at nuclear reactors. The ones at Torness used to produce the equivalent of millions of fires and needed plenty of water in their cooling systems. But I needed something more solid before I could lay into him.

"The song's a typical lover's complaint," I said innocently. "The guy's having a hard time with a woman who blows hot and cold." I gave the Ice Queen a quick glance and was rewarded with her normal glacial gaze.

Lewis Hamilton was shaking his head in annoyance. "What's the point? Isn't there any connection with drugs?"

"Not one that's hit me so far," I replied. "I'll need to think about it."

The chief boyscout finally decided that staring me out was a waste of time. "I trust you'll let us know when your thought processes bear fruit. Another point, citizen. Why was the head left on your door?"

Good question. I'd been wondering about that myself. The hooded man had followed Roddie Aitken to my flat, so he probably knew about my involvement from the beginning. The fact that he'd risked being spotted with his unsavoury bundle suggested either that he had something against me or that he wanted to get me in even more deeply than I already was. Which might explain the choice of "Fire and Water" as the latest musical offering.

"Well, citizen?" the senior guardian asked, his saintly features beginning to tighten impatiently.

"Well what?" I replied with a lot more impatience. "There are plenty of people who know I'm running the case. The murderer may be one of them."

"Plenty of people?" Hamilton's forehead furrowed like it always did when he came to a conclusion that offends him. "The murders haven't been publicised, Dalrymple. The only people who know about them are auxiliaries."

I let a wide smile blossom across my face. He'd just buried his foot in the shit. I didn't have to add another word, so I turned on my heel and left the boyscouts to it.

*   *   *

I let myself into the flat as quietly as I could and lit a candle. Then I sat down at the kitchen table, feeling its flimsy legs bend as I leaned on it, and tried to do some serious thinking.

The main problem was that this wasn't simply a multiple murder investigation, which would have been bad enough. There were too many things going on at the margins – like William McEwan's death, the new drug formula, the nuclear physicist who ended up at Katharine's farm, the Bone Yard. How the hell did they all come together? Could it be that they were all part of an agenda that did not include a future for the Council? Then there was the music. I had the definite impression that someone was pulling my chain, someone who knew how much I was into the blues. The first two pieces obviously referred to the uppers they'd called Electric Blues, but now there was "Fire and Water", which I reckoned was a reference to the nuclear part of the puzzle. But why? What was I being told? That there was some connection between the decommissioned power station at Torness and the new drug?

The bedroom door opened and Katharine stepped into the dim light of the candle. She rubbed her eyes, but I wasn't paying much attention to them. The only garment on the lower half of her body was a pair of knickers. Her long legs looked in good condition – that's what you get if you work on a farm where there's no machinery. I had a look at them then went back to the black material covering her crotch. Presumably an itinerant salesman had called at her place since the Supply Directorate in Edinburgh provides only off-white underwear.

"What are you doing?" she asked. "It's the middle of the night."

"I am a creature of the night, my dear," I said in an attempt at a Lon Chaney accent.

"Creatures of the night who've got any sense spend it in bed." She headed back into the other room.

I pursued her after a diplomatic gap of a second or two. By

the time I got there she was already back under the covers. I threw my outer layer of clothing off and slid under the thin blankets, shivering. Katharine was facing the other way but she pushed her rump towards me. I moved into the warmth that her body was making. Her legs burned against me. I couldn't tell if she'd gone back to sleep or not, but she was very still. Then I remembered the Cavemen and what she'd been through. Suddenly I didn't feel like making any further moves. So I absorbed her heat and fell into a surprisingly dream-free sleep.

Which lasted until about six in the morning, when I woke up to the realisation that I was going to have to take some life-threatening decisions. I felt even worse when I saw that the other side of the bed was empty.

"Morning." Katharine appeared at the door with a mug of coffee. "I thought I heard sounds of the kraken waking."

"You're up early," I mumbled, trying to clear a way for words. My mouth was gummed up better than a glue-sniffer's nasal tubes in the days when you didn't need a guard permit for adhesive substances.

"The life of the soil," she said, sitting on the bed and drinking from her own mug. "You've almost run out of this stuff. You're going to have to get Davie to pilfer some more."

"Do you mind? I earned that from a client who works in one of the tourist restaurants." I gulped the coffee down. "Anyway, I've got other plans for him today."

"Have you now?" Katharine looked at me severely. "And what about me? If you think I'm going to stay in this shithole . . ."

"Before you insult my home any further, one of those plans involves you."

"I hope you don't expect me to dress up as a guardswoman and spend the day with him."

"Not exactly. I'm going to tell him to get you an 'ask no questions'."

"Can't I use yours?"

"I might need it. Until you get it, do you think you'll be able to bear staying in my shithole?"

She shrugged, then nodded non-committally. I wasn't convinced she'd stay but I had more worrying things on my mind. Like disturbing the senior guardian's breakfast.

"So you'll sort out Katharine's 'ask no questions' and take it to her at my place, Davie?"

He was staring out at the New Town's Georgian houses in the early morning gloom and looking pretty unimpressed. "What are you playing at, Quint? She a bloody deserter. If the public order guardian finds out . . ."

"Well, you'd better make sure he doesn't." I slapped him on the thigh. "Lighten up, pal. She's given me some pretty useful information."

"Oh, aye? And where's it got you? I haven't noticed any murderers sitting in the castle dungeons."

I nodded slowly, feeling the wet greyness of the walls in Forres Street seeping into me like a dose of pneumonia. "Someone's playing games with us, Davie, and I'm not having fun. Especially since I don't know the rules."

"The great Quintilian Dalrymple doesn't know the rules?" he asked ironically.

I wasn't in the mood, so I did what I normally do when he takes the piss — assaulted him verbally using numerous words banned by the Council. He enjoyed it almost as much as I did. Eventually we got back to business.

"Something else, Davie. Do you know anyone in the Fisheries Guard?" The sum total of the Council's navy is half a dozen converted trawlers that protect the city's fishing boats from the modern version of pirates — that is, headbangers from Fife armed with ex-British Army automatic rifles.

"Those lunatics? Aye, I went through auxiliary training with some of them." He looked at me seriously. "What's going on?

You don't want to mess with those guys. They're a bunch of total psychos."

"Who don't pay that much attention to what the guard command centre tells them to do?"

Davie shrugged. "They don't need to. The captains have their own patch to patrol. They have carte blanche to deal with raiders however they want. All they need the castle for is to approve their ammunition supplies."

That was what I wanted to hear.

Davie was peering at me suspiciously. "What are you up to, Quint?"

"Me? I'm going to have a chat with the senior guardian."

"Is he expecting you?" Davie asked as I got out of the Land-Rover.

"Put it this way – I don't think he'll exactly be surprised to see me." I stopped and turned back to him. "Keep your mobile on. If you don't hear from me in an hour, come knocking on his door."

"What?" The idea of making an unauthorised call on the chief boyscout looked about as palatable to him as a plate of citizen-issue black pudding.

I walked down the slippery road towards the checkpoint that restricts access to Moray Place. All the guardians have their residences in the circular street that surrounds a small park. The original members of the Enlightenment had thought it appropriate that Council members live together, despite the fact that they'd cut themselves off from their families. Then again, living together didn't have any dubious connotation as far as they were concerned. My parents were both guardians in the first Council and they'd given up living with each other in any significant way years before the last election.

I flashed my authorisation at the guardswoman by the heavy gate. She was young and hard, her fair hair drawn back tight in the regulation ponytail.

"Which guardian are you visiting, citizen?" she demanded, her hand on the telephone in the sentry box.

I didn't want to give the senior guardian any advance warning. "Your boss, the public order guardian," I said with a winning smile.

She was very far from returning that. "The guardian is at the castle, citizen."

"I don't think so. He told me to be here at seven thirty on the dot." I was pretty sure the guardswoman wouldn't risk annoying Hamilton by checking on his whereabouts.

His temper was to my advantage again. She took her hand away from the phone and raised the barrier. "It's number seven," she said.

"It's not the first time I've been here," I said as I walked past her. "Unfortunately."

Around the corner she couldn't see that I carried on past the residence that Hamilton rarely used and headed for the senior guardian's. In the gloom before sunrise the streetlights, which are kept on overnight here for security reasons, cast sparkling circles of pale orange on the icy paving stones. I was thinking about the infrequent visits I made to my mother here. The last was after the end of the murder case in 2020. I was usually torn to shreds by her and I had a nasty feeling her successor was about to keep up the tradition.

I knocked on the black door. It opened before I could blink. The male auxiliary on the other side must have been as close to it as the Three Graces' chiffon wraps are to their buttocks.

He ran an eye down me and made to close the door again.

"I'm Dalrymple," I said, sticking my authorisation in his face. "The senior guardian's expecting me." Well, that was a bit of a liberty, but there was some truth in it.

"I have no record of any appointment," the auxiliary said, stuttering slightly. He must have been in his late twenties but he suddenly looked like he needed a nappy. You often get that with members of his rank when the bureaucracy fouls up.

"Look," I said, pushing past him. "It's bloody freezing outside. I told you, the senior guardian will——"

"The senior guardian will do what, citizen Dalrymple?"

I looked up to see the man himself standing halfway down the ornate staircase, a file under his arm. Apparently I was too late to interrupt his breakfast. Then again, deities don't need to bother with food and drink.

"I need to talk to you," I said. At my side I felt the auxiliary flinch as I deliberately omitted his superior's title.

There was a pause as the chief boyscout considered my fate. "Very well. I was just going into the library. Will you join me?"

I wasn't sure whether the excessive politeness was for the benefit of the auxiliary or whether he always behaved like this out of Council meetings. It knocked me off the course I'd decided on. But only for a few moments.

"You often came here when my predecessor was in office, I imagine," he said, sitting down in a leather armchair beside the open fire. The walls were lined with books as high as the ceiling. They seemed mainly to be scientific tomes. Over by the barred window was a row of gunmetal cabinets. I wondered if they contained the files that had been removed from the Science and Energy Directorate archive.

"Citizen?" the guardian said less politely.

"What? Oh, no, not often. I only ever came here on official business."

The guardian nodded, his ascetic face beneath the wispy beard expressing approval. "My predecessor took the regulations very seriously."

"Much more seriously than she took her family," I said, looking into the fire's dull flames. I could feel his eyes on me still.

"I'm sure she knew what she was doing." The guardian drummed his fingers lightly on the grey file on his knees. "What is it that you want, citizen?"

This was it. Crisis point. I'd tried unsuccessfully to work out a way to do this diplomatically. I had to go for broke. I linked eyes with him.

"What exactly is the Bone Yard, guardian?"

I was hoping I could provoke a reaction from him like William McEwan had done at the Hogmanay party. But there was nothing – no giveaway intake of breath, no sweat on the forehead, no trembling fingers. He looked at me with his saint's eyes, strong but strangely compassionate, then shook his head slowly.

"No."

I didn't understand and it must have been obvious because he said it again.

"No, citizen." Now his eyes were less compassionate, but they were still strong, as determined as the craziest guardsmen's, the ones who volunteer for permanent border duty.

That seemed to be it. He said nothing more.

"What do you mean 'no'?" I asked eventually.

"I mean no, you are not to pursue any line of enquiry about this subject." His thin body was taut now, coiled in the chair like a snake about to dart forward. "I mean no, the Bone Yard has nothing to do with the murders you are investigating. I mean no, you are not to discuss the subject with anyone else. Including any of my colleagues on the Council."

"But there are indications that the Electric Blues and this Bone Yard place are connected." I returned his stare but I couldn't do much to deflect it. Time for the killer blow. "And there are indications that your directorate is or has been involved."

Again, nothing. He was about as impervious to attack as a pre-Enlightenment prime minister with a massive majority.

"Indications are not evidence, citizen," he said imperiously. "And even the Council's justice system needs evidence."

For a split second I thought he was being ironical about the regime he ran, but the set of his mouth told me that was a vain hope.

"Let me put my cards on the table," I said, resorting to dishonesty – I had no intention of telling him about William McEwan's minute and what I'd found out about the nuclear physicist. "The song 'Fire and Water' that we found on, or rather in Raeburn 03 made me think of the old nuclear power station at Torness." I kept my eyes on him, but he was as solid as the Bass Rock. "I was wondering if it might be the Bone Yard I heard the former guardian talking to you about."

There was only the slightest relaxation in the chief boyscout's body, but it was enough to tell me that he thought he was off the hook.

"Really, citizen. William McEwan's mind had obviously begun to wander. I can assure you that the Bone Yard is in no way connected with Torness. You have my word on that." His eyes hardened again. "On the other hand, the murders do seem to have some connection with the drug." He stood up rapidly. "If you wish to remain in charge of the investigation, I suggest you make some progress with it quickly. And forget the Bone Yard."

"But what is it? What is the Bone Yard?" I asked desperately.

"Believe me, it is no concern of yours, citizen," he said firmly then pressed the bell for his secretary.

That was it. I was out of the house like a guardsman on a charge being marched to the latrines with a mop and bucket. But though I didn't show it to the auxiliaries and guard personnel who were assembling for the morning shift in Moray Place, I felt pretty pleased with myself. For one thing, I'd got out of the lion's den alive. For another, I was certain that the senior guardian's word was as worthless as a time-expired clothing voucher. It's never a good idea to tell an investigator that something isn't his concern.

Now I needed Davie's contacts in the Fisheries Guard more than ever.

Chapter Seventeen

———— >◦◦◦< ————

I got back to my place to find Davie and Katharine facing up to each other over the kitchen table. An "ask no questions" was lying between them on the surface. It looked like she'd given him a few choice suggestions as to where he could put it.

"Christ, am I glad to see you, Quint," Davie said, glowering at Katharine like a wee boy who's had his football nicked by a nimbler and much faster girl. "You can forget any chance of me working with this deserter."

"No, I can't." I looked at them as appealingly as I could. "I need all the help I can get."

"That's why I came back, Quint," Katharine said.

"Oh, aye?" Davie sneered. "You haven't done much so far."

I gave up and went over to my cassette player. After half a minute of Albert Collins playing "How Blue Can You Get" at full volume, they let go of each other's throats. I risked another few bars then shut the noise down.

"Got that out of your systems, children? Because I'm in deep shit in this investigation. And if my clothing's impregnated with the brown stuff, then so's yours." They seemed to be getting the message. Davie even looked mildly ashamed. Not Katharine — that would have been a major surprise. But at least she wasn't disagreeing.

"Would you mind telling me what's going on, Quint?" she asked, slipping the "ask no questions" into her pocket.

That seemed like a good idea. So I filled them in about where William McEwan's memo and the latest song were leading me. And about my meeting with the chief boyscout.

"I don't see what all this has got to do with the murders," Davie said, his face contorting as he tried to keep up.

"Neither do I. Call it a hunch, call it my genius for detective work . . ."

Katharine laughed. "Maybe we should go for the former so your head doesn't contract elephantiasis."

"Thank you." I smiled sourly at her.

Davie was still fighting it. "You just said the senior guardian told you to forget the Bone Yard and everything to do with his directorate. You're surely not planning on going up against him?"

I gestured to Katharine to keep quiet. I knew she'd have no problem working against the senior guardian. She probably kept herself awake at night longing for a chance like that. But Davie was different. He was a serving auxiliary, sworn to uphold the orders of the Council and its leader. And I needed his connections in the guard if I was to pull off what I had in mind.

"Look, Davie, I'm not saying the senior guardian's involved. But I don't believe his directorate has always been in the clear."

He rubbed his beard and looked at me dubiously. "What are you going to do then?"

"It doesn't work that way, guardsman. Either you're in or you're not. We haven't got time for committee meetings every half-hour."

He stared at me, glanced at Katharine then nodded slowly. "I suppose you'll need someone reliable to watch your back."

"That's a 'yes', is it?" I asked.

"Aye." He grinned and I grinned back. That's what I like about Davie. Once he's made a decision, he forgets all about the mental wrangling that led up to it.

"You're welcome to his back," said Katharine, unimpressed by this display of male bonding. "As far as I can remember, his front is much more interesting."

I didn't know whether to be encouraged by that or depressed by her uncertainty. It seemed best to move on.

"You asked what we're going to do." I looked at them both before I hit them with the big one. "We're going to take a trip to the old nuclear power station at Torness."

If the Supply Directorate hadn't rationed pins, you'd have heard several drop.

When we'd worked out as many angles as we could, Davie went off to talk to his friends in the Fisheries Guard. Katharine headed for the Central Library to pull a plan of the power station; I didn't want to risk going back to the Science and Energy Directorate archive. And I spent the rest of the day with Hamilton following up the few leads Machiavelli had left. Those didn't amount to much. There were several unauthorised absences from compulsory barracks philosophy debates, but he wasn't the first senior auxiliary to keep away from those. And we didn't find any traces of Electric Blues in the quarters of the few auxiliaries he was close to.

So the day passed, to be concluded by an uneventful Council meeting. I was keeping my head down in advance of the approaching night's programme of recreation and the senior guardian was so impressed by my reticence that he expressed only minor criticisms of my report. Not that I'd told him anything significant. The real fun was just about to begin.

We stopped at the retirement home on the way to Leith. I left the other two in the Land-Rover and ran up the stairs. The nurse made a half-hearted attempt to get in the way, but gave up when she saw it was me.

"Hello, old man," I said, gasping for breath as I went into

the room on the top floor. The only light was a pool of yellow on the desk.

My father looked up from his books. "Hello, failure. It's a bit late for social calls, isn't it?"

"Yes, well, it's not exactly a normal visit."

"I thought as much from the way you're twitching around," he said with a surprisingly lewd laugh. "Like a boy about to get his hands up a lassie's skirt for the first time." As he's got older, Hector has become increasingly scabrous. That's what you get from reading Juvenal all day.

"It's a bit more serious than that."

Hector stood up slowly from his chair and raised himself painfully to his full height. For all the aches and pains the old man suffers, he still has a commanding presence. "What exactly have you got yourself involved in, Quintilian?"

"Em, it's a bit sensitive."

My father's eyes flashed. "Are you going to tell me or not?" he demanded.

I smiled. "No, I'm not." I handed him a brown envelope.

"What's this? Pocket money like those arsehole MPs used to take in the old days?"

"What would you do with pocket money? You've got all the dirty books in Latin you need." I heard a single blast from the Land-Rover's horn. It was time to stop messing around. "Look, Hector, we're doing something a bit risky. It's all written down in there. Don't open it unless ... well, unless I don't show up again."

His expression was grave now. "That bad?"

I nodded. "And make sure you keep it somewhere secure. If it comes to the worst, your guess is as good as mine as to what you do with it."

"I'll think of something." He looked at me with a mixture of tenderness and annoyance. "You'll never learn, will you?"

I laughed. "On the contrary. I made sure I learned everything you taught me."

He shook his head. "I never taught you to be so headstrong, laddie."

I turned to go. "Oh, yes, you did."

"Quintilian?"

I glanced back at the tall figure. The lower part was out of the circle of light and he looked like a ghost whose nether parts had been removed. In his case, probably by my mother.

"This has to do with what Willie McEwan was saying, hasn't it?" he said slowly.

"Aye, it does."

"Good for you, lad." His voice was suddenly faint.

I left before the scene got too heavy.

"They'll be waiting for us in the docks," Davie said as I got back into the Land-Rover.

"Sorry."

Katharine looked at me in the dull light from the dashboard. "Are you all right, Quint?"

"Of course. Nothing I like better than breaking every regulation in the book as well as several that have never even occurred to the Council."

"Boasting again," muttered Davie.

We were lucky with the weather. Well, as lucky as you can expect to be in the perfect city in January. At least the sky had clouded over and the night was murky enough to give us the illusion that our activities were going ahead in private. The reality is that there are informers all over the place, though the Fisheries Guard base in the docks is probably as secure as anywhere. The fact that it was cold enough to emasculate a king penguin was in our favour too, but you'd have had a job convincing me of that as I jumped out of the Land-Rover and kissed goodbye to the circulation in my feet.

Leith began to get trendy around the time I was born in the 1980s, its old warehouses and merchants' offices metamorphosing into duplex apartments and wine bars for bankers and the like. There are none of them left now, just good citizens working in the Labour Directorate's facilities. I've always hated the place. Our family dentist lived and practised down here. He spent most of my childhood practising on me and never seemed to get any better. The dank streets outside the port area were quiet, the lights off as it was past curfew time. Leith is about as far as you can get from the tourist area and its inhabitants were all supposed to be tucked up in bed with a cup of what the Supply Directorate, with its vivid imagination, calls cocoa. A foghorn droned lazily as we waited for the gate to be opened, its melancholy sound sending a slow shiver up my spine.

"What's the matter?" Katharine asked. "Having second thoughts?"

"Two hundred and second more like."

Then there was movement ahead of us. The gate swung back and a beaten-up guard vehicle which bore a vague resemblance to a Transit van backed towards us at speed.

A burly guardsman, wearing – I'm not kidding – an eyepatch, stuck his head out. "Follow me!" he yelled, then set off like there was a time bomb in his cargo space. The fact that the head I glimpsed was completely bald and had a deep dent on the crown did nothing to settle my nerves.

"Do you know him?" I asked Davie, who was struggling to keep the Transit's single tail light in view.

"Aye, that's Harry – Jamieson 369. He's a complete nutter."

"What a surprise."

"You know what happened to his head?" Davie looked away from the narrow road across a swingbridge and grinned.

"Eyes front, guardsman," I said, holding on to the bottom of my seat. Katharine couldn't have looked less bothered if she'd tried.

"A couple of headbangers on a raiding ship had a go with crowbars."

"I suppose he didn't even notice."

Davie laughed. "How did you guess?"

We finally caught up with the other guard vehicle. Near the mouth of the old Imperial Dock – now called the Enlightenment Dock, of course – I made out a hulk alongside which must have been raised from the seabed very recently. Then I realised that guard personnel were carrying stores on board down a narrow gangway.

"Jesus, we're not going out in that, are we?" I asked, pointing my open mouth in Davie's direction.

"What did you expect?" he answered, putting his shoulder to the driver's door. "This is the Fisheries Guard, not the High Seas Fleet."

Katharine and I followed him out.

"Evening, Davie." The bald guardsman called Harry was standing on the damp dockside. He was wearing filthy oil-stained overalls. "These'll be your pals. No." He raised a hefty, blackened hand. "I don't want to see any ID." He grinned broadly. "That way, when you fall overboard, I'm in the clear."

"Very funny," I said. "Where's the captain?"

This time he laughed out loud. A bull with a hard-on would have bellowed more decorously. "Captain? Our magnificent vessels haven't got room for wankers standing on the bridge telling the crew what to do." He leaned towards me and I made the disturbing discovery that the stoved-in area on the top of his skull was pulsing like it had its own heart.

"But if you're looking for the guy in charge, that's me."

I commented on that under my breath, making sure my lips didn't move. Davie and Katharine were already walking the plank down to the rotting ex-trawler's deck.

"After you," said the skipper.

I set off, feeling my boots slip on the gangway and trying to remember when I'd last been on a boat.

"Down into the bowels," dirty Harry yelled, pushing me towards a door beneath the wheelhouse. Apart from a faded maroon heart painted on the superstructure, the ship would have had no problem masquerading as a raider.

"Right," the guardsman said, pulling out a bottle of barracks whisky and gulping from it before offering it round. "It just so happens that this vessel's going on routine patrol in eastern waters tonight." He looked at our faces one by one, holding his gaze on mine. "Eastern waters between Dunbar and Cove. Any good?"

I nodded. That covered the area of the power station.

"But you'll need to understand one thing," the bald man said, his face cracking into a grin again. "My business is beating a thousand kinds of shite out of fish thieves. That takes priority over your wee outing. They aren't very nice people, pirates, so if you're not into violence, you'd better keep your heads down."

"What makes you think I'm not into violence?" Katharine asked, taking hold of a fish knife from a rack on the wall.

Harry laughed like a kid who's come across the key to his father's booze cabinet. "My kind of woman," he boomed.

Maybe it was just me, but I had a bad feeling about the way the cruise was starting off.

We had moved out into the firth, six deck crew members taking positions at the vessel's bow and stern. They were all carrying light machine-guns. Fisheries Guard personnel are among the few who get their hands on the Council's small store of high-quality firearms. Officially guns were banned after the last of the drugs gangs were dealt with seven years back, but truncheons and auxiliary knives aren't much good against pirate ships. Until you board them, at least. I reckoned Harry and his crew had done that often enough over the years.

After we cleared the dock, Katharine and Davie had crashed out. I went up to the cramped wheelhouse and watched the bald man at work. He swung the wheel with the natural seaman's easy mastery, his mouth set in a solid smile suggesting he lived in hope that raiders would appear as soon as possible. He acknowledged my presence with an unconcerned nod but didn't waste his breath on talking. Eventually I decided to give it a go.

"Your people don't seem to give a shit about us or what we're doing on board, guardsman."

"What makes you think I do?" He grinned humourlessly. "Citizen." He managed to imbue that word with all the guardsman's loathing of ordinary citizens who get themselves involved in auxiliary business. I hadn't put him down as a bigot. A psychopath, yes.

"I was one of you lot once," I said, trying to impress him. "My barracks number was—"

"I know who you were." He leered at me in the feeble light from the navigation instruments, no trace of even a hard man's smile on his face now. "You were the fuckhead who got a lot of my mates killed in the drugs wars."

That was one way of looking at it. I decided to move the conversation back towards its original direction.

"Your people, they will keep quiet about this, won't they?"

Nice one, Quint. Judging by the way the skin on his scalp had gone all tense, I'd managed to insult him and his beloved crew.

"My people always keep quiet," he replied after a long pause. "Citizen."

I'd completely screwed up on the diplomacy front so I reckoned I had nothing to lose. "Like they've kept quiet about what happened at Torness a couple of years back?"

Now things got very subdued in the wheelhouse. The trawler's engine ploughed away beneath us and the waves belted into the bow, fortunately not too heavily. I looked ahead and saw nothing, not a single light. Or anything else. I hoped my companion knew where he was going.

"So that's what this is all about," the guardsman said eventually. "I thought as much." Then he clammed up again. This was like having a conversation with Rip van Winkle – as soon as it got interesting, decades of nothing.

"Were you out in eastern waters that night?" I asked,

trying very hard to pretend I knew what had happened at the power station.

"Out in eastern waters," he repeated. "That would be a good title for a book, eh? 'Out in eastern waters.' I like it."

"Great, why don't you use it for your memoirs?" I said, choking on my impatience. "So were you? Out in eastern waters?"

"Sure we were," he said, suddenly looking at me seriously. "I suppose you'll be wanting to hear the story."

Do the bears in what remains of Edinburgh zoo shit in the shrubberies?

So the bald man with the eyepatch and the dented head told me what he'd seen. End of wisecracks for a bit.

"I don't know why I'm letting you in on this. Still, Davie told me you're okay and I owe him one. That lunatic saved my life on the border when I was on my first tour. It'll be hours before we get there even if the pirates don't distract us and, now I think of it, I could do with telling someone the story. We were warned that we'd have a lifetime of shovelling coal if we ever opened our mouths and we haven't. But it isn't right. It festers inside you like something a surgeon should have dealings with."

"December 2019," I said.

"Aye. The fifth." Harry shook his head then spat out of the open side window. "It's not a date I can see myself ever forgetting. It was a night like this. Heavy cloud and no chance of making out the campfires on the hills over in Fife. I was pissed off. I wanted to practise my celestial navigation." He paused and reached for the bottle of barracks malt he had near the wheel. "That's why so few people had any idea about the explosions."

"Explosions?" I said, my gut going leaden.

"That's right, citizen. The fuckers had been messing about with the reactors, from what I could gather on the emergency channel. We were about five miles offshore when it started. Christ, the flashes were bright for all the cloud. The power station buildings suddenly looked like they were ten feet away."

"What did you do?"

"What do you think we fucking did?" He turned on me and I could see the rhythmic pulsing in his damaged skull. "I may look like a headcase, but I'm still an auxiliary. We went in to pick up the injured."

"What about . . . weren't you worried about the fallout?"

"I never even gave it a thought, pal." He glared at me again. "You did say you used to be an auxiliary, didn't you? We look after our own, remember?"

An image of Caro lying on the floor in the barn during the attack I planned came up in front of me, then disappeared into the murk that was all round the boat.

"What's the matter, citizen? Don't you want to know what we found?" the bald man asked, a dead smile plastered across his face. "Well, I'm telling you what we found even if you've lost the stomach for it." He gulped whisky again. "Fuck all is what we found. As soon as I radioed in my position I was ordered to return to base. Just like that. No discussion, no argument. Goodnight, Torness." He laughed bitterly. "Course, it didn't end there. A squad of special guards was waiting for us in Leith. We were confined to the ship until senior auxiliaries from the Science and Energy Directorate arrived and told us to zip our lips together about the firework show or else."

"One of those auxiliaries is now the senior guardian, isn't he?"

"I think I'll give that question the body swerve." He laughed, this time with a trace of humour. "In fact, I think I've told you all I'm going to, citizen."

I nodded slowly. He'd already said enough to make this freezing cruise worth while. "Thanks, Harry," I said, taking the bottle from his thick-fingered hand. "I wish you'd call me Quint."

The bald man glanced at me with his single eye. "And I wish I had the nerve to sail this bloody boat right across the North Sea. To hell with the fucking Council." He grabbed the bottle back and grinned malevolently. "And to hell with you, citizen Quint."

At least he'd managed to say my name.

After I swallowed some more whisky to help me get over the shock of hearing a serving auxiliary badmouth his lords and masters, I went down to the cramped cabin over the engine compartment and passed out with my head next to Davie's on the table. I woke to the smell of good-quality coffee. No doubt it had been looted from a raiding ship.

"It's dawn," Katharine said, handing me a metal mug so battered it could have come from Schliemann's excavations at Troy. "We're lying a couple of miles off the power station. The big man wants to know what we're doing next." She smiled faintly. "And so do I."

"Ah." I ran my hand through my hair and considered what Harry had told me about Torness. "My plans are in the process of being changed."

She moved away haughtily. "I'm sure you'll let me know when you've got them straight."

"No, I mean . . . oh, for Christ's sake, sit down, Katharine." I nudged Davie and was greeted with his version of a grizzly on the morning hibernation ends. "Time for a wee chat." I took a gulp of coffee and filled the pair of them in. By the time I finished, neither of them looked very happy.

"Are you sure about this?" Davie asked dubiously. "I never heard any rumours about explosions. If they were that big, wouldn't people in the city have seen or heard something?"

"It's a long way, Davie, and there was cloud cover. Anyway, if you don't believe me, ask your mate with the Grand Canyon in his skull." I turned to Katharine, wondering how many fearful thoughts had just passed through her mind. "Your farm's not many miles inland from Torness, is it?" I said softly.

She nodded, her face registering confusion rather than panic. "I wasn't there then, of course. But none of the others ever mentioned it."

I was trying to work out a way to broach the next difficult topic but Davie steamed in ahead of me.

"Any sheep with two heads?"

Katharine was obviously even further ahead than that. "No," she replied calmly. "And no unexplained illnesses or deaths either. Human or animal."

Feet pounded down the steps.

"Oh, you've finally woken up, have you?" Harry shook his head disapprovingly at Davie.

"You, being a member of the superior race, don't need to sleep, I suppose?" I said.

"That'll be right." Harry let out one of his roaring laughs. "So, have you changed your mind about going ashore for a picnic by the sarcophagus, citizen Quint?"

I felt Katharine and Davie's eyes on me.

"Doesn't sound like a particularly good idea after all," I said.

The bald man laughed again. "You got that right, pal. I wouldn't have let you go anyway. What I can do is take us in to about half a mile range so you can look at the place through binoculars. You're in luck. The cloud's lifting and the pirates must all be stoned. The sea's as empty as a foreigner's wallet after the Tourism Directorate has finished with it."

He thundered back up to the wheelhouse, leaving us to our thoughts. Mine would have done serious damage to a Geiger counter.

Grey, freezing morning that stung my eyes and laid waste to my circulation a couple of minutes after I went up on deck. Straight ahead of us stood the great rectangular block of the power station, stark and incongruous against the snow-covered fields behind. I looked through the binoculars Harry had handed me. The concrete end walls were heavily discoloured but between them bright yellow sheeting covered the entire extent of the central façade.

"Not much sign of damage," Davie muttered.

"Obviously they had to cover it up," Katharine said. "People in the tourist planes would soon have noticed if the place had blown up."

I nodded. "They must have rerouted them inland until they fixed the sheeting. But still . . ." I lowered the bins and rubbed my chin. "If there had been any serious radiation leak, monitors abroad would have picked it up. Not every country in Europe's as chaotic as this island."

Katharine moved nearer, running her lower arms along the rusty deckrail. "What are you getting at, Quint?"

I shrugged. "Maybe it was very localised. Maybe the reactor core wasn't affected."

Davie stood up straight and breathed in deeply, then thought better of it. "Christ, is the air safe around here?"

"I've been in this area dozens of times since the fireworks," Harry shouted from above, then bellowed out a laugh. "Do I look any the worse for it?"

Katharine and I exchanged glances.

"I'm not going any closer though," the big man continued. "So make the most of it."

We did. I scanned the high wire fencing. Yellow signs with the nuclear symbol had been hung every few yards. The fencing extended all the way along the pier which had given the only access to the power station. The Edinburgh land border is miles away and the technicians had to come by boat in the early years of the Enlightenment.

"Quint, what's that?" Katharine had grabbed my arm hard. "Over there by the gate."

I looked through the bins again. Surely not. The words I'd first heard William McEwan use to the senior guardian leaped up like one of the traps laid by the Viet Cong to skewer foot-soldiers in the jungle. It looked like Torness really was the Bone Yard. The unmistakable components of a human skeleton, completely bare of all remnants of flesh and clothing and splayed out in the shape of a St Andrew's cross, were clinging to the densely strung wire.

On the way back to Leith, Harry told us he reckoned the skeleton had been put there to scare dissidents or any other interested parties away from the power station. Maybe they were meant to think the fence was electrified, though there hadn't been much juice coming out of that edifice recently. The Science and Energy Directorate had apparently deserted the place completely. Left it and whatever nuclear nastiness was in it to the east wind and the fauna of what used to be East Lothian.

It was nearly dark by the time Harry navigated his pride and joy back into the Enlightenment Dock. I decided against reminding him to keep quiet about our trip.

"Good luck to you, Davie," he said as we started slithering up the frozen gangplank. "And to you, hard woman. Pity we didn't get the chance to see you fight." He let out a restrained roar. "I'm not wishing you luck, citizen Quint. You're way, way beyond the realms of luck."

I raised a finger to the daft bugger. He was right though. Even if I'd found the Bone Yard, I hadn't got anything to use against the senior guardian. Let alone the madman who'd been practising his butchery skills in the city.

"What are we going to do now?" Katharine asked as we got into the Land-Rover.

"Aye, what next, Quint?" said Davie.

"Stop ganging up on me, will you?" I yelled, burying my hands in my pockets and sinking my chin down on to the jacket that had done such a bad job of keeping the sea air out. I'd suddenly found myself thinking of Roddie Aitken. That was making me feel as blue as Mississippi Fred McDowall when he sang "Standing at the Burial Ground".

Chapter Eighteen

We headed down Ferry Road towards Trinity. I wanted to call in at the retirement home to let my old man know I was all right. On the way I turned my mobile back on. Less than a minute passed before Hamilton was on my case.

"Dalrymple? Where the hell have you been?" His voice was tense.

"What's happened?" My heart missed a beat as the idea that the killer had struck again hit me.

"Nothing's happened, man." That couldn't be right. He sounded like a ferret had crawled into his auxiliary-issue long johns. "I've been ringing your number every half-hour and getting unobtainable.".

"Oh." I tried to play it cool. "I've been checking out various archives. I forgot I'd turned it off."

"And where's Hume 253? I haven't been able to raise him either. What have you been doing with that 'ask no questions' I issued? I suppose you think I was born yesterday." With his heavy beard, he'd have been a big draw in the infirmary's neo-natal ward. "Anyway, what have you got to report at tonight's Council meeting?"

That was a good question. I turned the question back on him while I scrabbled around for something to fob his colleagues off with. Unfortunately he had even less than I did. It was going to be a fun evening.

❋   ❋   ❋

We were in luck. The senior guardian was preoccupied – I'd like to have known what with – and let Hamilton and me off the hook.

I went back to the flat and found Katharine asleep on the sofa. Her face wasn't tense like it was when she was awake and she looked much younger. I put my hand out and, without touching her, moved it slowly downwards above her short hair and the contours of her cheek and jaw. I had a sudden flash of her as she straddled me in my armchair a couple of years ago, her neck taut as she simultaneously forced herself down on me and bent her upper body back. The fact that I hadn't attended a sex session for nearly a fortnight suddenly became very apparent.

Then I heard someone begin to pound up the stair in archetypal guard fashion. So did Katharine. She was instantly awake, sitting up and at the ready. Her face was lined again, the moment of repose gone.

Davie shouldered open the door, carrying a large movable feast in both hands. "Guess what I've got here," he said, looking pleased with himself.

"Rations stolen from ordinary citizens?" Katharine asked with a sour smile.

"Shut up, will you?" I hissed, stuffing a tape of Council-approved folk music into my machine. I didn't want anyone to hear what we were about to discuss, let alone notice that I'd acquired a non-paying lodger who featured on the Deserters Register.

"You don't have to have any of it if your heavy-duty moral scruples get in the way," Davie said to Katharine.

That was it. I'd had it with them. "You're a pair of tossers," I shouted. "We've got our noses in all sorts of forbidden places and all you two can do is take the piss out of each other." I gave them the sulphuric acid glare I inherited from my mother. I've practised it a lot less than she did but it seemed to get through to them. "I'm not joking. Either give me some decent back-up or fuck off out the door."

They both looked pretty sheepish.

"So what have you got there, Davie?" I asked after a strained silence.

"Em, right, there's a pot of barracks stew, with decent meat in it "—he poked around in the dark brown contents of a cast-iron pan—" well, semi-decent meat."

Katharine's nose twitched dubiously.

"And wholemeal bread," Davie continued, "barracks beer, apple crumble and – wait for it – real cream."

"Real cream?" Katharine leaned forward, an interested expression on her face. "Where did you get that?"

"What's it to you?" Davie looked affronted. "You reckon I took this—"

"You remember where the door is, don't you, guardsman?" I said, burning him with the acid look again.

He glanced over his shoulder then sat down at the table. "It came from the guard kitchens," he muttered. "If it's any business of—"

"I'm not joking, Davie," I yelled.

We settled down to eat to the strains of bagpipes and fiddles. It could have been worse. At least there weren't any accordions.

"Right, team, we have to talk." I pushed my plate away and emptied my glass of barracks heavy.

Katharine took the armchair, leaving Davie to join me on the sofa. "It's about time we sorted things out, Quint," she said. "I haven't got a clue what we're doing and I don't think you have either."

"Thank you for that constructive opening."

"I'd have to go along with her there, Quint," Davie said, keeping his eyes off me.

"You as well? Now I really know who my friends are." I pulled out my notepad and started flicking through the pages. That didn't get me much further. "Okay. Review of where we stand. The cruise on your pal Harry's floating shipwreck wasn't a complete waste of time."

"That is reassuring," Katharine said.

It was her turn for the vitriolic look. "We've got confirmation that something disastrous happened at the power station near the end of 2019."

"Aye, but what's that got to do with these murders?" Davie said, opening his arms wide like a drunken tourist who's forgotten where his hotel is.

"That's the difficult bit." I drew a square on my pad, wrote "Torness" in it then sketched in the coastline. "How far's your farm from the power station again, Katharine?"

"About ten miles, I suppose. We never go that way because of the—"

"Because of the gangs," I interrupted. "In particular, because of the gang led by the headcase known as the Screecher?"

She nodded. "So?"

"So maybe the Screecher got nosy and took a trip over the fence."

"In which case, either they were his bones on the wire," said Davie, "or he glows in the dark."

"He might have sent one of his minions in," I said.

Katharine leaned forward and nodded her head. "He had a nuclear physicist in his gang, remember? Maybe the Screecher found him at the power station."

"Maybe," I said. "And maybe the Screecher used what he learned from him to put the squeeze on someone in the Council. By threatening to spread the word about the explosions."

Davie's hand came down hard on my knee. "Don't piss about, Quint. We all know the senior guardian's the most likely person to have had the squeeze put on him – Science and Energy is his directorate. Are you sure about this?"

"No," I said with a hollow laugh. "Except there are those files missing from the directorate archive. The ones you know who's probably got in his private library."

Katharine sat back, shaking her head. "Even if you sneaked a look at them, they wouldn't necessarily show any link to what's been going on in the last couple of months."

"True enough." I flicked through the pages again. This time I felt a couple of twinges. The first had to do with the toxicologist, but I let that one go for the moment. The second was much more pressing. Roddie Aitken had just made another appearance in my thoughts.

"What have you come up with?" Davie asked.

"Is it that obvious?"

"You're smirking like a kid who's got off border duty by playing with himself during his assessment."

Katharine yawned. "I'd have thought that would get him a permanent transfer into the City Guard."

"Children," I said, glaring them into submission. "Answer me this. As outlined in the manual I wrote for the directorate, what's the basic rule of investigating practice?"

Davie scratched his beard. "Always triangulate data?" he suggested without much confidence.

"Wrong, guardsman," Katharine said with a superior smile. "Always compare initial evidence and statements with subsequent data." It was a long time since she'd done her auxiliary training, but what I wrote in the *Public Order in Practice* manual seemed to have stuck.

"Very good. Unfortunately I haven't been following my own instructions."

"Meaning what?" Davie demanded, pissed off that a demoted auxiliary who was also a deserter had shown him up.

"Meaning that, in all this chaos, we've forgotten about the first victim."

Now Katharine was looking puzzled. "The young man? I assumed he had something to do with the Electric Blues."

I shook my head. "We never found any evidence of that. And he definitely didn't strike me as a drug trafficker."

Davie got up and went back to the table. What was left of the apple crumble did a disappearing act. "Me neither," he mumbled with his mouth full.

"What are you saying, Quint?" Katharine asked.

"I'm saying that tomorrow morning we hit the Delivery Department files and find out his movements over the last few weeks."

"But I've been through those files," Davie said.

"Yes, but we weren't particularly interested in where he'd been delivering, were we? Maybe he went somewhere that's linked with the drugs. Like, for instance, where they're produced."

He nodded, not looking too convinced. Soon afterwards he went back to his billet. Katharine went to bed and didn't move when I lay down on the other side. I left a space between us which she didn't move into. I didn't feel confident enough to stake a claim. As I drifted off, thankful at least that the bed wasn't moving up and down like dirty Harry's ship of fools, I remembered the oath I'd sworn. I'd been ignoring Roddie, but I was back on track now. I didn't care about the other two victims much, though even corrupt auxiliaries don't deserve to die the way they did. But I cared about Roddie and his killer was going to find that out. I slept surprisingly well that night.

The next morning was warmer and the snow was gone from the streets. It had turned into huge amounts of water that the works buses were spraying over citizens on the pavements. Their faces were even more sullen than they usually are first thing.

Davie steered the Land-Rover down to the Supply Directorate depot off the Canongate. In pre-Enlightenment times it had been part of Waverley station, but the Council blocked the railway lines leading in and out of the city soon after independence. That was part of their policy of securing the borders and getting a grip on the drugs gangs. The fact that it enabled them to control everything that went on in the city was purely incidental, of course.

The depot is gigantic, nearly half a mile long. The sentry at the gate took one look at the guard vehicle and waved us through without checking our IDs, which meant that Katharine didn't have to show her "ask no questions". I'd wondered about bringing her along – if we ran into Hamilton and he recognised her, we'd be in serious shit – but on balance it seemed safer to keep an eye on her. God knows what she'd have got up to on her own.

We drove into the great covered area. Rows of packing cases and piles of stores stretched away into the distance. In the early days the Council decided to concentrate all the city's supplies in one heavily guarded location to discourage thieving. That had the additional advantage of providing huge numbers of jobs for citizens involved in recording, packing and delivering the stuff. In fact, that may have been the only advantage because there's probably more pilfering and black-market-controlled stealing now than there ever was before.

Davie drove down the central passage towards the office section. We passed great heaps of potatoes and turnips, the bitter-sweet stink from the latter invading the Land-Rover; then boxes full of cheap clothes run up in the Council's sweatshops, not that the guardians refer to them as such; and finally, shelves full of the tattered books that are bought in on the cheap from other cities' ransacked libraries. Personnel from the Information Directorate's Censorship Department were sorting through them, tossing the rejects into crates marked "For Burning". The Council gets more heat from books than it does from the nuclear power station at Torness. There must be some sort of moral in that.

Katharine was shaking her head. "There's enough food in here to keep the city going for years."

Davie nodded. "Aye, and this depot doesn't handle the meat. You should see how much of that they've got in the cold stores at Slateford."

That reminded me of the Bone Yard. Not long ago I thought it might have something to do with the slaughterhouses in that part of the city. Something about that idea still nagged at me.

"So why are Edinburgh citizens all so thin and hungry-looking?" Katharine was saying. "Why doesn't the Council increase the entitlement to food vouchers?"

Davie shrugged, looking away as he pulled into a parking space beside a Supply Directorate delivery van that was held together with wire.

"Don't forget the tourists," I said as I opened the door. "They get first bite at the cherry. And at the sirloin steak."

Davie slammed the door on his side. "Sirloin steak?" he asked. "What's that, then?"

The deliveries supervisor, a middle-aged woman with grey hair and the wan look of someone who's seen it all and isn't convinced it was worth the bother, greeted us without enthusiasm. But at least she was efficient.

"All the delivery documentation pertaining to Roderick Aitken was removed from the main archive after his death. I will have it sent up to the meeting room for you to inspect." She gave Davie a sceptical glance from behind the stacks of files on her desk. "I hope you get more out it than you did the last time you were here, Hume 253."

We went up grimy stairs to a room furnished with a table and chairs that wouldn't have found space in a junk shop in the old days. No one could accuse Supply Directorate staff of creaming off quality goods to brighten up their place of work. I looked out of dirty windows at the scene that stretched across the depot's endless concrete floor. Forklifts raced around like crazed dung beetles, loading and discharging, endlessly moving things from one location to another. Armies of staff paraded around with clipboards, checking deliveries off and distributing bits of paper. The system seemed to work but it didn't exactly make you rejoice in the regime. A single computer would have saved an awful lot of hassle. But then there'd be citizens hanging around with nothing to do and the Council couldn't have that.

A couple of porters arrived with our very own collection of delivery sheets, waybills, receipts and rosters. We settled down to the kind of job that archivists dream about. I had some fun but the others struggled. After an hour we compared notes.

"There doesn't seem to be any pattern to the goods he delivered over the last three months," Katharine said, pushing away the files she'd been working on. "New carpets to tourist hotels, fruit, vegetables and other supplies to food stores, beer to the citizens' bars. About the only thing he hasn't delivered is sex aids to the recreation centres."

"The old hands keep that job for themselves," Davie said with a grin.

"What about you?" I asked.

He pulled a face that suggested he'd been wasting his time too. "No pattern with the vehicles he's been driving either." I'd put him on to that in case there were any Roddie had been assigned frequently; we could then have looked for a secret compartment where drugs might have been stashed. "Transits, Renaults, some Polish contraptions I can't pronounce the name of. They even had him on a bicycle distributing styluses for the record players in the tourist clubs." He raised his shoulders. "Nothing regular."

"Which leaves me," I said, giving them a triumphant smile. "And I've got several goodies."

"Oh, aye?" Davie came round the table.

"What is it, Quint?" Katharine kept to her chair, but her voice betrayed her interest.

"What I've got is three places where he made more than six visits in the last month of his life, i.e. December. I haven't gone any further back yet. I reckon any lead will be recent rather than months in the past."

"I wish you'd told me that," Davie complained.

"Why do you think the frequency of visits is important?"

Katharine said, ignoring him. "Surely he could have gone only once or twice to the place we're after?"

"You're right, he could have. But let's hope he didn't. Otherwise we're going to be driving around the city for the rest of our lives."

She nodded. "Fair enough. So where are these three places?"

"Number one, the zoo."

"Animal feed," Katharine said, checking her notes.

"Yup. Number two, a sawmill near a village called Temple about ten miles south of the city."

"Pine slats, two by fours and dormitory partitions."

"Right again. And number three, Slaughterhouse Four at Slateford."

"Don't tell me," said Davie. "Sirloin steak."

Katharine actually laughed at that. "Among other things. So where do we go first?"

I knew where I wanted to go first. It was finally time to check out the city's meat production facilities.

"How are we going to manage this on our own?" Katharine asked as we came out of the depot.

"We aren't," I replied. "If we're going to have any chance of finding the laboratory that's been producing the Electric Blues, we're going to need expert help."

She thought for a moment then turned to me with a satisfied smile. "The toxicologist."

"Correct. Head for the King's Buildings, Davie."

He turned down St Mary's Street, glancing at me as he span the wheel. "Won't we need some back-up, Quint?"

"You mean, shouldn't we inform Hamilton?" I asked with a laugh.

He wasn't impressed and gave both of us the benefit of his guardsman's assault glare. "That as well. I seem to remember a lot of references in your handbook to keeping senior officers fully informed."

"True enough," I said. "But that handbook was written for serving auxiliaries, not demoted ones like me."

"And me," put in Katharine.

"Also, telling Hamilton and calling in more guard personnel to help with the operation will mean that what we're doing gets leaked within half an hour. I don't want that. Don't worry, Davie, I've got to report to the Council tonight. I just don't want to give any advance warning of this line of enquiry."

I braced myself as he slammed his foot on the brakes at the junction with the Cowgate. Five or six cattle galloped nervously towards the Grassmarket, the herdsmen in medieval costume being applauded by a small group of tourists who presumably had nothing better to do with their time. At least those cows had escaped the city's slaughterhouses – for the time being.

I left Katharine and Davie in the Land-Rover outside the labs and went to find the chief toxicologist. This time he wasn't listening to Robert Johnson in his private quarters, but was supervising a team of white-coated, masked, rubber-gloved chemists who were siphoning off a clear liquid with extreme caution.

The toxicologist saw me through the glass panel. I gathered from his energetic semaphore that he didn't want me to come any closer.

"Citizen Dalrymple," he said as he eventually emerged, pulling down his mask. "You caught me at a very delicate procedural juncture."

Classic senior auxiliary gibberish. "What is it you've got in there?" I asked.

He looked around to see that we were alone. "It's a new variant of the e. coli virus. We found it in some salami that a Danish tourist imported illegally."

"Jesus. Has anyone been infected by it?"

He shook his head. "The man himself was repatriated the day he arrived and no other samples of the meat have been found."

"Thank Christ for that."

The chemist laughed, the folds of flesh on his face wobbling alarmingly. "Don't worry. It happens all the time."

"Right," I said, not particularly reassured. "If things are under control here, can you spare me some time?" I told him about the search for the Electric Blues lab.

He looked intrigued, then his face fell. "Wait a minute, citizen. Does the Council know about this?"

I pulled out my authorisation. "As you can see, you're required to give me all the assistance I want."

"You aren't answering my question," he said, his jowls quivering.

"Look, the Council will be briefed about this tonight." I could see he was wavering. I considered putting him on the spot for his addiction to banned music, then I thought of a better way. "Have you lost any senior staff in the last six months or so, Lister 25?"

He looked at me in surprise. "It's funny you should mention that, citizen. I was going to call you after your last visit but it slipped my mind. Lister 436. She was an excellent toxicologist – I'd been grooming her to take over from my present deputy. Then she was suddenly transferred to the senior guardian's private office last . . . let me see . . . last November, it must have been. Yes, late last November. I haven't heard from her since." Then he looked at me again, his wrinkled skin turning an even sicklier yellow shade than normal. "Surely you don't think she's been involved in the production of that drug?"

I didn't think it was necessary to answer that question. "Are you coming to see if we can find the lab?"

The chemist already had his white coat off. "If I find that a student of mine's been producing a substance like that, there'll be serious trouble."

He may have looked like an elephant that's been on a crash diet, but I wasn't planning on getting in his way.

Slaughterhouse Four is one of the many parts of Edinburgh that the tourists don't see. At first glance it doesn't seem like a place of death, unless the wind happens to be blowing towards you from it. The main block is a large Edwardian building with high windows and saucer domes at the corners. In the field and yards in front of it doomed sheep and cattle give a rustic touch to the rundown urban surroundings of soot-blackened housing and potholed roads.

"Right, we're going to have to be quick," I said as Davie pulled up outside the checkpoint. "If there is something illicit going on here, whoever's involved will clear out as soon as they hear we're about the place." I looked at the toxicologist on the front seat beside me. "I'm not going to spell out to the facility supervisors what we're after. When they see you, they'll probably assume it's something to do with hygiene or infection control."

"Are we going to split up?" Katharine asked from behind.

I nodded. "You go with Davie. If you see anything that looks like a lab, call me. Lister 25 and I will check out the resident science officer first."

As we cleared the sentry post, a heavy drizzle started to fall, weighing down our clothes with an evil-smelling spray in the few seconds it took us to get inside the abbatoir. Instantly the mild bleating and lowing from the animals ouside was replaced by the rattle of the machinery on the killing line and a high-pitched shrieking that made my stomach flip.

As I heard the heavy steel door clang behind me, I suddenly wondered where the butcher of humans had been since he decapitated Machiavelli. He'd been quiet for too long. I was sure of one thing, though. He'd feel very much at home in Slaughterhouse Four.

Chapter Nineteen

———◦◦◦◦◦———

I've been through a lot of post-mortems but they don't compare with Slaughterhouse Four. The most diligent serial killer would have to work weeks of overtime to get into the league of mayhem that's staged there every day. I'd consider turning vegetarian if the Supply Directorate could come up with alternative sources of protein, but soya and pulses don't exactly flourish in the city's farms.

The toxicologist and I put on protective overalls and walked up the killing line. The animals can't be stunned electrically because of the power shortages, so big men in blood-spattered clothing club them with round-ended iron bars. The petrified squealing is enough to make you lose yesterday's breakfast as well as today's. Then chains are lashed around rear ankles and the jerking carcasses are winched up. Slaughtermen with long-bladed knives wait for them down the line, yelling and joking to each other. You'd think they'd be disgusted by their work but people get used to anything. A spray of warm red liquid lashed across my chest, making me jerk backwards.

Lister 45 grabbed my sleeve and pointed to the right. There was a double door that had been secured with a heavy chain.

I indicated it to the auxiliary who'd been assigned to us. "What's in there?"

He put his mouth up to my ear and shouted above the din

from the conveyor belt. "The Halal line. For the Moslem tourists, you know? We're not allowed to go in from this side."

That sounded interesting. Even though the numbers of Moslem tourists has fallen recently because of the unrest in the Middle East, there are still a good few around. And the region does have a historical involvement in the drugs trade. Could there be a connection with the Electric Blues?

"Open it up," I said, beating the auxiliary's doubtful look down without having to pull out my authorisation.

He eventually managed to turn the key in the padlock and the door swung slowly open. The Halal line is in a poorly constructed extension to the main building, angled so it faces Mecca. There's no conveyor belt so the slaughtermen get very close to their victims. Pairs of bearded guys in bloody aprons were wrestling sheep to the floor and cutting their throats. In the background a Moslem clergyman was reciting from a book. All of them looked up and stared at us with undisguised hostility as we came in.

I walked past the holy man, who had rushed up and started to gesticulate wildly. There was a small room to the rear and I could see a couple of men in white coats through the glass door. They turned to me too, but they weren't aggressive, they were just proud of their work. They held their hands out to me as I shoved open the door. Each contained the glassy jelly of a sheep's eye.

"Thanks, but no thanks," I said, swallowing what had just arrived in my mouth.

The toxicologist came in, ran a practised eye around the place and shook his head. "We're wasting our time, citizen," he said. "Let's leave before these people get really annoyed."

We left the Moslems to it and rejoined the Enlightenment's atheist killing line. There isn't much to choose between them really. But as far as I'm concerned death isn't a religious matter – it's much more serious than that.

"Nothing," said Davie, pulling off his protective overalls. "We've been through the admin block, the packaging area and the coldstores. He shivered. "And they're bloody cold, I can tell you. There was no sign of anything like a lab."

Katharine nodded in agreement, gulping tea from one of the mugs that the supervisor had sent in to us. We were in what passes for a meeting room in Slaughterhouse Four. It must be one of the few rooms in the facility that doesn't have blood on the walls.

"Same here, I'm afraid," I said. "We did the sheep lines – ordinary and Halal – and the cattle." I'd discovered from the supervisor that pigs, poultry (including pigeons trapped at night in the city centre) and what are called "other sources of meat" (horses, donkeys and clapped-out camels and the like from the zoo) are processed in Slaughterhouses One to Three. But Roddie Aitken hadn't made many pick-ups or deliveries to those.

"Are you sure this is sensible, citizen?" Lister 25 asked, his wrinkled face partially hidden behind a mug. "I mean, if I were setting up a lab to produce illicit drugs, I wouldn't do so in a slaughterhouse."

I shrugged. "Maybe this was just a transit point. The Electric Blues might be made elsewhere then brought here for onward distribution." I looked round their pale faces and wondered how many of us would be stuffing our faces with meat that night. "And maybe I'm just following a lead up my own backside."

Davie turned up his nose. "In that case, I want a transfer back to the castle before you make me go the same way."

"Not yet, my friend." I headed for the door. "There are still two other locations to check, remember? Meanwhile, I've got to go and spin a yarn to the Council."

Outside it was pitch dark beyond the narrow ring of light by the slaughterhouse entrance. From the pens there came the sighing and coughing of invisible animals. They wouldn't be there for long. Like all the city's killing lines, Slaughterhouse Four works non-stop shifts. But the main beneficiaries aren't ordinary Edinburgh citizens. Our meat is rationed, while the tourists pay Third World prices for prime beef. That's the perfect city's version of equality.

Hamilton was waiting for me on the ground floor of the Assembly Hall. I'd deliberately timed my arrival to minimise his chances of picking my brains before the meeting.

"What the bloody hell have you been up to, Dalrymple?" he growled. "I heard a report that you've been poking around one of the slaughterhouses."

As I expected, it hadn't taken long for news of our activities to get back to him. "Don't worry," I said. "You'll hear all about it at the meeting."

"Did you find anything?" the guardian asked as we went up the stairs towards the Council chamber.

"Not a sausage," I said with a tight smile.

"What?" He followed me in, looking bewildered.

There was already a gaggle of guardians around the chief boyscout. He looked over their heads as I approached and watched me with a serene expression which didn't convince me for a moment.

"Well, citizen Dalrymple, have you anything to report?" he asked, an almost undetectable edge to his voice. "Anything at all?"

So that was the way he wanted it. "Yes, I have," I replied, smiling as he blinked involuntarily. I was sure he knew where I'd been, but it would be interesting to see how he reacted. I wasn't planning on telling him my line of thinking though. "We picked up a lead that linked Roddie Aitken with Slaughterhouse Four in Slateford."

"What was the nature of that lead, citizen?" The senior guardian was watching me as closely as I was watching him. The other guardians had stepped back a couple of paces to follow the duel.

"Supply Directorate records show that there were three locations that Roddie visited frequently. One was Slaughterhouse Four." No visible changes on the chief boyscout's face.

"Unfortunately, there was no sign of a lab capable of producing the Electric Blues."

"And what are the other two locations?" the senior guardian asked quietly. Too quietly, even by his standards. I reckoned there were knitting-needle teeth like a Moray eel's behind those saintly lips and I wasn't going to take any chances.

"The Three Graces club was one," I lied. "We've already taken that to pieces."

The chief boyscout kept after me. "And the other?" The tone of his voice rose a touch higher than the question required. I was sure he was desperate to know whether I was on to the lab.

I felt Hamilton's eyes on me. There was no option, but I felt a stab of guilt as I condemned him and a lot of his personnel to a wasted night. "The other?" I said, squeezing the moments for all they were worth. "The other is the City Distillery in Fountainbridge."

The skin on the senior guardian's face slackened just enough for me to know that he'd bought my dummy. So had Hamilton.

"The distillery?" he said incredulously. "It'll take us days to search that rabbit-warren, man."

It wouldn't, but he'd certainly be tied up long enough to give me the chance to check out the other places. I wasn't happy about messing him around, but I had to make sure the senior guardian knew nothing about where I was really heading until I had enough evidence to confront him.

"We'll get going as soon as the meeting's finished," I said, trying not to look too enthusiastic.

"The meeting has finished for you, citizen," said the chief boyscout, moving down the chamber with his flock of acolytes. "You are excused the rest of the proceedings as well, guardian."

Lewis Hamilton should have been embarrassed at being treated in that offhand way by someone so much younger, but as we walked out he was beaming more than a poor man who'd won the lottery in the days before the last British government rigged the draw in favour of cabinet members.

Obviously he hated meetings with the iron boyscouts as much as I did.

The next few hours needed careful planning. Before Hamilton and I went to the distillery with a couple of squads of guards, I called Davie and asked him to start checking out the zoo with the chief toxicologist. I also told Katharine to wait for me at my flat.

And then I pretended to be totally committed to the farce that I'd set up in the distillery. On the face of it, there was a reasonable chance that one of the city's two whisky-producing facilities concealed a drugs lab, given the presence of chemists and suitably equipped premises. In fact, it had occurred to me in the Council meeting that if the chief boyscout didn't have other things on his mind, he might have asked me why I'd visited the slaughterhouse before the potentially more suspicious distillery.

Hamilton and his white-overalled staff had great fun stomping around the ramshackle distillery. Thirty years ago it was a state-of-the-art plant, but during the Enlightenment it's been allowed to run down because of lack of funds. There's never been any question of cutting back whisky supplies to citizens and auxiliaries though, despite the guardians' own abstinence. Whisky and beer are the legalised opiates in their utopia.

After a couple of hours, I decided to leave Lewis to it. "There are some things here I want to check in the archives," I said, waving a sheaf of papers I'd abstracted from the facility supervisor's files.

"You can't go now, Dalrymple," the guardian said, looking round from a steel cabinet in the one of the labs. The distillery chemist was sitting in the corner with his head in his hands as one of Lister 25's staff painstakingly disassembled a maze of glass tubes, balloons and beakers. "We're making excellent progress."

Except you're going to find even less of a sausage than we did at Slaughterhouse Four, I thought.

"I won't be long." I walked away quickly and he didn't follow.

Outside, my planning hit a rough patch – transport. Davie had the Land-Rover at the zoo. I didn't fancy having a guard driver with me where I was going so I commandeered the nearest vehicle, a pick-up truck with more rust than is on what's left of the Forth Rail Bridge, and had another go at remembering how to drive. The last time Katharine almost bailed out. My technique didn't seem to have got much better. I swerved out on to the main road and missed one of the city's garbage trucks by the length of my forefinger – the one that's short a couple of joints.

I called Davie and asked how he was getting on.

"Nothing so far," he replied. "We've done the clinic, the foodstores and the admin block."

"Watch out for the peccaries," I said.

"What?"

"Nothing. I'm on my way to pick up Katharine."

"What are you driving?" he asked suspiciously. "More to the point, how are you driving?"

"Very safely indeed."

"Oh, aye."

I signed off. The jokes were over. Now I had to drive ten miles out of the city in pitch darkness through numerous guard checkpoints. I hoped it was going to be worth it.

The curfew was well under way and I had enough trouble even navigating to my own flat.

"About time," Katharine said as she climbed in. "I've been bored stiff up there."

I headed for the junction. "Jesus!" Katharine put her hands out in time to stop her head hitting the windscreen.

"Sorry. Bloody guard. They drive like lunatics."

"They're not the only ones. Didn't you see them, Quint?"

I was leaning forward like a myopic pensioner. "The lights on this thing are about as much use as a guardian in a drinking competition."

Somehow we made it past the checkpoints that the guard have erected at every mile-post without any more near misses. Katharine called ahead on the mobile before we reached each one and we only had to flash our "ask no questions". Apart from guard patrols, the roads were empty and completely unlit. It was like driving through a desert, although the temperature was a bit lower than the Gobi even on a bad night. Then we came out of a dip in the road about five miles out and were blinded by the lights of one of the city's coal mines. They work round the clock like the slaughterhouses. I spent some time down one after I was demoted. Cutting sheep's throats is probably only slightly more unpleasant, especially if being two thousand feet underground in a dripping, gas-ridden tunnel gets to you.

We turned off and were enveloped by the night again. Now there were tall trees on both sides of us, bending over the road ahead like great predators about to pounce. The pick-up's engine suddenly coughed, making both of us jump. You can be sure that the limited quantity of diesel the Council imports is the scrapings from the bottom of the oil companies' tanks; they don't give a shit about a city that has banned private cars.

We came to a crossroads that was unmarked. Since citizens' movements are carefully controlled and the drivers in the Transportation and Supply Directorates know where they're going, the guardians have dispensed with signposts. It takes you back to Britain during the Second World War, except that people knew who the enemy was then. These days that isn't so clear.

Eventually we reached the last checkpoint before our destination.

"Blue Sector Sawmill?" I asked the guardswoman on duty.

"Straight ahead, about three-quarters of a mile. What are you doing out here at this time of night?" She flashed her torch at us, holding it on my face.

I leaned out and pushed the beam down. The last thing I needed now was an eager auxiliary calling in to the guard command centre and reporting my presence out here. I held out our "ask no questions" and hoped that the guardswoman wasn't old enough to have known me when I was in the Public Order Directorate. There wasn't any sign of recognition. Usually young auxiliaries on their first tours of duty are the ones who get stuck on their own in the middle of nowhere. It's supposed to be good for their characters.

I accelerated away, following the road as it ran along the edge of a steep valley. I had a vague recollection of being driven out here to visit some friends of my parents when I was a kid. My old man told me that the village of Temple on the other side of the river had historical associations with the Knights Templar. I had a sudden vision of men in chain mail and white tunics emblazoned with red crosses, men who used a higher purpose like religion to justify slaughter. For some reason that made me think of the senior guardian.

"I can see a light ahead," said Katharine, bending forward to squint through the cracked windscreen.

It was the single maroon lamp displayed by facilities manned by City Guard personnel. We traversed a couple of humpbacks in the road, but that wasn't why I was feeling queasy. Davie hadn't called in with anything from the zoo, so this was it. If we didn't find something here, it would be back to letting the killer call the shots. And to being used as a urinal by the chief boyscout. Apparently even saints have to empty their bladders somewhere.

The auxiliary who appeared at the sawmill gate was built like a lumberjack, though the Supply Directorate hadn't managed to come up with an appropriate checked shirt. He rubbed his eyes and screwed them up when he saw the "ask no questions".

"What is it you're after?" he asked suspiciously, admitting us into a Victorian farm courtyard stacked with piles of wood. "We don't work a night shift here, you know."

"I need to see all the rooms in the facility," I said, putting on the standard do-what-I-say-or-it's-the-mines-for-you voice that undercover operatives affect when they're checking up on their colleagues.

The auxiliary wasn't impressed – he was old enough to have been through this kind of idiocy dozens of times – but he went into what was obviously the office and threw some switches. The steading was flooded in light, the ornate gables and casements looking as incongruous as a sober tourist in the Grassmarket after midnight. In the nineteenth century it wasn't a crime to embellish places of work. The Council prefers breezeblocks and concrete.

We followed the lumberjack, who turned out to be the sawmill supervisor, into the various storehouses, cutting yards, machine rooms and accommodation areas. The auxiliary dormitory was well-behaved, shiny-faced guardsmen blinking in the unshaded overhead light; but the citizen workers were rebellious, at first grumbling about being woken up then running their eyes hungrily over Katharine. They get drafted for month-long tours of duty and there are no sex sessions during that time, so I couldn't really blame them. Katharine returned their stares blankly and one by one they lowered their eyes.

All of which would have been fascinating for a social psychologist studying the effect of enforced labour, but it got us nowhere. The nearest thing to a sophisticated chemical lab was the wood treatment room and the nearest thing to dangerous chemicals were the drums of creosote lining the walls.

The auxiliary led us back to his office and offered us tea. "I don't suppose you want to tell me what that was all about?" he asked over his shoulder as he tinkered with a guard-issue spirit stove.

He seemed like a pretty reasonable guy. He was past middle age, probably one of the original breed of auxiliaries who used to believe in the Council's aims and now aren't so sure. I decided to satisfy his curiosity. You never know what you might pick up if you treat people like human beings.

"We're on the trail of some illicit material," I said. "There's a chance it moved between here and the main depot."

The lumberjack turned round and faced me. I suddenly noticed that the whites of his eyes were cloudy and wondered how much he could see. That was maybe why he'd been posted out here, where all the damage he could do was to his own fingers on the circular saw.

"What kind of material would that be then?"

"I don't think you want to know that, my friend."

"That bad?" He handed a mug to Katharine. "There you are, lady." He was running the risk of getting his head in his hands to play with using that form of address with her, but she didn't seem to regard him as a threat. Or a patronising arsehole. "Well, was there a particular driver involved?"

There didn't seem to be much harm in telling him that.

"Roddie Aitken?" he said, his face breaking into a grin beneath the shag pile of his beard. "Good lad, Roddie. What's he been up to?" Obviously the guard jungle drums hadn't been beating this far out of Edinburgh.

I looked down at the mug he was holding out to me. "He ... he had an accident." I didn't have the stomach to be more precise.

"Nothing serious, I hope." The auxiliary gulped from his own mug. "Must be a couple of weeks since I last saw him."

I nodded. "The manifests say he was picking up different kinds of wood."

"Aye, that's right." The lumberjack nodded, then his eyes shifted slowly away from mine.

It was one of those moments when you suddenly realise you're on the brink of something big. You don't get much warning, only a couple of seconds when the hairs on the back of your neck rise as if a barn dance has just started on your grave.

"Course, he wasn't only collecting from us," the auxiliary said, rubbing his afflicted eyes again then giving a strangely melancholic smile. "There were some packages that came down from the other place too. Only they never say anything about it in the documentation."

I was suddenly finding breathing difficult. "The other place?" I asked hoarsely. "What other place? I didn't see any lights except the one above your gate." I glanced at Katharine.

"Me neither," she said, her gaze locked on the auxiliary.

He shook his head. "Oh, there's no light over there at night. Most of the poor sods behind the walls prefer the darkness. Not that they have much choice."

I slammed my mug down on his desk, splashing hot liquid on the back of my hand. "For God's sake, what is this other place?" I shouted.

He gazed back at us then sighed like an aged wise man finally giving in to his disciples' demands for enlightenment.

"The other place?" he repeated in a low, unwavering voice. "You won't have heard of it. Most of the guardians don't even know it exists."

"What?" Katharine said incredulously. Even she was losing her cool.

The sawmill supervisor blinked his lustreless eyes. "They call it the Bone Yard."

Chapter Twenty

"So you have heard of it," the lumberjack said. He could obviously see more than I thought. He was smiling faintly at the expression of shock on my face. It must have rivalled Agamemnon's when his wife produced an axe in the bathroom at Mycenae. Then the auxiliary's voice hardened. "That means you must be working for the fuckers in the Science and Energy Directorate."

Still struggling to get my head round what was going on, I waved my hands at him ineffectually. "Public Order Directorate," I gasped. "Special investigator."

He sat down again, looking marginally less ferocious. "Well, there's plenty to investigate up there, I'll tell you that for nothing."

"Come on, Katharine," I said. "Let's get going."

Throughout this exchange she'd been motionless, an inscrutable look on her face.

The lumberjack let out a long, deep laugh that wouldn't have been out of place in a cemetery at midnight. "Your Council authorisation won't get you anywhere up there, citizen special investigator. The guards will be on to the Science and Energy Directorate before you can blink." He leaned forward and looked at both of us. "I get the impression you'd like what you're doing to stay a secret for as long as possible. Am I right?"

I nodded at him and smiled. There used to be a fair number of auxiliaries like him in the early years of the Enlightenment — people who hadn't forgotten what it was like to be a normal human being rather than a Council slave.

"There's a ten-foot stone wall with barbed wire on the top all the way round the place," the lumberjack said. "The only gate's in front of the old house. The wankers up there reckon their security's tighter than the prison on Cramond Island's."

"What exactly goes on up there?" Katharine asked.

The auxiliary examined his hands with their swollen fingers for a few moments. "What they say they do — not that they ever say much since they're a squad of specially chosen lunatics who never go back to the city and have as little to do with us as they can — what they say they do is dispose of cattle with new strains of BSE. That's why the place is guarded so closely. Supply deliveries and pick-ups are made here, supposedly to avoid any chance of contamination. We do see cattle trucks going up the road occasionally." He opened his clouded eyes at me knowingly. "Very occasionally."

I leaned forward into the ring of light round his desk. "But there's more to it than that, isn't there?"

"Aye, there is," the auxiliary said, nodding slowly. But I don't know what. You'll have to find that out for yourself." Suddenly he gave me a conspiratorial wink. "Bell 03."

His use of my former barracks number showed he knew who I used to be. I wondered if he'd recognised me the minute we arrived. Perhaps he'd served with me in the directorate. There wasn't time to ask.

"Can you get us inside?" I said.

He shook his head. "Forget it. I'm quite attached to this posting and I don't want to lose it. Not even for you." He smiled at me apologetically as he tugged his beard with his fingertips. At least he wasn't one of those guardsmen like Harry who held it against me that their friends had been killed in the drug wars. "But I will tell you the best place to get a look over the walls. After that you're on your own."

I glanced at Katharine. She shrugged, apparently unconcerned by the prospect of trying to penetrate a high-security facility. She was used to being on her own. So was I, but this was carrying things to extremes.

The lumberjack was unrolling a detailed City Guard map. Katharine and I gathered round like carrion crows alighting on a carcass. Except I had the feeling that this particular carcass still had a fair amount of life in it.

We went back the way we came for a mile then took the pick-up down a narrow lane that ran past a pine wood, driving slowly with only the sidelights on. The auxiliary reckoned the best way to approach the compound was from the rear, where the sentries were only placed every hundred yards. But we had to get there while it was still dark. We left the vehicle in a copse and headed off across the fields, following the compass bearing I'd worked out at the sawmill.

"Quint, why don't you call in Hamilton and have him pull the place apart?" Katharine asked in a low voice as we stumbled over the rough ground in the faint light of early dawn.

"I wish I could." Just after we started walking I'd tripped and landed in a ditch full of half-frozen water. Now my hands and arms were shaking uncontrollably. "But I'm certain that the senior guardian would put a stop to that before we got five yards beyond the gate."

"So the great Quintilian Dalrymple's going to act the hero." A smile played across her lips.

"No one's forcing you to be here," I hissed, peering at the solid mass that was beginning to rear up on the ridge in front of us. The truth was, I wasn't sure what I was going to do, even if we did manage to get inside. I'd spent so much time and effort searching for the mysterious Bone Yard and I was bloody sure it was the key to everything else that was wrong in the city. But

I was also in the process of committing the investigator's worst strategic error: getting close to the solution and then hoping that everything will work out for the best. Sometimes it's the only option you have.

The house inside the walls was built by a Victorian mines magnate who had political aspirations. According to the lumberjack, Gladstone had been a frequent visitor. Since the old Liberal's favourite hobby apart from rescuing fallen women was chopping up timber, it was surprising that the forest behind the wall was so thick. I wasn't complaining. The profusion of branches hanging down over the walls made life difficult for the sentries. From behind the ruined chapel outside the compound – no sharing a pew with the peasants in the village kirk for the original owner – Katharine and I took in the lie of the land. The sun was rising but there was a mist so we weren't as obvious as we might have been.

"What next, Quint? If we sling over that rope your friend gave us, we should be able to get on to the wall in that sheltered place."

I took a quick look at the sentry posts. They were built up on the inside with only a couple of feet of planking cut with slit-holes showing from where we were. I had a feeling that the senior guardian would not be canonising whoever was in charge. Like a lot of top-security facilities in the city its impregnability was a matter of rumour rather than fact.

"Okay, go for it," I said, squeezing her arm. "I'll be right behind you."

"You'd better be," Katharine replied, looking over her shoulder. "After all, you're the one who knows what he's doing here." She was away towards the wall before I could respond to that crack. Then the rope with the steel hook the lumberjack had given us flew over the wire on the top. It seemed to get a good purchase on something on the other side. I hoped it wasn't a passing guardsman's throat.

Katharine hauled herself up, the long skirts of her coat stuffed into her belt, then signalled to me to follow.

I stepped out and froze. There was a movement in the sentry box to my right. A period that felt like several decades, but in reality couldn't have been more than five seconds, ground by. I couldn't move back into the cover of the chapel wall in case that convinced the sentry that he or she had seen something. Swivelling my eyes, I satisfied myself that the maroon beret had drawn back from the slits in the planking. And ran for the wall like a frightened rabbit. It was only as I was halfway up the rope that the idiocy of the situation struck me. Taking refuge inside the walls of a top-security facility was carrying even my advanced appreciation of the bizarre a bit too far.

"Come on, for God's sake," Katharine said, holding out her hand as I began to struggle.

I took it without a second thought. I've never been much good at climbing ropes and I'm not proud either. There was a nasty moment when the barbed wire acquainted itself with my thighs, then I was over, pulling the rope up with me. We shinned down the other side and dived into the undergrowth. It was drenched in an icy dew.

"What next?" Katharine asked. "We can't see a thing from here."

"How do you fancy crawling through this?"

She pulled her coat skirts out. "No problem. I'm properly equipped." She glanced at my donkey jacket and soaked trousers contemptuously. "Unlike you."

So we crawled through the bracken and ferns till we reached the inner edge of the wood. In the distance at the far end of the enclosed land stood the main house, a large two-storey edifice in sandstone with enough windows to suggest that the man who built it either had an army of offspring or a lot of fawning friends who came to stay every weekend. Between us and the house was a fenced field where a couple of very sane-looking cows were chewing the cud. Away to the left was a much newer building, a long, low line of breezeblock huts with shuttered windows. Late period Council style without a doubt. And at the far end, a taller building without a single window from which a brick-built chimney rose high above the tops of even the oldest trees. That was where we were headed. Except we got distracted on the way.

The first thing we came across was a clearing in the wood. The surface of the ground seemed to be flat, then I noticed that it was covered by separate slabs of dull grey metal.

"What are those?" Katharine asked, looking around the open space. "There must be over thirty of them."

We went closer. And I saw a yellow-bordered symbol on each slab that immediately brought Torness to mind.

"Jesus."

"What is it, Quint?" Katharine asked again.

I went closer. There was no doubt about it. The international warning for radiation danger was on every slab. What's more, you didn't have to be a metallurgist to get the idea that the metal was lead, or an undertaker to recognise the slabs as grave markers.

"Jesus," I repeated. "This is it. This is the Bone Yard. Literally."

Katharine stared at me, then glanced away towards a narrow gap in the trees on the other side of the clearing. "Someone's coming," she said quietly.

I looked across the clearing and saw two figures approaching. The normal reaction would have been to melt back into the undergrowth and I almost did that. Then I realised that the figures weren't looking at us. They were dressed in citizen-issue grey coats that were several sizes too big for them and their heads were covered by the flat caps that absolve the Supply Directorate from providing the population with umbrellas. They were also concentrating so hard on the path in front of them that I began to wonder if there were mantraps under the worn grass. Then the leading one stumbled and the other person put out a hand

and supported his or her companion — it was impossible to tell which sex they were from our position. From their slow, unsteady progress, I got the impression they were very old.

Katharine nudged my elbow. "What do you think?" she whispered. "They don't exactly look dangerous."

We stood still as the figures reached the grave that was nearest to their side of the clearing. The lead slab was surrounded by a rim of fresh earth. The two of them stood staring down at the grave, arms round each other's back. It was then I realised that stooping seemed to be their usual stance. After a while one of them knelt down slowly and placed a small sprig of holly on the surface of the metal. There was a long silence, then a solitary crow cawed from behind us. The two figures raised their heads instinctively and looked straight at us.

I wanted to run across the clearing and reassure them we meant no harm, but that would have meant stepping over the graves and I didn't think that would endear me to them. Then it became obvious that they weren't disturbed by our presence. In fact, the one who was kneeling started carefully repositioning the holly on the slab. Perhaps they hadn't seen us after all.

"Come on," I said to Katharine under my breath. "They're the best chance we've got of finding out what the hell's been going on around here."

We circled the clearing and walked towards the figures slowly but without stealth. As we approached they finally seemed to register our presence, but they didn't speak — just turned and lifted their faces when they heard our footsteps.

I heard Katharine draw breath in rapidly. I could see why. The kneeling one was a woman. I knew that from the softness of her skin and the delicate line of her jaw and neck, even though her face was blotched with dark red lesions and her eyebrows had disappeared. Her male companion's face was also heavily marked and his limbs were shaking with rapid movements. But their eyes were what was hardest to look at. If the lumberjack's were clouded, theirs were almost completely opaque, like watered-down milk. That was why they hadn't noticed us for so long.

"What harm are we doing?" the woman asked querulously. "Alec's at peace now. You can't get anything else from him."

Katharine and I exchanged helpless glances.

"You're not doing any harm," I said. "We're not on the staff here."

An expression of what looked like joy flashed across both their faces, to be replaced almost immediately by a terrible sadness. It was as if they'd been waiting for this moment for years, only to realise as soon as it arrived that salvation from what they were going through was an impossible dream.

"Not on the staff?" the man repeated, his ruined features contorting as he struggled to work out who we were.

The woman rose to her feet with difficulty, holding on to her companion's arm tightly. "Surely you haven't come over the wall?" she said, her voice fraught with fear. "You'll never get out again, you know."

"We'll see about that," I said, trying to sound more in command of myself than I was. "In the meantime we need your help. Will you be missed for a few more minutes?"

The man laughed. It wasn't a pretty sound, but it raised my spirits. Whatever he'd suffered, at least he could still laugh. I saw that Katharine was smiling.

"They won't miss us. Now that we can't work in the labs or with the cattle, they're just waiting for us to join the others here." His head started to shake like his arms and legs. The woman drew him gently away from the grave.

"Come on," she said. "We'd better get into the cover of the bushes."

Katharine took her arm but she shook it off firmly. We let them move slowly ahead.

In the undergrowth they lowered themselves carefully on to the trunk of a fallen tree and sat hand in hand like a couple of kids who'd strayed away from a school picnic.

"If you're not on the staff, who are you?" the man asked suspiciously. "No one's ever volunteered to enter this place before."

"I'm Dalrymple," I said, preparing to launch into a sanitised account of what we were up to. I didn't get the chance.

"Quintilian Dalrymple?" they said in unison. I wasn't aware that my name had become part of a Gregorian chant. "The investigator?"

"Yes," I replied. "How do you know?"

"We haven't been here all our lives," the woman said. "Though it often feels like it. We knew about you when we were in the Science and Energy Directorate." She shook her head slowly. "Your mother was responsible for all this, you know."

I'd been wondering when my mother, the former senior guardian, would come back to haunt me. The lesions on the couple's faces were a silent reminder of the lupus that had ravaged her. But I suspected that what they were afflicted by was even worse than that.

"Don't worry," the man said. "We won't hold it against you." He sighed deeply like a torture victim who's tracked down his abusers but can't find the strength to avenge himself on them. "We're long past that."

"Tell us," Katharine said simply, squatting down on the damp bracken in front of them. "Tell us what they did to you."

"Very well," the man said. "This is our story. I hope you both find it informative." His voice broke towards the end of the sentence but I couldn't tell if that was the effect of emotion or his physical condition.

I settled back against the gnarled trunk of an ancient oak and shut out the harsh call of the crow that was still haunting the wood. Maybe it had found a rabbit — or something larger. Then I leaned forward and listened to the old man's soft, uneven tones.

"We're ... we were mechanical engineers. Specialising in

steam turbines. Before the Enlightenment we worked at Torness. Of course, after the plant was decommissioned, we had to retrain."

The woman laughed bitterly. "Coal. I hate the bloody stuff. We spent most of our time patching up what passes for a coal-fired power station in this benighted city."

Her companion nodded. "Until we were called into the Science and Energy Directorate in 2019 and told we were to be part of a top-secret team. They gave us false identities as ordinary citizens."

"To work on starting up the nuclear plant at Torness," I said.

They were seriously shocked. "You knew?" the woman exclaimed. "How? No one outside this hell-hole is supposed to have heard about the project we took part in."

I looked at their devastated faces. "Not quite no one. There were a few others. My mother and the science and energy guardian, for instance."

"Guardians," the man said. "Why would they talk?"

I considered defending William McEwan, but time was running out. The longer we were in the compound, the greater the chance we'd be caught.

"We heard your mother died, Quintilian," the woman said, giving me a surprisingly sympathetic look.

"She did. Last year." I paused for a moment, amazed that the woman could feel anything for the guardian who was at least partially responsible for what had happened to her.

"It would never have worked," the man continued. "All our colleagues were agreed on that. But there was great pressure on us to come up with a positive recommendation. The deputy guardian . . ."

That's what I wanted to hear. Some dirt on the one-time deputy science guardian who was now senior guardian.

"He was like a man with a mission. For him Edinburgh's very survival depended on the gas-cooled reactor." The man

PAUL JOHNSTON

lowered his head. His hands were shaking even more than they had been. "He forced us to break into the sarcophagus round the fuel elements. You see, the Council had been in such a hurry to close down the plant that it took the easy way out. Instead of spending money to make the reactor safe, it did the minimum. Then encased it in concrete."

Katharine had gone very white. "You mean it's still live?"

The woman shook her head slowly. "The original Council wasn't that irresponsible. Basic safety procedures were followed. It just wasn't a very good idea to break into the core." She was suddenly looking even frailer.

"There were explosions," I said softly.

The man nodded. "It could have been a lot worse. The radiation leak was minimised and the city was lucky. There was a south-westerly wind and the cloud was carried over the North Sea. There have been so many leaks from old reactors in Russia and the Ukraine that it probably hardly showed up on the monitors abroad."

"So the only people who suffered were us," the woman said, her voice shrill. "The forty of us who were in the immediate vicinity. We had no chance. Seven died on the spot."

Katharine put her hand on the woman's. This time it wasn't shaken off. "They brought you here?"

"They could hardly let us back into the city, could they?" said the man. "The tourists would have disappeared overnight." He looked at me with his milky eyes. "Besides, we've been useful to them. All the city's viruses and contamination have ended up here."

"BSE," I said, glancing away in the direction of the cattle.

"And worse," the man said, shaking his head.

There was something else I wanted to check. "Did you know the auxiliary Watt 103?"

"Oh, aye," the woman said brightly, then shook her head. "Poor Alasdair. He was even worse off than us. They made him stay at Torness. There were four of five of them. They

248

had to monitor the reactor after the sarcophagus was closed up again." Now she was looking at me. "Do you know what happened to him?"

Katharine squeezed the woman's knee gently. "I was with him when he died not long ago. He got out of Torness."

"I'm glad," the woman said. "He was a good man and he deserved better from the Council."

"So did you all," Katharine said, bending her head and resting it on the woman's thigh.

I was thinking about what the lumberjack said about the cattle trucks. "If they're monitoring BSE there must be a laboratory here."

"There are several labs," the woman said. "They had us working there before we got too shaky. Not that we know much about chemical procedures. We were nothing more than lab assistants." She laughed weakly. "Probably the most overqualified assistants in the world."

The man smiled at her, his mottled skin seeming almost to crack. For all the agonies and indignities they'd suffered, they were both undefeated. The iron boyscouts should have been shot for taking advantage of them.

"So chemists had to be drafted in?" I said.

The woman nodded. "There are three of them. The woman in charge is a toxicologist by specialisation. She's not been here long."

I was prepared to bet my entire collection of crime fiction that she was the one the chief toxicologist had been grooming to succeed him. I tried for a royal flush.

"When you were working in the labs, did you ever see any blue pills being produced?"

There was total silence for a few moments. Even the ravenous crow had decided to give it a rest. Then they both nodded.

"She called them Electric Blues," the man said. "I overheard her on her mobile once. She wasn't too pleased when she saw me, but who did she think I was going to tell?"

That was it. Time to call in the cavalry. I had my mobile halfway to my lips when Katharine sprang to her feet and cupped her ear in the direction of the clearing.

"Guards," she said, motioning to us to hit the ground.

I hadn't heard anything, but her experience of field operations was a lot more recent than mine. Then heavy boots came crashing through the bracken, getting nearer and nearer.

Until they stopped a couple of tree-trunks away.

"I'm fucking freezing out here," said a male voice. "Have you got that bastard whisky?"

"Aye."

A screwcap was undone, then gulping could be heard.

"Christ, that's better. Here you are, Jim."

Not exactly standard guard language, but the headbangers posted out here probably didn't give a shit about regulations.

"Where the hell are those stupid old fucks?" the first voice said. "Do you think they've croaked?"

I watched the faces of the ex-engineers. They were motionless, their lips slack.

"If they haven't yet, it won't be long. Their lead boxes are ready for them." A guttural, soulless laugh. "Come on. The commander'll be looking for us if we don't report back soon."

The sound of their legs brushing through the undergrowth faded.

Katharine helped the others to their feet. "I'm sorry you had to hear that," she said. "Those guardsmen are scum." She settled them on the fallen tree. "Won't you tell us your names?" she asked, looking at each of them in turn.

"Our names?" the woman said slowly. "Our names? The Council took those away from us years ago when we became auxiliaries."

"Yes, but surely you remember them."

The man turned towards her and smiled. "This is the Bone Yard. You saw the blank slabs. No one needs names here."

I swallowed hard then punched out Hamilton's number on

the mobile. For a horrible moment I thought I wasn't going to get a connection. At this range nothing was certain. Then I heard the buzz and breathed out.

"Dalrymple," I said when I heard the guardian's voice. I told him where we were, then lowered my voice. I was so wound up that I'd been shouting. "I've found the lab where the Electric Blues are being produced."

"You have? Well done, man. I'm on my way."

"Bring as many squads as you can," I said. "And don't take any shit from the sentries on the gate — this is a top-security facility."

"Are you sure? I've never heard of it."

"That's the wonder of top security, Lewis. Two more things."

"Go ahead."

"Bring a camera. In fact, bring several cameras. This place needs to be recorded for posterity."

"Right. And the other thing?"

"Whatever you do, Lewis, don't tell the senior guardian where you're going. It's a matter of life or death."

Chapter Twenty-One

Davie always did fancy himself as a racing driver. He caught up with Hamilton by the suburbs and called me again when the convoy of guard vehicles was approaching the gate.

"The guardian's demanding entry now, Quint. They don't look too happy on the other side. Hang on ... bloody hell, that was neat. The guardian just grabbed the sentry's mobile and smashed it against the gatepost."

It looked like Lewis was taking my point about the need for secrecy seriously. I just hoped there weren't many more mobiles inside the compound.

"Right, we're on our way in," Davie went on. "Where are you?"

"We're breaking cover now. Meet us at the labs behind the big house. Out."

I nodded to the others. "They're here."

Katharine was helping the man and woman to their feet. "It's over," she said, smiling at them. "You'll soon be free of this place."

They both shook their heads. "Where else is there for us? Our friends are all over there," the man said. The two of them looked over towards the clearing with its lead slabs as if their eyes were drawn by an ineluctable force. "That's where we want it to end. With them."

I couldn't argue with him. But I was going to use them first. I felt bad about it but I had to convince Lewis Hamilton that the senior guardian was even more off the rails than the last train that tried to cross the Forth Rail Bridge after independence.

"Can you take us to the labs?" I asked.

They nodded and we set off through the bracken. As we cleared the woodland, a shot rang out to our right. I made out a guardsman on the wall with a rifle and, further along, a sentry slumping back in his box. The guardian really was taking my warning seriously. Firearms are only issued in extreme cases. Then I saw the sentry's arm move upwards. There was another shot and he was still.

My mobile buzzed.

"Dalrymple? Are you all right?"

"Yes, Lewis. What's going on?"

"My people spotted one of the sentries with his mobile to his mouth. I hope he didn't get through to whoever he was calling. We think we've secured all the other mobiles."

"If you haven't we might be fighting a civil war." I signed off and led the others out into the open. In the enclosure ahead the cattle gazed at us without interest as they ruminated. They were in luck. Their date with the furnace and the tall chimney had been indefinitely postponed.

Guard personnel were swarming all over the place. Outside the labs a small group of white-coated figures had been assembled, their hands cuffed behind their backs. Hamilton was strolling around like an officer on parade. He'd been waiting for an operation like this for years. He was about to learn something about the chief boyscout that would make him even more pleased.

Davie came towards us.

"You okay, Quint?" he called, his eyes widening as he took in our companions. It looked like he'd made the connection between the state they were in and what had happened at Torness.

"Don't worry, lad," the man said, smiling faintly at him. "We're not as radioactive as that."

Davie realised his mouth was hanging open like a whale's in plankton-gathering mode. He closed it, stepped forward and took the man's arm, giving Katharine a grim smile. If it was safe enough for her, he wasn't going to hang back.

"What is this place, Dalrymple?" Hamilton shouted as I came into range.

"This is the Bone Yard, Lewis. Did you bring a camera?"

"Three, plus directorate photographers."

"Good. There's plenty for them to work on. One of them can start with these people here." I indicated the shuffling couple beside me. "You can send another over in the direction we've just come from. There's a clearing marked out with lead slabs that you'll be interested in."

"And the third?"

"There's a lab in there that should have a large number of small blue objects in it."

There was a sudden movement to my right. I turned and watched as the chief toxicologist's loose frame covered twenty yards at amazing speed.

"Is it you, Eileen?" I heard him say, his voice cracking. "And you, Murdo? I was told you'd both died a couple of years back."

"We're still going, Ramsay," the woman replied, clutching at his arm. "Not for long though."

The toxicologist's face was wet. "So this is what they called the Bone Yard," he said, shaking his head. "I heard the name a couple of times but I was told never to repeat it."

You didn't have to be Einstein to work out which of the city's scientists had given him that instruction. I left them to their shared pasts and went over to a tall young woman in a white coat. She had her head bowed as if the scene with her former lab assistants was causing her pain. There was more on the way.

"You're in a quicksand full of shit, Lister 436," I said to

her. "Your only chance of avoiding a long and unhappy life on Cramond Island is to come clean about the Electric Blues right now."

Her eyes jerked around for a few seconds, their dark brown colour in striking contrast to the ashen white of her skin. She was obviously wondering if selling out the senior guardian was a sensible option. A quick glance at Hamilton's miniature army helped her make up her mind. She led us in and showed us her chemistry set.

We had a council of war in the long conservatory that had been the staff's messroom. Old copies of the *Edinburgh Guardian* were scattered around the wooden floor, which was buckled all over as if moles had been trying to effect entry. Except no self-respecting mole would have wanted anything to do with the lowlife that made up the guard personnel here.

"Right, we've collected documents and taken photographs of everything," Hamilton said. "And all the Electric Blues we could find are in my Land-Rover."

"Make sure they don't fall out on the way back," Katharine said, making it sound like she had no faith in the guardian's competence.

I glared at her. I'd already spent more time than I should have persuading Lewis not to arrest her. Now he was doing his impersonation of Krakatoa seconds before eruption.

"It's one forty-three," I said, trying to move things along. "We can only hope that no word got out about our presence here. So the question is, what next?"

"We call an emergency Council meeting and divest the senior guardian of his powers forthwith," Hamilton said. He'd been overjoyed when we found papers in the lab linking the top level of the Science and Energy Directorate – i.e. the chief boyscout – to the drug production. But he was letting himself get a bit carried away.

"That might not be too clever," I said. "If we give the senior guardian the chance to defend himself, he might manage to turn this against us. The rest of the guardians think he walks on air as well as water. He did give most of them their jobs, remember."

"But we've got all this evidence," Davie said.

"We have now," I said. "But how long for? We're going to need as many copies of the photos as we can get."

"I'll see to that," the guardian said.

"And I've got to be sure I can make the bastard see reason," I said.

Hamilton looked at me quizzically. "Meaning?"

"Meaning that if he starts using staff loyal to him to locate our evidence, we have to stop him in his tracks." I had a thought. "Davie, give your mate Harry a call. Tell him we need his crews for a bit of shore-based headbanging."

Hamilton looked like he was lost at sea. I just hoped we weren't all going to end up as food for the fishes like the fat man in that gangster movie half a century ago.

"Lewis, I need you to find out where the senior guardian is." Katharine and I were with Hamilton in his Land-Rover on the way back to the city.

"Simple. He's required by Council regulations to advise the guard command centre of his whereabouts at all times." The guardian made the call. "He's been in meetings with a Chinese trade delegation all day and he's expected back in his private accommodation at four o'clock."

That was good news. If he'd been busy negotiating, he wouldn't have had much chance to wonder about what we were up to.

"Right, I'll land on him unannounced there. Somehow I think he'll find the time to see me."

"Dalrymple, surely you don't think the senior guardian's the killer," Hamilton said haltingly. "I mean, he's over-zealous and autocratic but he does have the city's best interests at heart. Even I have always been convinced of that."

I couldn't suppress a laugh. Over-zealous was a major understatement. The chief boyscout was so zealous he could have walked into a senior position with the Spanish Inquisition when he was at primary school. But Lewis had a point.

"No, I'm pretty sure he's not the murderer," I said. "At least not the one who killed Roddie Aitken and the female auxiliary. But considering he was responsible for everything that's been going on in the Bone Yard, I'm taking every precaution I can."

The sun was already low in the sky to the west. All around us sodden brown fields dotted with patches of half-frozen water stretched away into the distance, lined by bare trees with scarecrow branches. I shivered in the blast of cold air that was coming in the holes in the Land-Rover's bodywork. I found myself wishing I could put my arm round Katharine and feel the warmth of her. But she was sitting bolt upright in her long coat, her eyes fixed on the rutted road ahead. The Enlightenment wanted to get rid of the cult of the individual which had supposedly destroyed the United Kingdom's social fabric in the years around the millennium. All it achieved was to make us into even more self-reliant, emotionally illiterate citizens – and I speak from a position of considerable authority on emotional illiteracy.

"Right, Davie." We were round the corner from the checkpoint in front of the guardians' accommodation in Moray Place. I was leaning in the window of the pick-up which he'd driven in from the track where Katharine and I left it. "Have you got everything clear?"

"Do you mind?" he asked sardonically. "I'm a trained auxiliary."

"That's very reassuring, guardsman. Are Harry and his guys in the picture?"

"Aye. They're up at the castle waiting to be given copies of the photos and documents. Katharine and the guardian are handling that." He grinned. "Should be interesting to see if she ends up in the dungeons."

I gave him a frosty glare.

"Then Harry's people will take up positions near the six embassies you specified."

"And you've told them that if they don't hear anything by six p.m. they're to make the deliveries?"

"I have, Quint. Calm down, will you?"

"Calm down? That's easy for you to say. You're not the one who's got to squeeze the senior guardian's nuts."

He laughed. "You're having more fun than a guardsman in the barracks bar who's just come off border duty."

"Is that right? Make sure you come and join me if I'm not back in half an hour." I started to walk away.

"Quint? You don't want to forget this."

I turned back and took the object he was holding out. True enough, I needed to be properly equipped before I could contemplate facing the city's top dog.

Security around the guardians' quarters has never been exactly minimalist, but now Moray Place resembled the Red Square on May Day in the time before Moscow turned into an eastern version of Tombstone. It took me a lot of shoving to get through the serried ranks of guard personnel to the senior guardian's residence. It looked like someone was seriously worried about his personal safety.

The young female auxiliary at the door took an instant dislike to me. I managed to get my authorisation out before she could practise her unarmed combat skills on me.

"Where is he?" I asked, pushing past her.

"In his study." The auxiliary was already on the internal phone.

I headed up the ornate staircase, thinking of the times I'd come here to see my mother as I pulled on Katharine's coat. This meeting promised to be even more life-threatening than those ones. I slowed down outside the high door, took a deep breath, pulled up the hood and walked in with my head bent forward.

There was a sudden intake of breath then a long silence.

"Why are you wearing that coat, citizen?" The senior guardian's voice possessed almost its normal level of control, but there was enough wavering at the edges to make me sure my choice of apparel was having an effect.

"I thought it might set the mood for our meeting," I said, taking the coat off and moving towards the large mahogany desk. On my way I noticed the painting that the chief boyscout had hung above the Adam fireplace. Each guardian is entitled to borrow one work from the city's galleries and – surprise, surprise – his was the exquisite, sombre-toned El Greco entitled *The Saviour of the World*. Some world. Some saviour.

"Am I to understand that you have at last made progress in your investigation, citizen?" The guardian remained seated at the desk, his head resting on the high back of his chair like a king receiving a tedious courtier.

I spread my hands on the desktop and leaned towards him. "I spent the morning at the Bone Yard." I leaned closer, my eyes locked on to his. "It's time for the truth, you lying bastard." Spots of my saliva landed on his beard. I didn't offer an apology.

The chief boyscout was pale but still in command, at least of himself. "The truth? That's a notoriously slippery concept, citizen."

I slipped my hand round his beard and pulled his head across the desk. "The truth, you callous fucker, or you won't have to wait for the real hooded man to catch up with you."

His body had gone slack but his eyes were still hard. "Very well, citizen. If you would let me go . . ."

I pulled my hand away and watched as he rearranged himself in his chair.

"The truth," he said, his voice a lot less composed than he'd have liked. "If you've been to the special facility—"

"The Bone Yard," I shouted.

"The Bone Yard." He pronounced the words with a curious movement of his lips as if they were ones he should never have been forced to utter. "If you've been there, surely you know the truth, citizen."

"What I know is that you imprisoned the people who were exposed to radiation at Torness and directed all the city's muck, like BSE-infected cattle, at them." I felt my shoulders shaking. "And what I also know is that you set up production of the Electric Blues there. You realise that the drug's potentially lethal for people with weak hearts, don't you?"

The guardian shrugged then looked at me imperiously. "I see that my actions have failed to win your approval, citizen."

"Failed to win my approval? Jesus, don't you people ever speak plain English? What you did was criminal. Don't you get it? You forced those people to break through the sarcophagus, then you locked them up and used them as slave labour. Without bothering to mention any of that to the Council."

His eyes flashed. "The original decision to return to Torness was taken by my predecessors, Dalrymple. One of whom was your mother."

"Don't think I won't be carrying that with me for the rest of my life." A vision of the couple in the Bone Yard, their ravaged faces and crippled frames, had jumped up before me. "But that doesn't get you off the hook."

The guardian gave me a tight, totally humourless smile. "You're missing the point. As a demoted auxiliary, you obviously can't be relied upon to maintain your familiarity with the works of Plato so—"

"What is this bollocks?" I yelled, slamming my hand down on the desktop. This was exactly the kind of line my mother used to take when she had to explain herself and it pissed me off even more than queuing for food vouchers on a Friday afternoon. "Don't tell me the Enlightenment's favourite philosopher wrote something that justifies the bullshit you've been coming out with for the last two years."

He twitched his head at me impatiently. "Indeed he did. Don't you remember the noble lie, citizen?"

"Sounds like a major contradiction in terms," I replied, but something was stirring in the depths of my memory.

The chief boyscout rose to his feet like a preacher about to address his congregation, which made the prospect of listening even worse.

"There was a myth that human beings were formed from earth. Those destined to rule had gold mixed in with them, while warriors had silver, and farmers and artisans iron."

It came back to me, despite the fact that I always tried to steer the discussion in philosophy debates towards more mundane matters like how to eradicate the drugs gangs. "One of the many myths that indoctrinate people into believing their roles in life are predetermined, so they buckle down to their daily toil," I said. "I can see why it would appeal to the Council."

The guardian ignored my irony. "The Enlightenment has always given citizens the chance to better themselves."

"Oh, aye? Apart from selling their souls and becoming auxiliaries, what opportunities are there in the city now?" I suddenly found myself thinking of Roddie Aitken. All the Council's precious system gave him was an early cremation. "Anyway, what's the myth got to do with your noble lie?"

He smiled harshly at me again. Never mind gold or silver, he had enough iron in his soul to rebuild the Forth Bridge. "During the discussion it is suggested that rulers are entitled to lie in order to protect the interests of the state. Would you like the page reference to *The Republic?*"

"No, I fucking wouldn't." I leaned across the desk and grabbed his beard again. "You've got absolutely no chance of convincing me that the lies you've been telling are noble, pal." I pulled his face right up to mine. "In my book you're personally responsible for four murders. I don't give a shit about the two auxiliaries, but I care more about Roddie Aitken and William McEwan than you can even begin to imagine."

The chief boyscout didn't try to protest his innocence or deny that William had been murdered on his orders. For the first time he was looking frightened. Not an attractive emotion in a golden ruler but an emotion all the same. Maybe I was beginning to get to him.

"Listen to me," I said, loosening my grip. "When this is over there'll be nowhere for you to hide in Edinburgh, I promise you that. But there's still a lunatic out there and catching him is a fuck sight more important than what used to be your career." There was a flash of what I took to be resistance in his eyes. "And don't even think about arranging any accidents for me. I've got people ready to turn over photos of the Bone Yard and papers about the Electric Blues written in your own fair hand to a selection of embassies."

He nodded his head slowly in acquiescence and I let go of his beard.

"Right, I want to finish this investigation and I want to finish it fast. You've got some Electric Blues here, haven't you?"

He nodded, keeping his eyes away from mine.

"They're the ones the killer's been looking for all over the city, which is why three people have been cut apart and why you've turned Moray Place into Fort Knox. The killer was blackmailing you about Torness, threatening to tell the rest of the world what you've been covering up. He passed you the drugs formula and told you to set up production. Then what happened?"

"Whatever you may think, I am not a common criminal," the guardian said indignantly. "I had no intention of allowing that character to traffic drugs in the city. I enlisted the help of Raeburn 03 in the Public Order Directorate."

"And he thought it would be a bright idea to double-cross the hooded man? He got that wrong, didn't he? The killer reckoned Machiavelli had the Electric Blues. When he found he didn't, it was off with his head."

He didn't make any comment about the auxiliary's nickname. Perhaps he'd known about it all along. "That was unfortunate. The hooded man, as you've been calling him, wanted a woman when the deal was agreed. We gave him one of the Three Graces; she passed him a small sample of the drug as well as keeping an eye on him. The foolish woman also kept some of the pills for herself. We decided to lead him astray by making out that the delivery man Aitken was stealing the drugs on behalf of a rival dealer. The female auxiliary kept Aitken under surveillance too."

"By screwing him? You bastard," I said, raising my fist and watching as he jerked back into his seat. "You set Roddie Aitken up. When this is over, you'll be very sorry you did that." I managed to bring my breathing under control. "And you let me stay on the investigation in case I made things easy for you by catching the hooded man."

He nodded.

"I know more than you think," I said. "I know about the nuclear physicist Watt 103. He ended up in a gang run by a lunatic called the Screecher."

The senior guardian smiled humourlessly. "You have been busy. Apparently the Screecher got into Torness last year and killed the other scientists. He kept Watt 103 alive for his technical knowledge. I think he was planning to reopen the sarcophagus to strengthen his hand.

"Jesus. So who is the crazy bastard under the hood?"

He sat dead still for a few seconds then his face took on a supremely malicious expression. He looked like a bodysnatcher who's just come across a prime specimen dangling from a tree in a deserted wood.

"You know him, citizen," he said in a whisper.

I grabbed his beard again, feeling several strands come away in my fingers. "What do you mean I know him? Who is he, you fucker?"

Despite the damage I was doing to his facial hair, the chief boyscout seemed to be enjoying himself. Now the smile on his lips was so mocking that I badly wanted to lay into him. It's a hell of a long time since I've been violent. I applied long-forgotten auxiliary training to rein myself in.

"Let me describe him, citizen," he croaked, sprawling on the desk as I tugged harder. "Big man, over six feet two, at least sixteen stone . . ."

"Knows how to handle a knife and likes inflicting pain," I continued, unimpressed at being strung along. "Smart, judging by the way he chose the songs on the tapes, probably a devotee of the blues—" I broke off. Jesus, a devotee of the blues who was also getting himself involved in drugs trafficking. Maybe the bastard wasn't coming into it cold. Maybe he had plenty of experience in the business. I let the guardian go and rocked back on my heels.

"As I said, citizen. You know him." He was still smiling viciously, like a public executioner fingering the blade of his axe. Then he struck. "He stood watching while your woman friend was strangled by the Ear, Nose and Throat Man. He was that psychopath's leader."

I was back in the barn on Soutra seven years ago during the attack on the city's last remaining drugs gang; men turning to run and leaving a slim, shuddering form on the floor. Caro. She died a few seconds after I got to her.

"The Wolf," I said incredulously. Then I made the connection with the gang leader's name. The Screecher. No doubt he thought that was a really neat pseudonym for a blues singer.

I focused on the guardian again. "You're even sicker than I thought you were. You've been dealing with Howlin' Wolf? You set the Wolf on Roddie Aitken? You let the Wolf play games with me while he was cutting your own auxiliaries to pieces?"

I couldn't hold myself back any longer. It only took a split second. The head-butt spread his nose over his face like a ripe plum. That was the first instalment of his payment for the lives of Roddie Aitken and William McEwan.

Then I sank back into a chair and sat there quaking. The Wolf. Jesus. We really were up against Edinburgh's public enemy number one.

Chapter Twenty-Two

I called Davie in and got him to handcuff the chief boyscout to the arm of his chair. Now that I had him where I wanted him there was no need to use Harry's guys as postmen, so we called them off and got them to assemble at the castle. Hamilton and Katharine soon joined us in the senior guardian's study.

"What happened to him?" Lewis asked, bending over to examine the comatose figure on the desk.

"Remember those operations women used to get done before the Enlightenment to make themselves more appealing?" I asked. "He was in urgent need of one."

"Not only women had nose jobs," Katharine said sharply.

Lewis Hamilton seemed to be impressed by what I'd done to his boss. "I take it he was responsible for everything," he said, shaking his head in disgust. "What did he tell you?"

"Not as much as he might have. I got carried away before he finished." I filled them in on what I'd learned.

Hamilton looked even more disgusted when he found out that we were up against the Wolf. "Good God, man, I assumed that bloodthirsty lunatic left Edinburgh years ago and went to prey on the youth of some less stable city."

"Well, he's back home," I said. "The question now is how do we track him down?"

"Use the drugs?" Davie suggested. "They're what he wants, aren't they?"

Hamilton wasn't keen. "What are you proposing, guardsman? That we tie them to a tree in Princes Street Gardens and wait for him to pick them up?"

Davie shrugged. "It was only an idea."

"Bait," I said, nodding. "It's reasonable enough." I pointed at the figure that was still slumped over the desk. "We could use him instead of the drugs."

"I don't think I'll be able to sell either of those options to the Council," Hamilton said. "It's going to be hard enough to get them to accept that their hero's been concealing all these horrors."

"So how are we going to find the killer?" asked Katharine.

I went over to the window and looked out through the trees into the circle of grass in the middle of Moray Place. It was there that the hunt for the last killer ended. Something about that case was beginning to resurface in my mind, but it was like a deep-sea diver avoiding the bends: coming up extremely slowly. Whereas I was certain we needed to nail the Wolf quickly before he used his knife, let alone his teeth, again. Why had he been quiet for so long?

It was coming up to the time of the Council meeting. We were going to confront the guardians with the photos and papers that proved the senior guardian's guilt. Hamilton drafted in squads of guards to seal off the area around the Assembly Hall, just in case any of the chief boyscout's supporters were inclined to resist. Davie called Harry and told him to bring his people down to Moray Place. We needed an escort we could rely on for the guy with the flattened nose and they had the right qualifications.

In the Land-Rover surrounded by burly figures in oil-and salt-impregnated uniforms, the senior guardian was doing his best to look like an early Christian martyr. His long hair and wispy beard, the latter now matted with blood, added to the effect. He sat with his hands manacled to guards, his chin up and his eyes set in a glassy stare.

"What's the plan then?" Davie asked as we drove through Charlotte Square. It was so cold that the breath of the tourists around the gambling tents stood up from their mouths like periscopes above the surface of a dark ocean.

"Council meeting first," I said, glancing round at the senior guardian. "The last one for you." He made no sign of having heard me. "Then a detailed interrogation in the castle," I continued, turning back to Davie. "He knows things that'll lead us to the Wolf, I'm sure of it."

Katharine was crushed up against me in the front seat. I felt her arm and leg move. "How are you sure, Quint? Another one of your hunches?"

I didn't reply, just looked out as we passed the shops and restaurants on Princes Street. Their garish lights and banners were giving tourists the come-on like an aged tart in serious need of cosmetic surgery. Or even a total body transplant.

I turned to the senior guardian. "There's something I don't get about the Bone Yard. Why did you bury the bodies of the auxiliaries who'd been exposed to radiation? You could have burned them in the furnace there."

He gave me a brief, superior glance. "Scientists don't destroy material that might prove useful in the future, citizen."

I looked away in revulsion.

We skidded on the Mound's icy surfaces then pulled round the corner. Guard personnel waved us into Mound Place and Davie stopped by the railing separating the road from the steep slope of the gardens. An evening race meeting was in progress despite the weather. They use guard sprinters when it's too cold for the horses.

I ran my eye around the steps leading up to the Assembly Hall. A couple of guardians, one of them the Ice Queen, were looking at us dubiously, puzzled by the extra security. I don't know if they recognised the figure in the back of the vehicle.

"Right, get him out," I said to Harry and his men.

Doors creaked and the Land-Rover began to empty. I followed Katharine out of the passenger door and stopped to stretch my legs. During that process I made the mistake of blinking. I was aware of a sudden flurry of movement to the rear. That flurry came as the senior guardian wrenched the two guardsmen who were attached to him towards the railing. They stuck their free hands out to stop themselves, but he whiplashed forward like he'd been jabbed with a cattle prod. The point of the black-painted railing upright came out of the back of his neck, forming a small pyramid trimmed by strands of bloody hair. As cosmetic surgery goes, it was pretty radical. The irony of the city's chief official committing the heinous crime of suicide in front of the Assembly Hall wasn't bad either.

In the background to the right, the broken spire of the Enlightenment Monument rose up into the darkness, like a vandalised roadsign pointing to a utopia that no one believes in any more.

The Council meeting was pretty fraught. After the medical guardian had supervised the removal of the senior guardian from the railing and confirmed that he was dead, Hamilton hit his colleagues with the Bone Yard evidence. They were white-faced and quiet, like schoolchildren whose chemistry teacher had just drunk battery acid in front of them. It wasn't difficult for Lewis to get himself elected temporary senior guardian. Considering that had been his ambition for at least fifteen years, he was very cool about it. I wasn't surprised to hear them vote for a total news blackout about the Bone Yard and the chief boyscout's suicide as well. A report of the latter might have resulted in Edinburgh citizens dancing in the streets.

Afterwards we went up to the castle. No mutilated bodies had been discovered, there were no reports of violence. Christ, there weren't even any reports of "suspicious behaviour", the guard's blanket charge for citizens who get up their noses. So where was the Howlin' Wolf and what was he doing?

"Maybe he's crossed back over the border," Davie said. We were sitting at Hamilton's conference table tossing ideas around.

"Maybe he has," I said. I was looking out at the bright lights of the city centre.

"You don't believe that, do you, Quint?" Katharine said, leaning back in her chair. She had her coat buttoned up. Hamilton's idea of heating would have gone down well in ancient Sparta.

I shook my head then glanced across at the guardian's computer terminal. When in doubt, hit the archives. Except that in this particular case I knew I'd be wasting my time. I spent years trying to trace the Wolf and his gang members in the records when I was in the directorate, but he'd made sure they all kept out of the Council's bureaucracy from the second the Enlightenment came to power. I still got up and went over to the machine, unable to resist the temptation. Maybe there was something in the previously restricted files on the deceased senior guardian that referred to the deal with the Wolf.

But there wasn't. As I'd already discovered, the chief boyscout knew all about what to include in the archives and what to keep to himself. The filing cabinets in his study contained pharmacological reports and production schedules of the Electric Blues, but nothing about distribution or the Wolf. I did find out from the chief boyscout's personal file that his first sexual encounter was with a man who'd been a senior figure in the Church before independence, but he was hardly the only teenager who'd been down that path.

At midnight we called things off. Davie drove Katharine and me back to my place. As we swung round the bend at Tollcross and entered the blacked-out zone outside the tourist centre, I found myself dredging my memory for the thought that had eluded me earlier. It was something about the last murder case that being in Moray Place had provoked. The deep-sea diver was still controlling his buoyancy as carefully as a Supply Directorate clerk distributes ration books, but I was close, I almost had it.

We arrived outside my flat. I got out stiffly, forgetting how cold it was. The icy road surface did for me again and I landed hard on my arse, which put all thoughts of how to catch the Wolf temporarily out of my mind. The fact that Katharine was laughing at me didn't help the process of ratiocination either.

"Jesus Christ, what a day," I groaned, dropping on to the sofa.

"Don't forget last night," Katharine said. "And yesterday. It seems you need to make an application to get a night's sleep these days."

I reached out for the bottle of whisky on the table. "Two fingers for you and two fingers for me," I said, holding it up to the candle flame.

She raised an eyebrow but didn't refuse her share. "What happens next, Quint?" she asked, pushing my legs away and sitting down next to me.

The whisky had an instant effect. The faces of the people I'd been involved with over the last twenty-four hours flickered before me like the frames of an old film: the lumberjack who'd recognised me; the fragile inmates of the Bone Yard with their clouded eyes, their blotched complexions and their soft, sad voices; the toxicologist dashing to greet them, tears coursing down his wrinkled face; and the senior guardian, his face splashed with blood from his shattered nose and, at the last, his body hanging like a hooked fish from the railing spike.

"What happens next?" I repeated wearily. "We try to find the Wolf before he gets bored with selecting his victims and goes back to indiscriminate mayhem. He used to be an expert at that."

Katharine nudged me with her elbow. "That wasn't what I meant." She put the fingers of one hand on my chin and turned my face towards her. "What happens to us?"

My mouth experienced a sudden attack of paralysis. I could look at her, take in the way her eyes were wide apart and fixed on mine – but speak? No chance.

"You've been so distant, Quint. It's like I don't exist," she said, nudging me in the ribs again with enough force to make me wince. "I suppose you think I only came back to the city to tell you about the drugs formula."

The function of movement returned to my mouth but I was having difficulty forming a sentence with the words in the right order. Eventually I made the grade.

"Wait a minute, Katharine. You've not exactly been sending out too many signals yourself. What did you expect me to do? Listen to your story about the Cavemen then drag you to bed?"

Her face slackened and she gave me another smile. I'd seen more of those in the last five minutes than I had since she came back. "I'm sorry. You were so good about all the shit that happened to me." Her gaze dropped and her voice became less assured. "I suppose I just thought you'd be glad to see me again. Treat me like a long-lost lover rather than a psychiatric case."

I slid my hand over hers. She didn't move it away. "I thought you'd given up on men," I said. "You did kind of give that impression, Katharine."

She laughed. "I kind of gave that impression because I had given up on men, Quint. But you were never just one of them to me. I saved your life, remember." She moved her face close to mine.

I wasn't too sure where this debate was headed. "So because of that you have some kind of hold over me?" I asked, leaning my forehead against hers.

She nodded then put her lips against mine. At first she didn't make any attempt to kiss me and I didn't respond. Then we seemed to get used to each other and there was a lot of tongue contact.

Eventually she pulled away. "Come on, let's get under the

covers. Otherwise they'll find us like Captain Scott and his friends in the morning."

We stumbled into the bedroom, arms round each other. Her coat proved to be as big a source of trouble as it had been since I first laid eyes on it. We finally got our outer layers off and took refuge in my bed. It was dark under the covers but we didn't seem to have forgotten the general layout of each other's bodies.

"God, I haven't been near a shower for days," I said as my shirt came over my head.

"And you think I have?" Katharine replied from the region of my lower abdomen.

Once I was sensitive about what got up my nose, but years of weekly visits to the communal baths have put paid to that.

"Katharine," I gasped, suddenly feeling her mouth on my cock, "a condom, I've got one in the . . ."

A few seconds later her face came up to mine. "Too late," she said, her voice deep and alluring. "How long do you need to get hard again?"

"Twenty minutes?" The hard points of her breasts were rubbing against my chest and her groin was crushed against mine. I was forced to recalculate. "Quarter of an hour?"

"I'll settle for ten minutes," she said, breathing into my ear. "That's my best offer."

I closed my eyes and moved my hands down her back. "Done," I murmured, wondering exactly what kind of deal I'd just signed off on.

It turned out that I was party to an agreement similar to that entered into by Cleopatra and Mark Antony – something along the lines of "Forget the major crises taking place in the outside world, let's spend the rest of our lives screwing". Except that the rest of our lives in this case meant the next four hours. That was a long way beyond what I thought would be the limit of my energy reserves, as well as a strain on my stash of condoms.

I must have fallen into an abyss of dreamless sleep because the next thing I knew was the flailing sensation of coming up for air after a long dive. It wasn't just me waking up though. What also resurfaced was the thought that had been bothering me last night. Who says sex isn't good for the mind?

I sat up in bed, only vaguely aware that my shoulders were in the process of becoming a heat-free zone. My mind had just gone into overdrive. The murder case two years ago. Remembering that in Moray Place had set off the chain of ideas that I couldn't get hold of at the time. But now I had it. I'd made the connection I needed to identify that murderer by using information I'd got from a former member of Howlin' Wolf's gang who was a prisoner in the city's sole prison – the gang member known as Leadbelly. He might be able to help me again. But was he still alive? The last time I saw him he looked like he was a living skeleton and that was nearly two years ago.

I toppled out of bed and scrabbled around in my clothes for my mobile.

"What's going on, Quint?" Katharine asked, sitting up and rubbing her eyes.

"Lewis?" I said, waving at her to be quiet. "Are you in the castle? Good. I want you to log on to your computer."

"What are you talking about, man?" the guardian said in confusion. "It's not even six o'clock." You have to wake up very early in the morning to beat Lewis Hamilton.

"Don't argue, just get over to the terminal. Ready? Okay, do exactly what I tell you. Call up the main directorate menu. Got that?"

There was a long pause. "All right, it's on screen."

"Highlight the Corrections Department option."

"The Corrections . . . ?"

"Just do it!" I shouted.

"I have," Hamilton replied tersely.

"Highlight Cramond Island."

"Done."

"Highlight Prisoner Register."

"Done."

"Right. Are there any prisoners who entered the facility in 2015?" I couldn't remember Leadbelly's prisoner number but the year he was captured was burned on my memory permanently because of Caro's death.

"There's only one," the guardian said at last.

"Highlight his number."

"Done."

"Okay," I said breathlessly. "Scroll down the file and see if there's any reference to his drug gang name of Leadbelly."

There was an extended silence. I could feel my heart pounding like a bass drum played by a Sumo wrestler.

"Here it is," the guardian shouted, almost making me drop the mobile. "Code-name Leadbelly. Entered facility 23.5.2015."

It was him. Since he was on the register, the chances were he was still alive – unless the Corrections Department had failed to update its archives.

Hamilton was continuing to read. "Known confederate of Howlin' . . ."

I signed off, called Davie and told him to pick us up. It was a long shot but I reckoned it was worth it. Leadbelly had delivered the goods in the past and he was our best chance of finding the Wolf now. He was probably our only chance.

The tide was out so we were able to cross the causeway to the island. There was thick, freezing fog and I could think of numerous places I'd rather be. Starting with the Bahamas.

"How are your thighs?" Katharine asked from behind me.

"In need of a serious massage." At one stage last night she'd been on top, pounding up and down on them.

"I'll remember that next time."

I smiled to myself. "You reckon there'll be a next time, do you?"

"I do."

I looked over my shoulder and saw the grin on Katharine's face. Behind her Davie was trudging along with his head bowed.

"What's the matter with you, guardsman?" I called.

He raised his head. "Oh, nothing," he said morosely. "Being forced to watch a performance of *Romeo and Juliet* first thing in the morning is quite uplifting, really."

"Asshole," I said, realising as the word left my lips that Katharine had come out with it at exactly the same time. That was a bit worrying.

The guards at the gate knew we were coming. They admitted us to the prison yard. The place was like the set of a low-budget movie based on an Edgar Allan Poe story. *The Fall of the House of Usher*, perhaps. I almost expected the high walls to cant over at any moment and plunge us without a sound into the icy waters of the estuary.

Katharine stood on the flagstones, running her eyes round the cell windows. She'd spent three years on the island for dissident activities. It didn't look like she was overjoyed to be back.

One of the guards led us into the accommodation block and down damp steps to an interrogation room. The door slammed to behind us and in the single bulb's dim light I became aware that there was a hunched figure covered with a threadbare blanket on the floor in the far corner. No movement came from it.

"Leadbelly?" I said in a low voice.

Nothing.

Davie stepped up, ready to haul him to his feet. I shook my head.

"Leadbelly? It's me, Dalrymple. The guy who sent you the Huddie Ledbetter tapes." That had been the deal when he gave me information before. He'd been amazed that I kept my part of it. But that was nearly two years ago. God knows what life in the tomb of the island had done to his memory since then. The original Council tried to rehabilitate prisoners, but the iron boyscouts never gave a shit about the few remaining lifers.

Thin fingers appeared at the edge of the blanket, pulling it down to reveal a skull that Poe would have swooned over – hairless, unwashed, skin shrunken over uneven bone. An eye sunk deep in its socket glinted out at us.

"Huddie?" came a croak. "Huddie's dead and buried." There was a vacant laugh. "Lucky bastard."

I went over to him and knelt down, gagging at the stink that rose up to greet me.

"You remember me, don't you, Leadbelly?"

"Aye, I remember you. What the fuck do you want this time?" The words were harsh but the tone had a touch of the bitter humour that flourishes in hell-holes like this – until the inmates succumb to disease and malnutrition.

"Howlin' Wolf." I let the name sink in.

Leadbelly moved his head. Now both his eyes were on me. "What about him?"

"He's back."

I became aware of a grating noise that was gradually getting louder. When I saw the prisoner's shoulders shaking, I realised that this was his version of laughter.

"And he's been killing people."

Leadbelly didn't stop laughing immediately, but the noise and movement slowly came to a halt.

"What the fuck do you expect? He wasn't called the Wolf just because he liked the old guy's music." He began to crank the laughter up. "The Wolf does the business and suddenly Leadbelly's popular again. That's a real fucking joke."

I leaned forward into the pollution cloud that hung over him. "If you give me what I need, I'll get you out of here."

That shut him up. After a minute I began to wonder if I'd given him heart failure.

"I said, I'll get you out of here."

He jerked into life again. "I heard you." He let loose a manic cackle. "I was just trying to work out if I can trust you."

"I got you the tapes, remember?"

"Aye, you did." He thought about it again. "All right, what is it you want to know, man?"

"The Wolf, he had a lot of safe houses in the city, didn't he?"

Leadbelly nodded. As his head came down, I saw evidence of insect life on his scalp. "Let me guess. You want the addresses. You're fucking crazy, man. There were dozens of places over the years."

"Yes, but not in the last few months before we hit you at Soutra. We busted most of them and forced you out of the city, remember?"

The prisoner looked at me blankly, then nodded. "Aye, you're right. Seems like a century ago."

"Safe houses, Leadbelly. Or contacts — were there any friends or family?"

He cackled again. "We were a bunch of psychos, for fuck's sake. We didnae go back to our mothers for high tea on Sunday afternoons."

"I'll get you out," I repeated. Talking the Council into that would be the thirteenth labour of Hercules — the one the big man would have given the bodyswerve — but I'd think about that later.

"I reckon you might too." Leadbelly pulled himself to his feet. He was way beyond ordinary malnutrition. It looked like his bones had been on a diet. "Okay, here's the stuff. Two places you fuckers never found. A top-floor flat in the New Town. St Stephen's Street. I can't remember the number, but there was a tourist shop two doors further down selling Independent Edinburgh Rock and shite like that." He paused to draw breath. "And a house down beyond Jock's Lodge. What was it? Oh, aye. Mountcastle Street. It was number 35. I remember that because it's my prisoner number." He opened the blanket and showed the label stitched on his filthy striped tunic. "He used to take women there and give it to them." He looked over my shoulder and bared the rotten stumps of his teeth at Katharine.

"Let's go," I said, turning to the others.

"Here, what about me?" Leadbelly called.

"I'll be in touch. I said you could trust me."

A deranged baying followed us down the dank passage. Maybe it was just ironic laughter. Or maybe it was a salute from Leadbelly to the former leader of his pack.

Chapter Twenty-Three

━━━━◆◈◆━━━━

The tide was lapping at the sides of the causeway and we had to move quickly.

"All the flats in St Stephen's Street were turned into hostels for cheapskate tourists three or four years back, weren't they, Davie?" I said over my shoulder.

"Aye. There's no way he'd go there."

"Mountcastle Street's our only chance then. It's not so far from Roddie Aitken's flat and the palace ruins where he did for the female auxiliary." I was gasping for breath, the frozen cottonwool of the fog massing in my lungs. "He could have cut across the park."

Davie was suddenly right behind me. "Doesn't that street back on to the old railway sidings at Craigentinny?" he asked.

"Bloody hell, you're right. It's the perfect place to lie low."

Not long after independence when the Council was busy sealing off the city, a wagon carrying a tank of some highly toxic chemical had come off the rails at the sidings. The fumes killed a lot of the local residents, making the guardians even more determined to cut road and rail links with the outside world. The surrounding area was evacuated and the houses left deserted. As the citizen body was gradually reduced by desertion and illness, it never became necessary to repopulate the area. So the guard patrols it less regularly than most places.

"It's still a bit of a longshot, isn't it, Quint?" Katharine said.

I turned and looked at her. Our rapid pace across the causeway didn't seem to be affecting her at all. Her cheeks were red but her breathing was almost normal, whereas my legs were about to give way.

"Longshots are my speciality, remember?" I said, as we hit the mainland and headed for the Land-Rover.

She didn't look very convinced.

Davie turned off the Portobello Road and drove into the wasteland. None of the houses had windows or doors, none of them even had window or door frames. Since the Supply Directorate provides only the most basic fixtures and fittings, the houses have been easy targets over the years for citizens still hankering after the do-it-yourself superstores that used to enhance every suburb. The gaping holes in the buildings made them look like open-mouthed skulls whose eyes had long since gone to the carrion birds.

We coasted to a halt before the corner of Mountcastle Street.

"Are you sure you don't want back-up?" Davie asked, his hand on his mobile. "I've only got my truncheon and my service knife."

"I've got a blade too," Katharine said, lifting her sweatshirt.

"Whatever happens, you're staying here," I said to her with as much authority as I could manage.

"Who are you to give me orders, Quint?" she asked, her green eyes flashing. There was no sign at all of the night before's tenderness. "I saved your skin the last time we did something like this."

It was hard to argue with that. I turned to Davie to see if there was any hope of help from him, but he was deeply immersed in the view from his side window.

I weighed up the options. "All right. Call Hamilton, Davie. Tell him where we are and what we're doing. That way, if we blow it, he'll be here to pick up the pieces. You could let Harry know as well. Even the Wolf would think twice about mixing it with his guys."

I turned to Katharine as he hit the buttons. "I'm not giving you orders, for God's sake. But you're better off out of it. The Wolf and his gang killed women for fun." A vision of Caro lying on the barn floor with her leg twitching came up before me.

Katharine moved her face close to mine. "We're in this together, Quint. Come on, let's finish it."

The intensity in her voice surprised me. For someone who reckoned this was a longshot, all of a sudden she was very committed.

"Okay," Davie said, "they're all on their way." He gave me a serious look. "Why don't we wait for them, Quint?"

Katharine dug her elbow into my side. "No, let's check the place out now."

I wavered between them, then sat on the fence. "We'll do a recce. That way, if it's clear, we won't be wasting too many people's time."

Now it was Davie who was looking unconvinced. I shrugged at him and followed Katharine out of the Land-Rover.

We were crouched down behind the crumbling garden wall of number 33. The fog had risen a bit and we could see the open gap where number 35's front door had been. There was no sign of anybody, no sound because of the fog's muffling effect. Nothing but cracked paving stones, overgrown gardens and litter carried by the wind from the inhabited regions. The houses in the street were semi-detached and quite large. They must have had at least three bedrooms.

"Right, here's how we'll do it," I said. "Katharine, you go round the back and look into all the ground-floor windows there." I stared at her sternly. "Without going inside."

She nodded reluctantly.

"Davie, you and I'll go in the front. You take the upstairs and I'll take the downstairs."

"Quint," he said desperately, "they'll be here in a few minutes. Let's just hang on."

Katharine glared at him, then moved away quickly before we could stop her.

"Oh, for fuck's sake," Davie grunted, heading after her on all fours.

By the time we reached the front entrance, Katharine had already disappeared round the side. I stuck my head over the edge of what had once been a bay window. And swallowed back a surge of vomit. The carcass of a sheep lay spreadeagled on the floor in a pool of coagulated blood. All but one of the legs were missing and the belly had been split open and ransacked like a stolen handbag. The animal had probably been taken from one of the pens near the palace in the Enlightenment Park.

I tapped Davie's shoulder. "I think it's him. Get Katharine back to the Land-Rover."

He nodded and moved away to the side of the house. I took a deep breath and went in the front entrance. The floor was uneven and damp. I almost slipped as I looked cautiously into the right-hand front room. There were piles of sodden cardboard all over the place, but no other sign of habitation.

Then I heard it. The beginning of a shriek that was cut off. It came from the back of the house. I instantly thought of Katharine and ran down the corridor. To the left was what had been and apparently still was the kitchen. In the far corner were the remains of a fire and sheep bones gnawed clean of meat were strewn across the floor. But no people.

"In here, cocksucker." The voice from the other rear room was deep but strangely unsteady. "I've found myself an old friend." There was a harsh laugh. "Haven't I, darling?"

I felt a pain in my chest like I'd just been clubbed by an iron bar. I moved towards the doorway.

"Well, well. And now I've got another old friend." Howlin' Wolf was standing against the hole where a fireplace had been. I'd only ever caught a glimpse of him once, when he and the Ear, Nose and Throat Man turned away from Caro's body. He was big, almost as big as the animal who strangled her, his face and upper chest covered with a heavy beard. But it was the eyes I remembered – tiny, screwed-up sparks of malevolence. He had his arm round Katharine's neck. She was on her tiptoes, her cheeks blazing red as she fought for breath.

"The great fucking Quintilian Dalrymple," the Wolf said, grinning at me. "The shithead who chased me and my boys out of the city. Looks like it's time for some bills to be paid." Again his voice wavered. It was out of synch with his hulking frame.

I leaned forward on to the balls of my feet and tried to make things out in the unlit room. Katharine's head was twitching, her eyes fixed on me. She seemed to be telling me to stay back. But it was the Wolf's face that I was trying to see. The small patches of skin between the top of his beard and his piggy eyes were blotched with crimson, as was his forehead. I'd seen lesions like that very recently.

"You've found an old friend?" I said, playing for time and wondering where the hell Davie had got to.

Katharine struggled in his grip, her eyes protruding unnaturally.

The Wolf laughed again, like a demon looking forward to an eternity of pain. "The bitch here. I know her very fucking well." He pulled her round to face him. "Isn't that right?"

Katharine's feet were completely off the ground now and a harsh choking sound was coming from her. I stepped forward.

"Stand still, you," the Wolf shouted. "I've already seen one of your women die."

Bastard. I froze. Gradually he lowered Katharine's feet to the floor.

"I reamed this one's ass many a time, fucker." He coughed

and spat out a discoloured lump. "Maybe I'll ream it again in a minute. After I've cut her."

"You're the one who's reamed, Wolf," I said, trying not to look at the top of Davie's head which had appeared at the far end of the window. "You've got radiation sickness, haven't you? It's got much worse in the last few days. That's why you've been lying low." I gave him a bitter smile. "Don't worry, there are plenty of lead coffins available in the Bone Yard."

"The Bone Yard?" he said, coughing again. "You know where it is, fucker?"

"I found it, thanks to your cassettes. And I've got the Electric Blues. And the guard's top squad of headbangers is on its way." I wasn't planning on sparing him anything. "And I found you because Leadbelly told me about this place."

His head jacked upwards. "Leadbelly spilled his guts? Did he fuck, liar!"

I raised my shoulders with as much nonchalance as I could find. "How else could I have tracked you down? You had some kind of stash here, didn't you? What was it? Drugs? Weapons?"

He spat on the floor again. "Both. You chased us out of the city before I could clean the place out. There was a sack of ancient Es in the loft." He gave me a murderous glare. "And a set of butcher's knives that I'm going to use on the bitch and you."

Katharine's eyes bulged as the Wolf tightened his arm again.

"So you were the leader of the Cavemen," I said, trying to stall him. "And later you moved east and set yourself up as the Screecher."

He laughed again. "I like my people to live in fear. They know to keep away when I sing my blues."

I heard the noise of engines in the distance. Glancing over at the Wolf, I saw that he had his ear cocked.

"Running out of time, fucker," he said, pulling a long-bladed knife out of his belt. "Say goodbye to the woman." He didn't wait for me to speak, just raised the knife and brought it down with slow deliberation towards Katharine's abdomen.

The moment seemed to last for ever. Then there was a blurred movement from my left. Katharine immediately dropped to the floor like a stone. The Wolf stayed upright, his small eyes suddenly open very wide. For a couple of seconds it seemed he'd lost the plot. Davie was at the window, staring at the haft of his service knife. The blade was embedded in the wall an inch from the Wolf's head. Then the Wolf shook his head and looked down at Katharine. There was only one thing for it. I charged him, feeling the crunch as his own knife penetrated his chest and went right through into the plasterboard behind. I watched as his eyes slowly stopped twitching, then stepped back. The Wolf fell forward like a statue on to the cracked concrete, his head turned to one side with the hood of his coat lying partially over it. There was a long rattle in his throat then I heard the words "The Killing Floor", followed by a fading gasp. Trust the animal to die with the title of one of his namesake's songs on his lips. I stood up, giving him one last look. His eyelids were still wide apart but nothing else was open for business.

There was a stampede of auxiliary boots in the hallway.

"What happened?" Hamilton asked, taking in the scene.

Katharine got up slowly. Her breathing was still laboured and her whole body quivering. She raised her head. "Yes," she said quietly, "what happened?"

"The Wolf's dead," I said, moving my eyes away from her and feeling empty inside. "And we're even."

I shouldered my way through the guard personnel into the front room that didn't contain the sheep's remains. I suddenly had an intense desire to be alone.

Dirty Harry and his guys moved out, looking disappointed that they hadn't had a chance to deal with the Wolf themselves.

Hamilton came in after a few minutes. There was a mixture

of shock and delight on his face which made him look like a child in pre-Enlightenment times who'd discovered how easy it was to get away with shoplifting. "I can hardly believe it, Dalrymple," he said.

"What can you hardly believe, Lewis?" I said, trying not to lose my train of thought.

"After all this time, we finally got the scum."

I nodded. I obviously looked distracted enough to get his attention.

"What's the matter, man?" he asked impatiently. "This is a triumph. It's exactly what we need to get the Council back on an even keel."

Something gave way inside me. "Bugger off, will you, Lewis!" I shouted. "I don't give a fuck about the Council. If it hadn't been for the Council and its bastard leader, none of this would have happened."

The guardian retreated, muttering something about how the strain of the investigation had obviously got to me.

I turned away, dimly aware that the last of the guard personnel were leaving the house. My words to Hamilton took me back to what I'd been thinking about before. Was it right that the senior guardian was responsible for everything? He'd tried to keep what happened at Torness and what was done with the survivors secret, leaving himself open to blackmail by Howlin' Wolf. He'd set up production of the Electric Blues, even though he later tried to double-cross the Wolf. And he'd used people like Roddie Aitken without caring what happened to them. All that was clear enough. So it came down to the Wolf. He was clever; all the years he kept ahead of us when I was in the directorate proved that. And he knew about the blues, so he could have worked out the idea of the tapes in order to put me on the trail of the guardian and the Electric Blues. Obviously the idea was that I track down the drugs and the lab that produced them so that he could muscle in later on. But that didn't quite ring true. The Wolf was sharp, but he was also a psychopath. As the murders showed, he was at home with mayhem. I had the feeling that someone else was involved.

Katharine came in. Her neck was ringed with livid bruises. "Quint . . . I . . ." She wasn't looking at me. "I know what you're thinking. I'm not denying it . . ."

I went over to the hole where the window had been and stared out over the potholed road. There were criss-crossed tracks from guard vehicles all over it. "You're not denying that the reason you came back to the city was to track down the guy who abused you? You're not denying that you found out from the deserter who died at your farm that the Screecher used to be in charge of the Cavemen? You're not denying that you played me for a jackass just so that you could get a chance to pay the bastard back?" I glanced at her, trying to look indifferent. "I told you, Katharine. We're even. What more do you want?"

"Stop it!" she shouted, her face screwed up and her fists clenched. At first I thought she was going to hit me, then I saw the wetness around her eyes. "I'm not denying I wanted to kill him. He made me hate myself more than I ever thought I could." She gulped for breath. "But I didn't only come back for that. There was the drugs formula. It could have hurt a lot of people." She came closer. "And there was you, Quint. I came back for you as well. Even if you don't believe me, I did."

I was listening to her, but as she'd been speaking something else had struck me. The Wolf taunted me about Caro, made a crack about how he'd already seen one of my women die. How the hell did he know Caro was my woman? Because of auxiliary regulations we kept our tie as secret as we could. Only people who were very close to us knew about it. That made me sure about who else was involved in it all.

I took a step towards the door, then froze. There were a few seconds of silence then I heard the faint noise again. And again. Creaks on the ceiling and another sound I couldn't place immediately. A kind of muffled rolling. I raised my hand, caught sight of the stump of my right forefinger, looked back at Katharine then felt my mouth open even wider. There was someone else in the house.

I ran into the hallway, skidding and crashing my elbow into the wall. Then took the stairs three at a time.

Chapter Twenty-Four

———◆◇◆◇◆———

I raced into the upstairs front room like a greyhound after a hare and choked on what I inhaled. Despite the open holes in the walls, the room stank like a cesspit. Looking at the heaps of excrement on what was left of the floorboards, I realised that it actually was a cesspit. One inhabited by a misshapen dwarf on wheels.

"You forgot about me, Quint." The voice from the shrunken, chair-bound figure in the far corner was scratchy, like an astronaut's coming across the airwaves from a distant planet.

"I did, Billy." I watched as William Ewart Geddes, former deputy finance guardian and my oldest childhood friend, pushed his wheelchair forward a couple of feet. That was as far as the missing floorboards allowed him to go.

"But I never forgot you." The voice had hardened. Calculating eyes glinted at me from a filth-encrusted face. Billy's clothes were in tatters, his trousers open and streaked with shit.

"What's been happening to you?" I said, stepping closer. "What did the Wolf do to you, Billy?"

He laughed harshly. "The Wolf? The Wolf did nothing to me. He's been the best friend I ever had, Quint. The best, you hear?" His eyes were locked on me.

"But you need nursing, Billy. In your condition . . ."

"In my condition?" he screamed, spittle flying from his disfigured lips. "And who was responsible for my condition, Quint?" He'd obviously spent the time since I'd last seen him building up a major grudge against me.

"The blackmail and the drugs were your doing, weren't they, Billy?"

He nodded. "Oh aye. I was the best deal maker this city's ever had. The fuckers in the Council could have used me, but they turned their noses up at me and shunted me off to the home. I was going to get them for that. The Wolf was in this to make a heap of money but I wanted to wreck the regime."

"The Electric Blues would have killed plenty of innocent people."

"Who gives a fuck about innocent people? Nobody's innocent in this stinking city." He pushed himself backwards with surprising strength and banged into the wall.

"Not even Roddie Aitken, the first victim?"

Billy made an attempt at shrugging with his damaged shoulders. "That saintly hypocrite in the Council told us the boy was working for another gang. That made him expendable."

"Expendable?" I shouted. "He was set up, Billy. He knew nothing about the drugs or anything else. Jesus Christ, you didn't use to be like this."

He laughed again. "Exactly, Quint. You're finally getting the picture. I didn't use to be like this." He nodded down at the wheelchair, strands of filthy hair dropping over his forehead. "That's why I brought you into the game." He looked to one side of me. "Tell your friends to leave us alone. This is between you and me."

I motioned to Katharine and Davie to move back from the doorway. "You set all this up so that you could have a go at me as well, didn't you, Billy?"

"Don't flatter yourself," he said dismissively. "I had dealings with the Wolf years ago. He provided the city with essential products from time to time."

"Drugs, you mean."

He nodded. "Drugs and chemicals, mainly for medical purposes. He had contacts with other cities that we couldn't deal with officially."

"So he managed to get you out of the nursing home when he was looking for a lab to produce the Electric Blues."

Billy stared at me like a spider weighing up a fly. "Correct. And because I made a point of gathering information all the time I was in the Finance Directorate, I knew about the blast at Torness. I heard rumours about the Bone Yard. I ended up in this chair before I could find out exactly what it was."

"I found it, Billy. It was the chief boyscout's version of a concentration camp for the people affected by radiation."

He showed no emotion. "Was it there the drugs were produced?"

I nodded.

"So you worked it all out, you fucking smartass." Now there was a manic glint in his eyes. "Even where we were holed up. How?"

I told him about Leadbelly. "But I haven't found out everything, Billy," I said, trying to placate him so I could get closer without him snarling at me. "The songs were your idea, I suppose?"

"Of course. I knew you wouldn't be able to resist them."

"And 'Fire and Water' was to put me on to Torness and the senior guardian?"

"You made the connection?" He cackled triumphantly. "I knew you would."

I took a step closer. "But why did you do it so abstrusely, for Christ's sake? You could just have got the Wolf to scratch out a message in Roddie Aitken's blood."

"To turn the screw on the senior guardian. He had the Electric Blues and we wanted to make sure he didn't do

PAUL JOHNSTON

anything hasty with them." He looked at me as if I were a moron. "Anyway, do you think telling the Wolf what to do was easy? The only way I could sell him the idea of the tapes was by appealing to his extremely well-developed sense of the macabre. The guy wasn't good at taking orders." He stared at me blankly. "You killed him, I suppose."

The way he held his gaze on me made it clear that he meant "you" singular rather than plural. I nodded. "I'm not going to play a lament for him, Billy. When I got involved in the case, the Wolf started following me around, didn't he?" I was thinking of the time I'd seen the hooded man in Tollcross and the wheelchair tracks outside my flat.

"Sometimes he was totally out of control. The radiation did something to his brain. The stupid bugger got through the fence at Torness and started messing around with the damaged sarcophagus."

"I know."

"Of course you do." Billy laughed bitterly. "Shades of what happened at Sellafield years ago, eh? You'd better send some conscripts out to clean things up."

"Fancy taking charge of that operation?" I demanded.

"It would beat going back to the home I was in." Billy's eyes locked on to mine again. "The one you gave up visiting."

I inched towards him. "So why did the Wolf take you to my street?"

"I made the mistake of telling him who you used to be. He had it in for you in a big way since you'd dealt with most of his gang and driven him out of the city. I only just talked him out of confronting you that morning." Billy's lips drew back from discoloured teeth. "It was his idea to hang the auxiliary's head on your door." He spat out a malevolent laugh. "Not that I had any objection."

I moved closer, breathing in his stench. "You told him about Caro too, Billy," I said accusingly.

He didn't look away. "Everyone has their weak point. The Wolf wanted to know yours."

"You were her friend as well as mine, for fuck's sake."

He pounded his shrivelled arms on the wheelchair. "Exactly, Quint. I *was* her friend. You *were* my friend. But nothing lasts for ever."

"You twisted little bastard," I shouted, stepping over the gaps in the floorboards. "I'm taking you in front of the Council. This time it'll be Cramond Island for you, not a nursing home."

He looked at me placidly, a mocking smile on his lips. As I bent over him to get a hold of the wheelchair, I saw his eyes narrow. Then I remembered the set of butcher's knives the Wolf said he'd stashed in the house.

"Sit still, citizen." The medical guardian's voice was unusually sharp. I suppose I should have been grateful that she was stitching my neck herself.

"How many's it going to be?"

"Thirteen, I think. Lucky for some. If your assailant hadn't been in such a weakened condition, the meat cleaver would have severed your head. That would have been a pity." The Ice Queen looked even less compassionate than she sounded.

"The Torness survivors," I said. "Are they being looked after?"

She nodded. "They're in an isolation ward here." She shook her head slowly. "They won't need it for long though."

"So you're not even letting them die where they want to, near their friends?" I asked, wincing as I turned to look at her. "Does that make you proud to be a Council member?"

Her perfect features beneath the white-blonde hair were lifeless, as robotic as ever. I didn't expect an answer and I wasn't disappointed.

"Done," she said, snipping the thread.

I got up and headed for the door.

"Citizen," she called. "Nothing like Torness and the Bone Yard will be allowed to happen again, you can be sure of that."

I glanced back as I reached the door. "No, I can't, guardian," I said. "And neither can you."

I found it difficult to get too excited about the Council meeting that evening. Hamilton had the boyscouts well under control and it was pretty obvious that most of them would be back in auxiliary uniform soon. The Science and Energy Directorate was already organising an expedition to check the reactor casings at Torness. I let Davie report on the final stages of the investigation. It wouldn't do his career any harm and I was finding it difficult to care any more.

"Anything further?" Hamilton asked, giving me the eye when Davie finished.

"Billy Geddes – Heriot 03 as was," I said. "I want to recommend that he isn't sent to Cramond Island. He isn't up to it physically." I needed to clear my account with Billy. I was still guilty that I hadn't visited him often. Maybe the violence that Howlin' Wolf let loose on Roddie and the others could have been avoided if Billy hadn't wanted to get back at me so much.

Hamilton looked at me curiously and made a note. "It's not exactly your jurisdiction, Dalrymple, but we'll take your view into account. Anything else?"

"The prisoner known as Leadbelly," I said.

"Number 35 in Cramond Island," Davie put in, going for broke in the efficiency stakes.

"I offered him an amnesty."

Lewis Hamilton looked like he was about to explode, but eventually he made another note. Two down, one to go.

"And finally, there's Katharine Kirkwood."

"Don't tell me," the guardian said. "You want her desertion charge removed from the guard register."

I nodded, running my eye round the so-called iron boyscouts. Their faces were slack and pale, but whatever happened to them, they had a future, unlike the radiation victims from the Bone Yard. Katharine had done a hell of a sight less harm than the guardians and I'd have pointed that out if any of them had objected. They kept their mouths shut.

"Very well," Hamilton said, nodding and closing his note-book. "It only remains for me to offer you the thanks of the Council and the entire city for your good work, citizen Dalrymple. Should you desire to return to a senior post in the Public Order Directorate ..."

I raised an eyebrow at him and turned away. Then they started to applaud, which got me to the door even faster.

Outside the Assembly Hall I leaned against the railings and looked out across the city. The lights of the centre blazed as much as ever, burning up the city's precious coal reserves. The idea of bringing Torness back into service wasn't a bad one but anyone can have good ideas. It's how you put them into action that's difficult. I glanced to my right. A few yards in that direction the senior guardian had skewered himself. Thinking of Roddie Aitken and William McEwan, I didn't have it in me to feel regret for his suicide.

I heard voices from round the corner. A squad of cleaners appeared. Most of the citizens were laughing and joking despite having drawn the much hated night shift. All of them looked thin and drawn, clothes loose on their undernourished limbs. I thought of the Bone Yard. It wasn't just the place where the city's untouchables had been confined. The Bone Yard was Edinburgh itself. The citizen body was skin and bone, struggling to survive. But people still seemed able to make something of their over-regulated lives. They deserved better than they'd been getting from the guardians. But would the next Council improve anything? And did I have a part to play in the "perfect" city any more?

There was a rustle of clothing at my side.

"What are you doing out here, Quint?" Katharine's voice was hoarse, still affected by the bruising to her throat.

"I walked out on the tossers," I said without looking round. "Don't worry. You're in the clear."

I felt her eyes on me.

"I don't care about that." She laughed softly. "Anyway, I've still got my 'ask no questions'."

"You're all right then."

"Don't be like this, Quint," she said desperately. "I told you the truth. Okay, I didn't only come back for you." She moved up against me. "But the case is finished, isn't it? And I'm still here."

I turned to look at her. "Yes, I suppose you are."

She leaned forward and kissed me once on the lips.

"It's not you, Katharine," I said. "It's Edinburgh. Deep down inside I love this city. But it's the kind of love that makes you suffer and I don't know if I can take it any more."

"So come back to the farm with me," she said, touching the back of my hand with her fingertips. "There are none of the city's problems there. Just hard work and home-grown food."

"It's an idea," I said, nodding. Then I looked back out over the lights of Princes Street. But no matter how hard I tried, I couldn't conjure up fields of potatoes and kale. I kept thinking about the chief boyscout and the noble lie he'd quoted from Plato; that people's natures are predetermined and that their rulers have the right to lie in the interests of the state. It's a myth but like all myths there's some truth in it. In which case the next Council would be just as dangerous as the last one. There was one difference though. I wasn't going to get fooled again.

"Why are you smiling?" Katharine asked.

"I may just have rediscovered my vocation," I replied, turning to face the blackened Gothic façade behind us.

She looked at me, a smile gradually fading from her own

lips like the winter sun's last glow over an icy lake. Fire and water, I thought.

Davie ran down the steps and came towards us, his arm raised.

Katharine squeezed my hand once then walked slowly away, her long coat flapping in the wind. At the corner of the lane she stopped and looked back at me for a second before pulling up her hood and disappearing into the night.

WATER OF DEATH

Edinburgh, 2025 – an independent, almost crime-free oasis surrounded by anarchic city-states. Except global warming has turned the summer into the Big Heat and water, like everything else, is strictly rationed.

The ruling Council of City Guardians has been forced to become more user-friendly. Citizens now live only for the weekly lottery draw while serving the tourists in the year-round festival. So when a recent lottery winner goes missing, subversive investigator Quintilian Dalrymple is called in to deal with a minor case of the summer-time blues.

Then a body is discovered face down in the Water of Leith – the only clue to the death, a bottle of contraband whisky. Quint thinks he sees the first traces of a ruthless conspiracy to destabilise the city.

The Council, increasingly fearful of losing its grip on power, expects Quint to stop the tormentors dead in the water. But he is having serious difficulty distinguishing friend from foe during the Big Heat. Meanwhile the body count, like the temperature, keeps on rising ...

Don't miss Paul Johnston's new novel WATER OF DEATH available from Hodder & Stoughton in hardcover from June 1999.

Turn over to dip your toe in the water ...

WATER OF DEATH

Edinburgh, July 2025. Sweat City.

When I was a kid before independence, summer was a joke that got about as many laughs as a hospital waiting list. There was the occasional sunny day, but you spent most of the time running from showers of acid rain and the lash of rabid winds. To make things worse, for three weeks the place was overrun by armies of culture victims chasing the hot festival ticket. Now the festival is a year-round event – though a lot of the tourists are only interested in the officially sanctioned marijuana clubs – and "hot" doesn't even begin to describe the state of the weather. Over the last couple of years temperatures have risen by three to four degrees, causing tropical diseases to migrate northwards and bacteria to embark on a major expansion programme. Scientists in the late twentieth century would have got closer to the full horror of the phenomenon if they'd called it "global stewing" – except we haven't got enough fresh water to stew anything properly.

What we do have is a cracker of a name for the season between spring and autumn. To everyone's surprise the new-look, user-friendly Council of City Guardians didn't saddle us with an updated designation for the period (think French Revolution, think Thermidor). Our masters were probably too busy discussing initiatives to relieve the tourists of even more cash. As the blazing days and stifling nights dragged by, ordinary citizens gave up distinguishing between the months of June, July and August. And even though the classic *noir* movie hasn't been seen in Edinburgh since the cinemas were closed and television banned by the original Council, people have taken to calling this season the Big Heat. That kills me.

Still, in Sweat City we're really civilised. Unlike most states, we've done away with capital punishment and the nuclear switch has been flicked off permanently – the reactors at Torness were recently buried in enough concrete to give a 1990s town planner the ultimate hard on. On the other hand, the Council set up a compulsory lottery last year, turning greed into a virtue and most citizens into deluded fortune hunters. Deluded, very thirsty fortune hunters given the water restrictions.

Then some grade A headbangers came along and raised the temperature even higher than it had been during Big Heat 2025. Giving me a pretty near terminal case of the Summertime Blues.

Chapter One

I was lying in the Meadows with a book and heat-induced headache, making the most of the shade provided by one of the few trees with any leaves left on it. It was five in the afternoon but the sun still had plenty of fire in its belly. The rays glinted off a big hoarding in the middle of the park. It was advertising the lottery. Some poor sod who'd won it was dressed up like John Knox, a bottle of malt whisky poking out of his false beard. "Play Edlott, the Ultimate Lottery, and Anything Goes", the legend said. If you ask me, what goes, what's already gone, is the last of the Council's credibility. There's an elaborate system of prizes ranging from half-decent clothes, to bottles of better than average whisky like the one Johnnie the Fox had secreted, to labour waivers and pensions for life – but only for a few lucky sods. Edinburgh citizens were so starved of material possessions in the first twenty years of the Council that they now reckon Edlott is the knees of a very large Queen Bee. They even willingly accept the value of a ticket being docked from their wage vouchers every week. I think the whole thing sucks but maybe I'm biased. I've never won so much as a tube of extra-strength sun protection cream.

All round me Edinburgh citizens were lying motionless, their cheeks resting against parched soil that hadn't produced much grass since the Big Heat arrived. I was one of the lucky ones. At least I was wearing a pair of Supply Directorate shades that hadn't fallen to pieces. Yet.

I rolled over and peered at Arthur's Seat through the haze. People say the hill looks like a lion at rest. These days it's certainly the right shade of sandy brown though the desiccated vegetation on its flanks gives the impression of an erstwhile king of the beasts who's been mauled by a pride of rabid republicans. As it happens, that isn't a bad description of the Enlightenment Party which led Edinburgh into independence in 2004. But things have changed a hell of a lot since then. For a start, like the nerve gas used by demented dictators in the Balkans twenty-plus years ago, you can smell Edinburgh people coming long before you can see or hear them. Water's almost as precious as the revenue from tourists here.

I glanced round at my fellow citizens. If Arthur's Seat is a lion, we must be the pack of ragged hyenas that hangs around it. Everyone's in standard issue maroon shorts (standard issue meaning too wide, too long and not anything like cool enough) and off-white T-shirts. Those whose sunglasses have self-destructed wear faded sunhats with a Heart of Midlothian badge on the front. Up until the time of the "iron boyscouts" – the hardline lunatics who ran the Council of City Guardians between 2020 and 2022 – only the rank of auxiliaries was entitled to wear the heart insignia, which has nothing to do with the pre-Enlightenment football team. The present Council's doing its best to make citizens feel they have the same rights as the uniformed class who carry out the guardians' orders. Except the auxiliaries don't have to wear clowns' outfits.

The hard ground was making my arms stiff. I stretched and made the mistake of breathing in through my nose. It wasn't just that the herd of humanity needed more than the single shower lasting exactly sixty seconds which it gets each week. (One of the lottery prizes is a five minute shower every week for a month.) The still air over the expanse of flat parkland was infused with the reek from the public shithouses that have been set up at the end of every residential street. Since the onset of the Big Heat, citizens have had no running water in their flats. People get by one way or another and the black-marketeers do good business in bottles, jars, chamberpots – anything that will hold liquid. But the City Guard has to patrol the queues outside the communal bogs first thing in the morning. It doesn't take long for dozens of desperate citizens to lose their grip and turn on each other.

It was too hot to read. I lay back and let an old blues number run through my mind. No surprises what it was – "Dry Spell Blues". Before I could work out if Son House or Spider Carter was singing, the vocal was blown away by a sudden mechanical roar.

"Turn that rustbucket off, ya shite!" A red-haired kid of about seventeen jumped to his feet and started waving his arms at the driver of a tractor towing a battered water trailer. They come daily to refill the drinking water tanks at every street corner. It stopped about fifty yards away from us.

"Aye, give us a break or I'll give you one," shouted another young guy who obviously fancied himself as a hard man. The pair of them had done everything they could to make their clothes distinctive. They had their T-shirt sleeves folded double and their shorts stained with bleach, pieces of thick rope holding them up. Sweat City chic.

The driver had switched off his engine. Now that he could hear what was being broadcast to him, he didn't look happy. He was pretty musclebound for someone on the diet we get and the set of his unshaven face suggested he didn't think much of the Council's recent easy-going policies and their effect on the young.

"You wee bastards," he yelled, waddling towards the kids as quickly as his heavy thighs allowed. "Your heads are going down the pan."

There was a collective intake of breath as the citizens around me sat up and paid attention, grateful for anything that took their minds off the stifling heat. I watched as a woman sitting with a small child near the loudmouthed guys started gathering up her towels and waterbottles nervously.

Our heroes took one look at the big man coming their way, glanced at each other and turned to run. Then the tough guy spotted the woman's handbag. She'd left it lying open on the ground as she leant over her child.

"Tae fuck wi' the lot o' ye," the kid shouted in the local dialect which the Council outlawed years ago. He bent down to scoop up the bag and sprinted after his pal towards the streets on the far side of the park. "Southside Strollers rule!" he yelled over his shoulder.

The woman shrieked. Her kid joined in. The citizens nearest to them crowded round to help but nobody else moved a muscle. Even the tractor driver had turned to marble. It wouldn't have been the first time they'd seen a bag snatched by the city's new generation of arseholes. It wasn't the first time I'd seen it either. Maybe because I'd once been in the Public Order Directorate, maybe because I was theoretically still a member of the Enlightenment, maybe just because I fancied a run – whatever, I got to my feet and gave what in the City Guard we used to call "chase".

Bad idea.

After fifty yards they were still going away from me, dust rising from their feet and hanging in the air to coat my tongue and eyes. But after a hundred yards, when my lungs were clogging and my legs had decided enough was enough, the little sods had slowed to not much more than a stride. Evidence of loading up on illicit ale and black market grass, I reckoned. Then I cut my speed even more. People who get into those commodities at an early age usually learn how to look after themselves.

They turned to face me and started to laugh in between gasping for breath.

"Hey, look, Tommy, it's the Good fucking Samaritan," the red head said. Obviously he'd learned something in school, though the Education Directorate would have preferred something more in line with the Council's atheist principles to have stuck.

Tommy was rifling through the woman's bag, tossing paper hankies and the Supply Directorate's version of cosmetics away and stuffing food and clothing vouchers into his pocket. When he'd finished, he looked up at me and smiled threateningly. The teeth he revealed were uneven and discoloured.

"Get away, ya wanker," he hissed, raising his left fist. It had the letters D-E-A-D tattooed amateurishly on the lower finger joints. I was betting the right one had the word 'YOU'RE' on it, spelt wrong. "Come on, Col. We're gone."

He'd got that right. I took my mobile phone from the back pocket of my shorts and called the guard command centre in the castle. As soon as I started to speak, the two of them turned back towards me, their eyes empty and their fists drawn right back.

Like I said – bad idea.

"Are you all right, Quint?"

"What does it look like, Davie?" I took a break from flexing my right wrist and stood up to face the heavily-built guardsman who'd just arrived in a Land-Rover and a dust storm.

"Bloody hell, what did you do to those guys?"

I walked over to the bagsnatchers. The carrot head was leaning forward on both hands, carrying out a detailed examination of what had been his lunch. Tommy the hard man was still on his arse. Unfortunately he'd turned out to have a jaw that really was hard. I had a handkerchief wrapped round my seeping knuckles.

"Where did you learn to fight like that, ya bastard?" he demanded, trying to get to his feet. Then he ran his eye over Davie's uniform. "I might have fuckin' known. You're an Alsatian like him." The city's low life refer to the guard as dogs when they're feeling brave.

Davie grabbed the kid's arm and pulled him upright. "What was that, sonny?"

Tommy decided bravery was surplus to requirements. "Nothing," he muttered.

"Nothing what?" Davie shouted into his ear.

"Nothing, Hume 253." Tommy pronounced Davie's barracks number with exaggerated respect, his eyes to the ground.

"That's better, wee man. And for your information, this citizen is not a member of the City Guard."

"He fuckin' puts himself about like one," Tommy said under his breath.

Davie grinned at me. "And there was me thinking you'd forgotten your auxiliary training, Quint."

"Quint?" the boy said with a groan. "Aw, no. You're no' that investigator guy, are you? The one wi' the stupid name?"

Davie found all this highly amusing. "Quintilian Dalrymple?" he asked.

"Aye, the one who's in the paper every time you bitches cannae do your job."

Too much adulation isn't good for you. "So what are you going to do with this pair of scumbags, Hume 253?" I asked.

Colin the carrot finally managed to get to his feet.

"Cramond Island, I reckon," Davie replied. "The old prison'll be a great place to give them a hiding."

The carrot hit the dust again.

"You cannae do that," Tommy whined. "We've got rights. The Council's set up special centres for kids like us."

He was right. In their desperation to be seen as having citizens' best interests at heart, the latest guardians, or at least a majority of them, haven't only given citizens more personal freedom – apart from anything involving the use of water – and a lottery. They've organised a social welfare system that treats anyone who steps out of line as an honoured guest. To no one in the guard's surprise, petty crime has risen even faster than the temperature.

"Who are the Southside Strollers?" I asked.

"What's it to you?" Tommy said, giving me the eye.

Davie grabbed his arm and stuck his face up close to the boy's. "Answer the man, sonny."

"Awright, awright." Tommy had gone floppy again. "It's our gang. We all come from the south side of the city."

"And you spend your time strolling around nicking whatever you can?" I said.

Tommy shrugged nonchalantly, his eyes lowered.

A couple of auxiliaries from the Youth Development Department looking desperately eager to please turned up to collect the boys. Colin the carrot was busy holding on to his gut, but Tommy flashed a triumphant look at us.

"Just a minute, you," I said, moving over to him. I stuck my hand into his pocket and relieved him of the vouchers he'd taken, leaving a streak of blood from my knuckles on his shorts as a souvenir. "Oh aye, what's this then?"

The pair of them suddenly started examining the ground.

"What do you think, Davie?" I said, opening the scrap of crumpled paper and sniffing the small quantity of dried and shredded leaves.

Davie shook his head. "If it was up to me ..."

"But it isn't," the female auxiliary from the Welfare Directorate said, stepping forward and looking at the twist of grass. "Underage citizens are our responsibility, not the City Guard's. We'll see they're rehabilitated."

Davie looked at her disbelievingly. Like most of his colleagues, he had serious difficulty accepting the Council's recent caring policies. Not that he had any choice.

Tommy smirked then bared his teeth at me again. "You're dead, pal."

"Oh aye, Tommy?" I said. "And what does that make you?"

I handed the grass to Davie. We watched the miscreants get into the Youth Development Department van than I turned back to get my gear.

"The future of the city," Davie said morosely as he caught up with me. "Giving these headbangers special treatment is only going to make them harder to control later. Anyone caught with black market drugs should be nailed to the floor like in the old days."

"Hand that stuff over for analysis, will you?" We both knew that wouldn't make any difference. The guard's no longer permitted to give underage citizens the third degree so they probably wouldn't find out where the grass came from. I shrugged. "Stupid bastards. I told them to keep their distance but they had to have a go."

Davie laughed. "They weren't the only ones. You sorted them out pretty effectively, Quint."

"I'll probably end up on a charge. Unwarranted force."

"I don't think so. I'll be writing the report, remember."

The citizens under the trees were pretending they'd gone back to sleep. Davie's presence was making them shy. Even in the recently approved informal shirtsleeve order, the grey City Guard uniform isn't the most popular apparel in Edinburgh. The woman came to reclaim her vouchers, flashing me a brief smile of thanks. She probably thought I was an undercover guard operative.

"I'll give you a lift home," Davie said as we headed for his vehicle. "What were you doing here, anyway?"

"Trying unsuccessfully to find somewhere cool in this sweat pit to read my book."

"What have you got?" Davie took the volume from under my arm and laughed. "*Black and Blue*? Just like the state of your knuckles tomorrow morning."

"Very funny, guardsman."

"Isn't that book on the proscribed list?" he asked dubiously.

"The Council lifted the ban on pre-Enlightenment Scottish crime fiction at the end of last year. Don't you remember?"

"I just put a stop to crime," he said pointedly. "I don't read stories about it."

"That'll be right. You said something about taking me to my place?"

Davie wrenched open the passenger door of one of the guard's few surviving Land-Rovers. "At your service, sir," he said with fake deference. "Number 13 Gilmore Place it is, sir."

But as things turned out, we didn't make it.

Tollcross is as busy a junction as you get in Edinburgh. A guard vehicle on watch, a couple of Supply Directorate delivery vans, the ubiquitous Water Department tractor and a flurry of citizens on bicycles constitute traffic congestion these days. There was even a Japanese tourist scratching his head in one of the hire cars provided by an American multinational that the Council did a deal with. The lack of other private cars in the streets was obviously worrying the guy.

"Why were you frying yourself in the Meadows, Quint?" Davie asked. "There are bits of grass around the castle that actually get watered. It's quieter there too."

I looked at the burly figure next to me. He was still wearing the beard that used to be required of male auxiliaries, even though the current Council's made it optional. God knows what the temperature was beneath the matted growth.

"Quiet if you don't mind being stared at by sentries," I replied. "Since they moved the auxiliary training camp away from the Meadows, it's become a much more relaxing place."

"Asshole." Davie was shaking his head. "Anyone would think you hadn't spent ten years as one of us." He laughed. "Till they saw how handy you are with your fists."

My mobile rang before I could tell him how proud I was to have been demoted from the rank of auxiliary.

"Is that you, Dalrymple?"

I let out a groan. I might have known the public order guardian would get his claws into me late on a Friday afternoon. Not that his rank take week-ends off.

"Lewis Hamilton," I said. "What a surprise."

"Where are you, man?" he demanded. "And don't address me by name." Lewis was one of the old school, a guardian for twenty years. He didn't go along with the new Council's decision allowing citizens to use guardians' names instead of their official titles.

"I'm at Tollcross with Hume 253."

"Distracting my watch commander from his duties again?" Davie had been promoted a few months ago though that didn't stop him helping me out whenever something interesting came up.

"And the reason for your call is . . . ?" I asked.

"The reason for my call is that the people who run the lottery need your services."

I pointed to Davie to pull in to the kerbside. "Don't tell me. They've lost one of their winners again."

"I know, I know, he'll probably turn up drunk in a gutter after a couple of days . . ."

"With his prizes missing and his new clothes covered in other people's vomit. Jesus, Lewis, can't you find someone else to look for the moron? Like, for instance, a guardsman who started his first tour of duty this morning?"

Hamilton gave what passes for a laugh in his book. "No, Dalrymple. As you know very well, this is a high priority job. One for the city's freelance chief investigator. After tourists my fellow guardians' favourite human beings are lottery winners." I knew he had other ideas about that himself. As far as he was concerned, Edlott was yet another disaster perpetrated by the reforming guardians who made up the majority of the current Council. He particularly despised the culture guardian, whose directorate runs the lottery, for what he called his "lack of Platonic principles", whatever that means. I don't think Hamilton was too keen on his colleague's eye for a quick buck either. The underlying idea of Edlott was to reduce every citizen's voucher entitlement for the price of a few relatively cheap prizes. Still, the public order guardian's aversion to the lottery was nothing compared with the contempt he reserved for the Council members who forced through the measure permitting the supply of marijuana and other soft drugs to tourists. As I'd seen in the park, foreign visitors weren't the only grass consumers in the city.

"Any chance of you telling Edlott I'm tied up on some major investigation, Lewis. I mean, it's Friday night and the bars are . . ."

There was a monotonous buzzing in my ear.

"Bollocks!" I shouted into the mouthpiece.

Davie looked at me quizzically. "Bit early to hit a sex show, isn't it?"

I got the missing man's name and address from a new generation auxiliary in the Culture Directorate who oozed bonhomie like a private pension salesman in pre-Enlightenment times.

"Guess what, Davie. We're off to Morningside."

"What?" Davie turned on me with his brow furrowed. "You're off to Morningside, you mean."

"Your boss just told me this is a high priority job. The least you can do is ferry me out."

Davie looked at his watch and gave me a reluctant nod. "Okay, but I'm on duty tonight and I want to eat before that."

"You pamper that belly of yours, Davie."

He gave me a friendly scowl.

We came down to what was called Holy Corner before the Enlightenment. The four churches were turned into auxiliary accommodation blocks soon afterwards. They form part of Napier Barracks, the guard base controlling the city's central southern zone. The checkpoint barrier was quickly raised for us.

"Where to then?" Davie asked.

I looked at the note I'd scribbled. "Millar Crescent. Number 14."

He headed down the main road, the Land-Rover's bodywork juddering as he accelerated. Ahead of us, a thick layer of haze and dust obscured the Pentland Hills and the ravaged areas between us and them. What were once pretty respectable suburbs became the home of streetfighting man in the time leading up to independence. It had only been used again in the last couple of years and the parts beyond the heavily fortified city line a few hundred yards further south were still an urban wasteland. It was haunted by blackmarketeers and the dissidents who've been trying and failing to overturn the Council since it came to power. On this side of the line, the Housing Directorate has settled a lot of the city's problem families into flats that used to be occupied by Edinburgh's blue rinse and pearl necklace brigade. The Southside Strollers were the tip of a very large iceberg.

"Ten minutes, Quint," Davie said, as he manoeuvred round the water tank and the citizens' bicycle shed at the end of Millar Crescent. "That's all I'm giving you." Then his jaw dropped.

I followed the direction of his gaze. A young woman was on her way into the street entrance of number 14. She was wearing a citizen issue T-shirt and work trousers that were unusually well-pressed despite the spatters of paint on them. She also had a mauve chiffon scarf round her neck that had never seen the inside of a Supply Directorate store. She had light brown hair bound up in a tight plait and a self-contained look on her face. Oh, and she was built like the Venus de Milo with a full complement of limbs.

Davie already had his door open. "Well," he said, "make it half an hour."

We climbed the unlit, airless stairs to the third floor. The name Kennedy had been carved very skilfully in three inch high letters on the surface of a blue door on the right side of the landing. The incisions in the wood looked quite recent.

"This is the place," I said, raising my hand to knock.

"Where did she get to?" Davie asked, looking up and down the stairwell.

"Will you get a grip?" I thumped on the door. "Exert some auxiliary self-control."

"Ah, but we're supposed to come over like human beings these days," he said with a grin.

"Exactly. Like human beings, guardsman. Not like dogs after a ..."

Then the door opened very quickly. The woman we'd seen stood looking at us with her eyes wide open and a faint smile on her lips.

"Dogs after a ...?" she asked in a deep voice, her dark brown eyes darting between us. A lot of citizens would have made the most of that canine reference in the presence of a guardsman but there didn't seem to be any irony in her tone.

There was a silence which Davie and I found a lot more awkward than she did.

"Em ... I'm looking for citizen Kennedy," I said, pulling out my notebook and trying to make out my scribble in the dim light. "Citizen Fordyce Kennedy."

"My father," she said simply.

"And you are ...?"

She looked at me blankly for a couple of seconds then smiled, this time with a hint of mockery. "I'm his daughter." She hesitated then shrugged. "Agnes is my name."

"Right," I said. "So is he in?"

"Of course he isn't in," she said, her voice hardening. "That's why we called *you*."